AMBUSH

Wade jolted away from the bench, charged between two business buildings to an alley, and went
the opposite way. How in hell had they found him?
He turned into another alley behind some business
firms, small manufacturing, maybe. He was halfway down the alley when the Mercedes nosed in
behind him and sped up.

No way out.

He pulled his .45 and screwed on the silencer.
When the Mercedes came within fifty feet of him,
he shot four times at the front tire nearest him. His
third shot brought a loud bang as the tire blew out
and the big car twisted to a stop.

The silenced shots caused no alarm. Three car
doors opened and three men swarmed out of the
black rig.

Wade would have to do this the hard way.

He had no choice.

THE
SPECIALISTS

★★★★★★★

PLUNDER

Chet Cunningham

BANTAM BOOKS
New York Toronto London Sydney Auckland

THE SPECIALISTS: PLUNDER

A Bantam Book / December 1999

ISBN 0-553-58071-X

Published simultaneously in the United States and Canada

Bantam Books are published by Bantam Books, a division of Random
House, Inc. Its trademark, consisting of the words "Bantam Books"
and the portrayal of a rooster, is Registered in U.S. Patent and Trademark Office and in other countries. Marca Registrada. Bantam Books,
1540 Broadway, New York, New York 10036.

PRINTED IN THE UNITED STATES OF AMERICA

OPM   10   9   8   7   6   5   4   3   2   1

To my good friend and agent, Jake Elwell, and to my editor, Katie Hall, who "did lunch" one day in New York. The meeting resulted in this series. Also my appreciation to the San Diego Novelists Workshop members for their continuing criticism and support.

✶ THE PLAYERS ✶

WADE THORNE, thirty-eight, the Specialists team leader. He's six-two, 195 pounds, ex-CIA who quit to raise horses in Idaho. Eight years as a CIA field agent. He left the agency when a Russian agent killed his wife and daughter. He can fly anything with wings or rotors. He's a master with weapons of all types, in hand-to-hand fighting, stalking, silent movement, camouflage, and surprise attacks. He's also a class-four chess player, Formula One licensed race car driver, skier, loves to cook Italian food. Interested in Egyptology and has spent time there. Speaks Arabic, Italian, and French.

KATHERINE "KAT" KILLINGER, thirty-two, five-eight, slender, half-Hawaiian and half-English. She is second in command. A triathlon winner in Hawaii, a lawyer who has passed the bar in seven states, and an ex-FBI field agent. She has long, dark hair, a delicious golden coloring. She's gorgeous. Married at eighteen, divorced at nineteen, no children. Good with weapons, especially an automatic pistol. She has a sharp lawyer's mind, thinks well on her feet, uses karate, and has a historic Barbie doll collection. She's an expert on fifteenth-century Flemish painters and speaks German, Polish, and Spanish. She volunteers at a school in London tutoring students in reading.

ICHI YAMAGATA, twenty-four, six feet, 175 pounds. A Japanese American from Seattle. He's the arms expert for the team. He can repair, rebuild, customize, or create almost any small arm. He's a serious student of the Japanese Samurai warriors and a fantastic knife and short sword fighter. He is the silent killing expert for the Specialists. Had been a weapons expert for the FBI before being recruited for the team. Single, two years of college. A martial-arts expert. To relax, he flies exotic kites. He speaks Japanese and Mandarin Chinese.

ROGER JOHNSON, twenty-four, six-three, 210 pounds. An African American from the projects of New York. Kept out of trouble by playing basketball. Not quite good enough to be college recruited, so he joined the navy. Made it into the SEALs. Caught Mr. Marshall's attention and received a "special circumstances" discharge from the navy by order of the Chief of Naval Operations so he could join the Specialists. Knows various African languages such as Chichewa, Swahili, and Akan. Top demolitions expert for the team. Handles all explosives, timers, and bombs. He's the team's underwater expert.

HERSHEL LEVINE, thirty-one, five-nine, 145 pounds. Former Israeli Mossad agent who knew Mr. Marshall from the CIA. He's a computer whiz. Can program, hack into almost any system, rebuild, and repair computer hardware. Fantastic touch in researching on the World Wide Web. His young wife was killed in an Arab attack in Israel six years ago. Still has strong ties to Israel. Keeps some contacts with former coworkers on the Internet. Quietly efficient expert on all small arms. Speaks Hebrew, English, Arabic, Kurdish, and Persian.

DUNCAN BANCROFT, thirty-four, six-two, 165 pounds, blond, clean-shaven, soft-spoken, former English MI-6 agent who used to work with Mr. Marshall through the CIA. A team player. Top intelligence man. Knows everyone, has contacts and friends in most nations. Can help procure weapons in countries where they can't take in their own. A bit of a loner off duty. Has a Ph.D. in English literature from Cambridge. Loves to sail his boat. Is a competition pistol marksman. Is divorced with two girls in Scotland. Speaks Russian, Danish, French, and German.

★ ONE ★

BERLIN, GERMANY

George Silokowski looked behind him. The black Mercedes still followed him as if it were a weird game of tag. He wiped a bead of sweat off his forehead with one hand as he steered the 500-cc BMW motorcycle with the other. He roared down the narrow Berlin street, skidded around a corner on the cobblestones, and straightened it out with both hands.

Now wasn't the time to go down. Sweat trickled down his face and inside his helmet. Why were they following him? No, not just following, they were chasing him, scaring him right down to his gonads. Why the hell were they after him?

So far he had eluded them for almost twenty minutes. They had slid in behind him on a main strasse and gently bumped against him. He had taken off in a rush slashing through lanes of traffic so they couldn't possibly follow him. He lost them for a time, but then when he began to feel safe, they were on his tail again.

He had seen the sullen, unsmiling face of the man behind the wheel. The muted, almost expressionless visage and the eye patch scared him the most of all. It wasn't to be a mugging. They could have hit him with the big car and splattered him all over the street half a dozen times so far. They might want to kill him, but not here, not in such an obvious way.

George rode the cycle up a series of eight steps to the next level of a road and disappeared into a narrow alley. Now, surely they wouldn't be able to find him. He stopped the machine and put one foot down, but left the motor running. To his surprise he was panting. His blood pressure must be through the roof, his heart yammering like a jackhammer on a granite boulder.

Why were they chasing him?

At the far end of the street he saw the black car coming again. There was no conceivable way they could have found him, but there they were. Fucking magicians. He must have made somebody damn mad.

Two days ago he arrived in Berlin intent on learning more about his grandfather who had been born in Warsaw and escaped during the war into Switzerland after bribing some Nazi with four and a half million marks. Still the Nazis had sent his grandmother and her daughter to the gas chambers. George had visited two places asking questions about his grandfather.

Then this noon when he came out of his hotel, he had taken off on his rented motorcycle. At once he saw someone following him. They made no secret of it, as if they wanted him to know. A block later the Mercedes bumped him and the chase began. He wanted to ride right into the American embassy but he had no idea where it was. Even a police station, but he didn't even know what they were called.

He darted down another narrow street, but the Mercedes had enough room to slide through after him. They were wizards, that's what they were. Soon they were close behind him. One man leaned out the window and George expected to be shot, but nothing happened. They could have gunned him down right there and left him on the street. If they wanted to kill him they could have done it then.

Ahead of him he heard band music and then he saw the street fair. The whole area was clogged with people, stands, and booths. Eagerly he slid off his bike and wheeled it into the crowd and on through to the far side, then jumped back on the machine and raced away. For sure they couldn't find him this time.

Five minutes later he rolled down an unfamiliar street. He turned left and almost ran head-on into the same big, ugly-looking Mercedes. One man stood beside the car. He was tall, well over six feet, and solid. He wore a dark suit, a red tie, had red hair, and a patch covering one eye. George put his bike into a 180-degree skid, whipped it around, and raced back the way he had come. It was a move straight from his experience on the motocross circuit. His turn surprised them and they jumped into the big car and gave chase.

Two blocks away he saw two policemen get out of a car and head into an official-looking building. Yes, they were cops. He could stay with them. He stopped his bike in the parking lot near the building and ran inside.

Suddenly he was in the midst of twenty policemen. He thought it might be a shift change. He tried to talk to one of them. George couldn't find one who spoke English, and his German was worse than bad, since he knew only a few words. Why didn't anyone speak English?

He trembled and caught the sleeve of one of the cops. "You've got to help me. Some crazy men are chasing me in a big Mercedes."

The policeman looked puzzled, then shook his head. *"No sprechen English."*

"Come on, you've got to help me." His voice cracked and his eyes were wild now. This couldn't be happening.

The policeman shook his head, mumbled something, and went upstairs at the side of the room where the other cops had gone.

George tightened his fists and looked at the only other

policeman in the room. The cop sat at a desk on a raised platform. Maybe a sergeant or a lieutenant. He ran over to the desk.

"Sir, I'm an American and some guys are trying to kill me. You've got to help me."

"Englisher?" the policeman asked.

"*Nein,* American. These guys are chasing me."

"*No sprechen English.*" The cop held up a finger and used a phone, then said something in German. George had no idea what he said. George waited. All at once his kidneys wanted to explode. He looked at the cop again.

"Bathroom? Benjo, latrine?"

"Ah," the cop said and pointed down the hall. George rushed that way and made it just in time. When he came out of the bathroom two cops talked with the man at the desk. They smiled when he came up. One nodded.

"American?" he asked.

"Yes. You speak English?"

"Some little bit, yes?"

"At last. Some crazy men are trying to run down my motorcycle with their Mercedes. You understand?"

"Mercedes, fine car. Run good. You have?"

"No, the guys are trying to kill me."

"Mercedes good car. You want one?"

"No, some bastards are . . ." He almost gave up. "American embassy. Can you phone them? Phone embassy?"

"American embassy? Yes. One in Berlin."

"Phone them for me. I need to talk to them."

"Phone police business, yes?"

"The American embassy phone number. You have?"

"Embassy, yes." He stood there watching. Slowly George realized the man knew little English. He was mimicking the words that George used.

George knocked on the desk until the sergeant sitting behind it looked up. George decided he had to make a scene. Then maybe he'd get some help.

"Hey, you idiot," George screamed at the top of his

voice. "I want some help. Get me the American embassy. Some bastards are trying to kill me. I demand some help."

The cop who had tried to help and two other policemen came up beside him and walked him forward. Too late George realized they were throwing him out of the building. Back into the fire. They shoved him out the door and watched as he went to his bike.

George checked the scene. At least he didn't spot the Mercedes. Maybe the guys gave up with him in the station. Maybe.

All he wanted to do was find out more about his grandfather and how he got out of Germany in the middle of World War II when the Nazis sent his wife and daughter to the gas chambers. Also, he wanted to trace the nearly two million dollars someone stole from his grandfather's numbered account in Switzerland back in 1942.

He ran away from the front door to his bike, jumped on, started it, then glimpsed a walking path up the backside of the parking lot to the street above. No car could follow him up there. He took the trail slashing up the hill the way he had done hundreds of times in motocross racing. A cop yelled at him, but by then he was up the path to the street and charging away from the station and from the redheaded man who chased him.

Three blocks later, a small sedan slid in behind him as he cruised down the street, and two blocks farther along it joined forces with the black Mercedes. These guys were psychic. How did they do it? They must have radios. Then he remembered a spy movie. Maybe they put a tracking device on his bike. That would explain how they found him each time he lost them.

He rode too fast, barely getting around but keeping the bike upright. So he couldn't lose them. Maybe if he tried the autobahn, yes, that was it. This bike would do well over a hundred miles an hour. He could leave them in the German blacktop.

It took him ten minutes to find an on ramp to the high-speed roadway that raced along the edge of Berlin. Once on it, he kicked the bike into high gear and slashed out at eighty, then ninety miles an hour. The Mercedes behind him kept gaining.

George couldn't figure why he was targeted. He had a shouting match with a guy in one of the big German companies yesterday, but that was no reason to put a German killer squad chasing him. He had asked the man about the bribes that the Jews had paid to Nazis to get out of Poland and into Switzerland. That had set off a flurry of shouting and insults and his being escorted out of the building by security guards.

Damn that Mercedes. It gained more on him. He kicked the bike up to 120 and the Mercedes was still there. The super autobahn was made for speed. But George knew that if his motorcycle tire hit one small stick on the highway or one pothole, he would go flying a hundred feet and smash himself to death on the high-speed highway. He couldn't lose the Mercedes.

The big car came roaring up behind him. George did a fast lane change and got away. The driver was trying to jolt him hard with the Mercedes's bumper. One good smack and he'd lose control and skid for two hundred feet and grind his body down to the bone. He'd be dead before anyone found him. Just another crazy American riding too fast on the autobahn.

He kept changing lanes and kept the big car well behind him. If it came close enough to smash into him, the chase would be over and he'd be dead.

He looked at the German countryside. Maybe he'd be better off off the highway on a country road, or a small town where the Mercedes guys wouldn't want to be remembered? Yes. He slowed and took the next off ramp and wound into German farm country.

The big black car had to brake hard but made the off ramp and soon was right behind him. A half mile farther on, the small road came to a village. At once he slowed and turned down a side street, then down an alley. He shifted from there to a side street where he saw an auto mechanic's open door.

George almost stopped, then rolled slowly into an open bay and let the bike idle down. He looked around. A mechanic looked up from his work on a Volkswagen and pointed to a door that must lead to the office.

George looked back the way he had come. The Mercedes drove by slowly, but the men didn't look into the shop. Good. When the big car was past, George pushed his bike farther into the bay. He noticed that it was a drive-through type with doors on both sides. The mechanic wiped his hands on a cloth and started toward George. He said something in German.

George shook his head. "No German, *nein Deutsch*." He wasn't sure how to pronounce the word for "German" or even if it was the right one. The mechanic shrugged and went back to his project.

A moment later the Mercedes drove back the way it had come, slower this time. At the driveway into the auto shop the rig paused, then the driver turned the big car right into the shop's parking area. George was partly shielded by the doors. He gunned the bike's motor and raced out the back door, did a fast run around the end of the building and back to the street.

The big redhead saw him and jolted back into his car. The chase was on again. He rode back to the center of the small town and stopped in front of a store with a sidewalk display. The men in the car didn't seem to like an audience. If he stayed in town they wouldn't be able to hurt him, at least until dark. He looked over the fruit and vegetables, bought an apple, and sat on his bike beside the display eating it.

The chase car stopped half a block back. Yes, just as he thought. The chasers didn't want to be seen by the people here, and evidently they would do him no damage in front of all these witnesses.

"Englisher?"

He looked up quickly. A young woman stood near the display and watched him. She was in her twenties, blond and pretty. He shook his head.

"No, I'm American. You speak English?"

"*Nein. Sprechen Deutsch?*" She watched him with a shy smile.

"*Nein.*" He shrugged . . . "So, *tur?*" He hoped he pronounced door right. It was one of his few German words. If there was a door he could get through into an alley.

She frowned. "Motorcycle *tur?*"

George nodded.

The girl grinned and waved for him to follow. They went down two stores to a small opening between the buildings. George thought about it. If he left the village they would catch him. Why not just cool out there awhile. Let them sweat.

He shook his head at the girl. She said something to him in German he didn't understand. The girl watched him a moment, then motioned for him to follow her. They went back to her stand and he left the bike and she opened the door to the shop behind the street stand.

It was a store with the same fruits and vegetables and much more. She waved him inside and to the back where there was a small sitting room. The girl pointed at him to sit, and hurried away. She came back with a tray with drinks and some small cakes. He smiled. "*Danke,*" he said. She smiled. He thought that was German for thanks, but he wasn't sure.

He tried the drink. A cola of some kind. She watched him critically, then pointed.

"Coca-Cola," she said.

George stood. The bike. He had to find that bug or transmitter or whatever it was. There was time now. He hurried back to the front of the store, pulled the bike behind a short wall, and looked it over. George had no idea what he was looking for. Something that didn't belong there. Two minutes later he found the small device. It was held in place by a strong magnet on the inside of the back fender. He pulled it off and looked up the street. The front bumper of a car three feet away caught his attention. He ducked low and, keeping his back to the wall, raced to the car. He put the magnet on the bumper and went back inside the shelter.

Now he could get away from them. They wouldn't know where he was. He watched with satisfaction a few minutes later as the car he had put the transmitter on backed out and drove down the street away from where the black Mercedes still sat.

George didn't waste any time. He had to get away before they tracked down the car with the bug on it. He saw the girl watching him. George caught her hands, then reached in and softly kissed her lips. She smiled.

"I go," he said. He searched his memory. "I *gehen*."

She caught his hand. "*Danke*," she said and smiled.

George grabbed his bike and pushed it to the space between the buildings. The men in the Mercedes couldn't see him. He ran the bike halfway through, then kick-started it and rode the rest of the way into an alley and down to a short street, then into more streets until he had no idea where the highway was he came in on.

He paused. Now let them try to find him. George had to think about getting back to his hotel. He checked around but he was in a downhill section and could see little of the village. It had to be north. Yes, north.

He rode that way, passed one street he recognized, and then when he checked behind him, he saw the black Mercedes.

That was impossible. He had taken off the transmitter. He swore and headed south. Soon there was no more town, only a pasture and then fields with no fences. He raced into one, jumped a small ditch, and then was in grass up to his knees. He looked behind him. The Mercedes paused at the edge of the field, then turned and paralleled him on a dirt road.

Soon the road angled toward the field that grew narrower with a line of trees on his left.

The rifle shot caught him by surprise. He was a half mile from the village. Two more shots came in the clear, crisp German air. His bike wobbled, then skidded, and he realized that his rear tire was flat. They had shot it out.

Two men ran across the field toward him. Both had rifles. He dumped the useless bike and started to run away from them but a rifle round jolted into the dirt ahead of him. He stopped.

He'd find out what they wanted. At least they didn't shoot him. He was still alive and planned on staying alive.

The men with rifles ran up and motioned for him to walk toward the car. He went. One of them rolled the bike along behind, flat tire and all. At the car the man with the eye patch came out of the driver's seat. He put his fists on his hips and stared at George.

"You're a hard guy to catch, George."

George stared at the man. "How do you know my name?"

"We know everything about you, George. Now get in the car and stop wasting our time."

"How did you track me? I took that damn bug off the fender."

The eye-patch man chuckled. "Stupid. We had two of them on your bike in case you got curious and found one."

He watched as three men lifted the big motorcycle and stuffed it halfway into the Mercedes trunk. They tied it securely in place.

George looked at the tall man. He scowled and opened the back door and pointed inside. He had a .45 pistol in his belt so George could see it. George shivered as he stepped into the rear seat. The two men who had chased him slid in as well, one on each side of him, and closed the doors.

The big car ground over the lane back to a dirt road, down it a mile, then onto a highway. A short way down the road, the driver turned off onto a gravel track and headed into the back country.

"Where are you taking me?" George asked. One of the men in the backseat beside him punched him in the side.

"I want to know what this is all about. It must be about my grandfather. Is that right?"

The driver turned a moment. "Perhaps. Now shut up."

Ten minutes later the big car came to a stop at the end of the dirt track. There were no houses or buildings. All George saw was what must be an old quarry or rock pit.

"Out," the driver said. One of the men in the backseat pushed George and he stumbled out of the car. The tall man with the eye patch stepped in front of George and glared.

"You've cost us a lot of trouble, George. We don't like that. Now who else have you talked to about your grandfather?"

"No one. Just the one company I figured would know something about him."

The German with the eye patch hit George on the side of the head. The openhanded blow sent George jolting to one side, and he almost fell down. The other two Germans grabbed him and held him up.

"Don't lie to me, you little bastard, or you'll wish your hadn't."

"Not lying." George trembled. Nobody had ever hit him that hard. What were they doing?

"You have any documents, any papers, any reports that talk about our company? You talk to anyone about us?"

George knew then lying might save his life. "Hell yes. I talked to the American embassy yesterday. Told them all about your firm."

"Like hell you did, George. You're too stupid to have thought of that. You're lying."

George felt cold, a bone chill that dulled his senses. A dank, dark icing on his ability to think. He shook his head and squinted at the tall man with the eye patch.

The redhead used his fist this time. George didn't see it coming. It smashed into his jaw and drove him backward, dumping him to the gravel on the ground. He rolled to his side. For a moment he thought he was going to pass out. He fought back the black splotches and shook his head, then sat up and felt his jaw.

The man with the eye patch said something in German. The two men went to the trunk, lifted the bike out, and put it near the edge of the old quarry. George couldn't see the pit's bottom.

George looked up. "All this because I asked about my grandfather and his bribe to some Nazi?"

"Don't worry about it," the big German said.

George sensed the meaning behind the words. He jumped up and ran down the track of a road. They were going to kill him. They just had to find the right place. This was it.

He sprinted down the road. George ran twenty feet when one of the Germans hit him from behind. He went down, rolled once, and then the heavy German planted his big shoe in George's back. He couldn't even squirm.

"Let him up," the man with the patch said. They lifted him up and held him.

"Now, little man, one more question. Does anyone else know what you're doing here in Germany besides your family?"

He lied again. "Hell yes. The American embassy, and CNN, the cable TV channel, and the U.S. State Department. I told them all and named your firm as my prime suspect in robbing my granddad."

One of the Germans tripped him and he slammed to the ground scraping both hands in the crushed rock. This time the eye-patch man grabbed him by one arm and dragged him across the gravel to where his motorcycle sat.

"Too bad about the bike," the eye-patch man said. "I was thinking of keeping it." He nodded and the two men with him pushed up the kickstand, turned on the key, and ran the BMW bike toward the edge of the cliff. They pushed it over and watched it fall.

George heard the heavy machine hit the rocks far below. He lifted up to his knees. The eye-patch man still held George's wrist in a viselike grip. One of the men took a broom from the Mercedes and walked backward from the edge of the cliff, sweeping out all signs of footprints and then the car's tread prints but leaving the bike's tire tracks.

"So, no more bike, George. What do you think goes over next?"

★ TWO ★

POTTSTOWN, PENNSYLVANIA

Stan Silokowski put down the phone and wiped his eyes. He couldn't stop the gut-churning emotion that wracked him. He turned to his wife.

"It's true." He stopped and took a deep breath trying to control his voice. "The telegram from the embassy in Germany is true. George is dead." The fury of the loss boiled over him again and he cried. Then he took his wife Mary in his arms and rocked her back and forth. She sobbed again the way she had when the telegram came the day before.

Stan shook his head wiping at his eyes. He couldn't talk for a moment. He had made the arrangements to have their only son's body flown home.

"The police said George's rented motorcycle went over a bank into a rock quarry and smashed into rocks a hundred feet below." Stan stopped and blew his nose. His wife looked up, her face swollen from crying.

"There were no witnesses to the crash," he said. "Some people said they saw George in the small town of

Vertabaun the afternoon that he died. One woman said he bought an apple at her stand and seemed nervous."

Stan Silokowski patted his wife's shoulder. "We're going to get to the bottom of this. George would never ride a motorcycle off a cliff into a rock quarry. I bet Harley can help us. I'll give him a call."

He checked a number on a phone list, then dialed. He knew Virginia, Harley's secretary, and a minute later the congressman in Washington, D.C., came on the line.

"Harley, Stan Silokowski. I need a favor."

"Stan, that's why I'm here. How's Mary?"

"She's crying, Harley. You haven't heard. Our boy George was killed in Germany yesterday." He filled in the details he knew.

"Stan, George was a motocross rider, wasn't he? No way he would get into a crash on a bike and kill himself."

"What we figured, Harley. George went to Berlin to try to find out what happened to his grandfather's four and-a-half-million-mark fortune. We think my dad used it to bribe some Germans to get out of Warsaw at the height of the ghetto cleansing in 1942. It was supposed to be for the whole family to escape. But they must have lied about that and sent Grandma and her daughter to the gas chambers. Dad said he never saw them again. He couldn't find them after the war. George said he was going to ask enough questions to get some answers."

"You think there was some foul play, Stan?"

"Harley, there has to be. I think some Nazi sonofabitch had my boy killed so he wouldn't dig up any old dirt on the Nazis. Maybe some of them are now bigshot politicians or businessmen. Can you look into it for me?"

"Stan, I'm sorry for your loss. Please give my condolences to Mary. Yes, I saw George ride. He could make a motorcycle talk. He was good. I'll bug CNN, the TV news network. I have a button I push down there in Atlanta. This is the kind of story they'll love to follow up on. We'll do what we can from this end. Have you arranged to fly George home?"

They talked for a few minutes, then said good-bye and hung up. Stan rubbed his eyes again and took two deep breaths.

"Yes, Mother, I think we're going to find out just why George died over there in Germany. I'd bet you the farm that it wasn't because he made a mistake on that bike."

Mary Silokowski looked at her husband and tried to smile through the tears. Then she cried again.

KETTERING, ENGLAND

A few miles from the village of Kettering sits the twelfth-century Castle Baldermare. Overwhelmed twice in early battles, it had been rebuilt four times in the early days, and twice a hundred years ago, but fell again into a serious state of disrepair. Three years ago it was purchased outright by American industrialist and multimillionaire J. August Marshall. A royal land grant of twenty-five hundred acres surrounding the castle was part of the deal.

Marshall spent a fortune rebuilding the castle, following drawings and specifications of the original structure put up in 1130 by the first count, John Baldermare. The American had changed the interior from solid, cold stone and drafty corridors. Now it showed warm carpets and solid oak floors, air-conditioning and central heating, some lowered ceilings, a communications room with the latest in satellite communications, radio and television, faxes, and E-mail. The entire interior had been rebuilt.

One of England's top designers had brought in furniture and decor to rival the latest townhouses in London. More than twenty original oil paintings decorated the grand assembly hall and the living quarters in the castle's thirty-two rooms.

From the outside it was pure twelfth century, from the

inside the best in twenty-first-century luxury and up-to-date practicality and convenience. The three kitchens were a shining example.

J. August Marshall sat in his den on the third floor watching TV. It was a relaxing time for him, to pull his mind off his worldwide business ventures and companies. He clicked over the dial, watching the seventy-two-inch screen built into the wall over his desk. He stopped at CNN, the news network.

"Here in Berlin we are working on a developing story. A young man named George Silokowski has been killed in what officials call a motorcycle accident west of Berlin near a small town. Authorities there say it appears that Silokowski rode his rented BMW motorcycle off a bank and into a hundred-foot-deep rock quarry.

"A woman in the small town said she sold the young man an apple as he tarried at her stand. She said he appeared nervous as if someone were chasing him. She said he asked her if there was another way out of the street and she showed him a way.

"According to reports, Silokowski was in Berlin to try to track down his grandfather's fortune lost when he escaped from Warsaw in 1942 when the Nazis were shipping the Jews there to the death camps. CNN is investigating this case further."

J. August Marshall turned off the set and opened a file cabinet built into the wall. He took out four file folders bulging with material and settled down to read.

Marshall was more than just a rich American. He had served with honors for ten years as the head of the American Central Intelligence Agency. He retired two years ago and began a project of his own that he called THE SPECIALISTS. Few people outside his private secretary and those directly involved knew anything about this group.

Marshall had come up the hard way, made his fortune in electronics, then went into government service where he built a reputation as a hard-nosed manager who made the CIA into one of the best intelligence agencies in the world.

But he had restrictions. He wanted to do more and without the cautions and control of the American Congress and the President. He put his ideas together, quit the CIA on the best of terms, and began work on his grand plan. A man with a mission. Deciding he could work best from London, he bought this old castle, had it renovated and rebuilt using the same local quarry the first Count Baldermare probably did. At the same time he bought a small export import firm in London, opened it as the Marshall Export Import Company Ltd.

His mission: to put together an elite counterterrorist team. Covert operatives fighting terrorism, corruption, drug cartels, and any other evildoers anywhere in the world.

It took Mr. Marshall a year to select his group of Specialists. He had to have the best people in the world to do the job he wanted done. But a little over a year ago he had his team. The six members finally chosen underwent rigorous training for three months. There was ample space and seclusion on the wooded and slightly rolling grounds of Baldermare Castle so they could practice with automatic weapons, explosives, and mock attacks without anyone outside the boundaries of the estate able to hear them.

Now, Wade Thorne and his Specialists lay belly down in a patch of thick woods watching a run-down shack fifty feet ahead of them. It sat below an ancient oak tree. All six of the Specialists wore German-made black and green camouflage pants and shirts and cammie floppy hats. They blended in perfectly with the woods. Wade carried an H & K MP-5 submachine gun.

He waved the end man in their line farther out. Ichi Yamagata carried a Heckler and Koch G11 automatic rifle that looked like a chunk of two-by-four. It kicked out six hundred rounds per minute of 4.7 by 33mm caseless sizzlers. Ichi was a one-time CIA small weapons specialist. He ran twenty yards to the left and went to the ground with the weapon up and ready to fire.

Next to him lay Hershel Levine, a former Israeli Mossad agent now on the Specialists team. He carried an H & K MP-5 submachine gun with 9mm parabellum rounds that burned out of the barrel at eight hundred rounds per minute. Wade motioned for him to split the difference to Ichi and the man beside him. He did.

Wade moved the person on his far left out twenty more yards so they formed an arc around this side of the building. He motioned to Kat Killinger to move into that end position. Kat was the only woman on the team, and second in command. She was an ex-CIA agent, a lawyer, and a winner of the women's Iron Man triathlon in Hawaii. She was trim, fit, with long black hair and a pretty face. Kat held a Colt M-4A1, sliding stock carbine that fired .223 bullets up to one thousand rounds per minute and had a built-in 40mm grenade launcher under the barrel.

Wade waved Roger Johnson over more with his Colt M-4A1. Roger was a former SEAL for the U.S. Navy, and came over to the Specialists after he impressed Mr. Marshall on a SEAL underwater exercise.

The last man who lay near Wade was Duncan Bancroft, a onetime English MI-6 agent who brought to the team a world of intelligence and high-level government contacts. Today he carried an H & K 21A1 machine gun that fired 7.62 NATO rounds at nine hundred rounds per minute. It weighed in at 17.5 pounds.

The team members watched Wade. He threw a fragmentation grenade at the shack. When the 4.2-second fuse exploded the hand bomb, the Specialists opened up. They fired three- and six-round bursts, riddling the shack.

Twenty seconds later, Wade touched his shoulder mike twice, sending out a tsk-tsk over the radio net. Each of the Specialists had a radio speaker earplug and at once ceased fire. Wade signaled the two end men to rush the shack. Ichi and Kat charged the shack with their weapons at the ready, and kicked in the door. Ichi darted inside diving to the right. Kat charged in diving to the left. A moment later they both came out.

"All clear in the house," Kat said on her radio.

Wade waved the rest of the team forward. Three of them hit the leaf mulch on the ground ten feet from the shack and aimed their weapons outward in a perimeter defense.

"All clear and end of the exercise," Wade said. They all relaxed. "Comments?"

Kat looked up. "Right. We didn't all start firing at the same time when the grenade went off. Usually it wouldn't matter, but it could. We've got to concentrate on that fragger and when it pops, we fire."

"True," Wade said. "Most of our fire missions won't last more than ten to twelve seconds. When we get past that time, keep listening to your radio for a cease-fire. That's about it. Any complaints about the weapons? These will be your assigned weapon for the next mission."

Ichi waved the strange-looking automatic rifle. "Hey, I love this G-Eleven. Spits them out like crazy. Aiming is easy and no crawl."

"Good. We'll all have a chance to fire it before we move out again. I want everyone to be comfortable firing all of our weapons. Now it's time . . ." He frowned, reached down, and took out the beeper that Mr. Marshall insisted that he wear at all times. He checked the message: report to Castle.

"Okay, troops, on your feet, let's take a hike back home."

They hiked back in combat formation, with Ichi out front fifty yards as a lead scout, then Wade, and behind him Roger, Hershel, and Duncan. Kat brought up the tail end of the short column as rear guard.

Wade looked forward to getting to the Castle. It had been almost three months since they had been on a mission. They had needed most of that time to heal gunshot wounds, repair some damaged flesh, and train on the new weapons. Now they were ready.

Wade was the team leader. He was six-two, 195 pounds, and an ex-CIA agent who quit the Agency to raise horses in his ranch in the wilds of Idaho. He had eight years as a CIA field agent when a former East German agent killed his wife and daughter. Three years ago he came after Wade out of pure vengeance. When Wade wasn't home, the German hit at the two things the CIA agent loved the most.

Wade had been brought into the Specialists by his former boss at the CIA and helped him select the team, put it together, establish procedures, and supervise the special training. Now he had a smoothly working operation and he wanted to get back into action.

His second in command was a winner in almost any field. Mr. Marshall had known her when she worked with the FBI as a liaison with the CIA. He found out she was a lawyer as well as FBI. She was thirty-two years old and stood almost five-ten. There had never been any sexual tension on the team, and Wade intended to keep it that way. She was one of the guys, and could outshoot most of them. For pure physical stamina she could outlast any of the five men. Wade had been surprised to learn that she was an expert on fifteenth-century Flemish painters. What won him over was that she spent a lot of her free time tutoring low-income students in reading in London.

The Specialists had a standard hiking rate of five miles an hour. That meant they traveled a mile every twelve minutes. When they came up to the side door of the Castle, they were five minutes under their normal time.

"Work on your weapons in the supply room," Wade said. "I'll talk to Mr. Marshall and see what's happening."

Wade knocked on the open den door on the third floor as he always did. Mr. Marshall put down a file folder and waved him inside.

"Yes, Wade. How did the live firing exercise go?"

"It went well, Mr. Marshall. We're getting the new weapons matched up with our people."

"Good, we might need them soon. I've been going over a small problem. You may have heard of the significant gold plundering by the Nazis from the Jews during WWII."

Wade nodded.

"Seems there has been a lot of flack about it lately, including a two-and-a-half-billion-dollar settlement between Swiss banks and survivors of the Holocaust. Some say Switzerland in effect financed the last years of the war for the Nazis by taking in the stolen Jewish gold."

He peered over another file folder at Wade.

"Now there seems to be a slightly different development. A young man from Pennsylvania went to Berlin three days ago to try to get to the bottom of how his grandfather, a Polish Jew, lost more than four million marks to the Nazis in 1942. Half a bribe, half from a Swiss bank account. It's an extremely cold trail to try to follow.

"Evidently the young man stirred up a small firestorm. He had been in Berlin only two days when a farmer found him dead in a hundred-foot-deep quarry outside of Berlin. Both he and his motorcycle had taken a great fall."

"Maybe just a motorcycle crash."

"Probably not in this case, Wade. The young man's name was George Silokowski, and back home he was an expert professional motocross rider. Not a likely candidate to ride into a quarry."

"Probably not, no," Wade said. "Does this mean some people in Berlin are so touchy about the golden days of the Nazis that they will kill a kid who's asking the wrong questions?"

"Thought you might find that interesting. CNN ran a short story about the case just now. They said there will be a follow-up as soon as they can tie down exactly who the young man talked to in Berlin."

"Might be easier to say than to do," Wade said. "Also be easy to cover up and stonewall on it."

"I've been collecting clippings and stories about this gold problem for several months. Some of it might apply. I'll get the pertinent ones copied and give them to you.

"I'll give you the information I had faxed from Washington. It isn't much. The Agency has little on it. I've talked to the CNN people in Berlin and they have little they didn't broadcast.

"We know there was a Polish Jew named John Silokowski who avoided the death camps where most of the Jews were sent from the Warsaw ghetto in 1942. According to the family, he got away by bribing a Nazi in Poland with four and a half million marks. That man was George Silokowski's grandfather. George was the young man killed outside of Berlin.

"The elder Silokowski also had a Swiss bank account worth something like one and a half million marks. John gave an altered account number to the soldier he bribed, but thought he changed it enough. Evidently he didn't. That cash was gone, too, by the time John got to Switzerland. He barely had enough money for his passage to America. He may have known the name of the man he bribed, but we haven't learned it yet.

"We do know that hundreds of Germans became 'instant millionaires' during and just after the war. Many now think that this sudden wealth came from the stolen property, bank accounts, gold, and old master oil paintings that they stole from the Jews. They were routinely robbed and stripped of all wealth when they were sent to the death camps. That's our starting point.

"We'll need to cover the Swiss bank. We have the name of the one Silokowski used and it's still in business. The rest of the team can track down just what happened to young Silokowski in Berlin.

"We'll want to probe the death completely. He should be easy to track if he was chased through the German countryside, especially in the small town.

"I'll send someone from our Washington office to talk with George's parents in Pennsylvania. We need the name of the Nazi the old man bribed fifty-seven years ago.

"I want your team on the plane to Berlin first thing in the morning. You don't need to take weapons. We have plenty in our Berlin office. We'll need an early morning start; the jet will be waiting at Heathrow."

"Very good, sir. We have some getting ready to do. Won't need any cammies in Berlin. I'd say our usual Euro civvies should work out fine."

"Yes, quite. Please ask Celinda to come in. I need to get some copy work done. Oh, don't forget to draw four hundred marks for each of you before you go. Then we'll resupply you from our office in Berlin. Wade . . . good luck."

"Thank you, sir." Wade told Celinda she was wanted inside, then hurried down to the equipment room. Everyone was there cleaning and oiling the weapons they had just used.

"Team, time to get ready. We're off again. We leave for Berlin with the early birds in the morning. Civilian clothes. Take your usual gear. One suitcase for each. Now, gather around and I'll tell you what this mission is all about. At least we won't be out in the boonies on this one."

He told them what Mr. Marshall had said about their new assignment. There were questions.

"How can we follow a trail that's fifty-seven years old?" Ichi asked.

"We don't," Kat said. "We follow the lead we have this week about the death of the young man. If it's murder and not an accident, we have a big leg up. We find out who killed the boy, and we're well on our way to prying open at least one can of worms about Nazis plundering the Jews."

"That's it, then," Wade said. "Be ready to leave at 0400."

✷ THREE ✷

BERLIN, GERMANY

The sleek Gulfstream II private jet had delivered them quickly to Berlin's big international airport that morning. A waiting van from the Marshall Export/Import Company took them to the Berlin offices. They were in a business district and the place was a near duplicate of the London office except it was smaller. The business offices were real and operating, although actual transactions were few in number.

The attached building held the heart of the European operation. It had hotel-like rooms for ten people, a small food service, storage for a dozen vehicles, an armory with hundreds of various small arms and combat-ready equipment. There were uniforms of various sorts, a print shop to turn out documents and calling cards as needed.

The communications room had instant contact with London and several of the other Marshall firms throughout the world. E-mail was Mr. Marshall's current favorite form of communications. Six computers took care of business.

The Specialists were dressed in German-style business

garb. Three of the men had on business suits. Wade wore a sport coat and turtleneck. Roger Johnson was dressed more casually for working the street. Kat had on a tailored business suit.

They gathered in their office at the back of the Export/Import space. The room held two computers, three desks, telephones, a TV set, and various files, reference books, and a snack table that was filled when they were on-site.

When they arrived there were messages waiting for them. Mr. Marshall had E-mailed Wade a report from the U.S. interview with the Silokowskis. They said that George had called them the night before he died. He told them that he thought he had a good lead and that he was going to talk to people at three big German corporations the next day.

Wade gathered the team around him. They sat in chairs and on the edges of desks.

"So we have three immediate avenues of inquiry. We need to send someone to Switzerland to talk to the bankers there. For this one we need a diplomat with some bite. My suggestion would be for Kat to go and use her lawyer wiles to see what she can develop. This will be a sticky one, but we need to give it a try. Kat?"

"Sure. I'll enjoy crossing swords with those ultra-conservative money men. It might be fun to loosen them up a little."

"Good. Next we need to trace the last hours of George Silokowski. That's going to be tough. We can start with his hotel, people he might have talked to, the doorman, the clerk, or someone in a restaurant close by. I'll start on this part this afternoon.

"We need to check with the morgue and see if they discovered anything strange. Was there an autopsy and if so what does it show? Duncan, you work this one, along with contacting the German police who will say it wasn't their case, but they might have something. Then I want you to contact the CIA in town and do some telephoning to your intelligence community contacts and see if there is anything in the wind about this death.

"Ichi and Hershel, head out to the village of Vertabaun, the Silokowski death site, and see what you can discover about how he died. Talk to all of the locals you can find. See if they remember anything about someone following him. If so we need a description of the car and who was in it.

"Johnson, I've saved the best for last for you. Check out the word on the street. See what they know, what they've heard. Is there any talk about a killing, a chase, anything out of the ordinary. Okay? Questions?"

"What about transportation?" Ichi asked.

"Use what you need. Check out a car, get a cab. Kat, take the jet."

There were no more questions. "That's about it. Draw any weapons you need, sign out for a car, and let's get into action."

Just before the close of business that same day, CNN reporter Carter Franks walked into the large lobby of a giant corporation in Berlin. He had an appointment with the press relations vice president on the twenty-seventh floor. He signed in, was shown the right elevator, and whisked up to the floor. His escort opened the door and showed him in.

"This is Mr. Carter Franks, with CNN television network," the guide said. "He has an appointment."

The receptionist/secretary nodded and went to the door behind her desk. She opened it and spoke for a moment, then turned and told Franks in German that he was expected and waved him inside.

Franks checked the room. Big desk, clean on top, two chairs, modest-sized room, two doors leading out the back. The man he came to see was in his fifties, stern-looking. There was no nameplate on his desk. Franks began using his best German.

"Good afternoon. I'm Carter Franks, CNN television. I called and made this appointment. We're interested in learning more about a caller you had two days ago, one George Silokowski."

"Yes, Mr. Franks. We saw your newscast and of course we are concerned. Our people say that Mr. Silokowski left our offices early in the afternoon. We don't know where he went after that."

"If you have anything else we would be glad to hear about it. We'll give you and your firm complete credit for helping to clear up what must be a tragic accident."

"Yes, Mr. Franks, I agree. We have a data-gathering service in another of our offices across town. I have called for a car and an escort to take you through traffic. It's terrible this time of the day."

Franks frowned slightly, surprised. He was told there might be some resentment and problems with the people here. He smiled. "Well, that sounds outstanding. Yes, if it isn't too much trouble for you. Would it be all right to bring my cameraman along? He's waiting for me in the lobby." Franks watched the man. The cameraman ploy was a bluff, but it worked sometimes.

"Actually there's no need for a cameraman unless he wants to shoot a piece of paper with some figures on it."

A door opened behind him. He looked. "Yes, here is your escort now. After you look over the material, you can give me a call if you have any questions. We are glad to cooperate with CNN anytime."

"Thank you. We appreciate that." He motioned. "Which door is out?"

"This way, Mr. Franks," an attractive blonde woman in a business suit said. She smiled. "Right through here."

Once through the door the woman smiled brightly. "Mr. Franks, we'll be taking the freight elevator to the basement. It does drop a little fast so hold on."

At the basement the doors opened and three large men frowned at Franks. The woman nodded.

Two of the men grabbed Franks by the arms and propelled him across the basement parking garage to a car with the rear doors open.

"Hey, what the hell is going on?" Franks shouted. One of the men hit him in the face. "I'm a reporter with CNN, you guys let me go right now."

The other man hit him and blood spouted from his nose. They pushed him into the car. One man got in on each side of him and the car sped away.

The blonde at the elevator lifted her brows, went in, and closed the door.

The car with Carter Franks in the rear seat sped through the afternoon rush-hour traffic. Franks cringed in the seat between the big men. He'd never been treated this way in his life. Usually the name of CNN would get him and his cameraman out of most jams. This one looked bad. Why? He saw that the car's windows were tinted. No one could see inside. He shivered.

Then he shook his head. They would beat him up and throw him out of the car, the worst they might do. Yeah, he'd survive, and then he'd blast that company right out of the water.

The driver wore a black suit, white shirt, and red tie. He had red hair and a flesh-colored patch over his left eye. He checked on the man in the center seat. He would be no problem. Finding out how much he knew might be harder.

They drove for twenty minutes, then the big car pulled into an industrial section. They drove into a large warehouse near a canal and stopped.

"Out," one of the guards snapped. He left the car and pulled Franks out on his side. The newsman held his still bleeding nose.

"Look, I don't know who you think I am, or what I might know, but I'm just small potatoes. I'm working on a little public interest story. It's no big deal. If you guys don't know anything about it, fine. I'll cut my losses and get my nose to a doctor. It's broken, so I need a night in the hospital. Do we have a deal?"

The redhead hit Franks in the jaw with a heavy right fist. The blow knocked him to his knees. Before Franks could move, the redhead kicked him in the stomach blasting him over on his back. Franks gasped for air; he doubled over and sucked air into his lungs until they filled again. He gagged for a moment, then tried to sit up.

A foot on his chest slammed him back to the ground.

"Now, you little asshole," the man with the patch rasped. "Tell us what you know about George Silokowski."

"Nothing. Just that he died in a motorcycle crash outside of Berlin a ways. Two days ago. I was just doing my job. Looking for any details, anyone who knew him here."

"That's all?"

"Damn right. If I knew anything else, I'd tell you. I don't like to get beat up."

"We haven't even started on you yet," the only one of the three who had spoken said. "You still have all your fingernails. You ever had your fingers crushed with pliers? Most effective."

They were speaking in German. Franks shook his head. "I know absolutely nothing more about Silokowski. It's just a little story. Hell, we might not even file a follow-up. No story here. Nada, nothing."

"Then why did you come to the office?"

"My editor told me to, my boss. I had to come and ask."

"Too bad. Can you stand up?"

"I think so." Franks rolled to his hands and knees and heaved up. He was half bent over from the pain. Then slowly he stood upright.

Twenty yards away in the half-light of the afternoon in the big warehouse, a homeless man lay under some old sacks near a stash of his worldly possessions. He cradled a half-empty wine bottle. He had heard the car drive in and remained dead quiet. He hadn't liked what it looked to be. Now he blinked to clear his vision. He couldn't see them too well, but he could hear every word. He would listen to them. Above all he had to stay quiet or they would kill him.

The man with the eye patch grinned at Franks. "Hey, no hard feelings, right? We're just doing our jobs, too."

Franks had to tip his head up to see the tall man's face. He didn't see it coming. *It* was a double-fisted hammer blow to the side of Frank's neck. He gave a little cry and dropped like brain-shot steer in a slaughterhouse.

"Damn that was good," the big German said. "Drag him over to the door." The other two Germans caught Franks by the feet and dragged him to a big opening at the near side of the warehouse. It was a loading door, where barges once had come to disgorge their cargo. Now trucks had replaced the barges and the business went to another warehouse.

Franks lay on the rough plank floor, unconscious but breathing.

"Wake him up," the leader said. The other two Germans slapped his face, then found a bucket and filled it with the slimy water and dumped half of it on his face. He came awake sputtering and groaning.

The tall German knelt beside where Franks lay. "You have just one more chance. Why were you at our office today?"

Franks wiped his face. He felt giddy, half out of it. He shook his head. "George Silokowski was a professional motocross rider on bikes. Not a chance in hell he'd drive a bike off a road and get killed. Somebody must have helped him along."

The German swore. "Nobody told us he was a professional bike rider."

"He was on the tour. Won six races out of twelve. Damn good rider."

"Bastard!" the eye-patch man shouted. He slugged Franks in the face three, then four times before his sudden rage subsided. He stood and waved at his two helpers. "Stand him up," he told them.

They dragged Franks to a standing position but had

to hold him. He was almost unconscious. The big German stood behind Franks and hooked one large forearm around the side of Franks's neck. He moved his arm slightly, then let Franks sag against it until his whole weight was on the German's forearm. The big man nodded and waited.

It took almost four minutes before Franks stopped the arm movement as he fought for his life. The arm had cut off all blood flow to the brain's right-hand side via the right carotid artery. The "sleeper" hold is highly effective if used for a short period of time. When used for four to five minutes, it almost always results in a sudden cessation of the brain function and a shutdown of all body operations.

The man with the eye patch grunted and dropped Franks's corpse.

"Dump him in the canal out where the river current catches it. We want him downstream by morning."

"Take off his ID?" one of the others asked.

The big German hesitated. "No, leave it all on him. Then it will look more like an accident. He fell, hit his head, and drowned, or maybe he was dead before. Let's clean up here and get moving."

They examined each area where they had been, picked up anything that might tie them to the spot. Then they stepped into the big black Mercedes and drove out of the warehouse.

The man lying in the shadows stirred and sat up. He was beyond wondering about man's inhumanity to man. All he cared about was keeping a good place to sleep and finding enough to eat. Letting those men know he was there would not have been a help in either category. He had no doubts if they saw him, he would have been the second corpse in the canal. He turned over and tried to take a quick nap before time to go find his supper.

★ FOUR ★

ZURICH, SWITZERLAND

The Marshall jet had flown Kat to Zurich, Switzerland, just after noon. As the closest large Swiss city to Germany, Zurich was the depository of much of the gold and valuables stolen from the European Jews during World War II.

Kat had done preliminary research on the Internet and the World Wide Web before she left Berlin. There had been massive amounts of work done by thousands of people trying to track down the wartime plunder of gold and valuables from Jewish individuals. One search on the Web: Nazi plunder from Jews netted 116,054 matches. The most recent top ten documents were summarized. She was amazed at the amount of material that had been written on the subject. One report from the World Jewish Congress said that even today there were two tons of Nazi gold in the Federal Reserve Bank in New York worth about $28 million and four tons of gold worth twice that held by London's Bank of England. She would have to look into these reports in more detail later.

The Swiss National Bank of Zurich was located downtown. Rock solid and secure, it had been at that same site in much the same building for the past ninety-three years. One of the new additions had been discreet and carefully hidden security.

Kat wore the same beige tailored suit she had come in from England that morning. The jacket had been newly pressed at the Berlin office and she put on a fresh white blouse. Her card indicated she was from Marshall & Fenwick, Barristers, and a London address. The name on the card was Katherine Killinger.

"I wish to see your vice president in charge of records," she said to the guard.

"I'm sure you'll need an appointment," the guard said. "However I can show you to his secretary."

They were speaking German in which Kat was fluent. The secretary was male, about thirty, and checked her card with a wary eye.

"And what is the nature of your business with Mr. Harst, might I ask?"

"That would be best for Mr. Harst and I to discuss, however I appreciate your position. You might tell him that it has to do with a closed account that dates back to 1942. It is a rather urgent matter involving some litigation our firm is now undertaking. I flew in this morning from London and would like to move on this case immediately."

"Urgent after fifty years? Well now, I'll see if Mr. Harst can make time to see you."

Mr. Harst made the time.

He took her card and smiled. "Well now, Miss Killinger, just what is this urgent matter on an account closed over fifty-seven years?"

"We are searching for evidence that an account closed in this bank in 1942 was done so illegally, by committing a felony, totally without the knowledge or approval of the real account owner."

"Well now, you do have a cold trail to follow, Miss Killinger. Just how do you intend to prove all of this?"

"With your help. With the records of that account, when the deposits were made and when the withdrawal was made. We know this was a numbered account, but still there must be some notification when a sum of nearly one and a half million marks is withdrawn."

"Miss Killinger, our time-honored system of numbered accounts is slowly eroding, as you must know. However, in that day the only requirement for a withdrawal of any amount was the coded number of the account on a slip of paper. It was no business of ours who had the number or how it was used. The number itself was adequate for the transaction."

"I understand all of this. I also realize that by Swiss law you must keep complete records of all transactions from day one. For our case we will require a complete record of that account, including all deposits and withdrawals. We are working on the assumption here that a man known to the account holder discovered the number and emptied the account without the owner's knowledge or approval."

"As I told you before, Miss Killinger. That is simply not the bank's problem."

"Actually I think it is your problem. You see the account I'm talking about belonged to John Silokowski, a Polish Jew who bribed his way out of the Warsaw ghetto in 1942 when the Nazis were exterminating Jews across Eastern Europe. He got out for a four-and-a-half-million-mark bribe. The same Nazi who took the bribe, also found out the bank account number. Now, I am sure you are anxious not to attract the same sort of media attention other Swiss banks have recently come under, regarding the horrifying revelations that Swiss banks *did* have a role in financing the last years of the Nazi horror.

"If you feel you are unable to assist me in this matter, I am afraid I would have no recourse but to go to my good friends at CNN, and about a hundred other newspaper and media reporters across the globe, who would jump on this.

"You see," Kat continued, "it's complicated by the murder of the grandson of John Silokowski. You really should reconsider your position."

"I thought the worst of this was over. We did nothing wrong."

"But you did. You accepted gold that had been pounded out of Jewish skulls after the gassing, you took stolen bonds and stocks, and cash and diamonds taken from the Jews when they were herded out of the ghettos and onto the trains. You did a lot wrong. One phone call and I can have a hundred and fifty newspeople here. Do you really want that?"

Harst sighed. "Usually we require a court order to do this, but I'll see what I can do. It will take my people an hour to dig back fifty-seven years and find that one account. We have them cross-filed by name just in case the owner does lose his number. Not all of our banks did this, but we did. Give us an hour and then come back here."

Kat said she'd be back and went out for a quick salad and a cup of coffee.

She returned five minutes early and Harst was ready for her.

"Here is the account and the number, and the name John W. Silokowski. Deposits were made to the account for four years, prior to 1942. Then they stopped. Then on September 14, 1942, a withdrawal was made closing out the account. The amount paid was 1,365,227 marks. There was no signature on the withdrawal document, only the number as that's all that was required."

"But you must have some record of who you paid out that much money to. Was that the habit of the day?"

"I'm sure I don't know. Our banking laws and practices have changed a great deal since then. Now I must ask you to leave. I have completed my part of the bargain. I trust you will do the same."

"I still need to know who withdrew that money."

"I told you I have no way of knowing or finding out.

There was no signature; only the required account number. Now, if you'll excuse me, I have other work to do." He stood up.

Kat stayed where she was. "I still want to know. There must be some way to find out."

"Oh, there is, Miss Killinger. Ask the man who took the money out of the account. He will confirm it."

"Now look . . ."

Two men in guard's uniforms appeared at the door.

"Gentlemen, Miss Killinger was just leaving. Would you be so kind as to be sure she gets all the way out the front door."

Kat knew logic was on his side. She had gotten much further than she figured she would. She scowled, stood, and walked to the door.

"I'll be back, Harst, and you'll figure out some way to find that name for me."

Just outside the door one of the guards answered a beeper and moved quickly down the hall. They were on the second floor of the large bank. Kat looked at the guard, then in a speed of light move she grabbed the guard's arm and did a karate throw over her hip and slammed him to the floor. She dropped with both knees on his back pinning him down. She reached down and took his pistol from his holster and slid it down the hallway. She used thin plastic riot cuffs from her small purse and bound his wrists behind him and cuffed his ankles.

"Now, Herr Guard, you have a fine day." She smiled at him and walked down the wide staircase to the front door.

An hour later she was in the Marshall jet on her way back to Berlin. She went over it from every angle. The money was gone. They had the date, but there simply was no way to dredge up the name of the man who stole the money. It was a dead end. She hoped that the others in Berlin were having more success.

Kat did a quick critique on her day's work and decided she had played it right, had discovered all that she could. Satisfied, she closed her brown eyes and relaxed.

A soft, warm feeling slid over her and Kat knew she was doing exactly what she wanted to do. It was a great step up from the FBI. Now she had unlimited scope; she could function anywhere in the world.

She would miss her four students at the Thirtieth Street School in London for their weekly tutoring session in reading. They were progressing well, except for little Charles who had lost his mother a month ago. She just couldn't break through to him. For a moment she thought about children of her own. As always, she pushed the idea away. Yes, she wanted two kids, but not now, not yet. Maybe in five years.

Right now she had an exciting, important, and marvelous job to do. She would stay with it as long as it was so fulfilling.

Kat smiled to herself, looked out the window, and then fell asleep.

BERLIN, GERMANY

Late that same afternoon, an impeccably dressed man four inches over five feet tall marched into a conference room. As he entered the room, six men waiting there leaped to their feet and stood at attention. He moved at once to the head of the conference table. There were seven chairs around it. On the table in front of each man was a glass of ice water, a china plate with three small cakes on it, a pad of paper, and two ballpoint pens.

The short man sat in his chair and waited a moment for the others to sit. Imperiously, he looked around the room. None of the men would meet his gaze.

"Gentlemen, I am totally appalled. I gave strict instructions that no killings should occur. Now we have had two in less than three days. This is absolutely not acceptable. The first with the boy and his motorcycle barely passes as an accident. Let's hope it holds up that way. We can afford no bad press. None whatsoever. Is that understood?"

He looked at each man until that person nodded. The last man stared straight back at the short man. He was taller than anyone else in the room, and wore an Italian-cut suit, a white shirt, and a red tie. He was redheaded and had a flesh-colored eye patch over his left orb. At last he nodded.

"This second problem is more serious and close to home. A reporter from CNN was found in the industrial canal an hour ago. The authorities say he was not shot or strangled. There were no visible signs of trauma, but he was dead. An autopsy will determine the cause of death.

"Our problem is that he told his editor at CNN that he was coming to our company for a follow-up on the story about the dead American motorcyclist. That's a di-rect tie. We must have at least four people who saw the reporter leave the office after he signed out.

"Miller, get down to reception right now and arrange for those four and sign him out an hour after he signed in. Go."

The man darted out of the room.

"You five are my key corporate men. You know how important these next few weeks are. The President's an-nouncement is a week away. We must be pristine pure until that time. And then there is the confirmation a week later.

"This is the culmination of a great deal of work by you and many others in our corporation. At this stage we can't fail. There will be no more quick and fatal solutions to some of our small problems. There are many much better ways of taking care of any untoward incidents if any more do occur. Is this perfectly clear?"

Again he looked around the table, getting signs of agreement.

"Now, the task force will spin anything that happens in the next week. PR will be especially busy and working around the clock on the corporate end. You have your quota of men and women in the government to talk to, to consult with, and to convince. The largest event of our lives could be happening in a week. We must be low-key, positive, highly effective, and no mistakes."

The small man stood. The five others came to their feet at once. One so quickly that his chair toppled over backward. No one noticed.

"Now, back to your respective action offices and back to work on spreading the good news. Remember, there is no margin for error, there is no possibility of failure."

The man motioned to the redhead to follow him and the two walked swiftly out the door. The others waited a respectable time for their leader to be out of sight when they emerged, then they took elevators or rushed down stairways, their leader's dire warnings ringing in their ears.

While Kat was in Switzerland, Wade went over the newspapers the company had saved for him. The account of the dead American was still in the news three days after the crash. He remained something of a mystery. From the papers, Wade was able to determine where George had stayed.

He checked out a car from the Marshall garage below and drove to the hotel. He was surprised to find that the police had marked the room as a possible crime scene.

He tried his French on the cop who understood him.

"Look, I'm a journalist. I just want to take a quick look around so I can do a background story on George. What can it hurt?"

"No one allowed inside."

"Come on, this is my living. If I don't do this story I'll get fined and might even lose my job."

The cop lifted his eyebrows but said nothing.

"Okay, you open the door and come in with me and

watch me as I look around. What can that hurt? I'll give you fifty marks for your trouble."

The cop grinned and held out his hand. Wade peeled off the German paper bills and handed them to him. The cop smiled, opened the door, and they both went inside. It turned out to be a small suite, with a living room and bedroom. He tried the bedroom first. The cop stayed in the other room near the entrance, not wanting to be caught deserting his post.

Wade knew that the cops had been over the room. Evidently they had found nothing, or nothing they were talking about. He checked all the obvious hiding places, the underside of dresser drawers, in the toilet tank, on the back of the TV set. Nothing.

Resolving not to miss even the smallest hint, he reached for the phone book beside the bed. He riffled through it, but there were no inserts of paper. He held it tightly together, then dropped it on its spine on the bed. The book flipped open to a page where it had been creased. There was a pen check mark beside a name. He wrote down the name, address, and phone number.

Wade heard something from the other room and drew his hideout weapon, a Russian-made Stechkin 9mm Makarov. It held twenty rounds and could fire fully automatic. The sound came again, the *pffffft* of a silenced pistol.

Wade dropped low and peered around the open door leading to the small living room. A man bent over the cop who showed two bullet wounds in his forehead. There was almost no blood. The killer whirled, sensing someone behind him. He snapped off a shot as he turned, but missed. Wade fired one round from his unsilenced weapon. The 9mm caught the shooter in the right arm, knocking the weapon from his hand.

Wade lunged into the room, flattened the intruder with a downfield tackle, and rolled on top of him. He slashed the pistol across the side of the man's head.

Quickly, Wade used riot cuffs to bind the killer's hands behind his back, then tied his feet. He checked for a pulse on the cop. He was dead.

Wade eased the door open and looked down the corridor. Nobody there, but there would be soon. His shot would bring people running. He went out the door, wiping his fingerprints off the handle. It was the only thing he had touched beside the telephone book. No good prints there. He walked quickly to the far end of the corridor, found a back stairway to a parking area, and slipped out without being seen.

He walked around the block, found the company car where he had parked it half a block beyond the hotel. He had just pulled into traffic when he saw two police cars, their European cyclic horns blasting, race into the street. Smiling grimly, he eased down into traffic and was soon away.

A mile from the hotel, he found a phone booth and stopped and dialed the number he'd taken down from the phone book. There was no answer. He checked the address. After asking two people for directions, he found the place, which appeared to be an apartment building. When he knocked on the door it opened at once. A young woman looked at him curiously. He used what little German he knew to ask about George Silokowski.

At the mention of the name she waved him inside.

"You are English?" she inquired in English.

"No, American. Sorry about my German. You knew George?"

"Yes, he was my cousin, once removed we think, on the Polish side. He called me the first day he was in town and we had a good talk. He said he'd come see me before he left."

"Did he say he was frightened, or that anyone was following him?"

She frowned. "No. I'd never met him before, but he seemed at ease, not frightened at all. He told me he thought he had a small lead about his grandfather's fortune. The next day he was going to a big corporation to talk to them. He didn't say the name of it, but I think it was one of the huge conglomerates here in Berlin."

"Anything else? I'm a detective trying to find out what happened to him. My client thinks that he was chased and then killed and the whole thing made to look like a motorcycle accident."

"Oh, my." She put one hand to her mouth and slumped in a chair. She waved him to another chair. "I had no idea. The papers said an accident."

"I'm sorry, but that looks like what happened. If you can think of anything else he said that might give us a lead, please call me at this number. My secretary is there when I'm not."

She said she would and he went back to his car and drove to George's hotel. He decided to wait an hour, hoping that the police activity around the hotel and their dead cop would settle down, so that he could take one final look around.

But an hour later, there were still two police cars there. Despite its small size and being inexpensive, the hotel had a doorman. Wade had deliberately avoided him when he went in the first time so he couldn't identify him later. Now it didn't matter. He talked to the white-haired old man with his best, if poor German.

He showed him his card that said he was a special investigator for the Marshall Detective Bureau. The man nodded and kept the card.

"The boy who was killed in the crash, the American who rode the motorcycle. Do you remember him?"

"*Ja.*"

"Did he say where he was going the last day he left the hotel?"

"*Nein.* Say big corporation. No motorcycle that day. Ask about taxi. I tell him no taxi. Four big companies within four blocks of hotel. He laughed and gave me some marks and hurried away."

"Four big corporations so close?"

"City closed in around hotel."

"I understand. Did he say which one he was going to go to?"

"*Nein*. No say."

Wade thanked him and drove away. The police hadn't come out of the hotel as he talked. He was glad of that. They would be mighty interested to know who had been in the room when their comrade was shot. At least ballistics would tell them the wounded man was the killer.

He drove to the first big corporate-looking building he saw and parked a block away. The place was huge. He would stop in each one until he found out where George had signed in for a visit the day he died. He just hoped that the one George visited was one of these four.

⋆ FIVE ⋆

BERLIN, GERMANY

Security was extremely tight. Only a selected few in the Kunistan Corporation building knew that the Chancellor of Germany, Helmut Schmidt, would be there. He arrived at a back door, quickly entered a freight elevator, and was taken to the thirty-fourth floor to the conference room.

Moments before he arrived, a small man marched into the room, nodded to the others, and took a seat at the conference table. Behind each of the eleven men seated in the room stood an aide or a bodyguard.

Chancellor Schmidt swept into the room with two aides and his own security cadre. The men in the chairs jumped to their feet and applauded. Chancellor Schmidt smiled, then motioned for them to sit down. He remained standing.

"Gentlemen, I appreciate your coming today on such short notice. I know you have busy agendas, and I appreciate your help. You men represent the best of the new Germany. You are the movers and shakers in our nation today. Your firms and corporations control more than twenty-five percent of all the production and product of our great nation. That means that what you men decide and do can sway our nation one way or the other.

"You have been asked to bring with you today your blueprint for a greater Germany. We need to know what we can do now, next week, and next year to increase our economic growth, our prosperity, to help Germany to be more influential in world affairs. We in government look to you men to help us."

The small man in the expensive suit with the bodyguard behind him who had a patch over his left eye sat there listening to the others put forth their grandiose plans. He spoke barely at all and when it came his turn, he offered a mostly blue-sky plan to double Germany's exports to China who could pay for them in hard cash. It was a quick idea, not fleshed out, but it seemed to hit a responsive chord with the others around the table.

Mostly he was biding his time. The conference had been set for two hours. Then he was to have a private meeting with the Chancellor. It was the only reason he had come to this meeting.

Three of the men around the table were long-time friends. Their fathers went all the way back to the war together, and had served in the same outfit for a while. After the war the men kept in touch and socialized together, so the sons became friends as well.

Now all the old men were dead and the second generations ran the large businesses their fathers had founded. Now all four were established powers in the business life of Germany.

At last the talk was over, the Chancellor thanked them for coming and left with his aides. The businessmen talked for a few minutes, then all hurried away to other conferences of their own. The small man adjusted his papers on the table. He and his man were the last ones left in the room.

A few moments later, the Chancellor came back with one of his aides and closed the door.

"Yes, my good friend. Thanks for helping me on this

project. You are going to be a great asset to my administration. We will work well together."

"Mr. Chancellor, I will do my best for the good of
Germany. I come to you with clean hands. My business
background gives me great experience working with
people and with large sums of money and various aspects of national and international financial operations."

"That, my friend, is why we have chosen you. I have
dropped some trial balloons around the capital. You
are well thought of. There is no scandal in your life. You
are a perfect appointee. Unless something terrible happens in the next two weeks, you will be my choice for the
position of Germany's Federal Minister of Finance."

"Thank you, Mr. Chancellor. I will do everything in
my power to serve you and Germany."

"Good, good. Now I must be moving on to another
meeting. There is always another one. You'll get used to
that quickly. My thanks to you for coming."

The politician turned and left the room with his aide.

The small man in the expensive suit stood there
smiling. He had almost done it. With his hands in the
federal treasury, he could siphon off hundreds of millions of marks and no one would know the difference.
He could steal a hundred million a year with almost no
chance of being caught. Yes, the whole array of govern-
mental agencies and bureaus and committees were out
there just waiting for him.

He turned to the man standing behind him.

"To the office, Siegfried. We have much work to do to
get ready for the announcement by the Chancellor."

The first big corporate headquarters Wade walked into
was Bavaria Limited. He went to the reception desk in
the large lobby and smiled. In his best German he
asked if he could find out if a friend had been there three
days ago.

The woman cut through his bad German with English.

"You wish to know if someone signed in for an appointment three days ago?"

He grinned. "Thanks for the English. My German is terrible."

"Yes it is." She smiled back at him. "I'll have to talk to my supervisor. I don't even have the log from three days ago."

She spoke on the phone and a moment later a man in a severe dark blue suit came striding up. They talked a moment in German.

"He asked if you are a friend?"

"Yes, from America. His name is George Silokowski." Wade hoped the two were not up on the current news and recognized George's name. The supervisor nodded and handed the receptionist a bound book. Then he marched away.

She pointed someone else in the right direction, then turned back to Wade.

"You said the name was George Silokowski. Three days ago, or two?"

"Three."

"No, no sign-in on that date, I'll check two days ago." She ran her finger down two pages of names. "Sorry, nothing by that name. Perhaps he used another name."

"He wouldn't do that. Thank you." Wade waved at her and walked out to the street.

He found the next huge corporate office less than two blocks away. It was Germany World Wide. He went to the receptionist and a guard behind a counter and asked the question.

The young woman looked up quickly. "Yes, we have heard of that man. We have been instructed to call Public Relations for any inquiry about him. If you can wait a moment, someone will be right down."

He waited. Less than three minutes later a man hurried off the elevator and talked to the receptionist. She pointed at him.

"Sir, I'm Heinrich Mueller, with the public relations

office of World Wide. We understand that you are asking about Mr. Silokowski."

"Yes, I'm trying to trace his movements his last day."

"We know about his story. Are you a reporter?"

"No, a friend. A cousin in fact. We want to know what happened to him."

"I see. We have already checked and double-checked our sign-in records for the police. His name wasn't on any of them during the past four days."

"Couldn't he just walk in, take the elevator, and go upstairs?" Wade asked.

"My no, our security is very tight here. No one gets on the elevator without a pass, a badge, or a company escort. Your man simply wasn't here. Last year an unhappy ex-employee tried to blow the building up with a bomb. Since then we have been extremely tight with our security."

Wade thanked him and went back to the street. The next large company proved to be the opposite direction. He could see the tall building and walked back past George's hotel. Now there were three police cars in front of the building. Wade walked on the other side of the street and hurried past.

At the next large building he saw the name was Zedicher International Limited. He reached for the door just as a guard locked it. The guard shook his head and pointed to his watch. It was five o'clock. He let people inside come out, but no one else could get inside. This one would have to be first on his list the next morning. Wade found his car and went back to the Berlin headquarters of Marshall Export/Import and drove into the underground garage.

That same day, just after noon, Duncan Bancroft stopped at the Central Berlin Police Department. He still knew two of the top men there after all these years.

Deputy Chief Wilheim was a short, stocky bulldog of

a man with a drooping mustache, serious dark eyes, and a handgrip that was as strong as it had ever been.

"Bancroft you old doppelganger, I hear you threw over MI-6 and tied up with some private group."

"You heard right, Chief. It's been three or four years since I've seen you. You're looking as mean and nail-chewing as ever. How's Madeline?"

The chief's eyes closed briefly. "Of course, you couldn't know. She passed on a year ago. Cancer. At least it was quick. The kids are fine. How are those two girls of yours?"

"I'm sorry about Madeline. I'd go a million miles for her apple strudel. I wish I would have known." He caught the policeman's hand again and squeezed it. Then he brightened. "The girls couldn't be better, with their mother in Scotland. At least they are away from my bad example. Now, do you have time for some business?"

"So you are on a job."

"Right, Chief. What can you tell me about the American cyclist who crashed into a quarry three days ago and died?"

"We did have a report about such a person who stopped in one of our police substations. He tried to talk with an officer, but had no German. At last he got on his bike and rode away. We think it was the same man. Not much more we can tell you. We closed his room so the other department could check it."

"Did he say anything to your people about being chased?"

"They couldn't communicate that well. We don't have English-speaking men everywhere."

"No, not your fault. We Brits don't know as many languages as we should. We're on this for a private foundation. We believe . . ."

The chief grinned and Bancroft stopped. "What?"

"That would be the Marshall Export/Import Company, I would guess. Don't look so surprised. We want to know where we can get some outside help when we need it."

Bancroft chuckled.

"We did have some civilians report some outrageous motorcycle riding, going up steps, through narrow alleys, usually with a rider who kept looking over his shoulder."

"As if someone were chasing him?"

"Precisely."

"Chief, we don't think he died in an accident. The young man was a professional motorcycle racer, something called motocross. I believe they have such races here in Germany. Not the kind of a rider who would drive his bike off a hundred-foot drop."

"We agree, but there is nothing we can do about it. No crime took place in this jurisdiction. We don't have enough evidence to ask the Federal Police to investigate."

"Did you know the boy was in town to try to trace his grandfather's lost fortune? His grandfather was a Polish Jew sent out of Warsaw in 1942 during the genocide. He bribed his way off the death train to Treblinka and was sent to Switzerland. But there he found his numbered account had been raided. Altogether he lost more than four million marks."

"We keep hearing these stories, but it's out of our hands. The federal people are trying. That goes back almost sixty years. A cold trail. We wish you luck. Even your outfit will need lots of it to break into this kind of a case. But anything I hear, I'll be in touch with you at the export firm."

"Thanks, Chief. Our number is in the book." Bancroft reached out and took the cop's hand. "You take it easy. About time you retired and enjoyed those grandchildren."

"Ha, enjoy? They wear me out in half a day. Maybe next year when they are older." He smiled, stood with an obvious effort, and walked his friend to the door.

From the police station, Duncan caught a taxi to a tall building that he knew well. It was some kind of a bank if he remembered right, but he seldom had noticed that in the past. He went in the side door he always had used and took the self-service elevator to the eleventh floor.

Once off the elevator, he smiled. The same as before. There was no company designation. None of the doors had names or numbers on them. He glanced at the two high points and saw the video cameras were still there.

He walked briskly to the first door and stood so the camera could see him. He didn't bother knocking, and spoke plainly so the microphone would pick it up. "Duncan Bancroft. I've come from Mr. J. August Marshall. We need a small conference."

It took only a moment for the electric lock on the door to snick open and the door slid to the side into the wall. Same as usual. When the door opened, he saw inside the prison-sparse and operating-room-clean small room. It held one economy-size desk, a chair, and a pert young woman smiling at him. She rose and extended her hand.

"Mr. Bancroft, so good to see you again."

"Laura, as lovely as ever. Is it true that you're married?"

"Oh, I'm afraid not. Still waiting and watching. How is Mr. Marshall?"

"He's well, thank you. Except right now he's a bit upset about a matter I need to discuss with someone. Anyone still here who I know?"

"There's Warnick, Henshaw, and Hillary."

Bancroft smiled. "Hillary? Really. Is she tied up?"

"I'm sure she can make time for an old friend. Just a sec." She pushed a button on her desk and spoke softly into the audio pickups placed on three sides of her desk.

"Hillary, I have a Mr. Duncan Bancroft in the outer office. He's rather keen on talking with you."

Duncan had forgotten that Laura was British. She looked up. He hadn't noticed that she wore a different hairdo.

"Her nibs will be right down. She said not to let you move an inch. Sounds like she's glad to see you."

He smiled and waited. There were no windows in the room, no other doors that he could see. A moment later a panel in the rear of the room slid into the wall and a tall woman with short dark hair and a glowing smile hurried through. She held out her arms and hugged Duncan.

"Darling Duncan, it's been far, far too long. Come up to my office and we can talk about old times." She kissed him quickly on the cheek and caught his arm. She politely pulled him toward the door.

"Laura, if I'm never seen again . . ."

Then they were through the door. An elevator ride and a long hallway later, they arrived at Hillary's office. It was a suite, with an official area, a tiny kitchen, and a living room. She took him to the couch and they sat down.

"Now, tell me what you've been up to. Hear you're working with my old boss, Mr. Marshall."

"Right. Best job I've ever had. Not that my former employers weren't fine."

"I hear it pays damn well."

"True, but the kind of work we do is much expanded from the usual MI-6 operations." He stared at her. "Slim and trim and as beautiful as ever. How do you do it? Some fountain of youth somewhere? You must be well over twenty-four by now."

She laughed and kissed his lips and then eased back.

"Well thank you. That makes my day. You always were a darling. Now, damnit, to business. I'd guess you're here on a mission of some sort."

"The American motorcycle rider who died outside of town three days ago. You heard about it?"

"We did. I did. I'm on it for all the good it will do. We've hit dead ends everywhere. The police know nothing. There is no evidence of any foul play. Some talk that he was followed, chased by a black Mercedes, but there are thousands of them here in Berlin. We can't help you a bit."

"Who did you talk to?"

"The Berlin police, the village police near where he was found. The doctors who did the autopsy. The manager of the hotel where he stayed. He was in town only part of two days before he died. Not much to go on."

"No drugs or alcohol in his system?"

"None. No obvious wounds that would kill him. Just the mashing from the fall he took. A broken neck, broken back, both legs smashed, internal injuries they didn't even list, and a crushed skull. Take your pick for the cause of death."

"What about CNN?"

"We got most of our information from them. They were on it like vultures. Said something about a congressman who had the ear of one of their senior VPs in Atlanta."

"You know why the boy was in town?"

"Tracing his grandfather's history?"

"Part of it. His grandfather was a Warsaw Jew who dropped almost four million dollars bribing his way off the death train to Treblinka. The kid was here to rattle some cages and see who yelled uncle. Looks like he did and they did. Now we need to find out who."

"Nobody told us that part."

"You didn't need to know, I guess. You know nothing of any ties to anyone with that kind of a past?"

"Bribery. I've heard it was widespread in those days. Thousands of Nazis must have cleaned up. Gold teeth, old master paintings, diamonds, and gold. I can do some gentle probing, but this is still a tremendously sensitive subject with modern-day Germans."

"Yeah, what did your daddy do in the war, Hans?"

She nodded.

"Is this going to be all business?" she asked.

"At least for now. Maybe we can have dinner later."

"How's your ex and the girls?"

"Great, in Scotland in school. How's your ex?"

"I don't know. We don't keep in touch. No reason."

"I better go. Too early for dinner. Besides I have to report in."

"He's a slave driver."

"True, but we're willing slaves." He stood and she stood and he caught her face and kissed her lips deliciously.

"Later," he said. "Now you better lead me out of here so nobody shoots me."

As he walked away from the CIA building, Duncan thought of his girls in Scotland. He missed them. They were growing up so quickly. For no reason, that made him think of Cambridge. It had been early on. He had enjoyed the academic world. For a while. Then reality set in.

It had given him time for this boat. The summer sailing had been glorious. But no time now. He had sold the boat a year ago. He didn't even have time for competition pistol shooting. He had been moving up in the ranks. It was a tough sport.

The reverie came full circle as he thought of his two small girls again. What were they six and eight now? Time. It seemed to escape his clutches so easily.

☆ SIX ☆

Roger Johnson wore scruffy shoes, old pants, and a tattered windbreaker that had been thrown out twice. He left the Berlin Marshall office in a battered sedan, the worst-looking car in the fleet, and drove into the heart of the depressed part of town.

It had once been a thriving warehouse section, but economics turned the business another direction, and now many of the warehouses were abandoned until the owners could figure out a new and productive use for them.

Into the vacuum had poured dozens of street people of Berlin, those homeless who were further than down and out and desperately trying to hang on and find the food and the will to live for one more day.

Roger knew the feeling. As a black growing up in the New York City projects he had seen all of the worst that life had to offer those without enough money, without any incentive, with little family stability, and with no hope for a future.

Basketball on the school and public courts had been his salvation. He was good, but not good enough to be offered a scholarship to a college or university. Now, he parked six blocks from the heart of the homeless subculture and made his way slowly into the area. He carried a half-full bottle of cheap wine in a brown paper sack. He had poured the top half into the sink before he left the headquarters.

Roger was good at playing half drunk. As a Navy SEAL he had been one of the hardest drinkers in his unit until it almost killed him one night when he insisted on driving back to the base. After that he never touched alcohol again. Now he swayed a little humming a tune as he came to the first knot of bodies sitting around a small fire on the concrete floor of a partly fallen-down warehouse.

Roger spoke no German, but he figured some of these people would speak English or maybe French.

Somebody called to him in German. He stopped, swayed, and came to attention. Then he giggled. He spat back at the speaker a dozen words of Swahili, and a man laughed.

The speaker seemed to be the leader of this small band. He waved and said something in another language. Roger shook his head and held up the wine bottle.

"*Sprechen* this, you motherfuckers?"

"Ah, Englisher," someone else said, a woman. "You are a black man, aren't you?"

"I look like a white honkey to you, bro?" His words were slightly slurred, but understandable. Even today in much of Europe there is a curiosity about blacks. Many from Africa now live there but still most Europeans have never talked with a black person.

Roger tipped the bottle, swallowed a little of the strange cheap wine, and then held it high.

"Come on in, friend," the small woman who knew English said.

He walked to the group with the overly careful steps of a man who is drunk and knows it. Then he stumbled just before he sat down and the woman caught the bottle of wine spilling only a little of it.

She pointed at the bottle. Roger shrugged, then nodded. "Help yourself, pass it around. I can always steal another one." Two in the group laughed. Another one understood English.

"Why a dumb fire?" Roger asked. His slurred words were about the same.

"Our best provider promised us two chickens," the small woman said. "Told us to have the fire going, he'd bring the birds."

"He's late."

The woman translated and the ten others around the fire chattered a minute in derision. The translator was tiny, probably not even five feet tall, Roger guessed, maybe ninety pounds dripping wet. Her face was smudged and dirty, her hair hid by a bandanna, and grimy clothes covered her completely.

He took a candy bar from his pocket, opened it, and took a bite. Only then did he notice that every eye around the fire watched him. He shrugged and gave the rest of it to the woman.

She brightened. "Yeah? Thanks. I'm Magda."

"Roger," he said. Magda broke off a small piece of the candy and passed the bar to the next person. It went around six people. The others who didn't get any of it didn't object.

"What's happening?" Roger said.

Someone across the group growled, then stood. He was over six feet tall, a skinny two hundred pounds.

Madga said something sharply in German. She turned to Roger. "Ignore him. He thinks you're a cop. He's right. You're too fucking clean to be one of us."

Roger had forgotten that part.

"Hell, I fell in the canal yesterday, couldn't help it. Some of the damn dirt washed off."

Magda translated to the group and most of them laughed.

The big man came around the group and stared down at Roger. Without warning his foot lashed out in a kick aimed at Roger's side.

In a move just as quick, Roger grabbed the boot with

both hands, twisted it to the side, put it on his shoulder, and rammed it upward. The surprised German lost his balance, both feet went high, and he fell on his back and neck. Before he could gain his feet, Roger had both his knees planted on the man's chest and a six-inch knife pressing against his throat.

"You were saying?" Roger said.

Magda translated.

He said something in German and Magda told Roger. "He says you must be a cop to know a move like that."

Roger laughed, pulled back the knife, stood, and reached down to help the big man stand.

"Not a chance. U.S. Navy SEALs. NAVSPECWAR-GRUPONE."

Magda looked at him a moment, then translated. The big man hadn't stood. He sat on the ground and stared at Roger.

"SEALs, *ja*," the man said. He came to his feet and held out his hand. "Damn fine bunch, you SEALs. I'm Larry. I did a hitch in the U.S. Navy. On a carrier. Seen you boys operate. Sorry about the misunderstanding."

"No sweat off my balls," Roger said. They both grinned and shook hands.

"No more English-speaking surprises," Magda said.

"Good, so what's happening?"

She grinned. "You're no drunk, Roger. But no cop either. We can tell the German undercover guys. Their hair like yours gives them away. If it's clean and combed, you damn well ain't one of us. Next time mess up your hair and get some dirt in it. Now, why the fuck you here?"

He took out three more candy bars and started them around the circle the other way. A murmur of approval went with the candy.

"Straight?"

"As a string."

"You hear anything on the street about a killing? This American motorcycle rider who jumped his bike into a deep quarry three days ago."

"Heard about that. No buzz on the street about it being a snuff. Let me ask the guys." She talked to the others in German. Roger saw heads shake, a couple of "*neins*." Magda shook her head. "Sorry, nothing about that has filtered down to us."

"What about Crazy Otto," Larry said.

Roger looked at Magda. "Crazy Otto?"

"Old-timer we wouldn't let in our group. Crazy as a bulldog when he ain't drunk. Stays by himself. Somebody saw him early this afternoon. Claimed he saw three guys kill a man and throw him in the canal."

"Today?" Roger asked.

"From what he said. But then he's crazy."

"Who was snuffed?"

"Don't know. Nobody might have found the body yet."

"Yeah, might not." Roger frowned. Worth a try, he decided. "Where is Crazy Otto? Like to talk to him."

"You're joking," Magda said. "What good would that do?"

"I don't know. I'm digging into everything I can find. You know where he is?"

"Yeah. Stays in a warehouse just off the canal about two blocks over. You really want to talk to him?"

It took them twenty minutes to find Crazy Otto. Even though Magda knew where he holed up, she couldn't walk right to it. They found him under a fallen-down wall that made a three-foot-high protected cave. Rubbish nearly sealed the front of it.

"Any more candy bars?" Magda asked.

Roger took two candy bars and tossed them into the opening. Soon the shell of a man crawled out. He was grinning. Spouting German nonstop. Skinny as a nightstick, wore four sets of clothes even in the good weather. One set was dirtier than the other. He wore a motorcycle helmet without visor.

"See what I mean?" Magda asked. Crazy Otto began

shrieking, pointing at Roger, and screaming in German. Magda talked to him gently, repeated some phrases over and over.

At last she had him calmed down enough so she could ask him some questions. The crazy one cocked his head to one side and nodded. She turned to Roger.

"Okay, he says he did see three big men kill a much smaller man just before noon. They beat him up, questioned him about what he knew about somebody. He's forgotten the name. Then one man held his arm around the smaller man's throat until it killed him. Then they threw him in the canal out where the current would take the body downstream."

"Sounds like the old sleeper hold. Cuts off the blood flow to the brain. If it's held too long it can kill."

"That's about all he said."

Crazy Otto spouted more German and then laughed high and long.

"He says he remembers the name they asked the guy about. He will tell me for two more candy bars."

Roger was down to his last two. He took them out and held on to half of the bars and let Crazy Otto hold the other half. Crazy Otto giggled and then laughed and nodded. He said something in German and then a name that Roger knew.

"He says the man they killed was asking about a Pole. Crazy Otto said he remembered because it sounded like the name of his relatives in Poland."

Roger felt his blood pressure rise. "Ask him what the men looked like, what they wore, if they had a car what kind it was?"

She talked to him for several minutes, evidently asking him to try hard to remember. At last she lifted her brows.

"Well, he says there were three of them. The guy who seemed to be the boss had red hair and an eye patch. Looked out of place, that's why he remembered it. He said he was no more than fifty feet away when the car drove up and didn't move a whisker while they questioned and then beat up the guy."

The old man looked at Magda and shouted something from the lip of his own private abode. She nodded.

"He says one other thing. The car had German federal government license plates on it."

Roger thanked the old man, then he and Magda headed back to the fire. Roger gave Magda one hundred marks and told her to take the gang out for pizza.

She chuckled. "Yes, pizza. We know pizza. This time we buy it in front, not get the leftovers out of the trash in back."

Roger roamed the forgotten zone for another three hours, but could find no one else who had heard anything about a killing, in the warehouse or in a rock quarry, so he headed back to company headquarters.

It was early afternoon that first day in Berlin when Ichi and Hershel checked the small German village of Vertabaun. They had no trouble finding it and parked the small sedan on the main street and looked for the cart woman selling apples. They found her a block up the narrow avenue.

Hershel knew enough German to get by, and the girl behind the stand knew some English.

"Do you remember the American riding the motorcycle?" Hershel asked.

She frowned. "Yes. Police here in town ask questions. Three newspeople come, one with big TV camera. I say all I know."

"Did you see anyone following George?"

"No. He was nervous, frightened. I could tell."

"Was he handsome?"

"No." She laughed softly. "He was attractive. I liked him. Then he asked about how to get off the street. I show him, he leave."

"You saw no one who seemed to be following him, threatening him?"

She shook her head.

"Anyone else on the street who might have noticed him?"

"Yes, Klaus, the barber. He love motorcycles. He would notice."

They talked to Klaus in his shop four stores down. The barber spoke good English.

"Yes, I saw the lad. That bike, great one. Wish I had it. Not enough left to fix up. Rental firm came and took it."

"Did you see the motorcycle go through the walkway between the buildings?"

"Yes. Others have done it."

"You're not much help, Klaus."

"Did I tell you about the tall man with black suit and an eye patch?"

"No. Who was he?"

"I don't know. When the motorcycle went through the walkway, the big man with the eye patch ran the other way and got in a car. A big Mercedes sedan. Unusual, no?"

"Unusual, yes. *Danke*."

Hershel and Ichi ran back to the passage between the buildings and hurried through it. In back of the buildings were two rows of houses, then nothing but open space and a fenced pasture.

"Where would he go back here?" Ichi asked.

Hershel walked directly away from the passage. "I'd head out this way if I was running for my life. Power up and race down here past these houses."

They knocked at the door of the last house before the pasture. The woman who came to the door was in her seventies and spoke no English.

She chattered a moment in German and Hershel tried to follow it but couldn't. Finally he said the German word for motorcycle.

The old woman frowned, then slowly smiled. She waved at them to follow her. With short slow steps she walked to the end of the road in front of her house and to the ditch. There was no fence on this side. She pointed to the soft earth of the ditch and said something.

Ichi bent down and looked.

"Be damned. Motorcycle tracks. So old George cut across the field here."

Ichi caught the old woman's attention. "Gross Mercedes-Benz?"

She frowned again, started to shake her head, then nodded.

"Ja, Mercedes-Benz gross." She said something else, then motioned that it drove up to the ditch, turned around, and roared away.

They thanked the old woman and went back to town.

Ten minutes later they had driven past the old woman's house, found a road that went the same way the fence did, and followed where George might have ridden his bike crosscountry.

Two miles along, a four-strand barbed-wire fence angled in toward the gravel road. It would have forced George to come in close to the road.

Ichi pulled over on the road and stopped. "Maybe they shot him off the bike with a rifle," Ichi said. "Be easy to do at this range. Maybe we can find some rifle brass out here."

They walked the near side of the road for fifty yards, then Ichi gave a yelp. In the soft dirt at the side of the road they found tire tracks.

"Hey, heavy-duty tires, like a Mercedes would use."

They looked over the ground near the tracks carefully, then went over it again. Hershel found a single rifle shell casing in gleaming brass.

"So, they shot him or his bike here, pulled the rig over, and somebody rode it into the hills," Hershel said. "The report said they found his body ten kilometers north of here."

"We won't find anything out there," Ichi said. "The German police are good at that kind of thing. Let's try the town and Klaus again."

They parked at the end of the two-block main street and asked a dozen people about the big Mercedes. Nobody had noticed anything different that day.

Klaus was waiting for them. "Remember something," he said. "My friend Heinrich said he saw a big black Mercedes drive in and park. It had government license plates. Heinrich owes the government money so he hid. They weren't looking for him. Funny."

"Government plates. Was he sure?"

"Plenty sure to hide four hours."

Ichi gave Klaus fifty marks. The German nodded and stuffed the money in his pocket. "Remember another thing. The big man with eye patch over left eye also had red hair. Bright red hair like a carrot."

They thanked the German barber again and headed for their car. Ichi held out his hand and stopped Hershel twenty yards away. He saw feet sticking out from under the front of the Marshall company sedan. Ichi moved up quickly without a sound. Ichi stomped on one of the man's ankles, bringing a wail of pain.

At the same time Ichi grabbed both feet and pulled the man out from under the car. He squirmed free and tried to get away. Ichi slammed a straight right fist into his jaw and a kick into his belly. The man rolled over, whimpering.

Hershel put his foot on the man's back pinning him to the ground while Ichi checked under the car. He found a pool of brake fluid and a severed brake line.

"That first little hill outside of town would have been our last country drive," Ichi said. "No brakes at all."

Hershel kicked the man in the side, stood him up, and marched him down an alley. Hershel waved Ichi away. "You get a new brake line and I'll confer with our guest."

Ichi grinned and hurried away to find a new brake line or a garage that could fix the damage.

Hershel stared at the man a moment. They were in an alley with nobody in sight. Without warning, Hershel slammed a side of his hand into the sabotager's neck. He stumbled to the left but kept his feet.

"Why did you damage our car?" Hershel asked in German. The man looked straight ahead as if he didn't understand the question. Hershel opened his jacket so the man could see the .45-caliber automatic in his holster.

Beads of sweat popped out on the German's forehead.

Hershel jolted a short, vicious blow with his slightly closed fist to the back on the man's right side, slamming into his kidney. The German folded up at his waist and sagged to the ground.

In the meantime, Ichi found a small garage, showed the mechanic the problem, and in twenty minutes had a new brake line to replace the cut section. Ichi found Hershel sitting beside the German in the alley.

"Not a word," Hershel said. They handcuffed the man with his hands behind him and pushed him into the rear seat of the sedan. Ichi went in beside him and they headed back to Berlin.

Ichi called for a stop before they got to the autobahn.

"This one will be clean. No prints on file, no mug shot in the police records. They're too smart to use bad people. Let's strip-search him and dump him out naked as an Alpine blue jay."

They did on a small side road. In his clothes they found no labels, and no identification. Only twenty of the old German marks and a small slip of paper with two phone numbers on it. They were Berlin numbers.

At the first easy-to-use phone booth in Berlin, they stopped and tried the numbers. The first had an answering machine. They didn't leave a message. The second number produced a *"Ja?"* and nothing else. They would have to follow up on the addresses tomorrow.

It was dark by that time and they reported back to headquarters at the Marshall Export/Import office.

They parked the sedan in a no-parking zone at the back of the firm and walked around to the front door. Just inside was the usual hustle of end-of-the-day business. They nodded to some of the employees and walked to the rear of the complex where they took an elevator to the fourth floor.

When the elevator doors opened, they faced a small lobby with a desk with no one behind it, a chair, and two sets of doors. They looked at the first door and waited.

Behind the door a camera recorded their faces and a scanner quickly evaluated each man's iris. The technology was so new few people knew about it yet. A machine converted the colorful ring around the eye's pupil into a human bar code that is as unique and individualistic as fingerprints.

This system was far different from the old retina identification system that was used for many years for access to nuclear weapons. That one never caught on because you had to come within inches of the camera for it to work. The new iris-scanning cameras can work from a ten-to-twelve-foot distance with perfect results.

The system even functions correctly regardless of eyeglasses or contact lenses.

It took only a second or two and the iris ID had double-checked and approved the two men for entry. A light glowed near the door handle by the time the two men walked up to it. The RI had correctly cleared them for access to the next level of security.

Inside the door lay a larger room. Here four security men were on duty twenty-four hours a day. They checked ID cards, logged the visitor's name and time and person to be contacted.

With the two Specialists, they simply waved them through the electronically controlled door that rolled into the wall.

After walking down a long hall, the two came to the meeting room of the Specialists. Here there were six desks, a conference table, a variety of projectors, and a twenty-foot-long wall made up of fifteen feet of soft material bulletin board and the rest a green chalkboard.

Four members of the team were already there. Two were at their desks, and two at the bulletin board using push pins to tack up the results of their day's work.

Hershel and Ichi went to one desk and began to type out on their computer the pertinent accomplishments of their trip to the country town of Vertabaun.

Twenty minutes later, promptly at five-thirty, Kat Killinger went to the bulletin board and began to study it. The rest of the team grouped around her and read the results of the others' efforts. Long ago Kat had become the evaluator, the logic master, the person to gather together the facts thus far compiled and interpolate them and make decisions about what would be the best next step. Her lawyer's mind was devious at times, but usually worked through the chaff, and came up with good plans about what to do next.

Kat looked at the notes she had put on the bulletin board on the white sheets of paper about her work.

"Went to the Swiss National Bank, Zurich. John Silokowski account emptied and closed September 14, 1942. No signature on withdrawal slip. None needed at that time. No way to determine who withdrew the money. Dead end here. No more contact."

Kat moved to the next series of papers. They were from Wade.

"Located George's hotel. Bribed cop to get inside. Cop shot dead by intruder. I wounded the killer, left him tied for police. Found one name and phone number. Left by rear stairs. My weapon was not silenced. Followed up on phone number. Woman was distant cousin of George who had called her the first day he was in town. He told his cousin he was going to a 'big corporation' next day.

"Talked to the hotel doorman. Said George asked about a taxi to go to big corporate headquarters. Doorman said four of them nearby, no taxi needed. Checked out two huge corporate offices. Neither had any record of George visiting them. Two left to check."

Duncan's report came next.

"Saw an old friend, Deputy Chief Wilheim at the Berlin PD. He said no crime in his jurisdiction, so he can't help us. Then I went to the CIA headquarters in Berlin. Talked to a friend there, Hillary. CIA didn't know why George was in town. They say the CNN news group had inside information from a congressman. They were the main push. The CIA doesn't have a clue about George."

Ichi and Hershel's report came next.

"Checked the village near death scene. Several people saw George in town. He appeared frightened but not in a panic. Large Mercedes with government plates chased him. One man in the car was tall with an eye patch over left eye and had red hair. Found rifle brass where they could have shot George or the bike. Area of the death site in hilly country that's virtually deserted. Caught a man who cut the company sedan's brake line. Questioned him but he wouldn't talk. Found only two phone numbers that we'll follow up on. He was a local working for someone."

Roger's report read:

"Disguised as a homeless man, shared some wine with new friends in run-down section near warehouses. One man said he heard from a recluse that someone had been killed near his hideaway. Found the man. He said three men beat and killed a man and threw his body in an adjacent canal that led to the river. The headman of the trio was large, with an eye patch over his left eye and had red hair. They drove a large Mercedes with government plates."

Kat read the last report and made some notes on a pad. When all the Specialists had read the reports they looked at Kat.

"Okay, we know that the bank route is a fizzle. Nothing there we can use. His hotel room proved a blank, the police and CIA can't help us just yet. The bright spot is the ID on the man in on two killings. Tall man with red hair and a patch over his left eye. He showed up at George's motorcycle death and a dead man in the river. We need to find out who that dead man is and how he might be involved with George. Any questions or comments?"

"We're nowhere," Ichi said.

"Hey, we've been on the job for half a day," Wade said. "If this is a cover-up for some Nazi plunder, you can bet it's buried way down deep. We'll have to dig. We can be almost certain that George was murdered. We just don't know who and for sure why."

"Tomorrow?" Kat asked.

Wade watched his team. "I'll follow up on the other two large corporate headquarters near George's hotel. The proximity to his target is probably why he stayed at that hotel. Ichi and Hershel, I want you to go back to that village and find out if anyone wrote down the license plate number on that Mercedes with the government tags. Then try to see if anyone spotted the Mercedes and the cycle together.

"Roger, I want you to find out who that dead man was. The police should have something on him by now. Follow wherever it leads. There may be a connection with George. We need to know the tie-in fast. Not many men who have red hair and an eye patch running around Berlin these days.

"Duncan, can you do any more good with the cops or the CIA?"

"I doubt it. They have nothing on it. I don't think the Berlin cops want to get involved. The CIA is totally in the dark."

"You come with me on the corporate check. Kat?"

"I want to work the big newspaper financial editors. They must have a lot about this Nazi plunder they aren't printing. It might lead to some files on early millionaires coming out of the war who were working-class men going into it."

"Sounds good. Let's get some sleep and hit it hard in the morning. Mr. Marshall is going to want a report to-morrow night."

⋆ SEVEN ⋆

The next morning Wade and Duncan approached the third of the big corporate headquarters on Wade's list. It was the Zellerbach Corporation International. Wade wasn't sure what they did, but they said they had offices in twelve major European cities, in six U.S. cities, and in ten other worldwide capitals.

Two blonde ladies handled the information desk in the huge lobby. Both smiled at once.

"Do you speak English?" Wade asked.

"How lucky I'm here today," the closest one said. "My English isn't perfect but I can communicate. Yes?"

"Absolutely." Wade handed her his card from the Marshall News Service. "My job this morning is to find out all I can about a man named George Silokowski. What I need to know is if he checked into your building four days ago to see someone here. Would that be possible?"

"Yes, of course. I have a computer printout of the visitors for that day. Just give me his name and I'll pull up the file and do a search and have it in a minute if he's signed in during the last month."

"George Silokowski is the man's name." He spelled it for her as she pulled up the file and put the name in the search square. She hit FIND on the screen with the mouse and a moment later the screen flashed back.

"I'm sorry, sir, there is no record of George Silokow-ski signing in during the past month. Are you sure he came here?"

"Not really. I know he came to one of these big outfits. I'm trying to find out which one."

"You might try down half a block, Zedicher International Limited."

"Yes, we'll do that. You have a nice day."

"What?" she asked.

"You have a nice day."

"Oh, yes. American. She smiled. "We don't say that much here in Germany, but I like it."

On the way down the block, Duncan had an idea.

"Wasting time, two of us on this. Somebody said that CNN was a key on the first story about George. Why don't I go check them out while you hit Zedicher?"

"Good. I'll see you back at HQ about noon."

Two minutes later, Wade Thorne walked into the atrium lobby of the German industrial giant, Zedicher International Ltd. From the signs around, it seemed that they had an office in every country in the world. The soaring atrium was ten stories tall with fountains and living plants and huge glass sections to let in the sunshine. Hanging vines draped down five stories.

To the left he saw a reception desk on an elaborate vine-and-flower-covered pedestal. There were various signs as if each type of inquiry could go to a different worker. He chose one and held out his card.

The young woman smiled and said something in German he didn't understand. She took his card.

"*Sprechen English?*" he asked. The woman shook her head, held up one finger for him to wait, and slid out of her seat. Another woman, younger, prettier, came into the chair.

"Yes, Mr. Thorne," she said, reading off the card. "How may I help you?"

"I'm with the Marshall News Service. We're doing a follow-up story on the George Silokowski affair. We need to know if George signed in here four days ago to see some of your people."

"I'm sorry, sir, those files are confidential."

"Come on, a sign-in sheet confidential? May I speak with your supervisor?"

The woman stared at him for a moment, then evidently seeing that she couldn't dissuade him, picked up a phone and made a call.

"Mr. Schultz will be with you in a moment. If you'll sit in the blue chair right over there, he'll be here in five minutes."

Wade moved to the chair and stood beside it waiting. He didn't tap his foot but he might as well have. Sign-in list confidential? He'd never heard of such a thing. They must have it on computer. Why the hustle?

From habit he had clicked on his stopwatch when the girl gave him the five-minute deadline. Now he checked the readout. It had been four minutes and twenty seconds.

"Mr. Thorne?" A voice came from behind him.

Wade turned around and found a man four inches shorter than he, in an expensive suit and an all-business haircut. He wore glasses and smiled.

"You were inquiring about someone who signed in. This is a sensitive area. We have competitors who would like to know who comes to visit us. What was the name again?"

"George Silokowski. You may have seen it in the news. He died in a motorcycle crash four days ago."

"I'm not familiar with the name, but if you come to my office we can look for it. He wasn't a businessman, then?"

"No, he was just a guy from America trying to find his grandfather."

"Right. Let's go up to my office. The records are there or in the next office."

A few minutes later they walked off the elevator on the thirty-fourth floor and went down the hall to a room that had the door open. An attractive blonde woman in her twenties said something in German to the man.

"Yes. Mr. Thorne, this is Helga. She is in charge of our sign-in roster and our public relations applications. She knows the name you look for and will help you find it."

Helga held out her hand. It was cold as he took it and nodded in a short bow.

"Thanks, Helga. I'm sure you can do the job."

"I try. Little English. This way."

She led him into her office to a chair across a desk and looked at a file that lay open there.

"You say four days ago?"

"Yes."

"The name George Silokowski?"

"That's right. He came here that day to talk to some of your people. He may have come to public relations. I don't know who else he would talk to first. It was a rather delicate matter about his grandfather who escaped from Poland during the war, World War II that is."

She looked up and nodded. "I am sorry. I find no mention of Mr. Silokowski on my printout. Let me check the computer in the next office. Come right back."

Wade nodded at her and watched her walk away. It was an interesting geometric movement under a tight skirt. The whole day might not be wasted. He looked around the office. Bare of any personal touch. No pictures of family, no old school banners. One faded watercolor of a beach scene. That was it. German efficiency. Four metal filing cabinets, one desk, two chairs, and a desk lamp.

Helga came back in less than five minutes. She waved a sheaf of printouts and shook her head.

"Check five days ago, four days ago, and three days back. Mr. Silokowski not show on any of them. Sorry."

"Look, it's not earth-shattering. I'm doing a story

for a Pittsburgh paper about a couple's son who died over here. Figured there might be an angle with his coming here. His cousin told me he was going to meet someone here."

"Most sorry. No record. Our public relations people have no record of his visiting them. We are out of places to look. We have hundreds of offices in Germany. Maybe he come to another office, even another office here in Berlin?"

"Maybe that's it. I'll try some of the others." He stood to leave. She came up to him with a small white rose. Close up he could tell the rose was made of silk, but looked like the real thing.

"Small present since we didn't help you. We think image, yes? Small rose for you, think better of Zedicher International, no?" She pinned it to his lapel on his sport coat. Then she handed him a brochure about the company.

"Some reading for you, no? Yes. Now, must go. Sorry could not help more. You probably find him tomorrow." She stood so close he could smell her perfume. Wade smiled, took the four-color brochure, and stepped back.

"Yes, well, thanks anyway. Do I need a guard to get to the lobby?"

"No, no guard. Down hall take elevator to lobby. Can do?"

He nodded. "Can do. Thanks."

As he walked down the hall to the elevator he was curious. Both the man, then Helga, had written him off quickly. With a computer it would take only seconds to check the sign-in, but she was gone more than five minutes. Something didn't mesh. She dumped him quickly, as if there had been a red flag thrown up as soon as the Silokowski name was mentioned.

On the way down in the elevator he checked the brochure. The usual PR hype promoting the company as a whole. He folded it and put it in his sports-coat pocket. He glanced down at the white rose. It was a nice addition to his jacket. He decided to leave it there.

Once outside the building, he wasn't sure where to go next. He walked along the street casually, looking in store display windows, checking traffic. The sun was out, the weather warm, and he didn't have any pressing appointment.

From long habit he glanced into a store window and casually checked behind him. A balding man with a blue jacket suddenly found an item in a window interesting. Small warning bells went off. His CIA training came into force. He walked another half block and turned abruptly walking back the way he had come. The same man with blue jacket and hair loss turned and abruptly walked into a store.

If there was one tailing him, there would be two. He hadn't picked up the second one yet, but by the time he found him it could be too late. He reversed directions again at a slow pace, then darted into an alley and ran flat out the fifty yards to the other end. He turned right, ran half a block to another alley, and darted up that. He didn't see the bald man or any other behind him. He changed directions again, slowed to a walk, and found a small park where he sat on a bench watching both ways. No way they had been able to follow him.

A man appeared at the far end of the block, and Wade tensed, but he was walking a miniature schnauzer. Two minutes later, Wade had caught his breath and figured he was home free, when a large, black Mercedes came around the corner and drove slowly past him on the other side of the street. Three men in the car watched him. At the last moment he saw that the driver was a red-head with a patch over his left eye.

Wade jolted away from the bench, charged between two buildings into an alley, and went the opposite way the Mercedes had been headed. How in hell had they found him? He turned into another alley behind some business firms, small manufacturing maybe. He was halfway down the alley when the Mercedes nosed in behind him and speeded up.

No way out.

He pulled his .45 and screwed on the silencer. When the Mercedes came within fifty feet of him, he shot four times at the front tire nearest him. His third shot brought a loud bang as the tire blew out and the big car twisted to a stop.

The silenced shots caused no alarm. Three car doors opened and three men swarmed out of the black rig and gave chase.

Wade pounded down the alley another fifty feet, dodged again between two buildings, across a busy street, and down the far side to another alley where he vanished. He ran hard again, the .45 held tightly inside his jacket with his right hand.

He came to a large trash container in the deserted alley and paused just behind it listening. Soon he heard one man running hard up the alley. He bent low to the ground and took a quick look around the container. One man, the bald one. He looked behind the container and found a two-by-four three feet long. He held it like a baseball bat and listened for the pounding feet.

Not yet. No. He waited. The sounds came closer. The man slowed. Then came on. When Wade saw the first foot stride just past the trash container, he swung the two-by-four chest high like he was smashing a home run. The wooden club and the bald man came together in an instant. Wade heard ribs crack and break. The man gurgled with pain and stumbled, then went down in a flailing cauldron of arms and legs.

The two-by-four jolted from Wade's hands. He grabbed it and swung it just hard enough to land behind the German's left ear, knocking him out, but not enough to kill him. He searched his pockets and came up with a revolver. Wade pocketed it and ran again, down another alley, past a row of apartments, then into a park and through it and onto another business street. He went into a small café and was about to order some coffee when he saw the black Mercedes cruising slowly past.

How in hell?

He asked if there was a back entrance but no one understood him. He went into the kitchen, heard someone yell at him, and quickly moved through a storeroom and into the alley. This time he found a deserted place along the alley where there were no back doors and no people. He crouched behind a pile of boxes and a stack of wood and waited. They would come to him and this time he'd wait for them.

The car was a twin to the first Mercedes he had shot up. It nosed into the alley and stopped, then moved ahead slowly. Wade took the silencer off the .45 to give it more range and power. He waited.

When the big car was fifty feet away he leaned out and put six rounds from the .45 into the Mercedes's windshield. It starred and crumbled the way safety glass is supposed to, but the rounds went through first. He hoped that at least one found the mark. The car stopped. He slanted out from the trash, heard two shots behind him, but by that time he was around the corner and into the street, running hard again.

He slowed to a walk. He wiped his face with his right hand and as it came down he brushed the rose. He frowned. How could they find him? A bug? The damned rose Helga had given him? He unpinned the rose from his lapel and pulled back the petals.

Yes, a small, powerful sending device, a tracker, a bug. That's how they knew where he was. He hurried up the street to traffic and tossed the bug in the back of a pickup. Then he turned off the street and walked away. Now they would be following the pickup and they wouldn't find him again.

He walked for two blocks, entered a café, and drank a cup of coffee, then took a taxi. He gave the address of their HQ, but stopped the taxi about halfway there. He paid the man, got out, and walked another block before he took another cab. This time he was making damn sure that no one followed him.

Twenty minutes after Wade hurried into the team quarters he had showered and put on fresh clothes. When he went into the Specialists' workroom, he found Duncan on his computer.

"What's up?" Wade asked.

"Oh, CNN. They had a notice from Atlanta to get on the George Silokowski story. A directive. Some congressman has a close tie with some CNN big wig. So they sent a man to the village with a cameraman, and got part of the story. Evidently they found out he was going to go to the Zedicher outfit and ask some questions, so they sent a man there yesterday.

"That was the CNN reporter they pulled out of the river late last night. He didn't drown. The coroner or whatever they call him over here is hard at work trying to figure out why he died. I didn't tell them about our red-haired friend and our eyewitness source. Finished over there quickly and now I'm working on the Web to see what I can dig up on Nazi plunder from Jews."

"You might get a lot of entries."

"Tell me about it. On this one search I found 116,054 matches for the subject. I'm looking at the top ten. Might be something we can use. Look at this one:

"French Can't Estimate Stolen Assets. More like this. URL: Summary: The commission, led by Nazi concentration camp survivor Jean Matteoli, said the collaborationist Vichy regime systematically robbed Jews of their assets from 1940 to 1944. Writing of the 'aryanisation of Jewish assets,' the report said: 'This looting was partly led by the German occupiers and in coordination with the Vichy regime.' "

"That doesn't help us much. Anything on Switzerland?"

"Yeah how about this one: 'Hammerschlag Resource Center: Schlag Bytes. URL: Summary: Even the Austrians, who gave us Adolf Hitler, after years of official foot-dragging have finally acknowledged the plunder stolen from exterminated Austrian Jews and auctioned it off for the current survivors' benefit. Portugal too is fessing up to having received Nazi gold stolen from Jews, but the Swiss have yet even to acknowledge that they have billions of dollars' worth of Jewish property.' "

"Yeah, closer, Duncan. We need facts, figures, and names."

"This is as close as I can come so far: 'Yahoo!—Swiss Postpone Report on WWII Gold Deals. URL. Summary: Swiss professor Jean-Francois Bergier, chairman of the group probing Switzerland's wartime past, has said the report would detail to what extent authorities knowingly bought looted Nazi gold. The commission's survey in December confirmed earlier studies showing Switzerland accepted the most gold from Nazi Germany's central bank in the wartime years of 1939 to 1945.' "

"You're getting closer, keep looking." He told Duncan about his chase scene with the eye-patch man.

"So, looks like the Zedicher outfit is the one putting the pressure on George and anyone who asks about George."

"Like the CNN reporter did," Wade said.

"And you. Sounds like they were out to kill you."

"They tried. They might have lost some blood of their own in that windshield blast I gave them. But what now?"

"Now I'm going to try to narrow my search pattern. I'll go with Nazi plunder from Polish Jews. That should get me more specifics and better output."

He tried it. He had just over six hundred matches. The first ten looked good, but there was nothing they didn't already know.

Duncan tried a different tack. "Warsaw Jews Plundered by Nazis." That brought up 142 matches. He began to go through the first ten and found names of Warsaw Jews victimized out of their fortunes. Silokowski was not mentioned.

He began printing out the summaries of the articles. Later he could go back and key in on the WWW address for each article he wanted to read.

Three of the entries said some of the Jews who bribed their way from Warsaw to Switzerland said they had paid huge amounts of money to Nazis in the German Transportation Corps. This was part of the army that put the Warsaw Jews on boxcars and shipped them to Treblinka, one of the worst of the Nazi extermination camps.

Duncan printed out twenty-five summaries, then tried a different tack. He tried to dig out the latest on the 2.5-billion-dollar settlement Swiss banks had made to repay Jews. What he found was mostly speculation.

The plans were being drawn up but nothing would be done about it for another year. That seemed strange. More and more of the death camp survivors were dying every year.

He had an overload of information, but almost none of it was anything that he could use. He pushed the off button and tried to think of a new way to get at the information he knew was out there somewhere.

Kat had no trouble meeting with the financial editor of Berlin's biggest daily newspaper. His name was Hans and he said he liked to be on a first-name basis. Kat outlined what they were doing and began asking some pointed questions.

He held up one hand.

"This is an old saw with most Germans. We're tired of hearing about it. I would imagine it's something like the crimes committed against the black people in America in the thirties, forties, and fifties. A highly sensitive subject with most Germans. Yes, it happened, we're not proud of it, but it took place fifty years ago and there is not a lot we can do now to bring back six million human beings."

"I understand that, Hans. We're not here to stir up that pot of snakes at all. What we're more interested in are the reported three hundred everyday, working-class Germans who went into the war in 1939 or 1940 and came out of it in 1945 as multiple millionaires. That's the string we're trying to unravel."

Hans peaked his hands. They were speaking in German. He nodded and looked away.

"Yes, Kat, I know of some of these men. Rather, now I know the heirs of some of those millionaires. They flatly refuse to talk about how their fathers or uncles got rich during the war. Who can say for sure? The Nazis involved are almost all dead and buried."

"The problem remains. How did they become so rich, so suddenly?"

"The question has been asked a thousand times a thousand. The ones who truly know are dead or won't talk. Two I know of who are still alive are in private mental institutions. Unreachable. The heirs simply won't jeopardize their wealth."

"Jeopardize? Then there were misdeeds done in acquiring these fortunes?"

The financial editor squinted at her. "Kat, everyone assumes that. It's just what type of misdeeds and to whom and where they took place. Those are the questions."

"You tried to run down the answers?"

"For more years than I care to admit. Failure is not something I like to think about."

"But still that in itself is a story."

"I've told that one a dozen or more times. For the past two or three years the question has sprung up again. Switzerland and the gold problem. Other nations have the same situation only not with the massive proportions. Hundreds, maybe thousands of billions of dollars are at stake here. Gold once had a controlled price of about thirty-five dollars an ounce. After the war the price of gold was allowed to 'float' on the open market. It's now worth two hundred to three hundred dollars an ounce. That kind of tenfold increase in price alone makes the billions stolen skyrocket in value. Then think of the interest that would accumulate over fifty to sixty years on a measly million dollars."

"We're not that concerned with the large picture," Kat said. "What we're more interested in is one Jewish family. Did you hear about the young American who was killed on his motorcycle this week?"

"Yes, rode right into a deep quarry."

"The young man was a professional motorcycle rider, a champion motocross rider. Chances of him riding into that hole are about a billion to one."

"So?"

"We feel somebody murdered him. He came to Berlin to try to find out where his grandfather's four and a half million marks went during the war when he fled Warsaw in 1942 with the help of a huge bribe."

"So we get down to a case."

"Right. We wonder if the man who was bribed has left his issue a massive fortune."

Hans squirmed in his chair a moment and settled, then he folded his hands on his small belly and nodded. "How can I help you?"

"Names. You must have researched many of the huge corporate entities that mushroomed right after the war. Which started out from scratch with ten or twelve million marks while their fellow countrymen were reeling in defeat and trying to find enough money to put food on the table to keep from starving?"

"It would take some digging."

"For all of them, but you must know half a dozen off the top of your memory who were suddenly successful, against all odds."

"True. But the sins of the father . . ."

"Don't give the heirs the right to perpetuate the evil that their father did to gain his wealth."

Hans gave a short groan and sat up in the chair. "You're right, you're right. My own father must have been too honest or not lucky enough to become a millionaire that way. I'm not even sure what he did during the war."

"This has nothing to do with you. I wouldn't even think to ask you that."

"Miss Killinger, Kat. Are you a lawyer? I feel like I'm on a witness stand."

"I have been a practicing attorney, yes. Do you have six major firms that came about like the proverbial phoenix . . . only faster?"

Hans sighed again and stared out his window. Kat cleared her throat and moved her feet as if to stand. He looked back at her.

"Alright. I know four that seemed to have rocketed ahead of everyone else. Even right at the start. I researched them when I was in college. I'll write them down. Two of the men were generals in the army. I don't know about the third. The fourth one was a mere captain." He wrote out the names and gave them to her.

She took the folded paper and didn't open it to read the names. "Thank you. If we develop anything, you'll get the story first. It might be good to have your byline on the front page again, right?"

He smiled. "Yes. That would be good."

She thanked him, shook his hand, and left the building. She made sure that no one followed her.

✷ EIGHT ✷

Duncan and Wade worked their way through several hot pastrami sandwiches provided by the company kitchen and tested a large pot of coffee. Both had their work summary done and on the board when Kat arrived just after noon.

"Do I have a list to show you," she said, waving the folded paper. "These are the four biggest conglomerates who rose out of the ashes of WWII overnight. My editor friend said they are prime suspects for becoming instant millionaires during the war."

"Who?" Wade asked.

"Bavaria Limited, the telephone and telegraph people, Sweitzer Chemicals, First Security People's Bank, and our old friend, Zedicher International Limited."

Wade grinned. "It does give us another vote for our buddy Zedicher. Let's find out all we can about that company. Who is running it now, if the owner/managers are still the Zedicher family, how many of them, if it's a stock corporation or privately held. We need to know all we can about it. Duncan, you work with Kat on this one. Could prove productive."

Wade reached for his jacket, now without the traitorous white rosebud. "I have an idea, there's an old friend I haven't seen in several years. When I was stationed here before with the Agency, she proved to know who was doing what to whom. Hope she's still in business."

Duncan laughed and nodded. "I might know who you're talking about. The Marvelous Madam, we used to call her."

Wade chuckled. "The very same. Let's see if she's still in business." He went to the telephone and made three calls, then came back where the two were working the computers.

"She's still working. Perhaps she's moved up a notch or two in class. We'll see."

Outside the building, Wade took a cab. He didn't want to be tied down with a car. Marlena had a different address now, in a much fancier part of town. He stopped the cab a block from the address and walked the rest of the way. Two waiting limousines and an assortment of fancy cars across the street marked the address. He saw two diplomatic plates among them. Business as usual.

Prostitution is illegal in Germany, but as in most of Europe, the enforcement is not all it should be. With an operator like Marlena, there was never any trouble, never any unhappy clients, and no touch of scandal to taint the better-known customers.

During the Cold War, Marlena had been a fount of information to anyone who could pay her price. Everyone knew she worked all comers. Her establishment was a remarkably effective place to plant false leads and bogus operations. The opposition would have the material within hours.

From across the street, Wade checked the house. He guessed it had twenty rooms, walled, secure, with a locked front gate and a small manned gatehouse. There was no driveway inside. He spotted three small TV security cameras and was sure there would be a dozen or so more around the small estate. The place looked like old money that had fared well in post-war Germany.

Wade walked across the street and up to the entrance. He felt the camera on him and then a quality speaker came on.

"Yes, sir, how may I help you?"

"Tell Miss Marlena that an old friend is here, Wade Thorne. We used to do business together."

"Just a moment, sir."

In less than a minute the voice came on with an edge to it.

"Miss Marlena says she can see you for five minutes. Please open the gate when the buzzer sounds. Then proceed by the right-hand walkway to the rear of the building and go in the door marked 'Gymnasium.' Thank you."

The door clicked, he went in and to the gym. The elaborately carved oak door which featured a poised stag and two does stood open a foot. He nudged it wide, then took a step inside, sensing her presence before glimpsing her. She wore the same perfume she had years ago.

Marlena stepped out from behind a short wall that fronted an inside handball court. She was tall yet not gangling, with a Rubenesque figure. Soft blonde hair, cut short, radiated with hundreds of ringlets. She held a long cigarette holder in her right hand, exhaling a stream of smoke as she smiled.

"Thorne the Terrible. Haven't seen you in years. Heard you left the service."

He stepped up to her and kissed the proffered cheek.

"Yes, I resigned. You probably heard what happened."

"I did and that man was never allowed inside my place again. Unforgivable. So unprofessional." She smiled at him and held out her hand. "Come."

They moved out of the handball court, through a hall to a discreet door. Inside was an old-fashioned sitting room, complete with antique lamps, a settee, and a cuspidor. On one wall three old-fashioned split-bamboo fly rods were arranged to make an "N." On another wall hung a stag head with a ten-point rack.

"This was the previous owner's den. I left it much as it was. Nobody else ever comes here."

She eased down on the sofa and patted the place beside her.

"Now, Wade Thorne, tell me how your life is without the CIA."

"Much different. Have you heard of J. August Marshall?"

"The American billionaire who is dabbling in antiterrorist work." She cocked her head. "Of course. You now work for him. I know of two others, but I didn't expect you. Say hello for me to Duncan Bancroft and Hershel Levine. I have missed them both."

She shook her head sadly. "The good old days are gone, I'm afraid. There is no glamour, no danger in the work anymore. Even the secrets are not secret. I miss the marvelous days of intense competition and cutthroat operations—the little boy blood and guts of the Cold War."

"In a way, I miss it, too. But the range and scope of my new work is much greater than it was then."

She brightened, her smile glowing. "But my darling Wade, I am forgetting myself. You came for some entertainment, yes? To relax and forget your work for an hour or so. May I recommend Charlene? She is young but not too young. She is . . ."

She frowned as he shook his head.

"No, Marlena, I have no time. As usual, I come looking for information. Even now I'm sure you know most of what goes on in the official halls of German government and a thousand large corporate offices. Information is what I need most."

"Which, government or business?"

Quickly he told her his job there. She had heard of the American motorcyclist's death.

"Silokowski. A common name in Poland at that time. Might be thousands with the name. The government is keeping a hands-off policy on any Nazi plunder of the Jews in those days. Any laws broken are far, far out of the jurisdiction of the courts. The Jewish gold problem has festered for so long that the German public is tired to death hearing about it. It all happened so many years ago. It would be much like the early Americans' shameful treatment of the Indians during the westward movement."

"So what's left for us to dig into, Marlena?"

"You have any suspect names of firms? Many men became instant successes right after the war. Some think many of those phoenix-type birds were fueled by stolen Jewish money and gems."

"Do any large corporate names come to your mind?" Wade asked.

"Several. Let me think a moment. Yes, Düsseldorf Construction way over by the Swiss border. Then Bavaria Limited here in Berlin. Those two I know most about, and wished that I didn't."

"What about Zedicher International Limited?"

"I've heard some bad things about the little bastard running the place, but if there's Jewish gold in the roots of the huge conglomerate, I don't know about it. Maybe Zedicher is more secretive than the others."

"What else, Marlena? You have that slightly goofy look."

She laughed. "Thought I grew out of that. Might be nothing. I hear lots of vibes about Zedicher hobnobbing with the big princes and powerful. Lots of government types, federal bench, top agencies, even the Chancellor himself."

"Does Zedicher have political ambition?"

"Doesn't seem likely. He's out after the money. He deals in cash, not in good works or government niceties. Puzzles me."

"Puzzles me, too. So, I better get moving. I have many miles to go before I sleep."

"Just a moment, Wade. For old times' sake let me at least offer you a gift."

A door opened that he hadn't noticed and a woman came into the room. She wore her long black hair almost to her waist, and she was beautifully naked. Sculptured breasts showed in perfect balance with her slender figure. A pinched-in waist, flat stomach, sheaf of dark crotch hair, and long tapered legs completed the picture.

She lifted her head and smiled showing pale green eyes, faintly pink lips, and high cheekbones. Slender arms ended in hands with delicate fingers that posed prettily as she turned half to the side the way runway models do.

"Beautiful," Wade said. "You always did have the best in the business, Marlena." He peeled a fifty-mark note from his pocket clip and pushed it at the madam. "Give it to her." He bent and kissed Marlena's held-out cheek. "Be careful out there, lady. I'll try to see you again before I leave and give you the latest results."

"I'll probably see them in the tabloids if you're successful."

Wade took another long look at the girl who hadn't broken her pose, and then he walked quickly out of the room, through the hall, and outside to the gate. The steel barrier opened automatically as he reached for it.

At seven P.M. the Specialists gathered in the workroom. Each had a report on the bulletin board and was ready to expand on it as needed.

Wade gave his report on his visit to Zedicher's and the tailing, the bug they put on him, and how they tried their best to kill him. They laughed when he recounted how he discovered the bug and put it in the pickup truck. He said he saw the same man with the red hair and eye patch behind one of the Mercedes. It's a three-way tie-in with him and the other violent acts in this case.

"Then I talked to an old friend in the entertainment business and she suggested two firms that could be in the rags to billionaire class. Neither of them was Zedicher, but she said the nasty little man who ran the operation had been doing a lot of political politiking lately and that worried her. Oh, Marlena said to say hello to Duncan and Hershel."

"Yahooooo," Duncan bellowed.

"Well now, what a nice lady," Hershel said and grinned.

Ichi and Hershel reported that they had toured the small village again.

"We talked to dozens of people who remembered seeing the motorcycle and the Mercedes," Hershel said. "Trouble is, none of them saw the two together. Nobody saw the big car going up into the hills, or the bike either. It was either ridden up there by one of the men from the car, or hauled up in the Mercedes's big trunk.

"We did get more descriptions on the other two men with the redhead. One of them was shorter, stocky, a weight lifter type with lots of muscles and a crew cut. He had a big gold earring on the right side. The third one was slight, the shortest of the three, a sloppy dresser with long hair. Two people said they saw a pistol in his waistband. We didn't find anyone who could remember the license tag on the big car, other than that it was a federal government plate."

Roger had a quick report. "Worked the police station and they had an ID on the man from the river. He still had all of his papers, money, and ID with him. He was working for CNN as a reporter. His job was to dig out the story, then an on-camera person would come out with a crew and they'd film it.

"I went directly to CNN and they were shaken. They had been notified last night. They told me they knew that their man, Carter Franks, went to the Zedicher company that afternoon to see if he could find out who George Silokowski wanted to talk to there. That was the last they heard from him until the police called. While I was there, Duncan came and we talked to them for a while, but they had nothing more and we couldn't help them."

Wade scowled. "By the time the police get to Zedicher's the people there will have Franks signed out and at least six witnesses who remember seeing him leave the building by himself long before his body was found."

Duncan took over. "I called my cop friend and he was furious about the dead cop. He said they knew they had

the killer, but they wanted to find out who shot the killer
and tied him up with a ribbon. They want to question the
person and get a witness to the murder if possible. I told
him if I heard anything about such a man I'd be sure to
get back to him."

Kat looked at the summaries on the wall and the ver-
bals and shrugged. "So it looks like from all reports we
have our target. The Zedicher company is the offending
group here. The killer may even be this big redhead with
an eye patch. Is that a familiar description to anyone
from your previous employment?"

"I've known some redheads in this part of the world,
but they all had two good eyes," Wade said.

Duncan and Hershel both shook their heads.

Kat looked at the reports again for a moment. "I'd say
the next step is to find out everything we can about the
Zedicher company. We need to concentrate on the very
first company during 1945 when it started. We need to
know the founder's name. We need to find out what that
man did during the war. Germans have intricate records
and I'm sure most of them from WWII are maintained
somewhere. They should be open to inspection. That's
the direction some of us will move tomorrow."

She looked at Wade.

"Mr. Marshall is due here in ten minutes," Wade said.
"Let's see what we can dig up between now and then on
Zedicher. Kat, let's you and I do some thinking about
what direction we move tomorrow."

Twenty minutes later the door opened and Mr. J. August Marshall walked into the room. They all stood and
stopped talking. At first he ordered them not to do that.
Wade talked to him about it and convinced him it was
the right way. He said some of them had been military
and it was ingrained. The rest of them stood out of re-
spect. It was good for the team.

"Sit, sit. Sorry I'm late. Traffic. I thought it was bad in
London. From what I hear on my E-mail you have a suspect who might be Silokowski's killer. He works for the

firm that may also be the one started by the man who took the bribe and stole money from Silokowski and undoubtedly thousands of other Jews from Warsaw. Have I got this right, so far?"

Several members nodded.

"Knowing this is easy. Proving it will be the tough part. On my way over here I saw on CNN a long story about George Silokowski. It showed a lot of his motocross rides, his wins, his background. An on-camera narrator came right out and said that many people don't believe that George died accidentally by riding off a German cliff. It was a hard-hitting news story. They followed it closely by a bulletin that one of their reporters had been killed in Berlin when he went to a huge industrial headquarters building to talk to the public relations people about what happened to George Silokowski. In fact, that's probably why they're still paying so much attention to Silokowski's death. The story said they made no accusations, but that firm was the last place that anyone saw their reporter, Carter Franks, alive.

"So CNN is stirring the pot. We all must be careful. It could be that the Zedicher people have killed twice already. We don't want to give them a chance to strike again."

Again, several members of the team nodded.

"That's about it. I'm pleased with your progress. I have to go to the States tomorrow, so I won't be bothering you for a while. Keep me up-to-date with a nightly E-mail. I'll have my laptop and my cell phone with me. Now, any questions, any problems, any equipment or supplies that you need you can't get here?"

"Yeah, can we get Big Macs put on the company cafeteria menu?" Roger asked.

Everyone laughed.

"I'll talk with the chef." Mr. Marshall looked around. "Well then, looks like I have a few minutes before it's time to leave. Kat and Wade, could I see you in my office, please?"

They went through the door and up two flights to the top floor, to an office that was seldom used. Although it was past eight o'clock at night, his secretary sat at her desk in the outer office.

She held the door open to the inner sanctum. Wade had been there before. A high-tech office with computers, readout screens, all sorts of electronic gear on one side and on the other a soft couch and a putting green twelve feet long with a ball trap.

Mr. Marshall eased down on the sofa and pointed to matching upholstered chairs.

"Your progress sounds good, and it's come quickly. Good for you. Now comes the tough part, proving what you think you know. We can't go out on a limb like CNN did. They could get in huge trouble. They are sure they're right, but sometimes that's not enough. No public announcements from us, no news leaks, until you have it all tied up in a neat package, with enough hard evidence to convict. You know what I mean, Kat. Now, any problems?"

"Getting into Zedicher and digging out the truth about the past is our big roadblock," Kat said. "They will be gun shy now after the CNN story."

"Then don't go in," Mr. Marshall said. "Work everything from the outside. Research. There are fantastic German records going all the way back to Brunhilda. Work around them if you can't go through them."

"We'll certainly try to do that."

"Wade?" Mr. Marshall asked.

"I just need to come up with some good tracks and then follow them down. We've heard of a group in the German Army called the Transportation Corps, that evidently moved people from point to point. That will be a big research project."

"Good." Mr. Marshall stood. "I'm on my way. Tell the others good-bye for me. Don't worry about time. That's all we really have on this one. After fifty-seven years we can't be in a rush."

They said good-bye and went out his office door. His secretary took her laptop and went into the inner office as they left.

⋆ NINE ⋆

The next morning at the strategy meeting, Kat was adamant.

"I think I can go into Zedicher and tell them I'm from *Fortune* magazine, and I have been assigned to do a feature story on the internationally famous mega corporation. They will lap it up."

"Too dangerous," Wade said. "If they see through your ploy, you could be ridiculously and outrageously dead."

"Lots of people have tried to do that."

"You strike out once in this game and it's all over, for good."

"Hey, I know that. I think I have the right story idea, and that I'm smart enough to pull it off. I'll do some wild stuff first, then tell them my editor always wants to dig into the very first mark that the firm made. Who did it? Where was it? What was the product or service? Whose idea was it? How the company got started."

"What if it doesn't work?"

"I'll wear my .32 auto, draw, and walk out. None of them are going to shoot me on company property."

Wade paced the room. Roger, Duncan, and Hershel were all working various aspects of the Internet searching for the faintest beginnings of Zedicher International Ltd.

When Wade came past this time he stopped and stared hard at her. "If you get shot over there or caught, I'm gonna kill you myself. Only one way you can go—with a cameraman. Get three 35mm cameras for Ichi, one with a long lens. He knows cameras. He can cover for you in case of trouble. Agreed?"

"Yes, boss," she said with a sly smile. "Anything you say, O lord of the castle, our intrepid leader."

"I like the way you talk. You have four hours to get in and out, otherwise I'm coming in with the rest of the troops and we'll all have Uzis and H & K MP-5 subguns."

"Don't worry. We can get in and get out in four hours. I'll either get what we want or make them mad enough to clam up. I'll know either way and won't let it explode. Ichi, let's see if we can draw three cameras for you from the supply folks."

Wade watched them leave. He had some reservations, but by now he should know better. When Kat said she could do something, she did it. He raised his brows and cast aside the worry. There were others to get to.

Yesterday Marlena had mentioned that the Zedicher corporate leader seemed to be getting into politics. Should that be a worry on this project? Wade didn't see how it could affect their mission one way or the other. It might be bad for Germany, but the Germans would have to take care of that. Still, a chat with the political analyst on one of the big German newspapers might come in handy. Kat was the only one with good enough language skills to take on that job. Tomorrow. He glanced at his wristwatch. Almost nine A.M. He'd give her five hours, and then he'd start making big noises over at the Zedicher place.

Kat had set it up right. She called from the office pitching the idea that *Fortune* magazine wanted to do a full-blown feature on Zedicher. She had been put through at

once to the public relations people who sounded enthusi-
astic about it. She said that due to the deadline she had, it
was imperative that she and her still photographer come
right over to the company and begin their work. She told
them she was bringing along a cameraman so he could
get some idea of the picture potentials. They set up the
appointment for ten-thirty that morning on the twenty-
fourth floor with Herr W. Mueller.

At first it went fine. They showed their just printed and
cleverly aged ID badges. The cards were from *Fortune* magazine in New York City and said that Kat was a senior editor
and Ichi one of twenty photographers they kept on call.

Kat carefully worked around the series of questions
she had put together about the present situation of the
firm, about how many employees they had, about its
status on the stock market where it did well each year,
then more about the various worldwide projects that
Zedicher worked on.

That used up an hour, then Kat began to move into
how the firm had been established. "What was the name
of the founder of the huge firm?" Kat asked Mueller.

"He was Grant Zedicher, a great man with a great
vision."

"He was the right age so he must have been in the war.
What did he do in the army?"

"He was a clerk in one of the various wartime bureaus
in Berlin. His specialty was in following the production
of foodstuffs to be distributed to soldiers and sailors and
civilians." A man came in and whispered to Mueller. He
held up his hands and nodded. He turned to Kat.

"I'm sorry for the interruption, but you might be interested in this. One of my assistants has a series of pictures
he wants to show your cameraman. Maybe we can pro-
vide you with some vintage photos taken just after the
war of the first few firms that eventually led to all of this."

Ichi nodded. "Yes, good idea." He gave Kat a small
frown. She picked up on it.

"Yes, Ichi, you go with the man and get something

good. We'll want a combination of old and new shots. Any we can borrow now will save time later."

The two went out the door.

Kat looked at her notes in a secretary's spiral notebook. "Now, back to the subject. When was Mr. Zedicher discharged from the army?"

"As I understand it, at that time all was chaos. There were no actual discharges until years later. The soldiers just went home, if they had one to go to. The war was over. We had lost, our men began to try to make a life for themselves."

"Was Grant's father still living then? What did his father do for a living?"

"Yes, he lived for several years after the war. He was a bricklayer, and a good one. He ended his career as a foreman in a construction company."

"Let's see, the war ended May 7, 1945. Some of this material you furnished me about the beginnings of the company shows that the first small firm that Grant Zedicher established came into being on June 15, 1945. Less than five weeks after the end of the war."

"Yes, he was eager to get his business started. Those who knew Grant said he'd been dreaming about his own business for most of the war years."

"That makes a problem for me, Herr Mueller. The war was over and five weeks later Grant Zedicher opens up his first company. The background material says it was a small trucking firm with six dump trucks used for cleaning up the debris and wreckage of much of Berlin. The company had an initial funding of forty thousand marks. Even in those days that was twenty thousand dollars. Where did a German soldier at the end of a lost war get that kind of money?"

Mueller scowled for a moment. "It isn't important where he found the money, the main idea here is that he scraped it together and made a success of his business. A year later he invested almost a million marks in his new construction business."

"Mr. Mueller, *Fortune* magazine is read by wealthy, successful men who are interested how others achieved their success. How he got that first forty thousand marks and then the million a year later are vital to my story. I know my readers would love some details."

Mueller stared at her over his clasped hands. His chin dropped to his hands and he frowned. "Yes, Miss Killinger, I see your point. However there are certain aspects of any business venture that must be confidential. I'm afraid this is one of them when talking about Zedicher International." He watched her for a moment, then sighed.

"You're not going to be happy with that, are you?"

"No. It's my job to find out."

"All right, let's do it this way. The first cash came to him from an uncle who lived in the United States and who he contacted just after the end of the war. The man was not wealthy, but he had some spare money, and he loaned Grant Zedicher the forty thousand marks."

"What's that man's name?"

Mueller chuckled. "You never are satisfied, are you, Miss Killinger? I can't tell you that."

"Herr Mueller. I am not an innocent from America. My research staff at *Fortune* did a lot of homework before I called you. I know for a fact that the first operation of Grant Zedicher was not a trucking firm, but the construction outfit. It was a great business to have to help reconstruct Berlin and half of Germany. The initial investment in the contracting and construction outfit was slightly over seven million marks."

Mueller scowled and slumped back in his chair.

"We know this from German records of 1945. Zedicher wasn't a wealthy man when the war started. His family had no money. Then suddenly five weeks after the end of the war, Herr Zedicher shows up with seven million marks and goes into business. What I want to know is where he got the money?"

Mueller stood slowly. "Miss Killinger, if you don't believe what I tell you, we have nothing more to say to each other. I would think it's time for you to leave." He touched a button on the desk set.

"Did Grant knock over a bank somewhere when he was a soldier? Did he find a hidden hoard of gold in some warehouse? Maybe he stumbled on one of the old master oil paintings that vanished from occupied territories all over Europe."

"Good-bye, Miss Killinger."

Two large men in civilian clothes came in the door and stood waiting orders.

"Please take Miss Killinger to the street entrance. She is to see no one in the building or talk to no one. Now."

The men came toward Kat. She glared at Mueller. "You are a lousy liar, Mueller. You should at least get your story straight. You'll be seeing much of what we've discussed tonight on CNN television. Be sure to watch the six o'clock news."

One of the guards touched her shoulder and she lashed out her right hand that had fisted and jolted it into his chest. His eyes widened in surprise and he took half a step backward. Then both men caught her shoulders and marched her out the open door.

"Let go of me or I'll scream and make such a fuss you'll be the laughingstock of your buddies."

They looked at each other, let go of her, and ushered her to the elevator. They ordered two persons on the elevator off, then took her down a number of floors and opened the door. A short way down the hall they caught her by both arms and thrust her inside a room and slammed the door shut.

"Damn," Kat said. She still had her .32 automatic but the room was dark. She moved back to the door and searched around the right-hand side until she found a light switch. The light came on. The room was eight feet square without any furniture, just a square box. Like a cell.

Kat thought of shooting off the lock. No. The two men knew exactly where to come. They had used this

room for the same purpose before. She shivered. The
CNN reporter may have been kept in here while they decided what to do with him. The whole outfit seemed
touchy, sensitive, paranoid. They must have a lot to hide.
She looked around for a hidden camera. If there was one
it was one of the smallest she'd ever seen.

Kat sat down and leaned against the wall. She had po-
sitioned herself behind where the door would open
giving her some temporary protection. When the guards
came back, maybe she could shoot both of them and lock
them inside. She looked again at the door. There was no
knob of any kind on the inside.

Kat had pushed the timer on her wristwatch as soon
as she realized she was a prisoner. Twelve minutes. She
waited. Mueller was lying through his teeth. So she had
bluffed him on the seven million marks. She had made
that up on the run. It had worked. He fell for it so it must
have been something like that. No way an honest man
could come up with that kind of cash in five weeks.

An hour passed.

She heard someone at the door. She stood, pulled the
automatic, and pressed against the wall behind where
the door would open.

The door unlatched, then slammed viciously on the
hinges and smashed into her where she stood against the
wall. The blow hit her hand and jolted the pistol free and
it fell on the floor.

The same two men darted into the room. One snorted
and picked up the pistol. The other grabbed her and
pulled her toward the door.

"You make any kind of a disturbance and I'll knock
you out and carry you the rest of the way, understand?"
one of them said.

Kat nodded, and held her injured hand. She decided
nothing was broken.

They led her down the hall to a freight elevator. Moments later the doors opened and they were in the park-

ing basement. Mueller walked out from behind a car and scowled at her.

"Are you ready to accept my details about the starting of the company?"

"Hell no, you little shithead."

Before she could react, one of the guards shot her with pepper spray, sending her to her knees and bringing great wails of pain and fury from her as she tried to avoid more shots of the pepper-laced spray. Kat collapsed, pretending to pass out. They would have to carry her wherever they were taking her. It might give her a slight advantage. That's all she needed, just one small chance.

The men yelled a minute blaming each other for putting her down. Then Mueller said something quietly and she felt herself being lifted. A car door opened and she was stuffed inside, lying on the backseat, she guessed. The car started and eased along, evidently getting out of the parking structure.

Kat opened her eyes. They still hurt like hell but now she could see. No gun. Panty hose. Without a sound she pulled down her panty hose and took them off. She twisted the legs together like a cord and eased up so she could see. Driver, man on passenger's side.

The car was out of the garage in heavy traffic. Good. She eased up higher, then, in a lightning move, reared up, looped the panty hose around the passenger-side man's neck, and heaved backward with all 130 of her pounds. She pulled the cord as tightly as she could as she watched him. He didn't make a sound. The driver didn't notice anything for a few seconds.

"What the hell?" the driver yelped.

"Just keep driving and both hands on the wheel or this asshole is dead."

"Feisty little cat, ain't you?"

She felt the passenger go limp. She kept up the pressure for another ten seconds just like in training. He'd be out for at least half an hour, but not dead.

The driver had sneaked one hand down from the wheel toward his waistband. She grabbed her shoe and held the toe and slammed the two-inch sturdy heel down hard on the driver's head. He screeched, hit the brakes, and almost caused a wreck.

"What?"

Kat surged against the front seat and wrapped her arm around the driver's throat and pulled tight.

"Now, asshole, drive. Get out of this traffic, up a side street somewhere. Do it or I crush your larynx and you die in twenty seconds." Some extra pressure on his windpipe with her arm encouraged him to follow orders.

Kat leaned farther into the front seat and found the shoulder holster of the unconscious man and lifted out the 9mm pistol. She racked the slide back and heard a round snick into place in the chamber.

"This is your buddy's nine-millimeter in the side of your neck, stupid. Do you understand?"

"Yes, yes. Understand."

"You even start to reach for your weapon, you're one dead krauthead, you capisce?"

"*Ja.*"

"Now turn again, get us where there aren't a lot of people." As they drove, she pulled on her shoes and straightened her jacket and skirt.

They rolled along a half a mile into a mixed residential-business part of town and she had him pull over to the curb and stop. They had left her purse in Mueller's room. Nothing in it incriminating or that would tie her to the Marshall group, but she'd need some cash.

Kat left the car on the driver's side and kept the weapon covering the German. She opened the door and shielded the gun from anyone watching.

"Now, tough guy, give me your wallet and that of your out of it buddy over there. Do it now or you're dead meat."

The plainclothes guard shrugged, handed over his wallet, and then pushed the other man to one side and worked the billfold out of his back pocket.

She took both and held them in her left hand.

"The car keys. Give them to me."

The thug behind the wheel scowled, pulled out the ring with only two keys on it, and passed it to Kat. She took a .45-caliber automatic from the man's waist holster and stepped back and slammed the door. The window was down.

"Sit right here for a half hour. You even move a pinkie and I'm going to put six .45 slugs through your skull. You read me, you overgrown bastard?"

"Ja."

"Remember, I'll be watching." She faded toward the back of the car, then crossed the street and walked away. She watched the car as long as she could. Neither man moved. Half a block later she caught a cab. Both the men she had just left had considerable cash in their wallets.

It took the cab only twenty minutes to drive to the front of the Marshall offices. Two minutes later she hurried into the workroom and dropped into a chair. She rested her head on the table. Until right now, she had no idea how tired she was. She was the only one there.

A few minutes later, the telephone rang. Kat didn't know where it was. She found it on the fourth ring.

"Marshall Export/Import," she said.

"Kat. Ichi here. Where are you? Are you all right? I tried to find you, but Mueller said you had been called back to the office suddenly and couldn't find me. What the hell happened?"

"Tell you when you get here. Are you away from Zedicher's place?"

"Yeah, across the street."

"Good, come in out of the cold, young man. Mueller is a class A, number-one asshole."

"Oh, boy. When you start swearing, things aren't going exactly right. I'll be there in twenty minutes."

★ TEN ★

When Duncan, George, and Hershel came back from the company cafeteria a few minutes, later they found Kat with her head cushioned on her arms on her desk.

"Kat, what's the matter?" Hershel asked.

She lifted her head and tried to grin. It didn't quite come off. She shook her head. "No problem. Everything is fine."

"Yeah and pigs can fly. Where's Ichi?"

She sighed, looked at the three who had gathered around, and briefed her morning for them.

"The bastards," Roger spat. "At least we're certain of our target now. I'd say that the Zedicher brass is getting just as nervous as all hell."

"We've got a batch of printouts about early Zedicher International," Duncan said. "Some of it's from their own Web site so it won't help us much."

Ichi came in the door looking angry and worried.

"Kat, I knew I shouldn't have left you alone with them. Damn. At least you made it out." He sniffed when he came up to her. "Pepper spray? Yeah, you better get a shower and get the last of it washed off."

Kat sat there and stared at him.

"Hey, Kat, come on. Shower time." Ichi grinned. "Lady, am I going to have to strip you naked and scrub you down myself?"

Kat managed a small smile and shook her head. "I think I can manage a shower all alone, thanks. Just trying to figure out where we go from here. We need more data on that first year and how the firm started.

"Duncan, you know anybody in city government who could help us with early records? They must have had to post a bond, or be capitalized or something. See if you can dig up a figure for us."

"Can do. I've got a friend over in records."

Kat stood and wavered. Roger grabbed her shoulder but she straightened and nodded. "Yes, a shower. That does sound good. Then maybe some lunch. Who knows?"

Wade walked in as Kat was leaving. He watched her curiously for a moment, then held the door for her. Inside the workroom he pointed the way Kat had left.

"What's with Kat? She looked used up."

Ichi gave Wade a quick rundown on what happened at Zedicher's building that morning.

"Had a hunch not to let her go. Kat will snap out of her funk in a couple of hours and will be hell on wheels. I've seen her do it before. Well, now Zedicher has been alerted again that somebody is after them. I spent the morning at the Hall of Military Records. Learned a lot about the Nazi Transportation Corps. They worked all over the war. Had the total logistics of the war to take care of. A huge task, especially when Germany began gobbling up the small nations.

"They had one arm stationed in Warsaw and other centers of Jewish population. In effect, they used cattle cars to haul Jews to the death camps. There was a separate group to do this work called the Final Solution Battalion. Ugly job but the men and machines are all detailed in the office. It's going to take some digging, but with any luck we'll find out if some of the locals were in the corps in Warsaw and in that Final Solution Battalion."

Wade looked at the others. "How did the Internet search go on Zedicher's background?"

"We have some," Roger said. "Nothing much before 1950, though, and that's not what we need."

"Keep at it. I'll put in another half day on the Transportation Corps and see if I can find a listing of the staff in Warsaw during 1942."

After a quick lunch, Wade made a call to George Silokowski's parents in Pennsylvania. Mr. Silokowski came on the line.

"Yes, Mr. Thorne. I remember you. We hope that you will find out who killed our son. My wife hasn't recovered yet from the shock. I'm not the best."

"We're on their trail, Mr. Silokowski, but it's a huge corporation and we haven't tied down the specific man yet. We're working on that. I wondered if you have any more information that George told you. You mentioned once that there were some tape recordings, if you could find them. Did you?"

"Oh, yes, I forgot. We found three tapes. Two of them on long talks between George and his grandfather. My dad rambled on about what it was like in Warsaw when the war started. Then later on my dad talked about getting out of Poland. He even mentioned the name of the man he bribed."

"Do you have that name, Mr. Silokowski?"

"Yes, indeed. Remember it even. He was Grant Zedicher, a German Nazi in the Transportation Corps. Hope by now he's roasting in hell for sending all the Jews to their deaths in Treblinka."

"I'd guess he is. Grant Zedicher. Yes, that ties in with what we know here. Could you send that tape to me here at my office? Send it by FedEx, so I'll have it in two days."

"Yes, can do that. You'll keep me up-to-date on what's doing."

"I'll do that, Mr. Silokowski. And thank you. Get that tape off on a plane today."

They hung up and Wade told the others.

"Yeah, we're sure," Duncan said. "Now all we have to do is prove it."

"Or nail the redhead for two murders," Wade said.

A few minutes later, Kat came back in looking refreshed and in command. She had washed off more than the pepper spray. When she heard about the tape recorder, she let out a Rebel yell.

"Now we've got the bastards."

"I'll get copies of the records," Wade said. "Then we'll see if we can nail down Grant Zedicher as being on duty in Warsaw during that period of 1942. This will be for our own benefit and the media."

"I'll get to the city records people and try to find out how Zedicher was financed that first year from the records," Duncan said.

Kat fidgeted at her desk a minute. "Say you draw out a couple of million dollars from a numbered account and close out the sucker. What's the easiest, fastest, and least dangerous way to handle the money?"

"Deposit it again," Hershel said.

"Right, deposit it again in the same bank, so nothing moves except the figures. It's a transfer of funds from one closed out account to a new account. So, it's possible that the exact amount drawn out would be deposited that very same day. And maybe we can tie down the new depositor."

"Even fifty-seven years ago?" Wade asked.

"It's a reach, but worth another trip to Switzerland to talk to my little buddy there at the bank. I'll get out of here on the company jet in the morning and be back before dark tomorrow night."

"Works for me," Wade said.

Ichi, Hershel, and Roger went to the computers and dug out anything about Zedicher International that would help them.

Kat studied the bulletin board, making up a flow chart, looking for any holes, trying to figure out what they hadn't covered yet and how they could do it. Wade and Duncan left.

One problem nagged at Wade as he worked with two clerks at the Hall of Military Records trying to dig up the records on the Transportation Corps in Warsaw in 1942. An operation to swindle the Jews out of their life's savings would take more than one man. It had to be kept hidden from the German officials and the army, as well as softly whispered about among the Polish Jews. Would that take ten men? Twenty? He had no idea. When he found the right group of men in Warsaw shipping out the Jews, he would have to check carefully. He might want to dig out twenty names from the rosters and hope he found some other conspirators in the group. That would be after he located Grant Zedicher.

Everything was paper. Long ago, records were sealed in cardboard boxes to keep the dust out. The outer edges of the stacks of papers had yellowed. They checked labels on the outside and opened some parcels. Gradually they worked back to the year 1942. Then they had to find Poland, then Warsaw.

It was nearly eight o'clock that night when they found the first hint that they were on the right track.

"January, 1942, Warsaw, Transportation Corps roster," one excited worker said. Wade had paid both of the men well to keep working after their usual quitting time.

Now they all were sagging with fatigue.

"Let's quit for now," Wade said. "Tomorrow morning we'll dig into this section. I don't want to be so groggy that I miss what we need here."

They marked the spot in the records so they could find it quickly the next day and left.

High over Berlin in the penthouse of the Zedicher International home office building, G. B. Zedicher took off his shoes and wiggled his toes. He'd been wanting to do that half the day. He sipped the drink provided by his butler and stared out the huge windows at Berlin.

"Yes, Berlin. My Berlin." He laughed but it came out dry and cutting. After another sip of the drink he looked over at the man standing near one of the windows.

"Now, Siegfried, what is so important?"

"I told you about my contact with the tall American this morning. I knew I should recognize him. At last it has come to me. He looks different, but he's the same man. His name is Wade Thorne, and for years he was with the American CIA. I have worked against him more than once. The last time he shot me. It had to be him who ambushed me. That was when I lost my eye. Now I'm glad he's here. I have waited more than five years to settle my score with him."

"Siegfried. You will at once forget your private matter with this man. He is an enemy of Zedicher, not your personal target. Anything that happens to him will be to benefit Zedicher, not you. Am I clear on this matter?"

"Yes, sir. Clear."

G. B. Zedicher took his drink and walked to the window. "Today I own Berlin, the most important parts, anyway. Next year I could own half of Germany. Siegfried, the prospects, the rewards of this new venture, are staggering. There will be billions and billions of marks, enough for everyone. Your salary will triple. The benefits are literally unlimited.

"All I have to do is stay in favor with the Chancellor, and keep out of trouble for two weeks, and we are home free, with the prospects stretching out in front of us to infinity."

G. B. tipped the glass and drained the rest of the drink. A white-coated servant appeared at his side with a fresh drink. He took the drink but didn't thank the man or even look at him.

"Before that glorious time comes, we have a little bit of housecleaning to do. It should have been done long before now. At this time it is essential that we locate a black box. No, you have never heard of it. The box itself is not important. It is just welded steel. It's what's in the box that is vital.

"I don't have it, or know where it is. That leaves four others who may know. At least one of them must have an idea where it is, or knows who to ask about it. We must find the black box within a week."

"Yes, sir."

"There are three names for you to check. If that's not productive there is a fourth name. The three will know that you are coming, but not what it's about. This is not strong-arm work. These three men are lifelong friends. You know them. You must be diplomatic, low-key, but insistent. Make them understand that whoever knows the whereabouts of the black box must give you the information now, for the protection of all of us. Do you understand? This is the most important work that I will ever ask you to do."

"Yes, sir, Mr. Zedicher. I'll begin today, as soon as you give me the names and how to find them."

ZURICH, SWITZERLAND

Kat had to wait an hour before she was shown into Fritz Harst's office in the big bank only a few miles across the border from Germany. He was not pleased to see her.

"Yes, Miss Killinger. How well I remember your last visit to our firm. One of our guards is especially interested in seeing you again. He was the laughingstock of the guard force."

"I'm here on a much more important affair than the macho representation of some overmuscled rent-a-cop." She outlined what she wanted.

"Find a matching deposit that many years back? That would be virtually impossible."

"That's what you screeched when I asked to find the withdrawal. We located it. Now we go back to the same spot in the stored records and work forward. The new deposit must have been made the same day. You couldn't have had more than a few thousand deposits made that day."

"Or else what?"

"Or else I'll be terribly disappointed in you and decide that you really are trying to conceal a tiny part of your bank's hiding the Nazi plunder from those six million Jews massacred during the big war."

"Yes. You did mention that. Two hours. You can have four people to help you look for two hours. You realize what this little fishing expedition of yours is costing this bank?"

"Not a mark. You're paying them anyway. If you don't do it, do you realize the public relations scandal I can throw against your bank's good name to a world-wide television audience?"

Herr Harst lifted his brows and made two phone calls.

Two hours later in the musty records room, they hadn't found the deposit, but they had only a few over three hundred more to check. That size deposit, over 2.8 million marks, would be easy to spot once they hit the right page.

An hour later one of the German women yelped. "Here it is, almost three million marks . . . down to the same single digit. Made on the same day."

They carried the slender volume to an adjoining office and made a photocopy of it, and Kat thanked the ladies who put the record books away.

Minutes later, Harst looked at the perfect copy with the right listing that had been underlined.

"Yes, the same amount. Congratulations. You also have the number of the account."

"Now, I want the name that goes with the number. I know that you have a secret file with those names. Otherwise as bankers you would be unable to service any of the accounts."

Harst began to sweat. He mopped his forehead. He made a phone call and spoke so softly she couldn't make out more than a few words.

He put down the handset and stared at her. "Only in the most dire of circumstances do we even admit that there is such a list. Not all banks keep them. Our founder indicated that we must. I'd guess about half the Swiss banks can come up with a listing of name and address if they are pressed hard enough.

"The bank's directors are meeting now to make a yes or no decision on this situation. I've only seen it done once in my thirty-five years at this bank."

The phone rang. Harst picked it up and listened. There was a sharp intake of breath, then he said something and hung up the phone.

"You will have the name of the man who opened that account in an hour."

"I'll wait."

The messenger came less than twenty minutes later. He gave Harst a sealed envelope and left quickly. Harst looked at it, then silently handed it to Kat. She stared at it for a moment, then tore off the end of the business-style envelope and pulled out a single sheet of paper. Typed on the page was one name. She'd never heard of the man before. The name was Hans Derrick.

She darted a stern look at the banker. "This wouldn't be a ploy to throw us off the track, would it, Herr Harst?"

"Absolutely not. I am a banker, the most respected profession in Switzerland. We do not lie or cheat our customers, nor do we give out the wrong name for a numbered account. I'll stake my job and my life on the fact that this is the name that belongs to that numbered account into which almost three million marks were transferred in 1942."

Kat watched the man a moment. She'd been in court enough to know when a man was lying. Herr Harst was telling her the truth.

At the airport, the Marshall business jet wasn't ready to take off. It had to be refueled. Kat tapped her foot for a minute, then called the Berlin number on her German cell phone. The call went through on the first try. The switchboard found Wade deep in the bowels of the German Hall of Military Records.

"Wade, I have it, the name of the person who cleaned out the Silokowski numbered account and opened one of his own with the same amount of cash."

"Good. Don't show it to anybody until you get back here. We've been working the Transportation Corps records. I want you to come directly here from the airport. There is something I want you to see. Get here as fast as you can."

"Where is here?"

"The German Hall of Military Records building." He gave her the address. "Now get your little bottom moving and fly over here."

✷ ELEVEN ✷

BERLIN, GERMANY

Kat was impressed how short distances were in Europe. Three hundred and seventy-five miles and she arrived back in Berlin. That wouldn't take you halfway across the state of Texas. But then Texas was a state of mind.

She grabbed an airport cab and skidded to a stop in front of the Hall of Military Records a half hour before it closed. They took her directly to where Wade and his two short-term slaves worked on the files in the mustiest storage room Kat had ever smelled.

"We found him," Wade crooned as Kat walked in. "We found Grant Zedicher assigned to the Warsaw section of the Transportation Corps in the Final Solution Battalion."

"So we can prove that Zedicher was in the corps, but how can we prove a bribe that was freely given almost sixty years ago?"

"We won't have to. This one will never come before a court of law. My guess. Right now we're trying to figure out how many of the other two hundred men in the battalion were also involved in this Zedicher ring of bribery experts who moved a few Jews into Switzerland for many millions of dollars."

"You figure it would take six or seven men to handle all the details?" Kat asked. She thumbed through some of the musty records. At least there wasn't much dust on the files, which had been sealed with some kind of tape.

"I'm guessing six. The fewer to do the job, the fewer to share in the profits—even as huge as they must have been. Say a twenty million split for each man would be much better than ten million each."

"I agree. But how can we find your six men out of the one hundred and ninety-nine left in the pool?"

"I don't have the foggiest idea. Do you?"

"We might check one other name, see if it's in the battalion." She took out the envelope and handed it to Wade. "This is the name of the man who emptied out John Silokowski's Swiss bank account and redeposited the same amount of money the same day in a new numbered account."

Wade took out the sheet of paper and read the name. "Hans Derrick." Derrick? He looked puzzled. "I remember that name. As I think back we found two or three Derrick names in the battalion roster. Let's check again."

The list was alphabetical. Kat hit the end of the "D's" and found the first Derrick. "Here's one with Ludwig for a first name. Press on."

One of the German helpers found the right name a moment later. Each name was on a form that gave the rank, serial number, job specialty, date entered the army, and what jobs the man had held up to this point.

The other researcher pointed to the name and nodded. "Important man now in Germany. Runs huge business. Owns one of the largest telecommunications businesses in Germany. Call the company Bavaria Limited."

Wade grinned. "Hey, I paid those folks a visit yesterday. George hadn't been there. So, we have a tie with two current billionaires, whose fathers were in the same outfit in Warsaw in 1942. I wonder if they knew each other, or worked together?"

"Tomorrow morning I'm going to find out. Would anyone object if I get out of here? If I don't get a shower in another hour I'm going to dissolve into one huge dust ball."

Wade waved her out the door. Before he left the records collection, Wade and the two helpers wrote down all two hundred names in the Final Solution Battalion. Wade took the papers with him. He wondered how many more of these two hundred became rich industrialists right after World War II?

Later that night in their workroom, Wade put the names into his computer and ticked off Derrick and Zedicher. Then he scanned a section of the local paper to check on the business news. There was none about large firms in Berlin. Nowhere in the news could he find any of the two hundred men on the transportation roster.

Kat came in from her shower; her hair still wet and tied up in a towel. She wore a cover-up robe and worked at her computer a moment, then took a cup of coffee and went over to Wade.

"Fork in the road, boss. Now we have two who must have been involved in the bribery and theft of John Silokowski's fortune. The fact that Derrick knew the Silokowski money was in that numbered account and knew how to get it proves that he worked with Zedicher who was the contact man in the field. So now we have to learn as much as we can about the day-to-day world of those two men. If there are others, they might surface through contacts."

They wrote out a project load.

"Hershel will head a two-man team to work the computers for anything else on Zedicher and now work on Derrick," Wade said. "We don't even know the names of the current heads of those two big outfits. We get those and then we try to dig up everything we can. There must be a leak, an opening, a chance that we can strike some gold around here somewhere.

"Duncan is our best man at shadowing," Wade said. "We'll put him on Zedicher International to try to find out anything he can about the head man's current agenda and his travels."

Duncan dove into his job. He quickly found out the name of the CEO of Zedicher International. He was G. B. Zedicher. A telephone call to the business editor of one of the German newspapers revealed that G. B. was a small man, not more than five feet four inches tall, slender, impeccably dressed, and liked to play the rich man with parties, big dinners, and banquets.

He dug up a feature article on the man and read it twice. G. B. lived in the penthouse on top of the Zedicher building downtown. He traveled by limousine with driver, evidently had a wife and family somewhere in the country north of Berlin. He went there every second weekend. This weekend he would be in town.

A casual walk around the big building showed Duncan that there were three underground garage entrances. One for the general public to use at a ridiculously high hourly rental, another for the employees, and a third that evidently was controlled by a radio signal from outside and only the CEO himself used that door.

Duncan called one of the contacts he had used when he was with the British Intelligence Service. The man said they had little on Zedicher: he was rich, liked getting his own way, lately had been making political motions, but nothing had developed.

Driving the company car, Duncan found a parking space where he could watch the private garage door into the Zedicher building. It was in the rear of the block square tower. By that time it was eleven-thirty and Duncan took a bite out of a deli sandwich and sipped his noontime coffee. He'd been there only fifteen minutes when the garage door opened and a black Mercedes limo slid out and headed uptown. Duncan drove three cars behind. The big limo moved swiftly through traffic and a few minutes later came to a stop at the Count Borgia Restaurant.

The limo paused only a moment while the doorman opened the rear door and G. B. Zedicher stepped out. He vanished inside the fancy eatery.

Duncan parked and ran back to the restaurant. He hurried past the doorman and talked to the man at a stand-up reservations desk just inside the lobby. Duncan's German wasn't that good, but he made himself understood. The deskman knew G. B. Zedicher.

"Does he have a private dining room? Where did he go?"

The man paused while Duncan pulled out a twenty-mark note and slipped it to him. He looked at the denomination and shrugged.

"He is here. Where I'm not certain."

Duncan put two more twenty-mark notes on top of the first one and the man nodded.

"Sir, Mr. Zedicher is here for his weekly luncheon with his friend Roderick Selig. That's all I can say." He turned to four customers who waited behind Duncan.

Duncan grinned and walked out of the eatery. He had what he wanted. He remembered the name from former days in Germany. Selig was the CEO of the huge Kunistan Corporation Limited, another of the massive multinational outfits that had ballooned in action and growth after the war.

For just a moment he wondered if there had been a Selig in the list of men who worked in the Warsaw Transportation Corps during the war. He'd find out as soon as he got back to the office.

He parked his company car where he could see the entrance and waited.

•   •   •

Upstairs in the top floor of the restaurant, Roderick Selig welcomed Zedicher. He was already on his second cocktail.

"My friend," Selig said. "How is it going with you? I hear you are about to make a big splash in politics."

"Too many of my confidants aren't able to keep their mouths shut," Zedicher said. "Or did I tell you myself?" He shook his hand, took a drink a waiter brought to him. It was his usual and the waiter knew it.

They stood and watched the city through the seventh-floor window.

"The appointment, it isn't for sure. You know how politics are. It could all blow over or blow up, or I could be the Federal Minister of Finance within two weeks. It all depends."

They had the waiter set up the table over by the window and sat with another drink.

Selig began to chuckle. He was a large man, over six feet tall and solidly built with touches of easy living fat. His dress shirts always had stains under the arms and now, even in the air-conditioned room, beads of sweat showed on his forehead.

His chuckle continued.

"What's so funny, Roderick?"

"I'm remembering the old days our fathers must have had back in Warsaw. The good days they called them. They had the idea, then backed off, afraid that they would be caught. Then they decided all they had to do was give a cut to whoever found out about it and all would be well. They must have lost a million before it was started."

"Those fathers of ours were in exactly the right place at the precise moment in history so the plan would work."

"Work it did, to perfection."

"Until they ran out of, um . . . clients."

They both laughed. Selig had already ordered pheasant under glass for both of them, a special bottle of red wine, and two elaborate chocolate desserts, which were served with everything else. Then the waiters left the room and the door was locked.

The men didn't waste any time talking after that. They charged into the pheasants and the six side dishes until the birds were destroyed. Then they sat back and belched, sipped the wine, and Zedicher got down to business.

"With this political thing coming up, I figured it was time to take care of one small problem that we've had over the years," Zedicher said.

"The bastard black box," Selig said. "With all of the talk about Jewish gold in Switzerland, the black box has been on my mind, too. We need to find it and to utterly destroy it and the contents."

"Agreed, Roderick. I don't have it, do you?"

"No, or it would have been burned in my furnace a thousand times by now."

"Then who?"

Selig shifted in his chair, slipped his shoes off, and gave a long sigh of contentment. His face grew serious. "Last I knew of it was when Berthold had it. Remember the problem Berthold had with his brother Audwin about ten or twelve years ago?"

"Yes, that was a real big mess. Berthold must have the black box, then?"

"I'm sure he doesn't. I talk to him now and then. All is going well. Audwin is under control. Berthold told me he doesn't have the box and doesn't know where it is."

"Then Audwin . . ."

"He must have hidden it somewhere just before they found out what he was doing." Selig shook his head. "So we still don't know where it is."

"I want the matter settled as quickly as possible. This week at the latest. I'm taking no chances. I've put Siegfried to work on the problem. He may come to see you. If he calls, tell him we talked and he can save the time and effort of both of you."

"What about Penrod?" Selig asked.

"We talked a month ago. At the time he asked me about the box. He's concerned as well. I doubt if he has any information. He was never friendly with Audwin. I'm afraid Audwin has to be our main concern."

"Siegfried is a good man," Selig said. "If anyone can dig out that box, Siegfried is the one."

"What if Audwin really has gone crazy now and doesn't remember if he did anything with the box, and if he did, he can't remember where he hid it?"

Selig sighed and shook his head. He wiggled his feet back in his shoes and held up his hands. "If that happens, we will just have to wait and hope that nobody stumbles over it, and if they do, that they have no idea what the contents of the box mean."

They finished the wine, then lit cigars that Selig had flown in from Cuba. He thought they were the best in the world.

It was well over two hours after Zedicher entered the restaurant that the two friends stood and walked to the door. They would not be seen leaving together. They shook hands, then grinned.

"It has its critics, Selig, but the old German Third Reich has been remarkably good to us."

They both laughed and Selig went to the elevator first. Zedicher spent fifteen minutes staring out at Berlin, wondering where in all of Germany that damned box could be.

Over two hours after Duncan saw the industrialist go into the restaurant, the big limo wheeled up and G. B. Zedicher came out the front door and slipped inside the Mercedes. Duncan followed it.

The car went straight to the Zedicher building and vanished into the private garage entrance. Duncan parked again where he could monitor the door and waited.

He used his cell phone and called the workroom. Wade had come back and picked up.

"Wade, I have a name for you. Huge industrialist in town. I want you to see if his name is on that list of two hundred you have from the Final Solution Battalion."

"So, what's the name?"

"Roderick Selig. He and Zedicher just had lunch in a private dining room at one of the best restaurants in town. I've got my money on your finding a Selig on your list. Is it alphabetical?"

"Of course, German efficiency," Wade said. "Oh, yes, mother. There is one. Ludwig Selig. He was one of the transportation guys who worked the trains out of War-saw heading for Treblinka and the death chambers. Now we should find out if he was Roderick's father."

"That's easy. If he is, we've got three of them in on the bribery/robbery," Duncan said.

"I'm betting this case will never come to trial. It will blow up long before it could come to that. What we need is enough evidence that nails these guys to the wall, so the heirs of the swindled Jewish families can come for-ward and launch lawsuits against them."

"Should I hang out here and see what Zedicher does next?"

"Right. Stick with him. We know he sometimes stays in his penthouse mansion on top there. If he doesn't show by seven or eight tonight, hang it up and come in."

"Thanks, boss."

"Think nothing of it. I'm still trying to satisfy a strange itch I have about this redhead who works for Zedicher. Something grabs at me, but I can't quite figure out what. I'm heading for the Zedicher building to try to lure the red-topped guy out to chase me again. I want a real close-up look at the varmint."

"Not a good idea, Wade. Think that one through. Ask Kat about it. Those guys aren't playing checkers over there."

"Neither am I. There's a chance he could be some-body from my past. I didn't make a lot of friends back then. Happens when you have to shoot people. Don't worry, I've got my concealed weapon permit just like the rest of us do. I'm legal. I won't let this guy get in the way of our current project. Not in any way.

"Good work on Selig. Now we probably have three. Hang in there and tail Zedicher. I'll see you when you get back."

Wade hung up the phone and checked the .45 auto-loader under his left arm. He changed the magazine, using one that extended just beyond the handle and held twelve rounds. Might come in handy.

Wade took a taxi to the Zedicher building and coaxed the reception woman into letting him talk to the public relations people. He was from the Marshall News Service and he wanted to do a feature on the harvesting of seaweed for a nature magazine. She at last agreed to let him go up.

Once he was in the same office he had been in before, the same blonde woman recognized him and pushed a button on her desk. Two big men came in at once. Wade pulled his .45 auto.

"On the floor, all three of you, now. No more buttons. I thought we could do this like civilized adults. Don't any of you move for five minutes. I'll be watching you from the hall. You come out that door, you're dead."

He moved to the door, almost let it close, then leaned back inside. One of the big guys was on his knees. He saw the .45 and he dropped back to his belly on the floor.

Wade propped the door open six inches with a chair, then ran down the hall toward the steps. He had to get out of the building. They would have an alarm out within minutes. He saw the freight elevator open and charged inside.

✶ TWELVE ✶

One worker in the elevator looked at Wade strangely and he realized he still had the .45 in his hand. He pushed it back in the holster and hit the down button on the elevator. He let it go all the way to the basement.

He was confused for a moment, then he saw a loading ramp and ran to it, jumped down the four feet to the concrete, and raced out through the truck ramp and down the street. He didn't want to get too far ahead. The man in the freight elevator would tell them which way he went.

Wade stopped behind a solid-looking car and waited. He was screened from the direction he had come. He could see the front of the Zedicher building. Both big men came to the sidewalk. They were joined by another man. One ran the other way, and two came toward him. He wanted a good look at them, this would be it. He would see if the new man was the redheaded one. As the pair came forward cautiously, they didn't show their weapons, but he knew they had guns handy.

When they were fifty feet away, Wade could tell the larger of the two had red hair. Yes. It had worked. Now if he could get a solid ID on the man without being spotted.

He ducked low and peered through the window of the car. The big man was still coming. Closer now. Wade waited, ducked down, came up twice more but with minimum motion so he wouldn't be noticed.

Yes, it was the same redhead with the eye patch, watching to both sides. His left hand was in his pocket. Watching, waiting. The man's eye was intense. Wade stared at the redhead's square-cut jaw and the high cheekbones. Did he know him? The eye patch was throwing him off. But the face seemed somehow familiar. Then he saw the nose, twisted one way, then the other, a double break.

Wade dropped down, shocked, his anger rising. The man chasing him was Siegfried, a top former East German intelligence agent during the Cold War. The one man in the world Wade hated with all his soul. Siegfried had attacked Wade's family, butchered them, made a clean getaway. Wade wanted to lift up and shoot the man down right there. So his round in Berlin 5 years ago hadn't killed him—only blinded one eye.

His heart raced, Wade's hand stroked the big pistol in its holster, eyes narrowed as he watched the hated man ease past the car and check inside the next one. An unholy and totally animalistic surge of emotion billowed up in him and it was all he could do to keep from shooting the villain down where he stood. Then he slammed a cap on his runaway emotions and tried to calm himself. Wade pulled off his jacket and pushed it under the car. They would be looking for a man in a tan jacket. He walked slowly up the street after the two men were well beyond the car that had hidden him. The red hair had fooled Wade for a minute. When he had known Siegfried he had short blond hair. The fuller red hair was a beacon that no professional agent would wear. That and the eye patch made him stand out in any gathering. But now Siegfried had changed jobs, he worked for Zedicher. But he hadn't changed his line of work, killing.

The two Germans saw something ahead and raced

that way. Wade walked half a block down the street the other way, then went across traffic and strolled casually on toward the Zedicher building and away from Siegfried.

He hailed a taxi and rode toward the office. He couldn't believe it. The man was Siegfried, one of the best of the East German agents in the Cold War. He had been brutal, efficient, and deadly. Two years before Wade quit the CIA, he and Siegfried had come to blows in East Berlin.

Wade had been on a mission to turn an East German into a double agent working for the United States. He had almost succeeded when Siegfried showed up in place of the other agent at the next meeting and came out shooting. The contact had been set for a deserted area so none of the East German's buddies would know what he was doing. It was also perfect for a trap for Siegfried to kill the American agent who was trying to turn Siegfried's man.

The location had been a frozen lake in a deserted park. The shootout lasted five minutes and Wade was down to two rounds. They both conserved their bullets then and maneuvered to get a killing advantage. Just as he was about to slip away, Wade heard movement around a big oak tree. He waited. Siegfried stepped around it with his weapon pointing the other way.

Wade lifted his weapon and fired automatically. He saw the round smash into the East German's back as he fell down behind the tree.

Lights from East German patrol cars showed less than a block away and Wade hadn't been able to confirm the kill. He faded away through the woods and park and got away.

It wasn't until almost two years later that Wade realized that he hadn't killed Siegfried. He was shocked when he saw photos taken of three men entering the U.S. through the Washington, D.C., airport. All had been checked by immigration and CIA and passed through.

Only later did Wade tell the inspectors that they had goofed and let into the United States one of the worst of the East German spies and killers.

That same day, Wade moved his wife and two small girls to a new home in a gated facility that had twenty-four-hour roving guards and was a part of a housing area on a military base.

He checked in with his wife Vivian twice a day by phone.

One day Vivian told Wade that a deliveryman had left a package for them.

"Don't open it," Wade cautioned. "Get out of the house right now. Take the kids to a movie. Don't touch that package, it's probably a bomb." Vivian, as a wife of a CIA agent, was always extremely careful when it came to security.

Wade raced home and checked the package. It was from a firm he had ordered something from. He tested it, dropped it behind a rock wall. He could hear no ticking. He dropped it in a bucket of water. At last he ripped it apart with a spade and found a sweatshirt he had ordered ruined by his testing.

A week later another package arrived at his house. Again he told Vivian to leave it alone and go to a neighbor's house. He tested the package the same way. When he dropped it over the rock wall it exploded with killing force and knocked some rocks off the wall. He was not injured.

He moved his family again. This time into a gated, exclusive complex with double security. His wife said everything was fine when he called at three that afternoon. When he came home at six-thirty there were no lights on in the house that early winter evening. He tried the front door. It was unlocked. He pulled his automatic and went in fast. He found the girls first.

Both had been strangled and a large S letter had been carved in each small chest, "S" for Siegfried.

"Oh, God, no." Wade went down on his knees, his

arms around the silent naked forms. Tears washed down his face as he stared at each small precious daughter. Then he folded their arms, covered their bodies, and stormed out of the bedroom to find his wife.

"Vivian," he bellowed, but knew that she couldn't hear him. He wondered how Siegfried had done it. How had he found them? This hurt a hundred times more than if the agent had killed Wade. He raced into their bedroom, but it was empty and made up the way Vivian always did right after she got up. He stormed into the living room, the family room, then the kitchen. All were hauntingly empty. He knew she was there. Just off the silent kitchen was the laundry room. A small area no more than six feet square with the washer and dryer, furnace and hot-water heater. The washer was open; the front load dryer was closed.

No, impossible. He stared at the closed dryer for a full minute before his shaking hand reached the handle. He pulled the door open. One of Vivian's arms swung down from the cramped inside of the dryer.

He collapsed on the floor. Wade leaned back against the washer and let the sobs tear through his body time and time again. It was more than an hour before he stopped, before he could speak, before he felt that he could stand and not fall. He crawled to the dryer and gently eased Vivian from her hot death chamber. She wasn't a big person, five-four. Her arms and legs had been folded and then wrapped around inside the cylinder. He tugged gently until he had her out and lay her on the floor. Her face and head were bruised and had turned red from the heat.

For a moment he stared at her. They had warned him about getting married all those years ago. But he told them times had changed, his family would be safe.

He crawled into the kitchen and used the drawers and handles to help him stand. Then he picked up the kitchen phone and called his control at CIA.

No 911 call.

He knew that well enough. The Agency had two men and an unmarked van at his house within an hour. These men were the cleaners. Their job was to clean up after anything like this or worse, and not let a word about it leak out.

There would be a statement from the Agency in a week or so that a mother and her two daughters were killed in a car crash on a backcountry road. Evidently a tire blew out sending the vehicle off the road into a deep ditch that held ten feet of water. The funeral for the three had already taken place after cremation. The woman had been a secretary at one of the Agency's low-level locations.

The van eased in the driveway and up to the back of the house. Two neighbors stood on their lawns watching. They knew something had happened. The CIA men shielded any view of the bodies as they were carried out in body bags. There was nothing to clean up in the house.

Rob Hartley, Wade's control, led Wade to his bedroom where he packed a suitcase for him. He would be "in residence" at one of the Agency's several full-care facilities around D.C. There the Agency would give him as much time as he wanted. Years ago he had written out instructions for final arrangements for his family if they were ever needed: cremation and the ashes scattered over the Atlantic. No services. He wouldn't be involved. He couldn't stand to be there. It was his fault his family had been slaughtered.

After a week of sitting in his room at the facility he called Hartley.

"I'm resigning, Rob. Pull the plug on me this week. I have that small ranch out in Idaho with six horses. I'm going out there and raise horses and a few cattle and let somebody else save the whole damn world."

Rob had made the usual arguments about waiting, giving it more time, letting the wounds heal. They had put on a full search for Siegfried, but the last word was that he had slipped into Canada and was by then back in Germany.

Wade had only nodded. He took his Keogh money and his funded retirement and flew to Idaho.

Wade knew what he had to do. He pulled every string, every contact that he had in and out of the Agency. A week later he knew where Siegfried was assigned, knew his home address, knew he was at his office this week. Wade flew to Germany, infiltrated into East Berlin, and watched the East German agent's apartment.

It took him four days to make sure of Siegfried's routine. Every morning he came out of the apartment at seven-fifteen, stopped across the street for breakfast, then drove seven miles to his office. He always parked in a company lot a block from his workplace.

Wade usually followed him. Today he was in front of Siegfried, waiting in an alley through a block of small manufacturing plants.

Then it was simple. Siegfried came walking up carrying a newspaper. When the East German agent was three steps from the alley, Wade leaned out, shot him once in the face with his silenced .45. As Siegfried fell, Wade moved back into the alley and ran. His car was parked at the other end. He got in and drove away. There was little chance that Siegfried could survive. However, Wade wasn't sure of the kill. There were too many witnesses on the street to risk his checking on the body. A week later, Wade was back in Idaho worrying about one of his mares ready to foal.

He was in Idaho just over two years before his old boss, J. August Marshall, flew there in a chopper one day and talked to Wade about a new job. Wade had made peace with himself. His mistake couldn't be undone. His family was dead. Now he had to move on. He was ready.

When the taxi stopped in front of the Marshall office in Berlin, Wade eased out and paid the driver. He was still too shocked and angry to get any work done on the project. He walked away from the building and down the street.

He wasn't sure where he went, or how long the walk lasted. When he shook his head and looked at his watch, he realized that it was dark. He had to walk for ten minutes before he could find a cab. The long journey had been done mostly in a fog of anger, fury, and planning what terrible death he could arrange for Siegfried. Whatever else happened on this project, Siegfried would die. He knew that. The rest of the team didn't have to know it. He had decided the first few minutes of his walk that he wouldn't tell the others about Siegfried. It would be his secret, until the time came to shoot him down with as much pain as possible. He'd heard of one sadistic Russian agent who had shot an Israeli spy forty-two times before he killed him. It was a record Wade would love to try to break on Siegfried.

By the time Wade made it back to the Marshall company workroom, all but Hershel and Kat had turned in. Both were still working on their computers and they told Wade they had some interesting news.

Kat looked up, her dark eyes flashing. "I've found some early things on the Bavaria Limited outfit. Fifteen years ago there were two brothers running the place, Audwin Derrick and his brother Berthold. Now for the past ten years or so, all documents are signed by Berthold, all announcements are made by the same man. No mention at all of the other brother, Audwin. Now I find that terribly interesting."

Wade had to pull his mind back to the project. He could still see Siegfried's face and he trembled. "Damned interesting, Kat," Wade said. "Anything unusual we can dig up about these big three will be ammunition we can use in all sorts of ways. Some even legal. Keep digging."

Hershel had been checking the names of big corporate CEOs against the list of men who had worked as Nazis in the Final Solution Battalion in Warsaw in 1942. He had come up with ten solid matches.

"But then some of these names are the most common in Germany. There's a chance that most of these men had nothing at all to do with robbing the rich Warsaw Jews. But it is a list that is growing as we dig into this problem. We have our three solid ones, and that's a great place to start."

Hershel frowned and stared at the screen for a minute, then looked back at Wade.

"Hey, boss, what happens when we get one or two or all of these guys dead to rights that their fathers swindled and cheated and robbed the Warsaw Jews before sending them to the extermination showers in Treblinka? Do we try to broadcast what we know and pull down these big corporations? Jeez, that would be like dismantling GM, IBM, and AT&T because their fathers were all criminals. That would leave a huge hole in the German economy. Can we do that?"

"First we get the evidence that we need, the hard incontrovertible facts that these bastards did the deed," Wade said. "Then we'll figure out how to put the matter as straight as it can be put. We aren't trying to make anybody pay for the six million dead. Nobody can ever repay a debt like that. But maybe we can crack one chunk out of this German stonewalling about the stolen gold and the riches."

⋆ THIRTEEN ⋆

At the meeting that evening in the back workroom, the Specialists assembled with a lot to talk about. Kat and Hershel had worked the printouts from the Web again and again. Each time they came up with the names of five men who seemed to have no cash at the start of the war, but millions quickly after that.

All of them worked on reconstruction in some way. Part of this work was paid for by the World War II Marshall Plan. No relation to the Specialists' Mr. Marshall. The men quickly became rich, then richer, and now headed mammoth international corporations.

Kat had winnowed it down to five names as most promising. Two of them were already on their list, Zedicher and Selig. They would be checked out in every way possible. Derrick at Bavaria Limited was a probable, but they had to check it out in detail.

Two of the Specialists went to work on each of the three remaining names. Ichi and Duncan drew the Diffendorfer Electronics giant. They telephoned ahead the next morning and asked about doing a major feature story on the firm for a huge U.S. electronics magazine. The public relations people were delighted.

An hour later they showed up with cameras, tape recorders, and notebooks. The PR person at the German firm even spoke English. She was tall, blonde, and extremely German but her English was better than Ichi's.

"So you are a magazine team, right? You want to know everything about Diffendorfer. It will take us at least three days. Do you have the time?"

"Hey, we can work here a week if we have to," Ichi said.

They plunged into the history of the firm. There was a short film, some books of pictures, and lots of newspaper articles. The girl's name was Louise. She said to call her Lois. They worked through the morning, had a free lunch in the company cafeteria, and went back to the history. Just after the break, Hershel zeroed in on the vital element.

"Just how did Mr. Diffendorfer get started so soon after the war? I've heard that conditions were terrible. Most of Berlin lay in ruins. Where did he get the money to go into business?"

Lois beamed. "Good, good. I'm glad to tell you. He started his business with one bicycle. There were no cars then, no trucks, or even any streets. People needed to move faster than walking. The bicycle suddenly became the best form of transportation. Mr. Diffendorfer found bikes, bought them, fixed them, made new parts for old ones. He would walk miles to find a broken bike and buy it cheaply, fix it up, and sell it. He started all this in a bombed-out building's basement.

"After a year he had enough funds to begin importing bicycles from other countries and selling them. Two years later he saw that electronics would be the wave of the future and he learned all he could about them, and bought a small firm that had been making irons for women to use."

"So he had no huge benefactor who gave him a few million marks to get started?" Ichi asked.

"Absolutely not. Here are three volumes of photos

and early newspaper stories about the firm's early days. They prove our founder started slowly, painfully, and only after ten years did he have much of a business going. From then on it exploded with the electronics age. Of course now there are computers, and software and radios, television, camcorders, and military electronics."

Ichi looked at Duncan. Duncan nodded and the two stood.

"Hey, I'm sorry about this, but we have another appointment we have to go to," Ichi said. "We weren't sure if we could get to see you today or not. We'll call back when we have this other problem straightened out."

"Thanks for your help telling us about the company here," Duncan said. "We do appreciate it."

They left with all of their equipment to the surprise of Lois, the public relations person.

"No sense wasting time here," Ichi said when they hit the street. "This old boy did it the right way, so he probably isn't involved."

Several miles across town, Kat and Hershel worked the TV news feature ploy on Griswold International Construction. They had arranged the preliminary discussion with the public relations department and were two hours into a general survey of the operation when Kat moved the questions into the firm's history.

"One thing our viewers want to know on big corporations like this is just how they got started. Was it one man, or a committee, or a whole group of people working together?"

Rolfe Gerber frowned for a moment. "I had planned on getting into that aspect of the corporation this afternoon, but I guess I can switch gears a little."

"As I understand, Griswold began right after the war in 1945, is that right?" Hershel asked.

"Yes. It was one man who had the vision to begin a new firm that would help rebuild Berlin and all of Germany, then the rest of Europe."

"That would be Mandel Griswold?" Hershel asked.

"Yes, Mr. Griswold had just come out of the German Army and he was determined not to have to work for someone else the rest of his life. He told everyone he was tired of taking orders, he wanted to be the man to give them."

Kat checked some notes she had made from her Internet search on the computer. "Now I've read that Mr. Griswold joined the army right out of school, so he had no real trade or skills. His father had been a carpenter all his life. So essentially it was a lower working-class family. Is that right?"

"Yes, a carpenter. That's where old Mandel must have received his early training in construction."

"Now, Mr. Gerber, as you must know we do a lot of research on a firm before we decide to go ahead with a story on it. Part of our research was in the old records showing business applications and original funding, and permits and that sort of thing for a new business to get started. Even right after the war the efficient German ethic was in full force and records were kept and businesses were set up the right way.

"Those early records show that Griswold Construction began with a business funded at a little over seven million marks. That was late in 1945. This is a recorded fact, Mr. Gerber. What we need to know is how a common man like Mandel Griswold, just out of the army and without any big family money behind him, could set up a corporation worth seven million marks?"

Gerber frowned, took off his glasses and polished them, and put them on carefully.

"Actually there is a lot of confusion about the beginnings of the corporation. It didn't start in 1945 as some sources say. It was more like 1955 before it was finally incorporated and began to work in the construction industry. By that time Mr. Griswold had saved some money, and had contacts where he could borrow . . ."

Kat held up her hand. "Mr. Gerber. What about the Berlin city records? They show plainly that the firm under Mandel Griswold opened for business in December of 1945 with an incorporated value of just over seven million marks. What are you trying to hide? Why not just tell us how the financing was arranged? That's all we're looking for right now. We must have that as the basis for the whole story."

Gerber stood from behind his desk high in the Griswold building. "Please excuse me a moment. I'll have to clear this with another party. It will be just a few minutes." He nodded and left the office.

Kat looked at Hershel and nodded. "Shook him up right down to his gonads," she whispered. "He must be going for reinforcements."

Hershel stood and walked to the window. He could see half of Berlin from that height. "It's a beautiful city. Never think that it was a flat bombed-out ruin just fifty years ago."

Two guards in security uniforms came into the room. Both had side arms. Rolfe Gerber came in right behind them.

"If you please, you must leave the building at once. We have no time to play your American games. These guards will escort you to the exit. Please do not try to come again. You will not be welcome. I have nothing more to say."

He gave a curt order and the two guards motioned toward the door. Kat shrugged.

"Why not, Gerber. You've already told us what we needed to know by throwing us out. Thanks."

Ten minutes later, Kat and Hershel sat in a company car across the street from the big Griswold headquarters building and sipped at their paper cups of coffee.

"Lying through his teeth," Hershel said.

"True, but how do we prove it? We have copies of the original business license and the funding of seven million marks. But that's not enough. That doesn't say that he didn't borrow it from a friend or a bank. We need evidence that he didn't borrow it from anyone."

"That still doesn't prove that he was part of the bribery/robbery detail in the corps in Warsaw."

"Don't remind me. We have to get back in there and dig out what we need to know."

"How? They all have name tags with ID and secret coding on them. The codes on the chips probably limit the areas they can penetrate. We'd need to get into what area?"

"Old records, early day journals."

"Kat, not even a crazy German is going to write down that he stole seven million marks from the Warsaw ghetto Jews."

Kat scowled as she nodded. "That's the hell of it. How do we tie this one down?"

Hershel finished his coffee. "Who runs this outfit now?"

"Penrod Griswold, fifty-three, a post-war baby," Kat said, looking at her notes.

"So we grab Penrod and make him confess he knew where his daddy got the cash to start his business."

"He'd never admit it."

"So, are we stalemated?"

"Just temporarily." Kat pointed. "See that woman who just got out of the car parked in the no parking area? She's wearing a uniform of some kind and the outside security are treating her like she's royalty."

Hershel put down his binoculars. "She got out of a car that has a sign on the door. 'Personal Couriers.' The ad under the logo says: 'We specialize in For His Eyes Only correspondence, small packages, confidential matter'."

"Yes," Kat said. "We have our gimmick. See if she gets a badge or pass or anything from the guards."

"Yep, right at the door, the last security man clipped a three-tier badge of some kind that must give carte blanche to the place."

"Let's move, driver man. Get me to the office on time. We've got some work to do before the four-thirty rush hour."

On the way back to the office, Hershel grinned as Kat laid out her plan.

"You going in there alone?" Hershel asked.

"How many people does it take to deliver an envelope?"

"Maybe I could meet you at a side door and we both could work on it?"

"Not with the security we saw around there today. Remember those badges? We don't have time to dummy up one of those in an hour. You see to the rig. One of our newer small sedans." Kat had worked over the classified section of the telephone directory and came up with a name.

"We'll be Lightning Couriers Inc. 'When it has to be delivered on time, Lightning strikes.' Good slogan but it's too long. Let's just use the Lightning Couriers Inc. painted on the driver's door panel."

By four o'clock they were ready. The art department had come up with some important-looking labels. They used an expensive padded envelope with thirty pages of stapled blank paper inside. On the return address area, something had been typed in on a label, but then rubbed out with black marking pen. It looked important. On the bottom in fancy script were the words: FOR HIS EYES ONLY. HAND-TO-HAND DELIVERY GUARANTEED.

One secretary used to this sort of job spent almost an hour on the phone trying to find out the name of the head man on the history of the Griswold firm or corporate beginnings. At last she tied down the name of the man who was the supervisor of historical records. The package was addressed to him: Herr Hermann Albrecht, Records Division, then the firm's headquarters and address.

Both of them would go in the newly painted car to the headquarters. Hershel drove. He stopped in a no parking zone and when a guard came to talk to him, Kat got out of the car and spoke briefly. The guard waved her forward.

She talked to the men at the front door, showed them her package and her company ID. She waved at Hershel and the "company" car drove away.

"That's what it says," Kate said, sounding miffed. "I have to deliver it from my hand to his. We guarantee that. Surely you've had our people bring in deliveries like this before. We're the best couriers in town for sensitive material."

"His eyes only," the guard said. "Looks legitimate enough. I can issue you a pass to the twentieth floor where our records department is. I've never heard of that man, but he's not an important name around here."

"I do need to get it up to him as soon as possible. What do I sign, or where do I get a badge? I notice that you wear one."

"We could escort you up there, but I'm short on men right now." The German scowled, muttered something, and reached in a drawer in his stand-up desk and took out a company badge.

"This is good for working hours only. Leave it at the reception desk when you leave. You have only forty-five minutes so don't get lost. If he's not there, or out sick or something, just leave it for him."

"Not a chance," Kat said. "I can't just leave it. It has to go from my hand to his. That's why we get paid so well."

He clipped the badge on her jacket lapel and waved her forward.

Kat smiled at him and went inside. Her badge was like a passport into the company. People smiled and nodded. She took the elevator to the twentieth floor, located the right office, and saw that there was a guard stationed inside the door. She went in and asked if this was where the bookkeeping people were. The guard shook his head and gave her instructions.

She listened and went out into the hall. Two doors

down she found a women's rest room and hurried inside. Timing. It was only 4:38. It would be twenty-two minutes before the guard left and the rooms were locked up for the night. She wondered about security on the doors.

Someone came in the rest room and Kat stepped into one of the stalls and closed the door. She stood for a while, then sat down to wait. Four more women came in, and left. Then eight or ten came in chattering with each other. When the last woman left the rest room, it was almost ten after five. Kat came out of the booth and took a quick look out the door into the hall. Two men walked the other way.

Late workers. There might be a lot of them. When should she try the door to the records section? She had carefully noted the door lock when she left. It was a common type with easy to change keying if something went wrong. It would take her twenty to thirty seconds to pick it with her ring of handy wires and probes.

At twenty after five, she walked out of the women's room, met two women coming toward her. She nodded and continued. At the records door, she looked both ways.

No one.

Do it now. She had the picks in her right hand. She bent down and pushed into the keyhole the first two slender probes with right angle turns on the tips. For ten seconds she worked them, heard a click, then inserted another probe and turned it and the door came open. She slipped inside and closed the door.

She remembered it was an inside office with no windows and now it became absolutely dark. She took out a small pencil flashlight from her hand purse and shone it around. No light would show out from this room. She turned on the switch. She made a slow check of the files and the phone list on the receptionist's desk.

Under corporate records she found a phone number and a note beside it, Room 12-B. She opened one door and looked down a corridor. Doors showed on both sides.

The door she had come in suddenly rattled. Someone

must be checking to see that the doors were all locked. This one would automatically lock again once it closed. She tensed, waiting, then the guard must have moved down the outside hall.

Kay walked quickly from door to door. The numbers started at six and worked up. There it was, 12-B. She tried the doorknob and the panel opened. Inside it was dark. She snapped on the overhead light. Again, no windows. The light was safe.

The room was jammed with filing cabinets. Some were built into the walls. Three rows of cabinets six high went nearly from wall to wall, with only room to slide around the ends. All were labeled.

It took her five minutes to find the section on corporate history. Kat paused and considered it. If this were her company and something underhanded had happened to get it started, would she keep any record of it? Absolutely not. Still these were Germans, world renowned for their efficiency and total and complete record keeping. She checked in the files. One said "1945 to 1950." She looked in it. Early sales reports, commissions, reports of purchases. Then she found a file marked "First Business." The file showed a ten-story building that was shattered. The next pictures of it showed it being restored. She took two of the pictures and put them in the big envelope she carried. If the envelope passed the test to get in, it should also qualify to go out.

Kat kept looking. She found a copy of the first business license. It was marked August 1945. The firm was incorporated for seven million marks. She took that document as well. She adjusted her shoulder strap purse. She carried little in it beside her picks and her new Walther P88 9mm parabellum pistol and its silencer. Its weight of just over three pounds was reassuring.

Kat worked for another half hour and found nothing more that would help. She was just ready to give up and leave when a guard sprang into the room, his pistol out and aimed straight at her.

"What the hell? I'm working overtime and you come point that gun at me?"

"No good," the guard said. "That's a visitor's badge not good after closing time. Come away from the files easy and into the corridor. I'm going to enjoy searching you."

He was over six feet, blond, under thirty, and looked like a weight lifter. She clutched the package in one hand and the straps of her purse with the other and moved slowly out of the file room into the hall.

"Now, I don't know what you're talking about. The man who gave me the badge said he would be right back to help me research. Now he must have the right kind of employee badge. Oh, there he comes now."

The guard frowned and started to look back, changed his mind and watched her.

"Hey, I'm over here, Heinrich. Come tell this gun-happy guard . . ."

The guard turned then, giving Kat enough time to swing her purse on the three-foot straps. The heavy Walther-filled purse swung out like a ball and chain of olden days and hit the guard on the side of the head just as he looked back toward Kat. His pistol went off, but the round missed Kat. His eyes glazed, then his knees buckled. He sank to the floor and then sprawled out on his stomach.

Kat grabbed his pistol and hurried to the outer door that led into the main hall. She was on the twentieth floor, might have killed the guard, had his gun, and was stealing documents. Not bad. Also she had gained entry under false pretenses. Not even a misdemeanor. She tossed the guard's gun in a wastebasket.

She checked both ways, slipped into the hall, and headed for the elevator.

Some kind of an alarm went off. She had to ignore it. She wasn't about to walk down twenty floors.

At the elevator bank there were six lifts. Two went past going down, not stopping at her signal on the button.

One came up and passed her floor. The next one came up, stopped, and the door slid open. There was no one inside.

She stepped in, punched the lobby button, and the doors closed. Somebody down the hall shouted but by then the doors had shut and the elevator moved downward.

Twice more it stopped on floors, but there was no one to get on.

In the lobby she walked out with confidence. She had resealed the package and had her story straight.

Someone at the reception/guard desk called to her and she walked up to the guard.

"Miss, your pass. This isn't good after closing. What was your business?"

She showed him the package. "I came in just before quitting time, but the guard said I'd have time to deliver the package. It's For His Eyes Only, which means I have to deliver it in person. Then his secretary couldn't find him and she kept me waiting. She stayed until five-thirty but we still couldn't find him. She said I'd have to come back tomorrow."

The guard frowned, made some notes on a sheet of paper, and had her sign out on the form. She signed. A phone rang. The guard picked it up.

He listened for a moment. "No, nobody has come down. Well, one young lady from a courier service. Nobody else. Yes. I see. All right." He hung up and shook his head.

"Miss, I'm sorry, but there's been some trouble on the twentieth floor. My supervisor says he wants to talk to you. Would you mind waiting a moment to keep him happy?"

Kat had the Walther out of her purse and showed it to the guard. "I would mind. Now come out from behind there and take me over to the main door and let me out. If you don't, you won't have to worry about your pension, you'll be shot dead and under six feet of good German dirt."

☆ FOURTEEN ☆

The security man at the front desk was about forty, he'd seen a lot in his time. He shook his head and smiled at Kat who held the pistol pointing directly at him.

"Now come, miss, you don't want to do that. I'm sure it's just some kind of a misunderstanding."

Kat fired a silenced shot into the file cabinet beside him. The man's eyes went wide; he slid past the opening in the reception desk counter and walked the way Kat pointed. She headed him for a smaller side door, moving closely behind him. Now and then she poked the nose of the silencer into his back.

"Easy, take it easy, lady. I have a family at home. You want out, I can let you out."

They walked to the door at the side of the lobby. Another guard came into the big open space and watched Kat and the guard. The man leading Kat hadn't seen the other guard.

They stopped at the door and the man held up a key and turned it in the side door away from the huge main doors. The door eased open. Kat pulled back the pistol and slammed it down against the guard's head dropping him to the floor. She edged out the door to the sidewalk and ran to the right holding her purse and the large envelope in one hand and the Walther pistol in the other.

A guard came around the far end of the Griswold building and stared at her. She now held the pistol inside her jacket. She called to the guard.

"Something is wrong back down there. I heard a gunshot."

The guard frowned and ran forward, past her and toward the main doors. When she looked back, six men in guard uniforms poured out the side door and ran after her. She darted into the first alley. Quickly she ripped open the large envelope, took out the two sheets of paper she needed from the Griswold files. She hesitated a moment, then folded them in half, unbuttoned the top two buttons of her blouse, and pushed the papers inside the light blue garment. She buttoned the fasteners, discarded the envelope and blank paper, and ran.

Three teenage boys played marbles in the dirt halfway down the alley. Two bicycles lay on their sides. She grabbed one, righted it, and amid the shouts of the boys, rode away down the alley. Kat wondered how quickly they would have cars out hunting her. She rode across the first street into the alley on the far side, then at the next street she turned left away from the tall building she had just left. Five blocks more and she put the bike down near the next street and walked across to a small café with sidewalk tables.

Kat strolled inside, bought coffee and a roll, and sat at a table near the back. She took off her tan jacket and sat on it. They would be looking for that jacket.

Five minutes later two Germans in Griswold guard uniforms came into the small café and looked around. She kept sipping at her coffee with the cup covering half of her face as they stared at everyone. They didn't waste any time on her, moving past to the next woman, then a couple. Two minutes later they were gone.

Kat had been holding the silenced Walther under the table as the guards checked out the place. Now she unscrewed the sound suppressor and put the weapon and the long tube in her purse. She finished her coffee and roll leisurely, then unhooked the shoulder strap from her purse and put it in the seat. Now she had more of a clutch purse. She left the tan jacket in the booth with the purse strap and walked outside as casually as she could. Kat knew that she looked considerably different than she had at the Griswold company office.

She could see no one watching the eatery. There were no police or cars with Griswold logos on them prowling the block. She let out a held-in breath and looked for a taxi.

Twenty minutes later she was back in the Marshall Export/Import office. She looked for the list of the Nazi Transportation Corps. The name of Mandel Griswold had to be on the list. Where was that envelope? She found it on Wade's desk. A quick look down the names and she stopped at the Gs. Yes, there it was, Mandel Griswold. They had the fourth member of the group tied down as sure as they could at the moment.

That morning, Wade and Roger took on the fifth name on the list of firms, Bavaria T&T Limited, a huge telephone company in Germany.

"We need a new gimmick," Wade said. "How do we get past the door and into the PR guts of things without them getting suspicious?"

"We tried the TV show and the magazine spread, and good old CNN network," Roger said. "What's left?"

Wade grinned. "Roger, my man, I hear you worked on two or three movies when you were a SEAL with the navy."

"Yeah, it was a blast. Not your ordinary service day when the movie folks were in town."

"We're in town again, Roger. We go over as a movie scouting team, trying to pick out a big corporation we can give a hundred million dollars' worth of free publicity worldwide. We want to use Bavaria Telephone &

Telegraph Limited as our home for the film, the background, the realism of all the rest of the big action adventure show with a top flight star cast out of Hollywood."

Roger grinned. "Yeah, I can get one of those shoulder cams, the kind the TV reporters use, and keep shooting as you talk to their PR department."

"Yeah, and we don't take just two of us. We'll take three of the secretaries and two of our guards with us in our contingent. Drive up in a big black Mercedes. Let them know we're coming. Yeah, I like it."

"Then somewhere after we have them hooked on a fifty-million splurge of free publicity, we smack them with the facts," Roger said. "We want to show the company as being founded on gold, money, jewels, and old master paintings, stolen from the Jews in the Warsaw ghetto in 1942."

"Let's put it together," Wade said. "First you'll need a telephone to find that TV camera. Be careful with it. The damn things cost about seventy-five thousand dollars."

By two that afternoon they had the secretaries dressed in thigh-high mini-mini skirts, three-inch pumps, white peasant blouses with scoop necklines, show business makeup, and all with their hair piled high on their heads. Wade made his call that morning and got through to the PR people who liked the idea of the worldwide publicity. The PR manager said to come see him that afternoon just after two o'clock. He said he'd meet them at the front door, outside.

Wade and Roger both wore blue jeans and T-shirts with advertising about other movies on them. A Hollywood uniform for producers and directors. Roger would be the film's director.

They drove up in the big Mercedes and all streamed out. Wade led the parade to the front door, with Roger shooting footage of the trip. He'd had a cram course in how to run the camera. As Roger shot, Wade used a bullhorn to get his team into place near the front door. The PR man was there.

He came up to Wade quickly. When Roger talked to him on the phone the man said his name was Wilheim Reuther. The man was all smiles and waves.

"Do you need the bullhorn?" he asked in English.

"Damn right. You Reuther? Need the horn to get all of our ducks in a row here. I think my people are ready, what about yours?"

"Yes, Mr. Thorne, all ready. Let's go in the main door. I see your cameraman is taking pictures of our corporation. We're the second largest corporate entity in all of Germany."

They trooped inside. All security and badges were brushed aside. They were taken up to the seventeenth floor in two elevators with Roger still shooting with the camera.

They all clustered in one conference room, with four representatives of Bavaria Limited. They were so eager for this kind of publicity that Wade could feel the vibrations zinging through the air.

Wade made an opening statement that was translated into German and then he asked Roger to give some of the scope of the storyline.

Roger frowned, then nodded. "It's a love story that goes wrong, how a young, innocent girl gets mixed up with a powerful old-money German family that is ultimately influential. There has been talk of a questionable past about how the family's main business had been started just after the war, but the young girl refuses to believe it. She is enthralled with the handsome grandson of the firm's founder and is on the verge of marrying him, when something happens that makes her pull back.

"A young American Jewish man smashes into the scene on a motorcycle screaming that the family had robbed his Jewish grandfather during World War II, just before they sent him into the gas chambers at Treblinka. He screams in front of TV cameras that the Derrick family fortune was founded on the fortunes of Jews in the genocide perpetrated by the Nazis during World War II, and especially those who had been sent out of the Warsaw ghetto in 1942."

Reuther jumped up from where he had been growing increasingly more agitated as Roger talked.

"No, no, it can't be. You said you would change the names of the company. This is a slander against our founder."

Wade stood up and waved his arms. "Easy, easy, Wilheim. This is just an idea, a treatment. It will change a hundred times before we even get to the script stage. We're scouting locations and firms that want to cooperate with us in exchange for a hundred million in free publicity. We thought your firm was the one."

"We are, but the name has to be changed. The idea that our founder stole money from those poor Jewish people on their way to their deaths. That's slanderous." He nodded. "But as you said, it is just a treatment, an idea. We like the idea of the young girl and the moneyed youth from the family. *Ja*, that is the good part."

"Wilheim, you reacted so strongly about the Jewish plunder money. Are you protesting too much? Is there something real here that we may have stumbled upon. Is the Bavaria Limited corporate structure all based on those millions of dollars, maybe billions, that were stolen from the Jews out of Warsaw alone?"

Wilhelm straightened up, his back stiff as a ramrod now, as he glared at Wade.

"Absolutely untrue. Absurd. Unthinkable that you even ask such a question. Our founding is easily established with the facts of the case. They are on file."

"So, where did Hans Derrick find the eight million marks that he used to start his company?"

"He didn't find it. He borrowed it from six different sources. It wasn't eight million, it was six hundred thousand that he borrowed from old-line German families that had taken money out of Germany long before the middle of the war."

"Swiss numbered bank accounts?" Wade asked sharply.

Wilhelm squirmed, scowled, then put his fists on his hips. "Yes, some of them. Some invested in England, some in America."

"Isn't it true that Hans Derrick was a member of the Nazi Transportation Corps during the war and was assigned to the Final Solution Battalion at the Warsaw ghetto?"

"No, absolutely not. No." The anger and the command had slid out of his voice. "Out of here. All of you Americans and movie people. Out of here. There will be no movie about Bavaria Limited. Absolutely no movie. That is all trash talk. It is calumny of the first degree. I won't permit it on company property. Get your equipment and get out of here."

Wade paused near the furious German publicity maven and stared at him. "Hans Derrick was a member of that Transportation Corps. German records prove that. What I wonder is how many of the two hundred men in that group were robbing and murdering the Warsaw Jews?"

Wade gave him a challenging look and hurried past, ushering his three miniskirted secretaries out to the elevator. Armed security men made sure that Wade and his group all went directly to the front door and out to the street. The big Mercedes was still there. They all stepped inside and drove away.

"Looks like we just lost another friend," Wade said.

Roger laughed softly. "Oh, yeah, we sure did. Can you imagine the inner office memos that are going to be flashing around that place today."

"E-mail will be hot."

The invitation from Siegfried to Berthold Derrick was emphatic: there would be a meeting with the two of them that same day just after three P.M. in the public park some forty miles north of Berlin in the boathouse on the lake. Siegfried had made the phone call that morning.

"What's so important it can't wait until we can meet over dinner somewhere a bit more civilized?" Berthold Derrick had asked.

"Mr. Zedicher instructed me to ask you to be there at that time as a special favor to him. You'll have to ask him what it's about. I'm just the messenger."

Derrick frowned at the phone. Zedicher had always liked being the boss, the officer, the damned leader. All right, one more time. He was getting tired as hell waiting on the man. Yes, this would be the last time he let the little general push him around.

"You tell Mr. Zedicher that I'll be there, alone as you suggested before. Some sort of security problem, you said. Yes, I'll be there."

Now Siegfried waited inside the boathouse in the deserted public park. There was little activity around the lake this time of year. Most of the boats had been put up and the rest would follow in a month. Siegfried had parked his smaller Mercedes-Benz around the corner of the dirt road and walked to the shed. He was a half hour early. Derrick had a history of being late to every meeting, luncheon, or formal dinner. He would be late this time as well.

Siegfried shook his head. The damn black box. He was not certain what it contained. All he knew was that he had to find it.

He knew that Mr. Selig and Mr. Zedicher did not have it and had no idea whatsoever where it could be. That left three, Griswold and Berthold and Audwin Derrick. If Derrick had no idea, the next step would be to talk to his brother and Griswold. One of them had to know. Somebody had to know.

Siegfried heard a car drive in near the boathouse and stop. A door slammed. Just one door. Good. Derrick would come inside as ordered.

A moment later the latch on the wooden door lifted and the door swung outward.

"G. B.? Are you in there? It's dark."

"This is the place, Mr. Derrick. Please come inside and close the door. This isn't a topic we want the whole world to hear."

"Siegfried? That must be you. Where is G. B.?"

The man came in and closed the door. The room was only half lit by the window, but Siegfried had been accustomed to the light for a half hour. Derrick was taller than he had remembered, but thin and sickly looking. No threat. Mistake. Derrick always carried a pistol for protection, everywhere. Some said even to bed and in his shower.

"Mr. Zedicher is not here. He was called away unexpectedly. He has given me the matter to discuss with you. There are chairs to this side, and some glasses and a bottle. Shall we sit?"

He could see Derrick wince and then set his arms akimbo, before he relaxed, nodded, and moved to the chair.

Siegfried poured whiskey in both glasses and sipped at his.

"Mr. Zedicher is extremely anxious to find the black box. You are highly aware of its importance and the dangers that it contains, that involve all of you. Mr. Zedicher has given me a deadline. I must find the black box within a week so the four of you can join together and jointly destroy it."

Derrick gulped down his shot of whiskey and wiped sweat from his head. "Oh, I agree. I agree. I haven't had a good night's sleep since the box was lost or, God forbid, stolen. It's been ten or twelve years, perhaps more since we have had control of it."

"Precisely what we are trying to do. Mr. Derrick, do you know where the black box is?"

"No, positively no. I don't know where it is. I had thought one of the others had it, but then we don't talk as much as we used to, and the issue went from vital to less than vital."

"You have no clue whatsoever, Herr Derrick?"

"None whatsoever."

"If you are lying to me, Derrick, I'll have to kill you here, this afternoon."

Derrick jumped up and drew the pistol quicker than Siegfried thought he could. As he drew, he fired and the bullet tore into the wooden table two inches from Siegfried's hand. Siegfried never even flinched. He simply stared at the man. When the sound died away, Siegfried picked up his glass and sipped at the whiskey.

"Mr. Derrick, if I was going to kill you, you'd be dead long before now, before you had a chance to take a warning shot at me. Now holster your piece and sit. We have much to talk about before we're done."

Derrick frowned at him, waved the pistol.

"Put your weapon on the table," Derrick said, his voice soft, unsure.

"Naturally. I'll have no use of it. You are certainly no value to the partners dead and sunk in the lake." Siegfried put the big .45 on the table and smiled at Derrick.

"Another whiskey? I thought so." He poured another whiskey in the man's glass and refilled his own.

"Now, sit down and we'll continue to talk. I have many questions to ask you."

Derrick shook his head, and then changed his mind and put the pistol in his belt holster and slumped in the chair.

"So, when was the last time you saw the black box?"

"That I remember. The five of us were up in the mountains at a party, no wives allowed. We were on a hunting expedition we told them. We had the box there and we went over the records and told the stories our fathers had told us. It was a fine time we had."

"Who took the black box home with him?"

Derrick rubbed the back of his neck. "I . . . I can't recall. I know that I didn't. Those were the days when Audwin and I both ran the corporation, so he was along on the hunting trip as well."

"Do you remember anyone saying that he would take

care of the box until the next time you had a similar gathering?"

"No, no one. We had the meet, we each had two women in our rooms, we entertained ourselves the rest of the day and the night, then we went home the next afternoon. Not a shot had been fired at any of the wild beasts in the general area."

"That's the last time you saw the box?"

"No, it was in our home company safe after that. I saw it from time to time. Then one day it was missing."

"That was what ten or twelve years ago?"

"Yes, about ten."

"Now, the trouble with Audwin. That came just after that mountain orgy?"

"Yes, now that I think of it. He must have been at it for a year or two when I discovered the problem, and stopped him."

"Then came the confinement in the psychiatric clinic?"

"Yes. That date I remember. Ten years next month. It was the decision of the group. That was the lesser of the two solutions—so I voted to confine him."

"He's about the same now as he was?"

"About the same. The drugs over ten years have taken a toll. He's weaker now, that's for sure, but his mind is still strong and his determination is like a burning coal that won't go out."

Siegfried stood with his glass and walked around the small boathouse. "We still have two problems, then, don't we? Finding the black box, and silencing Audwin forever."

"No, he's my brother. I will never agree to that."

"Nobody asked you to agree. Sometimes what must be done, must be done. Now, for a simpler question, Mr. Derrick. Do you think that Audwin might have taken the black box home with him from that hunting trip?"

"Yes and put it in our company safe. Then later he used it in his shenanigans. He may be the one who knows where it is today."

"Which is the best reason in the world for our not harming your baby brother, Derrick. I think we're finished here." They both stood. Siegfried took one last drink from his glass and put it on the small table, then his right fist lashed out with a thunderous blow to Derrick's jaw. The smaller man went down on the boards of the boathouse floor. He sat up and touched his jaw.

"Derrick, don't ever shoot your weapon near me again, or I'll kill you on the spot, with no questions asked. You've already earned two black marks. One more and you're little more than worm food in some unmarked grave. Do you understand me?" As he said it, Siegfried drew the big .45-caliber automatic pistol and eased the muzzle against Derrick's temple.

"I . . . I understand."

Siegfried turned his back on the man and walked out the door. Berthold Derrick didn't even think about reaching for the loaded pistol where it hung at his waist.

Wade gave out new orders at the office. "We know there are four men who were in the same outfit. However there were over two hundred in that unit. Did these four men know each other then? In any military unit there are so many men it's impossible to get to know everyone. In wartime it is a hundred times worse. Even if these four men did know each other at that time, did they conspire together to rob hundreds of Jews of their fortunes? We need to find these answers. It will be hard.

"One way is to shadow the sons of these four. Even if they play bridge every night together this doesn't prove their fathers knew each other back then. But it could turn up something new we need to know.

"Duncan, you stay with Zedicher. You know his lair. Kat, I want you on Derrick, he doesn't know you. Hershel, you keep working the computers, the Internet, and your contacts in town to see if you can dig up any contact points between the four.

"Ichi, you tackle Selig and, Roger, you go with Griswold. Anything they do might mean something. I'm going to try to bait their killer, Siegfried, again and get a line on him. I'll tell you about him one of these days. I owe him big time. Any questions?"

It was after eight o'clock that evening before Zedicher came out of his rooftop mansion and left in the light blue Mercedes out of his private garage door in the huge headquarters. Duncan stayed with him to one of the government buildings. The dapper little man left the car with a taller, sturdier man right behind him, went in the side entrance, and vanished. Duncan discovered the building was the Treasury Building. He found a good parking spot, took out his night-vision goggles, and settled down to wait.

Inside the building, G. B. Zedicher was met and escorted up a set of stairs, through huge double doors, and into a conference room unlike any Zedicher had ever seen before. It was a formal room, just missing garrish. There were huge oil paintings, beautifully upholstered furniture, a mural painted on the high ceiling, and dozens of vases filled with an amazing variety of flowers. He smiled and looked around.

Zedicher didn't know everyone, but he figured that all the cream of the German government officials were in that one room. He was with them, one of them. It was time to circulate, to talk, to lie, to praise, to be one of the gang. He knew that role and could play it to perfection. Zedicher smiled and went forward and took the offered hand of the Chancellor, the head of the German government.

"G. B. Zedicher, I'm pleased to see that you could attend. It's going to be an interesting evening."

★ FIFTEEN ★

"Chancellor, I'm honored to be here. This is a magnificent room, and it looks like everyone who is involved in the government is here. I'll be delighted to meet as many of them as I can."

The Chancellor gave Zedicher a knowing smile and they moved on. G. B. Zedicher was not widely known outside of his firm. Now that was going to change. He worked the room like a veteran politician, shaking hands, memorizing names, becoming awestruck when he met high-ranking government officials.

G.B. didn't know he could be so informal and engaging. He spent an hour and a half talking about everything from global warming, to the safety of the German oil supply and on to the use of the Euro across the nations in Europe.

The informal time lasted over another half-hour, then they were called to dinner in a formal dining room. Even Zedicher was impressed. It was set up like a state dinner, with all the trimmings: the best china, ten pieces of silverware, two napkins, and even finger bowls. To his surprise, Zedicher found himself seated at the right hand of the Chancellor. He saw several politicians in the area looking at him and soon there was a buzz with much of it wondering who this stranger was in the second spot.

The dinner came and Zedicher was so on edge he didn't even know what was served. Then he settled down and realized his new position. Zedicher felt strangely at home, as if this was what life was supposed to be for men like him, and the rest of them—the leaders of Germany.

As the men and a few women settled down to taste their fancy dessert, the Chancellor rose and used a sterling silver spoon to ring a crystal wineglass.

"Ladies and gentlemen. Please don't let me interrupt your dinner. The dessert is as fantastic as it looks. There are some introductions I want to make before any of you run out on me."

He went through the top six men and one woman in his cabinet, then continued.

"Tonight I want to introduce to you a man most of you already know who has been a leader of Germany for the past twenty years, a leader in the field of business and industry. A man who has shot to the top and developed a strong sense of values in the financial area." The plaudits continued for another two minutes, then the Chancellor introduced Zedicher.

"Herr Zedicher. Perhaps you would honor us with a few words about your views on the German economy."

Zedicher had been warned that the request would be made and he had conferred with his top economists for three hours as they put together a brief, yet thorough evaluation and prediction about the direction of the economy. He spoke without the aid of notes or cards.

In short fashion Zedicher predicted a slow but steady growth of the GNP, that inflation would top out and remain at under four percent, and that the Euro currency would be a boon to all of Europe and help make their manufactured products more attractive to world consumers. He closed by promising if he had anything to say about it, he would lower taxes on business and industry to encourage continued prosperity and full employment.

He sat down to a rousing ovation from the politicians.

At the end of the dinner there was brandy and more schmoozing and talk. Several men congratulated Zedicher on a great speech.

An hour later, an aide to the Chancellor touched Zedicher's shoulder and motioned to him.

"The Chancellor would like to see you, Herr Zedicher."

Zedicher smiled. Good news he hoped. They went into an adjoining room, then into a smaller one where the Chancellor worried an unlit cigar.

"G.B., I'm proud of you. That was an outstanding performance. If we had to take a vote right now, I'm sure I could get you approved as Minister of Finance on the first ballot."

"Thank you, Chancellor. I appreciate it. I felt right at home here tonight, like I belong here. I can get along with the others in your administration. No problem there. Anytime that you are ready to make the announcement, I'll be ready to come into your administration."

"Good, good, Zedicher." The Chancellor stopped and scowled. "There is one problem. Karl Krueger was not here tonight. He's having more physical problems. I have talked to him about stepping down, but he says this is a temporary setback. He claims he'll be up and moving mountains again in six months. What he doesn't understand is that a lot needs to be done before those six months slip away from us. Once they are gone, we can never catch up with them."

"I'm ready whenever you want to make the appointment. I understand about Minister Krueger."

"This might take six or eight months. When I spoke to you about the job earlier, I thought Krueger was worse off than he actually was. I figured he would be pleased to resign so he could concentrate on regaining his health." The Chancellor paused and reached out his hand. "Well, G.B., it's been a good launching of your political career. Don't let this one small holdup distract you. I talked to many of the men here tonight and they were impressed with you as a person, and your grasp of the economic life of our nation. Be hopeful, and we'll have you in the Finance Minister's chair before you know it."

Zedicher said something appropriate. As he watched the Chancellor and his bodyguard adviser leaving, he promised himself that the Finance Minister's chair would be his long before the Chancellor figured.

Halfway along on the drive home much later that evening, Zedicher smiled. He would call on Siegfried one more time. Exactly how the situation would be resolved would be up to Siegfried. But it would be done, and quicker than anyone expected. If he knew Siegfried, it would be cleverly—if brutally—accomplished.

Earlier that day, Kat had checked in with Berthold Derrick. She had tried to make an appointment through the phone connections to his private office. His secretary said he was tied up all day and had an engagement that night. Could she leave a name and number and perhaps he could call her the next day?

Kat declined and moved from her car toward the parking garage at the side of the big building. There was a guard at the entrance. She waved at the guard and walked up to him.

"Would it be possible to leave my car in your garage here, or is this only for employees? I don't see any sign."

The guard grinned at the pretty lady and shook his head. "Afraid not, miss. No parking here except the company big shots. Old Berthold Derrick himself parks here. Course he has about three spaces in the slot right beside his private elevator."

"So, does he still drive that mile-long limo, the extended Mercedes?"

"Oh, no, he turned that in months ago. Now he's in one of the new Rolls-Royces, Cloud Fire or something like that. It's a soft blue with gold trim. Hey, I never get it mixed up with the Mercedes and Porsches."

"But you say no parking for us common folks. Damn." She looked closely at the guard. He was in his thirties and had been staring at her chest. She stood a little taller and smiled at him. "Well, I guess I'll just have to find a lucky spot. If you see me driving around and around, I'm searching for a parking spot."

"I'll wave," the guard said.

Kat had found out what she needed to know. She had parked the company sedan halfway down the block where she could spot the garage exit. Now it would be a waiting game to see just when the big boss came out of the tower and where he went.

It was a little after ten in the morning. Kat settled down in the car. She had brought along a sack of fruit to nibble on, and a German picture magazine. Both came in handy.

She sat there until almost four that afternoon when she saw a large motorcycle come out of the garage exit followed closely by the latest model Rolls. She started the engine and saw the big car turn away from her. Kat did a fast U-turn on the street and settled in three cars behind the Rolls.

A motorcycle escort, now there was a twist for a big shot. Everyone would wonder who was in the car that way, and nobody was going to try to cut you off in traffic. They drove for ten minutes, then wound into the raunchier part of town that seemed to cater to the less-moneyed drinkers and revelers. The Rolls pulled into a no parking zone and stopped. The motorcycle had turned and parked directly in front of the big car. The rider stepped off the cycle and began a slow walk around the car.

Kat had stopped fifty feet in back and parked in front of a tattoo parlor. "Ten marks, any class A tattoo anywhere you want it. Yes, anywhere!" the window sign read.

The far door of the Rolls opened and a tall, thin man stepped out. He wore a flame-red shirt and pants. Over the shirt was a black vest adorned with silver baubles. He had on fancy sunglasses and carried a short riding crop in his left hand.

The car was in front of a club of some kind. The inside door showed just past a cashier's window. A huge man stood there watching the people on the street and the door. He checked two young men and let them into the club. Three more men had lined up at the window.

The man she assumed was Berthold Derrick stood six feet one and looked to be far too thin. She left the car and walked toward the Rolls. Now she could see Derrick plainly. His face was pale with that almost wasted look of the perpetually ill, but his movements were precise, quick, and he moved toward the glass cashier's window with a short tap-dance routine.

The bouncer/guard at the door pushed the three young men to one side and opened the door. Derrick must be known there; he didn't have to pay at the ticket window.

Kat waited behind a car twenty feet away. She had dressed on the conservative side, her blend-in ensemble. Black pants, soft brown blouse buttoned to her throat with a matching brown jacket. Her long dark hair curled around her shoulders and brown eyes matched her blouse. She hadn't tanned any this year and her skin tone was that of dry Hawaiian sand. The tan purse holding her pistol had long straps over her left shoulder.

When the clients cleared the door, Kat walked up and headed toward the pay window.

"*Nein,*" the German word came as an order from the bouncer. She turned to him and spoke in German.

"It's a free country, haven't you heard. I pay, I go inside."

The big guard laughed. "Lady, this is a joint for men only. No women, not even one as pretty as you are. Unless you're cross dressing, which I'd bet you're not. No way to get inside here except through me."

"You'd touch me if I tried?"

"Absolutely."

Kat came up within three feet of the man who stood, legs apart, hands at the ready, his eyes watching hers with such intensity that it told her a lot about his background and training. Special Forces, she'd bet a buck on it.

Kat glared at him for a moment, then shrugged. She saw him relax as she started to turn away. In a millisecond she spun back, her right fist slamming into the side of his neck like a two-by-four, jolting the big man to the left. In almost the same motion she kicked out hard with her right foot. Her solid leather upper on the two-inch pumps connected with his scrotum driving the testes upward and smashing one against solid bone, bringing a screech of pain and fury from the guard. He glared at her a moment, then both hands went to his crotch as he dropped to his knees, then forward on his face on the sidewalk.

Kat walked to the door, stared at the man behind the ticket window. The buzzer sounded and Kat hurried inside. The lighting was nearly nonexistent. A row of peep shows lined one side of the long room. On the other side were cages with nude women in them. They writhed and wound themselves around cushioned poles and chairs. A man stood in front of a big black woman. His hand pumped hard inside his pants. Kat moved on. At the end of the line of naked women she found rooms that were more private.

Each room had a bed and a dresser, and a woman lounging on the bed wearing little or no clothes. Kat watched a man insert bills into a slot in the door, which at once clicked open. The shade over the window closed and the man slipped inside.

Farther along there were triple X-rated movies with lounges provided and a group of semidressed girls looking bored waiting for customers.

One of the girls looked up and noticed Kat. "What the fuck are you doing in here?"

"Looking for that skinny guy in the red shirt."

"He's in the blood room," another girl said. "Saw him

go down a couple of minutes ago." She pointed down a dimly lit hall. Kat reached in her tan purse and fisted the Walther before she walked down the dark corridor.

She heard a wail of pain from directly ahead, then nothing. A woman cried out in sudden anguish, but the sound cut off. Another twenty feet down the dank tunnel, Kat saw a gleam of light. She walked toward it on silent feet.

A groan came, then another high-pitched scream that stabbed through the darkness for only two or three seconds.

Blackness, a stream of light, another wail of pain.

In a sudden burst of light the door jolted open, six hands grabbed Kat by the arms and legs, lifting her, carrying her forward into the room of pain and blood before she could pull out her pistol. Then she had it out but at once a heavy fist slammed into her right hand and the Walther jolted to the floor.

★ SIXTEEN ★

The room into which Kat had been carried plunged into total darkness. She felt a cloth cover her head and face and a cord drawn tight around her neck.

Slowly the hands that held her lowered her into a chair. She was aware that the lights came back on when she saw fringes of less than total darkness through the cloth.

A voice shouted at her, evidently from someone only inches from her ear.

"Mere woman, why do you violate our sacred sanctum? How can you come here and not die for your trouble?"

The hood was ripped off her head and Kat closed her eyes at once from the shock of intense floodlights that burned into her retinas.

"Why?" the voice boomed again. Male and heavy with anger and mistrust.

Kat opened her eyes in fits and starts, opening and closing. Once she saw a woman directly ahead of her tied to a cross on the wall. She was naked to the waist with bloody gashes across both breasts and down her belly. Blood seeped down her body.

Then Kat closed her eyes again and waited. One eye at a time. Now, at last both eyes.

"We have asked you a question. We demand an answer."

Someone held the Walther in front of her.

"Are you police?"

"No, idiots!" Kat bellowed in her best parade-ground voice. "You miserable goat-sired bastards. You wretches of the underside of darkness and despair. You misbegotten shitheads of the universe. You dare to ask me why I am here?"

She felt hands that had been holding her letting go. A moment later she felt the last hand pull away. She motioned at the two strong floodlights that keyed on her. "Out," she demanded. The lights snapped off.

She sprang to her feet and slowly looked around. Four men stood in the room, all naked. Four women had been tied against the walls, two on each side. All four showed bloody cuts on their torsos.

Kat whirled and faced two of the men and marched toward them, crowding them back against the wall. One of the two was the man who had been wearing the red shirt and pants—Berthold Derrick.

"Where is your master? He can be none of you dregs of human flesh. You are egregious, pathetic examples of poor discipline and no true belief in the one spirit of blackness. Where is your master?"

"We have none. We are non-affiliated." The voice was the same she had heard before and came from Derrick.

"You are orotund bastards, merely playing a game with the eternal fire of hell that can turn you all into whimpering goat-dogs yelping at your true master's feet."

Kat whirled, saw her pistol on a small table, and walked deliberately to the table and picked up the weapon. She held it pointing at the floor. Her finger stabbed at two of the naked men.

"You and you, untie these unholy women victims and

take them away. Don't be so insouciant in your rituals, or the next time I will be your master and you all will suffer the thrill of a thousand slices."

She paused as the women were cut down and led out the door. Their eyes showed her their gratitude.

Kat pointed at the other two men concentrating on Derrick. "You with the shifting eyes of a common thief and the penis of a goat-bred incubus. Get out of my sight. Now." The words thundered in the room and Derrick scuttered across the room after his clothes.

"No, no clothes. Get out of here as foul, naked, and ugly as the moment you were born. Go."

Derrick took one long look at Kat, then rushed for the door and hurried through it.

The last man in the room was five-nine, going to fat, about forty-five with a potbelly and almost no hair on his genitals.

"Ugly little man. Why are you here?"

"The group . . . the four of us rent the room, no questions. We get physical . . . nothing serious. Never have killed one of the girls."

"Girl toys?"

"Yes, like that."

He shivered, looked at the stack of clothes, and then glanced away.

"Get out of here. Go the back way. I'll follow you so I'm sure you leave. You understand me, you naked excuse for a human being?"

"Yes. Yes, ma'am."

"Go, now."

He headed for the door, looked once more at the clothes, then went out the opening and on down the dark corridor. Kat followed, watching her back. They came to some lights, then more rooms and ahead a door with a red light on it. There was also a sign:

"No exit. This door has an alarm. For use in fire emergency only."

"Open it, idiot. This is the largest emergency you may ever experience in your miserable lifetime."

He opened the door. The alarm went off, a ringing bell, and the two hurried out and closed the door. The alarm stopped.

The naked man rushed off down the alley. Kat turned the other way, found the end of the narrow passage and the street, and within five minutes was in her car and driving back toward the headquarters. She smiled. Herr Derrick must have caused quite a stir as he ran naked through the building and outside to his car. At least he had a driver to get him home.

Back in the Specialists room, Kat found Ichi hard at work field-stripping and oiling a half-dozen weapons spread out on a table.

"What happened with Selig?" Kat asked.

"He and his staff are on a two-day sensitivity training session up in the mountains. I decided not to go along. So I figured these little sweethearts needed some attention. I mean, they sit over here six months at a time without even getting oiled. They need some care and maintenance the way any good machine does."

"Not my idea of a fun afternoon," Kat said.

Ichi grinned. He was in his element; these weapons were what he lived for. "Hey, lady, you shoot them, I'll clean and maintain them. Good deal all the way around."

"Roger came back from tailing Griswold yet?" Kat asked. Ichi shook his head. "I'm going to have a shower. You wouldn't believe where I've been this afternoon. That place still makes me feel dirty even now."

Roger had taken a Porsche convertible from the company garage that morning to use while tailing the head of Griswold Construction, Penrod Griswold. Telephone calls had established that he had meetings today at two locations and would be tied up all day.

Roger took a chance and watched the guards around the garage area. When he saw unusual activity, and a three-car convoy pulled out of the garage, all stretch limos, Roger figured that would be the top dog. He had a description of Griswold and drove by the first meeting spot just as the big German exited the center limo and walked into one of his suppliers. It was Griswold.

They must have had lunch as well, since the CEO of Griswold Construction didn't emerge until just after three that afternoon. His convoy of two empty cars and his in the middle of the sandwich drove back to the company headquarters and vanished. That was the last that Roger saw of the top dog. About seven that evening he gave up and went back to the Marshall Export/Import Company and turned in his car. At least it had been a good afternoon for a drive.

Siegfried had done his homework. Finance Minister Karl Krueger's secretary had been quite specific about it. Mr. Krueger was not to be contacted in any way. He was home recuperating and his deputy was handling all vital functions at this time. It was expected that Mr. Krueger would be back to work in about two weeks. He was stronger now but his doctors advised more home rest. After all, the man was almost seventy years old and not as able to bounce back from illness the way a younger man could.

Siegfried had thanked her and grinned. He drove a different car tonight, a sleek BMW, so new it still had that new car smell. He looked up Krueger's address. He had a town apartment and another home just outside of Berlin to the west. That's where Krueger was recovering. It was an exclusive area with no estate less than twenty acres and the restrictions in deeds and practice were holding to that standard.

Hills dotted the area and Krueger lived on top of one

of them some ten miles of twisting roads and more hills from the main highway west.

Siegfried planned on arriving just after dinnertime. Krueger was a widower with no children at home. He had a cook and housekeeper, but she left every evening after cooking his supper. There were no other servants.

Siegfried waited until he saw the old sedan the cook-housekeeper used roll down the hill and away to the east. He drove up the hill slowly with his lights off and arrived at the house he was sure without being observed.

He tried the front door. It had been locked. Country thinking, no one trusted the neighbors. Siegfried picked the simple lock, turned the knob, and slipped inside the house. It was one of the older ones that had been entirely reworked. The place was magnificent. Two night-lights showed in the front hall and in the living room. Down another corridor he saw a light that must be coming from a den or first-floor bedroom.

The German agent moved down the carpet quietly and looked inside the door.

Krueger held a .45 automatic pointed directly at the intruder's heart.

"Siegfried, isn't it? I knew you when you were with the East German intelligence people. You weren't all that good then, and you certainly aren't much better now. Take out your two weapons gently by the butts and lay them on the floor, then sit down and cross your legs. I'd say it's time we had a good long talk. It was stupid of you to make such a long call to my secretary. All calls that come into my office are automatically traced, that new instant readout of the caller's number. We wondered why G. B. Zedicher was so concerned with my health. Then I remembered the rumors about him and I heard about his little speech to the gathering last night and it all became so clear.

"I should shoot you right now, but out of curiosity, I want to see what you'll say and what you'll try to do."

✷ SEVENTEEN ✷

OUTSIDE BERLIN, GERMANY

Siegfried smiled at the much smaller man. He hadn't shown the flicker of an eye at his surprise of being discovered and under a gun. He'd been there many times before.

"Well, Herr Minister Krueger. There is no need for the weapon. I would feel undressed without my own hardware so I'll have to decline your invitation to put down my guns. I'm sure you understand. Let's just leave things the way they are now. I knocked on the door but no one came. I wondered that you might have taken a turn for the worse, but I see you're looking much better."

"How would you know? You've never seen me ill. Now out with it, why are you here?"

"I like the direct approach, Minister Krueger. As you know I work for Mr. Zedicher, and he wondered if there was anything he could do to help you out during this time of illness?"

"What a liar you are, Siegfried. What a pile of bullshit you talk. I know Zedicher is doing everything he can to get my job. I also know that I'll be well enough next week to get back to the office and catch up on my work. I love my job. It has many rewards, and that's one thing that your G. B. Zedicher isn't going to get. He's achieved almost everything else that he's wanted. Not this time."

Siegfried started to move and Krueger waved the weapon.

"Easy, spy. Stay exactly where you are."

"Minister Krueger, you have me wrong. I am no longer a spy or in the intelligence service. I'm a businessman now, working at a trade, helping a firm to gain success and hold on to it. Yes, the work is a lot different than before."

"Your work is to kill people. I know that. Why are you here?"

"Mr. Zedicher asked me to bring you a message. He says he realizes this puts him in an awkward position: with the Chancellor wanting Mr. Zedicher to be the Federal Minister of Finance, while you are still here and alive and getting healthier. Mr. Zedicher said he has no wish to embarrass you in any way. He will not strive for your position. He will do everything he can to dissuade the Chancellor from moving in that direction."

"I could almost believe you, Siegfried, if I weren't completely aware of your history, your work with the East German spy machine, and your continuing work with the Zedicher corporations. A leopard can't change its spots, any more than you can change your attitude, your beliefs, and your work habits. Once a killer, always a killer.

"I asked you before to take out your weapons and put them on the floor. If you don't now, I'll shoot you. I'm warning you I'm not a good shot with a pistol. No practice, but I can hit your broad chest."

Siegfried moved cautiously, reached under his jacket, and lifted out a Heckler & Koch P7M10. He lifted the 9mm parabellum shooter by the butt with a finger and thumb and put it on a small coffee table near him.

"The hideout on your left leg," Krueger said.

"You have been reading up on me, Mr. Krueger. I'm flattered. May I bend down to retrieve the piece?"

Krueger looked at him, then at the H & K pistol. He nodded. He was six feet from the killer, a small coffee table between them.

Siegfried bent down to loosen the weapon from his left ankle. Then, so quickly that Krueger could do little but gasp, Siegfried grabbed the light coffee table with both hands, surged upward with it, and charged Krueger with the table shielding him.

Krueger fired, but the round buried itself in the top and leg of the coffee table a half a second before Siegfried smashed the table into the recovering Krueger. Krueger went down, jolting backward over a chair and sprawling on the floor. He still held the pistol. Siegfried's vicious kick spun the weapon from Krueger's hand and smashed his wrist.

Krueger wailed in pain. He sat up and held his right hand. "You bastard, you broke my wrist."

"You should be more careful not to fall while you're recuperating. Now, I have some suggestions for you."

"Get out of here or I'm calling the police."

"Not a good idea, since I now have a weapon and you don't. Sit there and listen. I never say anything twice."

Sweat popped out on Krueger's forehead. He tried to wipe it away but had to put down his right hand and he moaned when the hand fell to his lap.

"You bastard. Somebody is going to kill you sooner or later. I just pray that it's sooner."

Siegfried sat in a soft chair across from where Krueger cowered on the floor.

"That won't be quick enough to help you much, old man. Here is the proposition. Yes, Mr. Zedicher will be the Federal Minister of Finance with or without your co-operation. The scenario goes like this. You've not been recovering as quickly as you think you should and you're depressed. You know you're not doing your job now, and it looks like you won't be able to handle it for at least six months more. Germany needs a strong man at the financial helm. That's why you're going to resign and suggest that G. B. Zedicher would be a good man to replace you."

"Never in a million years," Krueger blurted, his face red with fury. "Zedicher is nothing but a money-grubbing machine. I've watched him muscle his way into one industry after another. He uses his money like a club."

"Glad you noticed that, Krueger. For your resignation, Mr. Zedicher will transfer to your numbered account the sum of two million marks. When you do recover and want to go back to work, there will be a continuing position for you in the most plausible of the Zedicher companies as a vice president. You will have a salary of eight hundred thousand marks annually."

Siegfried looked up at the man who was frowning. "How does it sound so far?"

"Like you were buying me out. Hell, I can make three times that much a year by offering friends certain contracts and business deals. Then there are all of the bureaus and committees and departments to deal with for a fat fee, on the side of course."

Siegfried knelt in front of Krueger. "You're old and sick but at least you aren't stupid. Mr. Zedicher is thinking along the same lines, only ten to twenty times as big as you are. He figures your office should be worth a billion marks a year . . . on the side as you say."

"Sounds like him. He'll get caught and hung."

Siegfried slapped Krueger hard across the face. The older man swayed to one side, put out his right hand to catch himself, and bellowed in pain when the broken wrist gave way and he sprawled on the floor.

He pushed himself up with his left hand until he could sit. He held his right wrist again, tears seeping from his eyes. "You unholy bastard. Fucking maniac that's what you are."

Siegfried punched Krueger solidly in the face, smashing his nose, bringing spurts of blood as the Minister of Finance jolted backward and fell to the hardwood floor.

"Now, old man, I'm getting tired of this. I'll give you

one last chance to be a wealthy man for the rest of your life. Will you send a letter with me tonight to give to the Chancellor that you're ready to step down when he suggests?"

"No," the word came out softly. Krueger's white face now splattered with blood, pain, and the sudden realization that he was going to die that evening. "No, and you won't win. Someone will find you and kill you. The deal with Zedicher will blow up in your faces and everyone will know what double-dealing thieves and scoundrels you really are."

Siegfried leaned down and pushed the muzzle of his pistol into Krueger's mouth. The elderly eyes went wide for a moment, then a kind of acceptance came that death was near. He closed his eyes waiting for the shot that would end his existence.

It never came.

Siegfried pulled the weapon free, stood, and kicked Krueger twice in the head with his heavy soled shoes. The Minister of Finance was unconscious after the first kick. The second one was for good measure.

Siegfried checked the old body. Yes, he was still alive. Now he had to clean up the room. He found a towel in a bathroom and mopped up the blood off the floor. If there was no appearance of a struggle they wouldn't investigate the place critically. He put the coffee table back where it had been and looked at the bullet hole.

In the kitchen he found brown shoe polish under the sink and used just enough to conceal the splinter and the hole where the bullet had entered. It didn't come out. He took Krueger's pistol and made one last inspection. Yes. It would pass.

Siegfried picked up the unconscious minister and carried him to the Mercedes in the garage. He checked the house again, made sure everything was back in good order, then turned out the lights and snapped on a lock that activated when the door closed.

In the garage he put Krueger in the passenger's side,

started the car and drove it out of the garage, then closed the door. He had picked out the hill he would use when he drove in. It was two miles down the road toward the highway. It was perfect. The road clung to the side of the mountain on a curve with nothing but two hundred feet of space below to the rocky outcroppings.

At the curve he stopped. No cars had come past since he left Krueger's house. He pulled Krueger into the driver's seat, left the motor running, and pushed the rig into gear. Carefully he guided the car on the slight downhill slope to the side of the cliff. He jumped aside and let the car plunge off the road into space.

Siegfried didn't wait to hear the crash far below. He wiped out his footprints near the tire tracks in the soft dirt at the edge of the road, then crossed over and began jogging back to where he had left his car at the Krueger place.

With any good luck at all, no one had stopped by at the man's house, and no one had seen Siegfried's car parked there.

It took Siegfried twelve minutes to jog the two miles back to his car. He slid in, wiped sweat off his face, and drove back to Berlin.

The next morning the news was all over the radio and TV.

"Friends said this morning that they had no idea what happened to Finance Minister Karl Krueger. Police in the district said sometime last night Krueger evidently drove his heavy car off the road and it plunged 180 feet into a canyon. Air rescue brought the Minister to Central Berlin hospital about nine o'clock this morning where he is listed in critical condition. Doctors will not make any predictions.

"A friend who found the car early this morning while on a bicycle ride said that Krueger was so badly smashed up with massive head and chest injuries that there must be little chance that he could live long."

Siegfried nodded and switched to another channel, then to an all-news channel that had a continuing story

on the minister, his life, his work, and his recent illness. A
neighbor came on-camera and told what a good man
Karl Krueger was.

"Then there was the time my car froze up in winter
and he came over and helped me unfreeze it and when it
still wouldn't start, he loaned me one of his cars so I
could get to work. He is a wonderful man."

The neighbor on the other side of Krueger said he hadn't
been driving much since his illness. His housekeeper did
all of the errands. "It's just a mystery to me why the man
was driving at all, let alone at night. The housekeeper usually left about six-thirty after she got his supper ready. I
have no idea where he was driving. What would he have
to do at night that couldn't wait until morning?"

"District police were also at a loss to explain the late-
night drive. They said they could find no note, no list of
items to purchase, or any note from anyone asking him
to come. An empty prescription container was found in
the wreckage, but there was no date of issue and it could
have been there for some time. There was no place in the
immediate area where he could have had the prescription
refilled, police said."

Siegfried stretched, built himself a large breakfast,
and ate it with relish. Then he took a shower and dressed
carefully. He might just ask Mr. Zedicher for a raise this
morning. The way he counted it, the two-million-mark
gift to Krueger, and ten years of eight hundred thousand
marks salary, meant he had saved his boss over ten million marks. Yes, a good time to ask for a big bonus, say a
million marks to put in his retirement fund. Siegfried was
in an excellent mood by the time he parked at the
Zedicher building and took the elevator up to his office.

BERLIN, GERMANY

That same day the Specialists gathered in the workroom
and heard the news about Krueger. It meant nothing spe-

cial to them and they went back to their main target, the four Transportation Corps men who had become instant millionaires after the war.

They each gave a report, compared notes. Kat made a summary of each report and tacked it to the bulletin board under the right heading.

"So, where are we?" Wade asked.

Kat shook her head. "Without a case against any of them. We have circumstantial evidence, nothing more. Not enough even to get an arrest warrant if we were in that situation."

"But isn't it likely, almost certain, that the fathers of these four, and probably a lot more, made fortunes during the war robbing and bribing Jews out of Warsaw?" Roger asked.

"Almost for positive," Ichi said. "But how do we prove it? They aren't about to confess that their fathers told them one night when they had been drinking too much just where that multimillion-mark windfall came from right after the end of the war."

"Nowhere," Hershel said. "Damnit, we're nowhere."

"We've been here before," Duncan said. "So we settle down, look at everything again, and get with the program."

They all stared at each other for a minute. Then somebody snickered. A moment later all six were laughing until they cried.

"What's so funny?" Hershel asked.

Nobody knew. Then they laughed again.

Wade came out of it first.

"Anybody check the late news, something about the Minister of Finance driving his car over a cliff and winding up almost dead and in intensive care."

"Sounds familiar," Roger said. "Almost the same way that George Silokowski checked out."

"So much for coincidence," Kat said.

One of the secretaries came in and handed Wade a note. It said, "Check the TV news."

Wade turned on the TV set and they turned to the Berlin all-news channel.

". . . so what happened today isn't earth shattering in itself, but the promise downstream is tremendous. A company spokesman said that Mr. Zedicher will make a similar donation to the schools until each in Berlin has a library that the students and teachers can all be proud of. The five thousand books donated today by Zedicher International Limited. could be the start of donations that would impact every one of the three hundred eighty-four schools in the city of Berlin.

"Zedicher said that this great country has been good to him and his family, and now he wants to do a little paying back. No guess was made of the cost of this first donation from the company, but the librarian who accepted the books said that she estimates that the books would cost the school system about eighty-five thousand marks to buy, even at school discounts.

"That figure times the three hundred eighty-four schools would be a tremendously large donation by a commercial firm toward the education of our youth, the future of Germany."

Wade turned off the set.

"What in hell?" Roger asked.

"He's got another motive, not just giving back," Kat said.

"Trying to buy his way into heaven?" Duncan asked.

"Not a chance, something else."

"You guys. He's just misunderstood and not appreciated. Now he's trying to get in our good graces." It was Hershel's idea.

Ichi threw an eraser at him. "When pigs fly."

Kat stood and began pacing. It was her lawyer's mode. She said she could think better on her feet, as if she were in front of a jury on a final argument.

"Motive. What is it? Would this be a one-of-a-kind gesture? Not a chance. It's probably the start of a whirlwind of good deeds, of a massive PR campaign to give

G. B. Zedicher an image whiter than snow and purer than chewing gum. But what is his damned motive?"

"Let's try the TV again," Wade said. "There might be something to clue us in."

The set came on in the middle of a commercial. A beautiful blonde showed the benefits of a skin lotion. She turned around smiling prettily and was topless. There was little more than a flash of bare breasts but three of the men cheered. European commercials were much more relaxed about nudity than are the U.S. types.

"Back to the ten A.M. news," a conservatively dressed woman newscaster said. "An update on the Minister of Finance, Karl Krueger, who is in intensive care at Berlin Central. His doctors say now that he is in extremely serious condition. His family has been called to the hospital.

"Chancellor Helmut Schmidt said only moments ago in a news conference that the German people do not have to worry about the Ministry of Finance. He is appointing the deputy minister, Brun Harloff, to serve as acting minister until the situation regarding Herr Krueger is clarified. There was no indication that Harloff would be promoted to minister, but there was no closing the door to that chance either."

"In other news, the three men who fell into the river last night after a drinking bout have been treated and released from the hospital. None suffered serious injury in the . . ."

Wade turned off the set.

"So life goes on. Now what do we make out of this mess? Just what facts have we to go on, as well as speculation and extrapolation?"

"Tell me what them big words mean and I'll take a crack at it," Roger said. "Hell, us SEALs don't go for them big fancy-dancy words."

That brought another laugh, then they all settled down to a think-tank session of give and take, wild theory and shooting them down. It would be a long morning.

✳ EIGHTEEN ✳

John Silokowski took hesitant steps as he approached the office of the Transportation Corps, the Nazis who selected those Jews who would go on the next train. The people from the Warsaw ghetto were crowded into cattle and boxcars bound for "relocation" somewhere to the east. The Nazi headquarters had been a women's clothing store before the war. Now it stood fifty yards from the Umschlagplatz, the deportation point, where many thousands of Warsaw Jews had already been taken away. They had been selected, pushed into boxcars of trains that quickly departed.

John had heard rumors and wild stories about whole trainloads of Jews who vanished into the countryside and were never seen nor heard from again. John had no idea where they were going, but he knew for certain that he didn't want to go there with his family. The Nazis treated the Jews getting on the trains no better than cattle, and he had a cold fear in his heart that some of the rumors about death camps were actually true.

At one time there had been more than 315,000 Jews crammed into the Warsaw ghetto. He heard that over a hundred thousand had already been shipped out. No one had heard from more than a handful of them again. John knew of one man who had bribed some of the Transportation Corps soldiers and escaped to Switzerland.

He had to do everything he could to save his wife and small daughter, Ruth. He had been told by some of the Transportation Corps officers that the man to see was Captain Grant Zedicher, who was in charge of one of the sections of selection and transport. John went inside the building and shuddered. The transformation of the place was frightening.

Huge Nazi flags and banners covered the walls of the forty-foot-square room. Under a large picture of Hitler sat the man he was to see. He was behind a desk that sat on a three-foot platform. This gave Captain Zedicher a superior position, with the person he talked to having to look upward at him.

A German soldier pointed to a chair beside the near wall and John sat there. A Jewish man stood in front of the desk talking with the captain, and John Silokowski could hear the conversation plainly.

"Yes, yes, yes. You have explained your situation in too much detail already, Horowitz. I know your mother is ill and your two children are sickly. I can only do so much. The arrangements are the same and apply to each person. This is all done at considerable risk and danger to me and my men. I hope you realize that."

"Yes, Herr Zedicher. We do indeed. We simply ask that you allow the children to go without the usual favors. This would make it possible."

Silokowski looked around. There was no one else in the large room. Three desks grouped at the far wall. Two other doors had been closed permanently. The private who stood near the door had a submachine gun slung around his shoulder so he could bring it up ready to fire in a fraction of a second.

The risk here was pregnant, so volatile and acrid that John could taste it. If the idea of this safe transport was discovered by the German commanders, the men in this corps could be shot down on sight without any investigation.

John frowned. Or perhaps the commanders were a part of the operation already. Yes, that must be it. Such an arrangement would make it all possible. It would take several men to do what he had heard could be done.

Switzerland!

He shuddered just thinking about it. Switzerland and freedom. Freedom for his wife and his child. Eventually passage could be arranged to America or to Canada. Yes, freedom.

The private nudged him and pointed to the empty space in front of the captain.

"Sorry," he said, stood, and hurried to the man who could save him and his family.

The strange face looked down at Silokowski. The man's eyes were too close together, his nose small and cheekbones too low in his face. His lower jaw seemed to be slightly out of place.

"Well?" Captain Zedicher said.

"Captain, may I get right to the point. I understand that for a large consideration, you can arrange for transportation for a man and his family to Switzerland. If this is true I wish to discuss this with you and make any arrangements needed. We are ready to leave Warsaw on one hour's notice."

"Your name is John Silokowski, is that right?" Zedicher snapped.

"Yes, sir."

"You were a prominent merchant in Warsaw before the war?"

"Yes."

"You have retained some of the wealth that you built up in the good years for commerce?"

"That's right, Captain."

"Are you aware that because of the terrible risk my men and I are taking that this program is expensive?"

"Yes, sir, I'm prepared to make a generous offer."

Captain Zedicher laughed, but there was little humor in the sound. It made John Silokowski cringe.

"We don't take offers, Silokowski. We have prices. For you, your wife and daughter, the price is four million marks. Do you have that much?"

"Yes. But that's almost everything I have."

"Can you show me some proof?"

Silokowski reached inside the patched and repatched jacket he wore and pulled a thread. Inside the lining he took out a small leather bag with a pull string. He opened it and let six diamonds fall into his hand. They were three to five carats each, perfect blue-white diamonds without a flaw.

"These stones have been appraised at a little over four and a half million marks," John said.

Zedicher came down from the platform and checked the quality of the stones. He nodded.

"I agree, these are valuable diamonds. But what is to stop me from shooting you dead on the spot and taking the gems?"

"Only the fact that others know where I am and why I'm here. Many know of your service. If you were to kill me, no more of my people would come to you and your get-rich program would be at an end."

Zedicher nodded and went back to the tall desk.

"You are correct, Silokowski. You are a smart man. I'll see that you and your wife and daughter are driven to Switzerland. It will be about a week. Be ready. We always leave just after midnight. Have the stones with you when I send a messenger to bring you."

Silokowski hesitated and looked up.

"Something else?" Zedicher asked.

"A question. Everyone says the trains when they leave here with our people are going to labor camps. Is that right?"

"Absolutely. This way you won't have to do hard labor for the rest of the war. You'll be contacted." Zedicher smiled as the Jew left. He saw that there was another Jew sitting in a chair waiting to see him.

Private Selig came up to the captain and grinned. "Looks like we grabbed another big one, Captain."

"That we did, Selig." They spoke in low tones so the man in the chair couldn't hear. "He will get transport. We have to let one of them get through from time to time to keep the hopes alive of the rest of them. We have to work fast, Selig. I hear they'll be done here in another two months. We must hurry to make Jewish money while the Nazi sun shines."

They both grinned and Private Selig went to tell the next Jew that he could talk to the captain.

John Silokowski hurried home to the crowded flat where twelve of them lived together. Some of the people were relatives. He hadn't let on to them about the rescue. He had to be sure it would happen first. He had known of at least three men who had made it through to Switzerland. It would happen for him and his family.

Sarah met him in the corner of the room that they called home. It was separated from three other families in the room by a blanket. He kissed her and smiled. "It's all arranged," he whispered. "Your jewels will buy our freedom. He will take them all, but at least we will not be in a forced labor camp somewhere, or something worse. I've been hearing more bad things about the people who are selected and put in the boxcars."

Sarah's eyes glistened with tears as she hugged John. "I prayed that you could reason with the man. He must have some feelings. I know, I know, he's a German, a Nazi. Still there must be one tiny shred of . . ."

John Silokowski put his fingers over her lips. "Don't even think it, Sarah. The man is a machine with no feelings whatsoever."

He looked round. "Now, are we going to have some supper here or not?"

She shook her head. "We're sharing with the Levines, tonight. They received an allotment of food. They always share."

He settled down on the floor and leaned back against the wall. "In a week we should be in . . . we should be there. Then we won't have to worry any more about food, or being shot for no reason, or being sent to a work camp packed on a train like animals." She put her fingers over his lips.

Ruth, their four-year-old, stirred in her sleep on the doubled-over blanket on the floor. She had short, soft black hair and big eyes. She looked like her mother and for that John was eternally thankful. He picked her up and she came fully awake. "Papa. My toy bear? Did you find it?"

He looked at his wife who shook her head. "I'm afraid that Barney the Bear is still hiding from us. We'll look for it tomorrow. Now we have to get ready for supper."

He wanted to tell her how much he loved her and how they would be going soon on a long car trip and then they would be free. But he couldn't. Instead he used a borrowed needle and stitched the diamonds back into the lining of his coat. They were the salvation of his family. Less than a week.

"But, John, when we get there how will we live? Our money will all be gone."

The whispers again. He smiled. "For ten years I have had a bank account in Switzerland, a numbered account. We will draw out the money and sail for America. No, I didn't tell you about it. It was a business account for emergencies. Now it will take us to America and help us get started in a new business."

Two days later, a Jewish friend said he had a message for John. He was supposed to go to a certain street corner and wait. Someone would contact him there. The friend had no idea what it was about.

John kissed his wife and daughter good-bye, said he

would be right back, and went to the corner. At once another Jew John didn't know motioned to him and led him down an alley and then in a roundabout way to the rear door of the Transportation Corps headquarters building. John didn't even know there was a back door.

No one was inside except the same Private Selig and the captain. They sat at a table with a black box, which they quickly closed. It was about a foot wide and two feet long, maybe a foot high. John didn't give it another thought.

"Why am I here, Captain?"

"Need a word or two with you. Our committee met and turned down your family to be moved. Not for the four and a half million. We need more money for your daughter. You said the stones are worth four and a half. That means you're still short a million and a half marks for your daughter. You can decide to leave her here, that's fine with us."

John ran to the table and pounded on it with his fist. The captain stood quickly and unholstered a pistol but kept it aimed at the floor.

"You can't do this. You are charging us all the money I have. You can't split up my family. It's not right."

"Oh, but we can, Jew, indeed we can. The fact is we split up families here all the time. On every shipment. It means nothing to us. We're just doing our job. Now, to get to Switzerland you need another million and a half marks."

John lunged toward the captain. Before he came close, something hit him from behind. He felt the crushing blow against his head, then the lights flickered on and off as he fell to the floor. He never quite passed out. He stared up at the three men looking down at him.

"Oh, pardon me, Herr Silokowski. I don't believe you've met Sergeant Mandel Griswold. That was his rifle butt that clobbered you in the back of the head. Sit up, you're not hurt that bad. Griswold knows what he's doing."

John groaned and sat up. His head pounded.

"Now, we need to talk about the money. We know that you do have more resources. Any Jew with that kind of jewelry must also have other resources such as a numbered Swiss bank account."

"We made a deal," John shouted from where he sat on the floor. "You told me the gems for my family. A package deal, all of us for all the diamonds."

"We have a deal when I say we do," Captain Zedicher shouted. "I say you owe us a million and a half. It's the going rate. You have your choice. You give us the access numbers to your Swiss bank account, and you and your family have a free ride to Switzerland. You don't give me the number and I kill you, your family gets shipped out tomorrow on the train, and we keep the diamonds. Make up your mind."

"Bastards!" John shouted. Sergeant Griswold kicked him in the stomach and he sprawled on the floor. Slowly he sat up.

"All right, my family for the jewels and the account. You take out the million and a half marks and leave the rest there."

Captain Grant Zedicher of the Nazi Transportation Corps grinned. "Done. I'm a man of my word. Now, give me the number. You memorized it, right?"

"Of course." John Silokowski had to take several breaths to get his body working right. He almost vomited but kept the flow down. He swallowed again and recited the number. The captain wrote it in a book.

"Now, give me the name of the bank and the town. Then the number again. If you can't, I know you made this number up as you went. What is it again?"

Silokowski repeated the number. It was the same. Then he gave him the name of the bank in the Swiss town.

"All right, John Silokowski," the captain said. "You've just bought yourself a ride to Switzerland. The car leaves in just about an hour. I'll send a man to bring your wife and daughter. No one will know anything about it. Now, get the diamonds for me out of your coat and we'll take you out to the car."

Silokowski nodded. So far so good. He knew the Nazis would clean out his bank account. That was still better than dying and letting his family go into the trains. Anything was better than that.

He stood up slowly, kept his meal down, and went with Private Selig into a back room where he waited for the car.

A half hour later, the private came in again and told him to get outside into the alley. He went. The car pulled up and he stepped inside. His wife and daughter were not there. He looked at the private.

"Where is my family?"

"They're coming. Get in and relax."

John Silokowski stepped inside and the soldier swung the door. Silokowski caught it. "Where the hell is my wife and daughter?"

Someone stepped in beside him. Something hard smashed into the back of his skull and he fell back into the car.

"He's unconscious, he won't give you any more trouble. Drive out of here now," Captain Zedicher said.

"Won't he try to get out of the car once he realizes his family isn't going with him?" Selig asked.

"He'll try, but there are no door handles in the back-seat. Not a chance he can get away. We have two Swiss numbered accounts now. I should set up a trip to that neutral country soon. Let's wait for one more. We can do three accounts just as easily as two."

The next morning in Warsaw, the selection committee was out in force. They had a quota to fill. They simply went through the buildings in the ghetto and pointed at individuals and families. One pointed at Sarah Silokowski and Ruth.

"I can't go, my husband is missing," she shouted. She was told to pack one small bag for both of them and be at the deportation plaza in an hour or she would be shot.

Sarah had asked everyone she knew if they had seen John. It wasn't like him to stay out all night. Nobody had seen him. Ten people from her room were on the next train. She packed the bag carefully, put in what food she had and a bottle of water. She'd heard things about the trains.

The long walk to the plaza went quickly, then she and Ruth were checked off on a list and they were pushed into a boxcar. There were so many people in it that nobody could sit down. They crowded into one another apologizing, some crying. They stood there crammed together like a flock of sheep.

"We're all going to be killed," one old man kept wailing. "Why treat us like cattle if they aren't going to slaughter us?"

Two days later the train arrived at the Sobibór railroad station in Poland. There were only a few buildings. She saw a forester's hut and a barn. The people were pushed out of the boxcars, separated into groups of men on one side, and all the women and children on the other. Then they were all marched off.

The women and children were all sent in one direction. The men were checked, and those who looked strong enough to work were sent to a separate compound.

An hour later a nice lady who spoke perfect Polish talked to the line of women. They were outside a building that was built solidly and low to the ground.

The Germans used Sonderkommandos to talk to the people. They were Polish and spoke the language flawlessly. This was to keep the people calm and relieve any anxiety the people might have.

"We must have cleanliness here," the Polish woman said. "We are in the undressing chamber now. You all must remove all of your clothing and put it in a stack. Be sure to remember where you put it so you can come directly to it once you have bathed and been deloused."

At that point Sarah Silokowski didn't know what to think. She went along with the authority, as she had all her life. She was a follower. She held her baby in her arms and walked into the bathing chamber that had shower-heads installed along the walls.

Then it seemed to Sarah that there were too many women there for the number of showerheads, still more and more women and small children came into the chamber.

Suddenly, the Sonderkommando and the SS Nazi soldier jolted out of the door of the chamber and it was slammed shut and bolted down.

When the first hiss of gas came in the chamber, Sarah knew for sure that she would never see her husband again. She held tightly to her baby. Ruth began to cry, not sure what was going on. Sarah held her tightly, then a moment later she fell to the concrete floor as the gas fumes overwhelmed her and baby Ruth.

⋆ NINETEEN ⋆

BERLIN, GERMANY
1999

The Specialists worked over everything they had on each of the four suspects. They categorized and organized, they tried one flyer after another that might get them some hard evidence. Zedicher was the prime suspect; they had him tied directly to two murders.

"No hard evidence," Kat said again and again. After the third time she held up both hands and led them in the chant of "No hard evidence."

They broke up just before noon when one of the secretaries brought in the three afternoon newspaper early editions. Two of them had front page features on G. B. Zedicher. One paper asked the question: "Is Zedicher the Berlin Man of the Year?" Both papers had similar stories.

"These are public relation releases rewritten to make them look like the paper's own stories," Duncan said.

Wade scowled at the stories. "Why right now? He's been a force in this town for twenty years. Why is he so hot right now that the TV and newspapers are giving him all of this space?"

"Is he political?" Kat asked. "This looks like a coordinated PR push for an election campaign. But there are no elections scheduled in Germany for two years."

"Maybe it isn't for an election," Duncan said. "Remember the elected officials in a democracy represent less than one-tenth of one percent of all the workers on the government payroll."

"But what would need a PR campaign?" Ichi asked.

"An appointment to some high office," Hershel chimed in. "Say a Secretary of State, or director of the security program or defense, something like that."

Duncan knew the most about German politics. The rest of them looked at him. "Hey, nothing that I know of is coming up, no office or minister's spot to be filled. There could be a big one we don't know about."

"And this Zedicher bastard is trying to get appointed? Who does that, the President?"

"Here it's the Chancellor," Duncan said. "He wields the power."

Wade turned on the TV set in the workroom. All four of the local stations with noon news had picked up the newspaper stories and had put crews in the field to get in-person reaction of viewers and on-camera development of the stories. Each station took a slightly different tack and it was soon obvious that Zedicher himself was getting weary of the interview process, considering that he must have done six or eight sessions that morning.

"Pure puffery," Kat said. "It looks like an exercise for first year broadcast journalism students. They have no story. They are simply rehashing the PR statements. Zedicher stands there softly telling everyone he has no idea how the Man of the Year thing got started."

Roger had been reading to the end of each newspaper article. He looked up. "Hey, nowhere in these articles does it say anything about what Zedicher's family did during the war. Isn't that convenient. Nothing about Zedicher's humble family before the war. Just all of the fine things he's done for Berlin and Germany after he got rich."

"I'm surprised nobody asked him about that," Kat said. "Maybe I can sneak into his next press conference."

That afternoon the assault on the TV news and printed media continued, with more than a dozen smaller stories about Zedicher and what he had done to promote literacy, how he had welcomed the handicapped into his business firms—always careful to protect everyone with a disability.

Hershel shook his head. "This man G. B. Zedicher is a saint. I'd say he'll be canonized at the first chance by the Catholic Church, even though he's probably an atheist or a Lutheran."

That afternoon the barrage continued of articles, stories, picture features, and some comments from Zedicher on some of the current problems with the German economy. None of his advice was profound or original.

Wade shook his head. He waved at Duncan and Hershel. "Get over to the capitol as soon as you can and wring out all of your contacts there. See what's happening we don't know about. Zedicher must be getting the good guy treatment because he's on his way into some important appointment. See if you can find out what it is and why. He's shown no hint that he would go into the political arena up to now. Dig it out in a rush. Maybe there's something we can do to even up the publicity score."

Siegfried had been trying all morning to get an appointment with Penrod Griswold. The billionaire worked sometimes, other times he played golf or drove his sports cars in the mountains. He liked the thrill of taking hairpin turns twice as fast as anyone else.

By three o'clock, Siegfried at last made contact. Griswold was on a cell phone about twenty miles out of Berlin on some kind of a location, time, and distance race.

"No, not speed. You have to hit the mark, take the

right route, get checked off at each point, and make it back to the starting point. The winner is the one who checks in closest to the exact hour, minute, and second that is designated for the tour to take."

"Mr. Griswold. This is tremendously important. Mr. Zedicher asked me to contact you. We're hunting a highly important item that has a long history. I don't like to mention the color over the air this way. When can I talk to you about this highly sensitive matter?"

The air was silent for a moment. "Oh, yeah, that. Been wondering myself. Tell you what, Siegfried. I'd normally let it ride, but if old fuss-budget G.B. thinks it's this vital, we better have a talk. I have some ideas. This will be over in an hour. Another hour back to town. Meet me at five-thirty at the Baron and the Bear Café on Wonderloft Street."

"Yes, sir, Mr. Griswold. I'll be there five-thirty. I'll be waiting for you."

As it turned out, both men were late getting to the meeting. Griswold had a small fender-bender crash when his bluff failed at a country road and a major highway. It took an hour to fill out the accident report.

Siegfried made it to the meeting spot half an hour after the time because he had to shield Mr. Zedicher from overzealous press and photographers when he dedicated a new school reading wing at a small facility in one of Berlin's slum areas.

Siegfried never drank when he worked. He had just drained the second spring water drink when Griswold came in, talked a moment with the head bar man, and headed for Siegfried's table near the back. It was well away from any other drinkers or diners.

Griswold stared hard at Siegfried before he sat down. He nodded and slid into the booth.

"Yes, Siegfried. I remember you with G.B. on several occasions. You were with East German Intelligence ten years ago. We had all sorts of material on you. Glad you are on our side now."

A waiter came and Griswold ordered a drink, then stared at Siegfried. "You were hinting about the black box. I know it well. What I don't know is where it is. Have you talked to the others?"

"I have. None of the four of you have any idea what happened to it. The last we knew it was in the Derrick company safe inside a separate container that was double-locked. You remember what Audwin Derrick did about ten years ago?"

"Yes, some of it. About ten years ago, we tried to find the box, but it was no longer in the safe, and no one had any idea where it could be," Griswold said. Those were times of upheaval and reunification and many changes and remarkable opportunities. Everyone became so wrapped up in business that the box had little importance.

"Now it's quite important to Mr. Zedicher that we find and destroy the box and everything in it."

Griswold sipped at his drink, then smiled. "So that's what's stuck up G.B.'s ass. All this Man of the Year propaganda. He doesn't want his lily-white image tarnished." Griswold laughed. He shook his head and roared. It ended in a coughing fit that brought a concerned waiter. Griswold waved him away.

When he had recovered enough, he had a drink of water, then some of his mixed drink.

"Oh, yes. What tangled webs we spin." He shook his head and looked at an attractive young woman who walked by. He lifted his brows. "What's that song lyric? 'Pretty girl, walk a little slower when you walk past me.' Yes, that's it. At least I can watch these lovely creatures and remember what once was and dream of what might be."

He sipped at his drink. "You'll have to tell G.B. that I have no knowledge whatsoever about the box. I agree that it should be found. We should have found it ten years ago. The key to the whole episode seems to be Audwin Derrick. I thought we should have taken care of him permanently ten years ago. I still think we should if you're taking a straw vote. After he tells you where the box is."

"Mr. Griswold. Let me brief you on exactly where I am in the investigation. None of the four principals know where the black box is. Berthold Derrick says he knows that his brother Audwin knew it was in the company safe after they put it there for safekeeping more than twenty years ago.

"All the partners knew where the box was and considered it to be in a safe position.

"One day Berthold was in that particular safe and checked on the box without any reason. He found the box and its protective packaging were gone from the safe.

"A short time later, Berthold discovered that the company had been systematically looted for the past two years. Audwin had been giving away Bavaria Limited money in huge amounts. An audit of Audwin's books revealed that over sixty million marks were missing or paid to nonexistent accounts. Audwin wouldn't say why. He was removed from the corporate structure, and kept guarded until the investigation had been finished.

"They discovered that Audwin had used the black box records to try to find descendants of those men named in the book. If he could find them, he gave them each two million marks to compensate them for their loss during the war. When he ran out of names, he gave huge sums to Jewish relief organizations and Zionist causes and other Jewish charities. All gifts were anonymous.

"The truth of where the money came from to start the various corporations right after World War II had evidently at last taken a toll of Audwin and had driven him to this repayment idea.

"They asked Audwin where the box was, but could get only incoherent mumblings from him. The four of you voted not to kill Audwin, but to commit him to a private sanitarium where he would be kept safe, and where he should become well enough to tell them where the box was hidden. They kept trying to find it, but Audwin wouldn't help them. The four of you had no idea if he was insane or just pretending to be. The short stay in the mental facility stretched out, and now is over ten years long.

"So, my next move will be to question Audwin with all of the experience at my command. If he is faking his insanity, I will know it at once and soon convince him to cooperate.

"My one instruction from the others is not to kill Audwin until I have the black box in hand. Do you agree with and approve of my plan, Mr. Griswold?"

"I do. I'd never known the complete story. Sixty million. Damn. Ten years ago that was important money." He finished his drink, nodded at Siegfried, stood, and left. Siegfried snorted, and pulled some bills from his pocket to pay the tab.

Early the next morning, Wade stood near the employee entrance to the Zedicher building and watched people arrive for work. About eight-thirty a flood of people came through and security loosened as many without their employee badges hurried through the doors and to the elevators.

Wade wore a floppy hat, large dark glasses, and a fake heavy mustache as he waited and watched.

Five minutes later he saw his target. Siegfried with his red hair neatly combed and the black patch over his left eye walked briskly into the building. Wade hurried in behind him careful not to make eye contact with the guards on the door. Again, dozens of people crowded at the door and the guards stood back and waited.

Wade forged ahead, and made it into the same elevator that Siegfried did. More than twenty persons were crowded in and Wade managed to be well away from him.

Wade left the lift on the same floor Siegfried did, the

thirtieth, and watched as he went into room 30114. There was no name or any other indicator on the door.

Wade reversed his course and left the building by the same side entrance he had entered with not even a second glance from the guards. Now he was in for a long day of waiting. He went back to the workroom and tried again to reason out some hard evidence that a court or at least a newspaper would look at. He could nail down nothing.

He had decided the day before to follow Siegfried. Perhaps he was their best hard evidence. If they could prove that Siegfried killed the CNN reporter and George Silokowski, and that he had done so on orders from G. B. Zedicher, they would have most of the hard evidence they would need.

So, he wanted to follow Siegfried back to his apartment or hotel room. Once they knew the location, they would be able to work a variety of surveillances. They could plant bugs in the rooms with a repeater outside his building that would send every word spoken in the rooms to a voice-activated recorder in the workroom at Marshall Export/Import. They could follow Siegfried every day and see where he went. They could try to move into a room adjacent to his and use TV cameras put through the wall. They could harass him with late-night calls, weird noises, sleep-preventive sounds that would leave him sleepless and groggy the next day.

Now all Wade had to do was follow him when he came off work and hope that he went straight home.

That afternoon, Wade thought he must have missed Siegfried. When Wade arrived at his waiting spot at three o'clock there was a stream of office workers leaving the building. None of them was Siegfried. He waited. A few kept coming out. Then at four that afternoon another rush of workers departed.

Siegfried was one of the first. He walked away from the building, ignored cabs, and hurried across a busy street against the light. Then Wade saw that many people did that so he did too, and was barely in time to see

Siegfried stop in a bistro of some kind that featured roast pork and drinks.

Siegfried sat at the bar and had two drinks. He downed them quickly, said something to the bar keep, and left by the side door. Wade left shortly after he did and caught him turning right.

After that it was a walk of about three-quarters of a mile, Wade figured. It quickly led them out of the main business section into an area of a few old houses, some new apartments, and mixed small businesses. Siegfried went up three steps and into one of the newer apartment buildings. Wade waited five minutes, then tried the door. It came open. Inside in a small lobby there were call buttons. One was by the name of Siegfried Mierhoff. Room 212. Wade left the area and hurried back across the street. He found some shrubs that grew next to an abandoned shop and edged in behind them. He was concealed from the street and the building across the way, but he could watch the entrance.

Wade nibbled on a candy bar he had brought with him. He prayed devoutly that Siegfried had an active social life, and that he would need to leave his apartment quickly. Wade felt the package in his oversize pocket. He had everything he needed. The recorder was set up in the workroom. All he had to do was place the three or four pickup-sending devices in the apartment, then establish the larger relay transceiver on the building or a pole within a hundred yards of the bugs, and they would be in business.

What Wade really dreamed of putting in the spy's apartment was a pair of antipersonnel mines. Both would go off the second that Siegfried opened his bathroom door and would tear his body into jagged pieces scattered around the room. For the flash of a second Vivian's lovely face seared across his memory's inner eye, then it was gone. Damn him. Damn Siegfried Mierhoff.

The killer left an hour later. He had changed into what looked like a more expensive suit with black tie and a white handkerchief in his breast pocket. Probably a formal affair with Zedicher. Good, that would leave plenty of time for Wade's work.

As soon as Siegfried vanished up the street toward honking taxi horns, Wade left his protection and hurried across the almost dark street. He went into the apartment building, caught it lucky with someone just coming out, and pretended to hit a button, then grabbed the open door and nodded his thanks.

He went up steps to the second floor and looked for 212. Down toward the street. At the door he checked the lock. Newer, but not good enough. In forty-five seconds he had the door picked and was inside. He planted the bugs in all four rooms: one in the kitchen beside the refrigerator, one under the telephone stand in the living room. One on top of the medicine cabinet in the bath, and one next to a picture in the bedroom.

He slipped a ski mask on as he finished. An old habit. He checked the places. He couldn't see any of the bugs. Then he walked toward the apartment door.

A key rattled in the lock and the door swung open. Siegfried let out a bellow of rage and charged at Wade. Neither of them had time to pull out a weapon.

✯ TWENTY ✯

Less than a second and a half after the door swung open and the two men saw each other in Siegfried's apartment, they stormed together in unarmed combat. Both were experts. Their first contacts were quickly thrown punches with little preparation behind them. The blows were blocked but there was no room for any classic follow-up kicks. They parted and stared, then circled slowly in the small living room.

Neither spoke. A move by Siegfried toward his belt holster brought a flurry of kicks and thrusts by Wade to keep the slightly larger man off balance and his hand free of the pistol. When Wade made a move for the weapon at his side, Siegfried kept him busy with a charging attack of kicks and side-of-the-hand slashes.

Wade had tangled with this man before. He knew that with Siegfried's height and weight advantage it would be a close fight. That wasn't what he wanted. He wanted out of there and for the bugs to work perfectly. Getting caught on the site was a bush league play.

They had circled once in the small living room. Now Siegfried was in front of the couch with a low back. Wade decided his strategy in a tenth of a second. He drove straight ahead, his strong legs pumping, his fists out like battering rams. The move caught Siegfried by surprise. It wasn't a beginning of a contest maneuver. It was one to use when you're tired and want to take a quick break.

Wade's fists were pounded away by Siegfried's blows as Wade expected. Wade kept powering forward, lowered his head, and rammed it hard into the German's chest. The force of Wade's driving two hundred pounds slammed Siegfried backward. Usually he would have wrapped his heavy arms around Wade and tried to throw him. This time Siegfried's legs hit the seat of the sofa and ruined his balance. His arms flailed to each side to keep his body upright.

But the power was too great and Wade's jolting force slammed the big man over the sofa and dumped him in back of it.

The second Wade saw that Siegfried was going over the sofa, he lunged for the apartment door, slammed it shut after him, and raced down the hallway to the steps and to the front door. He dumped his jacket and the ski mask in the small mailbox room and stepped outside and walked down the street away from Siegfried's apartment.

Nearly a half block behind him, Wade heard a bellow of rage. The big man was on the sidewalk. Wade ignored him, knowing without his jacket and ski mask he looked much different. He walked calmly into a store, worked to the back, and went out a rear door into the alley. Then he ran full speed away from the scene, went across the first street into the next alley, and ran through it before coming out on the third street where he hailed a taxi and cruised toward the company office.

He had a big dinner at a fancy restaurant with Kat, then waited until midnight. He and Kat went back to a telephone pole a block from Siegfried's apartment house. They had laughed about the surprise visit by the German.

"What if he'd taken your ski mask off?" Kat asked.

"Then we probably would have had a fight to the death

one way or the other. He must have forgotten something and come back in a hurry to get it. I bet I spoiled his whole evening."

That afternoon, Wade had put the transceiver relay device together. It was calibrated to pick up signals from the four bugs in Siegfried's apartment. The relay was about the size of a paperback book. All Wade had to do was fasten it to the pole. It had its own battery and an antenna. It was activated by any sound it received from the bugs. It was powerful enough to relay the signals five miles across town to the company office.

Wade drove two screws into the pole through slots in the relay and secured it. No one would notice it up ten feet except a telephone lineman who happened to be climbing the pole. Then he'd probably ignore it. If it hung there for a week, it should have done its job.

Kat frowned on the drive back. "What about Siegfried? He's going to be curious about who had broken into his apartment. Are you sure he couldn't ID you?"

"He might. He may know that I'm in town. He had enough chances to see my face before today. But from those few seconds tonight he couldn't have done it. He could guess it was me. But why would I be in his apartment?"

"You didn't steal anything," Kat said. "Of course he'd have to figure he came back too quickly for a thief to make a good haul. If he figured it was you, he'd be looking for bugs. How many did you plant?"

"Four. Let's get back and check our relay and printout."

"If he thinks it might be you, he'll scour that place good. Might even sweep it with an electronic searcher."

"Let's hope he doesn't do that. I figure he'll find two or three and think he's done. Let's hope that's the worst scenario."

Back at the home office they checked the relay's receiver and the automatic printout it hooked up to. It had actuated. They saw some words that didn't make sense, then someone, evidently Siegfried, swearing.

The next entry on the tape came a moment later.

"Well, well, well. What do we have here? In the bath-room no less. Number two. You're getting sloppy in your old age, Wade, damn sloppy." Then the page went blank.

"Damn. He knows it was me. Could be bad."

There was a loud crunching sound.

"He stepped on the bug," Wade said.

"That could leave two. We'll have to hope he doesn't find them."

They waited ten minutes but there were no more transmissions. It was just after one-thirty A.M. when the pair gave up and headed for their rooms.

"We'll check it out in the morning," Kat said.

Slightly after two A.M. Siegfried settled down at his small desk and telephone in his apartment. He'd done his duty for Zedicher, now it was time for some personal work.

He picked up the telephone, then put it back and checked around. Two damn bugs he'd found. There could be more. Usually two were enough, but, this must be that damn Wade Thorne. He checked along the walls, the picture frames, and on the bottoms of chairs. Nothing. Tomorrow he'd get in a specialist he knew to sweep the place. If there were any more bugs, the electronic sweeper would find them.

He put on a light jacket and went to the corner phone booth and made his call.

"Yes, I know it's extremely early in the morning. That's why I call now. You know who this is. I want everything you have on Wade Thorne, about thirty-eight, thirty-nine, American ex-CIA. He's in Berlin. I want to know why, who he works for, his address, everything. I need it yesterday. Stay up the rest of the night and have it to me on my E-mail before six A.M. You understand. I need it damn bad. Everything."

Siegfried returned home and started to make another call, then stopped. Don't be stupid. Sweep it first. He nodded to himself and went to bed.

The next morning, Siegfried shunned the telephone at home and hurried to the office early to make some calls. The first went to an old friend who agreed to sweep the apartment.

"You need a key?" Siegfried asked.

They both laughed. "Yes, true. When did you ever need a key to get into my apartment? You know the address. Have it done before noon and earn yourself an extra fifty."

"Done."

Siegfried made two more calls. Both went to former intelligence people now in German government. He had strong contacts with the current and previous intelligence communities.

"I need to know all you can tell me about a former CIA man named Wade Thorne. You should know him. He's in town. I need to know who he's working for and why."

"Of course we know of him. He was a thorn in our side for years. We'll find out and get back to you at this number."

Siegfried settled in his chair and smiled.

Hans Doreffer carried his equipment in two suitcases. He really only needed one, but he liked to have a backup. Then too, he had his wife's homemade lunch in the second case. Hot soup, sandwich, fruit, and cookies. His wife always surprised him with something special in his lunch.

He took out his electronic equipment and began the debugging operation. He found the first bug in the kitchen and put it in his pocket. He would put it near the public telephone half a block away, and the people who planted it would get a steady stream of phone calls from the general public. One of his little jokes he played on these high-tech types.

He swept the bedroom, but found nothing. He had

just started on the living room when his indicator went blank. Why? He checked the switches. Sometimes he turned the sweeper off. No, it was still in the on position. He checked two more points, then looked at his battery. Dead. Damn, must be a direct short in it. He stared at the room. He'd tell good old Siegfried that he'd done the job and found one more in the kitchen, no more. Hell, Siegie would never know.

Hans put his gear away, opened the second case, and took out his lunch. He found a cold beer in the refrigerator and helped himself. Oh, yes, but he had a fine lunch. That would take up the rest of the morning before he went back home and got a new battery and a spare to carry in the second kit.

By ten that morning, Siegfried had the report from his overnight contact. "Yes, Thorne is in town. He's been working for some industrialist lately on routine industrial espionage, and other pet projects of the owner. I couldn't find out who the boss is. Thorne has a squad of five who go with him. I couldn't find a hotel where they are staying in town. I drew a blank there."

Siegfried thanked him and looked at his notes. Wade Thorne and five men to back him. That could be trouble. He tipped his hand when he tried to bug the apartment. Siegfried nodded and grinned. Yes, and when he found out the location of Thorne and his team, he'd hit them hard.

The last bit of information came by phone to Siegfried's office just after one that afternoon. His intelligence source speaking off the record said that Thorne was working for J. August Marshall, the billionaire industrialist, who had taken a strong stance lately against terrorism and any kind of crime that attacked the innocent, and the women and children of the world. Marshall had an office here, Marshall Export/Import.

It took Siegfried only ten minutes to assemble his hit squad. The other two men were from the old days. Knew how to do a job and keep quiet about it. Siegfried went to a special room deep in the third parking-level basement of the Zedicher Tower. The locker was behind a locked door and then past two more. Inside the locker were automatic weapons, explosives, hand grenades, and enough ammo to start a small war. Siegfried picked out the weapons he wanted, put them and sufficient ammo in a box, and had it taken by hand truck to one of the Mercedes reserved for him in the executive parking level.

He met his two men a block from the Marshall offices and they moved up close enough and parked so they could spot people going and coming. It was not a popular place with the public. Then he saw Wade Thorne enter the office with three others. Two looked like ex-military and the third was a tall woman. He signaled and the three left the car. They each carried South African-made BXP submachine guns. The weapons were a little over sixteen inches long and hung on a cord around the men's necks and kept hidden under jackets. They spit out 9mm parabellum rounds at a thousand rounds a minute, or almost seventeen rounds a second.

The men moved up to the door and went in all at once. They had target areas and each looked for the large man they had just seen enter the offices. It was a twin design setup, with desks and partitions on both sides of the central door. All three men wore ski masks that hid their heads and faces.

Siegfried and a second man ran to the left.

"Where are the four who just came in here?" he demanded. The clerks and secretaries looked at the weapons in stunned silence. Siegfried sent a six-round burst into the ceiling. Six of the women dropped off their chairs and hid under their desks. The three men ran into the workstations and found nothing.

Near the back of the section one of the secretaries reached to the side of her desk and removed a safety holder and pushed a red button. All doors leading out of the main office area into the secret sections automatically locked and an alarm bell rang in the workroom and other secret Specialists' areas.

Siegfried fired again, spraying bullets over the unmanned desks. The other men shook their heads. They had not found the men they wanted. He looked for rear doors, but found only closed panels that might hide anything. He fired into one of them, then motioned and the three men hurried out the front door, with one covering the area behind him in a rear guard position. Then they vanished into the street.

Wade Thorne and the rest of the Specialists heard the alarm in the workroom and knew at once the office section had been invaded. They couldn't go through the usual doors to get there. All six ran out of the side door and around half a block one way, then half a block the other way to the main doors. By the time they got there, the three invaders had left. The Specialists stormed inside with their weapons ready.

"Friendlies here now, folks," Wade bellowed. "Lock down the front door, kill the lights. Did anyone get hurt?"

"Over here," someone called. "Greta's bleeding."

Wade charged that way. Kat met him there. She knelt beside the woman sprawled on the floor. A pool of blood showed under her face. Kat touched Greta's throat and looked up at Wade.

"She's gone, I'm sorry."

Two women came up then. One had a bullet through her shoulder, another had been grazed.

"Put a closed sign on the door," Wade ordered one of the unhurt women. "Company vacation." He grabbed a phone and dialed a remembered number.

"Yes?"

"Hillary, please. In the clear."

"May I ask what . . ."

"No, damnit, get me Hillary."

A moment later a soft voice answered.

"Hillary here in the clear."

"Hillary, Wade Thorne. I'm in Berlin. We need some cleanup. Your old boss's HQ. Rather urgent."

"Just cleanup?"

"For now. Be a big help. Thanks." He hung up.

Twenty minutes later a knock sounded on the front door. Wade had been there waiting. He opened it and two men came in. Wade didn't know either one.

"One KIA and two wounds," Wade said. He led them to the dead woman.

"You have a rear closed entrance," the shorter of the two CIA men said. "Get it open now. Send a man to direct our rig."

Wade pointed to Duncan who ran to the front door with the other CIA man.

Twenty minutes later the front offices of Marshall Export/Import looked nearly normal. The blood was cleaned up; the woman had been transported in the CIA special van. She would be found some distance away with an empty purse and clothes in disarray: the victim of a rape, robbery, and murder.

The two wounded women were treated by a German doctor who worked with the CIA and didn't report gunshot wounds to the police. The Marshall maintenance people were on hand filling in bullet holes, repainting, repairing all damage so the place looked nearly back to normal.

Two part-time workers would report tomorrow to take over the duties of the hurt women. All of the workers knew the real job of the office and were warned there might be some danger. One woman quit and said she wouldn't be back.

The Specialists met in their workroom. They had debriefed the women. Nobody could describe the three men. The ski masks had taken care of that. The only data was that one of the three was four or five inches taller than the other two. The shell casings proved only that the weapons were 9mm submachine guns.

"Siegfried," Kat said. "With his former connections

in this town he must still have a lot of pipelines he can tap. He recognized you, then all he had to do was ask enough people until one knew who you worked for now."

"Keep the closed sign on the front door until this operation is over," Wade said. "We'll use the rear entrance." He stared at the board with the rivers of notes. "Yes, Siegfried, tit for tat. His tat was a little tougher than ours."

"Let's check the printout on that bug," Kat said. They found the electronics working in the outer office. The number window showed twenty-eight calls Kat grabbed the printouts from the bug and checked them. A moment later, she snorted.

"He found another bug all right. He must have put it in a public telephone booth somewhere. I'll have Olga read these as they come in and if there is anything from Siegfried, she'll sort those out."

"Maybe he didn't find the other bug," Duncan said.

Back in the workroom they concentrated on the Zedicher problem. There had been another gush of puffery publicity about the man and his company and dozens of charitable works.

Ten minutes later Olga came in with two printouts. "These were different," she said.

Kat read the first one out loud.

"Mr. Zedicher."

"Yes."

"My next interview is with Audwin. I've talked with the other men but they didn't have any idea where it is. I'll be driving up tomorrow morning to talk to Audwin and to convince him now is the time to find that box."

"Yes, do that. I'm busy with this other project, which is moving along nicely. Oh, with Audwin. Remember, he's one of the group. Don't damage him in any way or Derrick will raise hell. We have to know the location, however, so use your own best judgment."

"Don't worry, Mr. Zedicher. Just leave everything to

me. By tomorrow night your worries about that black box will all be over."

Wade looked at Kat. Kat ran to the bulletin board.

"Yes, here under Derrick. We have Audwin. He's the one who was on the books until about ten years ago, when suddenly he's gone and big brother is signing all the checks."

"Okay, Audwin was one of the team, but got put down and out, but not dead," Wade said. "Why?"

"What's this black box he mentioned?" Ichi asked. "Have we heard anything about that before?"

Kat scanned the note board where all the daily notes on every aspect of the case had been tacked up in family sections.

"Nothing that I can see," Kat said.

"This Siegfried said by tomorrow night all Zedicher's worries about the black box would be over," Roger said. "What is the black box?"

"He said the other men didn't know where the box was," Hershel said. "Could those be the four men who worked together in the Transportation Corps?"

"Sounds like we're starting to get some results from all this work," Duncan said. "Siegfried worked with two other guns today. Will he take them with him tomorrow?"

"No," Kat said. "He'd use them only when necessary. Tomorrow he goes into a familiar zone. He'll do it himself."

They looked at Wade. "Maybe. My suggestion is that we take our full crew in two cars loaded for bear. Weapons of choice, plenty of ammo." He paused. "Weren't there two messages?"

Kat picked the second one up where she had put it on the table.

"Glad old Siegfried didn't find that other bug. Here's the next call." She read it out loud. "It rings five times and he leaves a message. 'Hey, stupid. Told you to stay home afterward. Yeah, need you tomorrow. My place at noon.' "

Wade nodded. "All right, two of them. We'll be loaded and out of here at eleven A.M. Half hour to find his apartment and secure a good pair of parking spots. Then we follow him two on one ten cars back. It should be easy that time of day. Get your weapons picked out tonight. The company cafeteria is open in twenty minutes."

☆ TWENTY-ONE ☆

The next morning at eleven A.M. there was some discussion about which cars to take.

"We take the armored jobs they won't be able to stop us with a lucky shot," Roger said. He referred to the two armored Mercedes with bulletproof glass in all windows, steel plate protection around the engine and in the door panels, and special "run flat" tires that had sidewalls so strong they can run fifty miles at seventy mph without breaking down even if all the air escaped from the tire.

"If we do this right we shouldn't have a confrontation," Wade said. "Anyway, that big Mercedes Siegfried usually drives could run away and leave us if he knew he was being tailed. Those tanks of ours won't do over a hundred."

They took the two Mercedes with three Specialists in each rig. They both found parking spots where they could view the garage to the apartment where Siegfried lived.

Twenty minutes after Wade arrived, two men walked into the front entrance to the apartment house. Five minutes later a big Mercedes with government plates rolled out of the garage. Wade had his twenty-five power 50mm binoculars up watching. They auto-focused at once and he smiled.

"That's Siegfried at the wheel and he has one man with him." He spoke into a small mike on his shirt collar. "Let's roll, car two. You hang back until I have to fade away, then take over. You get his license plate?"

The Motorola personal communications system responded to the small speaker in Wade's ear. It was connected to a cigarette-sized transceiver on his belt.

"That's a Roger, car one," Roger Johnson in the second car said. The ex-Navy SEAL talked them into using the Motorola gear. It had pulled them out of more than one tight spot. Each of the Specialists had one of the sets and could talk to all the others.

The first fifty miles north out of Berlin were routine. Every fifteen miles the two tailing cars would change places, hanging ten cars behind the big black Mercedes. It was easy to see and stay with. Siegfried must not be in any hurry. He seldom went over a hundred miles an hour on the autobahn, and when he turned off on the four-lane highway he kept his speed under eighty miles an hour.

A short time later they left the highway taking a narrow road that led to the village of Wriezen.

"We're near the Polish border here," Hershel said on the radio. "It's certainly out of the way."

They drove through the small town with Wade holding back. He almost missed Siegfried turn, but at the last second saw the Mercedes take a short lane off the street and come to a stop at a heavy iron gate with a guard in front of it.

Wade drove past slowly, saw Siegfried talk with the guard, and watched the electronic gate roll back to let the car pass.

Kat saw a sign near the entrance. "It's called the Berlin Clinical Sanitarium . . . Private. About what we figured. Old Audwin isn't here of his own free will, I'd bet the ranch."

Wade kept driving. A quarter of a mile past the gate, the eight-foot-high chain-link fence ended. Wade pulled into an opening beside the road. A moment later the second car slid in beside it.

Windows rolled down. "Looks solid," Hershel said.

"Over that fence in ten seconds," Roger said. "Or we could blow a hole in it."

"We keep it quiet," Wade said. "First we put one car where we can see the driveway without attracting attention."

"Ain't none, Cap," Roger said. "Let me drift back through the trees and find an OP. From there I can contact you by Motorola if they move anyone out."

"Good," Wade said and passed over the binoculars. "Low-key, quiet."

"Hey, us SEALs are the silent warriors. They don't see us until two seconds before we kill them. I'll keep in touch."

The car door clicked softly as it closed.

"We drive on up another mile," Wade said. "The Motorolas are good for that far on the level. We won't be able to go in until it gets dark, unless Siegfried tries to move him."

Kat frowned, then lifted her brows. "They will have Audwin on heavy drugs. It'll take them six or eight hours to bring him off of the drugs to halfway normal. That's when they can start to question him. My bet is that they didn't phone last night to take Audwin off the juice."

"So we have some wait time," Wade said. "We need anything else?"

Duncan used the radio. "Just as we left the area, I saw a pair of dogs strolling along the wire. Dobermans. We have any joy juice for puppies?"

"Good catch, Duncan," Kat said. "I should have thought of that. I'll go into town and find some at the drugstore. We used Exorphinanine last time. It worked fine."

"Take this car," Wade said, moving out the door. Kat

slid over. "Keep your helper. If you find a café you could bring us some hamburgers and fries."

Wade checked his watch. It was only a little after four-thirty. Roger would be up-to-date with what they were doing by way of the radio. Wade told the rest of them to stay put, and to scrunch down if any cars came by. He took off on foot to where they saw the last of the sanitarium chain-link fence and turned where it turned into the middle of a thick wooded area. Be an easy place to get over the fence with the trees, but how close to the sanitarium buildings would they be?

The fence ran a quarter of a mile, he figured, then turned another ninety degrees and went back toward the buildings. He was within fifty yards of the last building when he saw a blur against the fence and two large, black Doberman pinschers crashed into the fence, snarling and barking. Something set off an alarm that sounded twice as loud in the country quietness.

At the first sight of the dogs, Wade backtracked into the heavier woods, and stood directly behind a large oak tree. He edged to one side and glanced around it.

A Jeep bounced over a rough-cut road to the spot and a man from the rig gave the dogs a soft command. They stopped barking and sat beside his feet. He fed each of the dogs something, then gave them another command and they trotted on down the trail next to the fence.

The man lifted binoculars and studied the woods beyond the fence. Wade pulled in until the trunk of the tree shielded all of his body. He waited.

It was nearly five minutes before Wade heard the Jeep's engine start and the vehicle pulled away, tracing down the rough road along the fence.

Wade wondered if it was vibration sensors or the contact with the fence that set off the alarm. Intrusion alarms of some kind. They would have to watch for that. They would be going over the fence, probably in two places. How would they attract the dogs without setting off an alarm? He wasn't sure.

"Roger, do you read me?" Wade asked his Motorola.

"Softly, Cap'n. Nothing going on down here. No new cars. Can't see the Mercedes. Two delivery rigs have come in. They weren't even questioned, just waved through the gate."

"Might be an idea."

Wade walked back where he could see the fence and made a note where a sturdy tree branch had grown over the fence. It would be one entrance point. He touched base with the people in the car, then checked out the fence along the road. High up near the corner where the car was he found another good entrance point.

Back at the car, he sent Duncan down to relieve Roger. The ex-SEAL came back promptly.

"Want you to check out the security along the fence," Wade told him. After twenty feet, the intrusion expert stopped.

"Yeah, they got some. See that thin wire along the top of the fence? That's a break to make circuit. You pop that wire and the alarm goes off. It pinpoints the exact location of the break on a screen in security."

Wade told him about the dogs attacking the fence when they evidently saw or heard him.

"Yeah that would do it." He stared through the fence at the ground. "Don't see any vibration sensors. You step anywhere within fifty feet of some of them dandies and they wail like a welfare mother who has to go to work."

Wade showed him the two places he wanted to get over the fence.

"Oh, yeah. Limb is high enough we can crawl out on it or hand over hand, get past the wire and drop. Piece of cake."

"Kat?"

Roger flashed his grin. "Hell, Cap'n, if we do it, Kat will bust her bra to do it too. And she will. No worry about Kat."

Back at the car, Kat had returned with the goods.

"Didn't have what I wanted but I got some tranquilizer for horses. Should knock out those puppies in two minutes."

By that time it was dusk. Wade briefed them on what they would do. They brought handguns, but only two of them; Roger and Wade would take in the H & K MP-5 submachine guns.

"We get in, we find Audwin, and we take him out. Hershel, your turn as driver. I want you to take both cars down near the main drive. When we call on the Motorola, you bring up one car and get it through the gate any way you can. Just don't kill the guard. When I call, we'll be three or four minutes from the gate."

"Right. On your call."

It was dark by the time they headed for the fence and the best get-over spot. Kat took out the tranquilizer already mixed into the raw hamburger. She tossed it over the fence in inch-thick balls, then used a dog whistle. Three short bursts they couldn't hear.

"Hope the dogs hear that," she said. A minute later the dogs came toward the fence. The Specialists all had scurried back out of sight. The dogs sniffed, saw no danger, then smelled the hamburger.

Two minutes later the two big Dobermans lay stretched out and snoozing on the woods' floor mulch.

Roger had a coil of strong nylon rope around his shoulder. He went first to the tree, climbing up it, then hand over hand on the limb until he was over the fence. He dropped and put plastic cinch tie strips on the front legs of the dogs.

Kat went up the tree next. When Roger dropped off she worked her way out, hesitated just over the wire, then surged on out and dropped.

When all were across they saw a Jeep driving toward them with lights on. They hid just past the fence in some brush and waited.

"If they spot the dogs we take them out as silently as possible," Wade said.

The Jeep came around a small bend and its light played on the two dogs down and out.

"What the hell?" the driver snarled. He jumped from the Jeep and ran to the dogs. Another man in the Jeep pulled back the pump on a shotgun and a round slapped into the chamber.

Roger had vanished to the rear of the Jeep the moment it stopped. As soon as the second man stepped from the rig, Roger slammed a pair of punches into the side of his neck and the German collapsed. The shotgun fell toward the ground. Roger grabbed it with one hand. If it hit the ground it would have discharged.

"Somebody's got to be inside, Harry," the first guard said in German.

Wade wasn't sure what he said, but he knew it wasn't good. He charged the man, coming out of the dark into the light of the headlamps. The guard got his hand up and reached for a pistol in his waist holster, but Wade slammed into him before he could draw. Wade's pistol jolted down against the guard's head and he slumped on the ground unconscious. They bound both men and gagged them and rolled them into the brush. Ichi drove the Jeep a hundred yards farther along the trail, left it with the lights off, and hurried back to the rest of them.

"We're in, but we don't know where they have Audwin. We find him, we take him out. Simple."

They headed for the lights they could see through the brush. At the edge of the woods, they stopped. They were at the back of the place. Three floodlights bathed the whole area like it was day. There were two doors leading to small patio areas.

Kat took Wade's MP-5, screwed on a sound suppressor, and shot out the closest floodlight. It went out with a loud pop. She aimed and took out the next two.

"Door on the right," Wade whispered and they ran through the darkness toward the patio and its door.

Before they made it, they heard voices. Two men ran round the side of the building calling to each other.

Kat interpreted. "They say, 'What the fuck happened. How could all three bulbs burn out at the same time.' "

Wade touched the door handle. Locked. He took out his picks and worked quickly. It was a by-feel job. Twenty seconds later he had the door unlocked, turned the knob, and edged it open.

"These black clothes aren't going to win any contests inside," Kat said. "We need some whites to pass. Wade, you and I will try to find some clothes. The rest wait here, but keep the door cracked."

Wade nodded and the two slid inside. It was the end of a corridor. To the right were three doors. Kat grinned and opened the middle one.

"Linens," she whispered. They slipped inside and closed the door. Wade found the long doctor coats. They took off black shirts and slipped into the coats. Kat turned her back and Wade grinned. Once in the white coats, they gathered up three more and took them to the Specialists outside. They changed.

They moved down the hall. It soon divided into two wings. Kat, Wade, and Ichi took the left-hand hall, Duncan and Roger the other.

"Find Audwin Derrick," Wade whispered.

Kat led the way. Ahead they saw a nurse's station. One woman sat behind the counter. She looked up and frowned.

"What is this?" she asked in German.

Kat waved it aside. "Things are different tonight. I'm replacement nurse for Audwin Derrick. Which room is he in?"

"One forty-two, but no one said anything about a new nurse. Who are these men?"

"Orderlies in case the patient gets violent again."

"He's never violent."

"Come with me, now," Kat commanded the woman. "Show us where his room is." Kat snapped the last order. The woman didn't move. "Bring her," Kat said in English to Wade, who darted behind the counter and pulled her along.

Kat checked the numbers. One twenty-two. Twenty more rooms. It was only a little after seven o'clock. The corridors seemed strangely empty, Wade thought. But this was a psychiatric facility. Wade pushed the nurse ahead of him. She looked for a way to escape but there wasn't one. Ichi brought up the rear watching behind them.

Just around a corner, Kat saw the right number. A guard sat on a chair in front of the door to 142. Kat walked up quickly. The man looked up at her. He had a pistol in a belt holster.

"I'm the nurse for Derrick, he needs some new meds," she said in German.

"Yeah, why's that?"

"It's time. His new medication."

"Don't think so," the man said. He started to stand. Kat hit him a glancing blow with her pistol and he slumped in his chair. Ichi came up fast and pinned the man in his chair. Kat tried the door. She edged it open and looked inside.

It was a double hospital room. Siegfried sat in an upholstered chair, his mouth open and snoring softly.

★ TWENTY-TWO ★

WRIEZEN, GERMANY

Wade saw Siegfried the same time Kat did. He edged her to one side and eased open the door. It squeaked.

Siegfried came alert at once, lifted the subgun just as Wade lunged forward and slammed it out of his hands with a smashing right fist to the back of Siegfried's right hand.

The German killer swore. The two big men faced each other in the confines of the double hospital room. Kat had out her pistol but Siegfried never even looked at her.

"You won't shoot," he said. "That would bring all of my men in a rush and the ten guards on duty tonight. I hoped you might try to find me."

"It's Audwin we want, not you. Killers like you are a dime a fistful."

"To get Audwin you go through me." Siegfried's hand darted to his pocket and brought out a switchblade knife with a five-inch honed sharp blade. He flicked his wrist and the blade opened and locked in place.

Wade pulled a five-inch bladed knife from a scabbard on his right leg and faced the slightly larger man.

"So come get me," Siegfried said.

Wade held the blade like a rapier, so he could stab forward, or slash to the right or left, up or down. Siegfried held his knife the same way.

"Ichi, silencer. If he puts me down, kill him and get out of here with Audwin."

Siegfried drove in at Wade then, a slashing, fencing type thrust with one foot forward and ready to spring either way. Wade feinted one way, lunged the other way, missed the swinging blade, and cut a small gash on Siegfried's knife-hand arm. The German hissed in surprise and sprang back moving in a tight circle to the left.

This time Wade attacked first, a stutter step and two changes of directions before he drove forward with a killing thrust at the larger man's chest. Siegfried twisted away, taking only a slice through his white shirt but missing skin.

Kat stood to one side with the German nurse held by one arm. She stared wide-eyed at the two big men with knives. The nurse shook her head, wailed softly, and fainted. Kat put plastic strip cuffs around her hands and her ankles, a gag around her mouth, and pushed her to the side of the room.

Ichi threw Wade a towel, which he wrapped around his left hand and arm giving him a place to take a cut when he bored in for a damaging thrust.

They traded two more attacks without drawing blood. Both were expert knife fighters. On the second one a chair tipped over and a small coffee table jolted backward two feet.

Wade smashed into the German's face again, this time with no feint, only power as he held his left arm out to take a thrust. Siegfried slammed his knife blade against Wade's arm on the side of the blade, bounced it off, and slashed at Wade's throat. The honed steel missed by half an inch. With the opening Wade lunged to the side and upward stabbing forward, his blade lancing two inches into Siegfried's left shoulder.

Wade had seen Ichi following the fight with his 9mm pistol. This was not an Olympic contest in fair play. Ichi watched the fighters another few seconds, then tracked Siegfried and shot him in the right shoulder just after he had withdrawn from an attack. The soft *pfffffft* of the shot would not travel outside the room.

The powerful slug cut into the German's shoulder, smashed a bone, and shattered the lead into a half-dozen pieces, some breaking free of skin and tissue, some driving downward into the biceps.

Siegfried's hand slowly relaxed dropping his knife. His face blanched with pain and he fell to his knees. Wade jumped in front of him and gave a powerful upward knee thrust, catching the former spy under the jaw, snapping his head backward, and plunging him into unconsciousness.

"Tie him up and gag him," Wade said. He used the lip mike and called the others. "Duncan, Roger, come back to our hallway. We have Audwin. Quickly."

As soon as Siegfried dropped to his knees, Kat hurried to the bed on the far side of the room where a man lay. He mumbled something and then tried to sit up. He came awake slowly. The drugs were wearing off.

"Audwin Derrick?" Kat asked.

The man blinked. His hair fell around his shoulders. He had a full beard. His eyes showed soft blue but guarded. "Go away," he said, then eased back on the bed and his eyes closed and steady, even breathing took over. He slept.

"He's not all the way clean of the drugs," Kat said. "What do we do next?"

Ichi and Wade finished tying Siegfried.

"Wish I could finish it with this bastard Siegfried right now," Wade said. He kicked the unconscious man on the leg. "We'll meet later. Audwin won't wake up, so he can't walk." He looked around the room. To the side stood a walker and a wheelchair. He pointed. Ichi brought the chair to the bed and he and Kat lifted Audwin into the wheelchair, put his feet on the foot rests, and wrapped a three-inch safety belt around his chest and the back of the chair.

The door edged open and Roger and Duncan came in. They took in the situation at a glance. Roger grabbed the handles of the wheelchair and looked at Wade.

"Which way out?" Kat asked.

"We found a door that led outside on that other wing," Duncan said. "We could see the front gate across the lawn."

"Sounds good, let's go before somebody stumbles in here and complicates the problem," Wade said.

They were halfway down the second hallway aiming for the outside door, when two uniformed guards came out from a side corridor. Both had their weapons out. One gave a cry, and shouted out an order.

"He said to stop where we are," Kat interpreted. "Let's stop and let them come to us. Keep your weapons hidden."

"Wound them only," Wade said. "We don't want to leave any innocent bodies behind."

When the two guards had advanced to within fifteen feet of the group in the corridor, Kat lifted her pistol and slammed a round through the closest guard's gunhand shoulder. He wailed in pain as the other guard lifted his revolver, only to see three handguns and two submachine guns aimed at them.

"Drop your weapons and walk ahead of us to the door," Kat ordered them in German. They put down their revolvers.

The small crowd moved cautiously now, watching behind and ahead. The guards knew something had happened. They must have found the dogs and the tied-up guards on the perimeter.

At the door, Duncan went out and checked around. This area was not highly lighted. There were only two small lights on a concrete walkway that circled through the parklike area.

Duncan waved and the team worked across the lawn.

It was tough pushing the wheelchair. Wade took over, lifted the small front wheels out of the grass, and balanced the chair doing a wheelie across the thick, just cut lawn.

The Motorola spoke.

"I've got two bogies to the right, just past the end of that wing," Ichi reported. He had moved out as a scout in the darkness.

"Hold it here, people," Wade whispered into his lip mike. "Ichi, move up and put them down."

The main party froze in the darkness.

Five minutes later Ichi came on. "No chance, skipper, to do it quiet. How about a diversion?"

"Roger, good idea." He swung up his MP-5 with the grenade launcher under the barrel and took out two HE 40mm rounds from his back pocket. He loaded a round and aimed it in the woods behind the last wing. The explosion in back brought an immediate response. Wade fired one more 40mm round and waited. The two men guarding the end of the wing stormed across the lawn fifty feet in front of Wade as they charged the site of the explosions. They must have thought it could be someone blowing a hole in the fence and invading the place.

Wade heard two car engines start and saw headlights bouncing round the perimeter fence.

"Now," Wade said and the team moved forward with its guest. Audwin still wasn't fully conscious. The cooler night air had revived him some, but he mostly held on as the wheelchair tilted backward more and rolled across the grass.

They were still fifty yards from the lighted main gate. The barrier was closed tightly. Wade was about ready to call for Hershel to bring up the car and broach the gate when a Jeep with four men in it rolled to a stop between them and the gate. The four men spread out in a military formation and went prone in the dim light. Wade could see that they all carried rifles.

The caravan stopped. The Specialists hit the grass and watched.

"Blocking position," Roger said. "We've got them outgunned. Maybe a demonstration will convince them to back off."

"How?" Wade asked.

"We all fire into the ground twenty yards out. The rounds will kill out in the turf without hurting anyone, but the muzzle flashes of those two subguns will scare the shit out of those homeboys."

"Let's do it," Wade said. "As soon as you hear my fire, everyone cut loose. Give it twenty rounds on the subguns and ten on your pistols. Remember, into the ground."

The Specialists responded through the Motorolas. Wade pushed the lever to automatic fire on the MP-5, aimed it carefully twenty feet ahead of him, and pounded off a three-round burst. In the beat of a hummingbird's wings, the others joined in. The firing lasted ten seconds, then the sound faded.

"Lay down your weapons and run back the way you came, or you're all dead," Kat bellowed in the sudden silence after the weapons stilled.

They heard some excited German talk, and then one man lifted up and ran for the wing of the hospital forty yards away. A cry came, then the other three followed him. Their silhouettes against the gate lights showed none of them had his rifle.

"Let's move, fast," Wade said.

Roger had the wheelchair. He tipped it up and jogged across the grass. Two ran ahead of him watching for any dips or ditches. There were none.

Wade went to the Motorola. "Hershel, get the gate, now. We're on our way, maybe two minutes away."

Seconds later they heard an engine growling, then tires squealing to a stop at the gate. Three pistol shots slammed into the night quiet, then they could hear the gate rolling open. Wade sprinted for the opening.

As he came up, he saw the two guards flat on their stomachs near the sides of the gate. Hershel finished cuffing them, then peered into the darkness. He ran back to the Mercedes, turned it around, and backed it halfway through the gate position and opened all four doors.

Far behind the five runners, they heard shouts and then shots. No lead came their way. They charged into the gate position. Kat and Wade tugged Audwin out of the wheelchair and into the backseat of the big car.

"Kat, Ichi, run for the other car, drive out the way we were before and wait for us. We'll be there."

Wade and Roger watched the others get into the car, then when there was room for two, they fired a dozen rounds from the subguns into the air, jolted inside the Mercedes, and it surged away from the gate. Behind them they saw two uniformed guards running up to the gate with their handguns out but already the car was out of range.

Around the bend of the drive, they saw the taillights of the second car ahead of them. Together the two Mercedes powered down the country road. They didn't know the area, and turned twice trying to get back to the main road. They angled for the lights of the small town, then ahead of them they saw two cars with their lights on completely blocking the road from ditch to ditch.

"Back the other way," Wade shouted into the mike. Hershel hit the brakes, twisted the wheel, and let the big car skid around in a near-perfect 180-degree sliding turn. He gunned the engine, straightened out, and raced back the way they had come. Behind him the lead car had tried the same thing, almost made it, backed up, and then churned ahead with gravel flying as they got back on the road and left the roadblock behind.

"They must have radios," Wade said into his mike. "So the folks at the home ranch will know we're coming back. Watch for any road to the right or left so we can miss that confrontation. This time it would be three or four of their Jeeps and an ambulance or two."

A half mile later, they realized there was no other road. They would be up against the homeboys again at the driveway into the sanitarium.

"Let's hope they haven't brought in the local police," Kat said on the radio.

Wade frowned. "I doubt they would do that. They want as little publicity at this point as possible. Then they would have to explain who the patient was who got away."

They drove slower then, trying to figure out what to do.

"The road and that turn-out is more than sixty feet across right there," Hershel said. "Take a lot of rigs to block it."

"My guess is that they'll try. Their jobs are on the line if Audwin gets free."

A minute later they saw the lights of the cars and trucks that had been pulled on the road in front of the sanitarium. Wade had given instructions. The two Mercedes pulled up beside one another fifty yards from the barricade. They saw pickups, vans, two ambulances, and three heavier cars most sideways across the road and the drive out.

"We'll get as close as we can, then on my order, we do it," Wade said. Thirty feet away, the two cars stopped and six people stepped out of the cars and five watched Wade.

"Let's do it," Wade said. "Now."

✶ TWENTY-THREE ✶

The six Specialists threw grenades so they landed just in front of the barricade. Then they looked away and put their hands over their ears.

In the open, the flash-bang grenades don't create the absolute panic and confusion that they do inside a room, but the results were still productive. The weapons exploded, then a series of brilliant flashes pulsated through the night sky followed by a series of seven cracking explosions that would deafen anyone nearby for several minutes.

When the flash-bang grenades went off, the Specialists rushed back into their cars. The weak point in the barricade was the left. The first Mercedes nudged up to the Jeep parked sideways there and pushed the front. The big Specialists' Mercedes's rear tires smoked for a moment, then the Jeep pivoted endways and rolled out of the way. Both Mercedes boiled through the opening and were a hundred yards down the roadway before the surprised barricade people knew what had happened.

Wade used the Motorola. "Everyone on board and in one chunk?"

They all chimed in one at a time the way the small net was supposed to work for quick checks.

"Good. How is our friend?"

Kat had moved into the car with Audwin. She had been tending him since the grenades went off.

"He's almost awake. That must be a powerful drug they had him on. In two hours he should be alert and my guess is hungry."

Two hours later, the twin Mercedes wheeled into the back garage door at the Marshall Export/Import firm and the door rolled down behind them. They all relaxed. Wade had been on a cell phone on the way in and had a friendly doctor on hand with a wheelchair when they arrived.

Audwin could talk now. He jabbered at Kat who had been listening and responding for the past ten minutes. She told him he was safe now.

"Where is my brother and Zedicher?"

"We don't know, but they can't hurt you now. We want you to be checked over by a real doctor. He won't give you any kind of pills or shots. We won't drug you. That's all over. You're free now, Audwin."

"They will kill me."

"No they won't. It's our job to keep them from doing that."

They took Audwin into the complex to two rooms set up as an infirmary complete with a lot of emergency-room equipment. Kat started to leave the room, but Audwin protested.

"No. No, Kat. You must stay with me. I trust you. I can talk with you. Stay."

She did. The doctor checked Audwin over and found him to be in good physical shape.

"His blood pressure is down a little, but the drug they had him on could do that. He's a bit listless, but a good meal and some exercise and he should be as good as new."

The doctor was led out and the group assembled. Audwin looked at them. "Who are these people?" he asked Kat.

She told him.

"Why? Why did you rescue me from my prison of ten years?"

"We knew you were being held against your will. That's not right. We wanted to help you."

He listened to Kat and smiled. "Help me, if I will help you, yes?"

"We can talk about that tomorrow. Don't you want to get some sleep?"

"I slept for the past ten years. I want to learn how to walk again. Will you help me?" Audwin still wore the hospital gown they had found him in. Ichi vanished and came back with a pair of pants and shirt and underwear. He was about the same size as Audwin. Hershel provided some shoes and socks.

They left the room as he dressed. Then he knocked on the door and Kat went back inside. Audwin had walked to the door and he laughed softly.

"Now, big brother, you and your three friends are going to get what's coming to you."

Kat let it pass and took him into the hall. They walked up and down for a half hour, and then she took him back to the same room and asked if he wanted to sleep.

He nodded, then pointed to the other bed across the room. "You sleep there and I'll feel really free."

The next morning Kat woke up early and watched him sleep. She set up a small microphone near the table and went to freshen up and change clothes in her room. When she came back Audwin sat on his bed, dressed and a little glassy-eyed.

"What would you like for breakfast?" she asked him.

"Steak, hash browns, four eggs, and orange juice," he said. Then he watched her closely. She picked up the phone and dialed three numbers, gave the order to the kitchen, and smiled.

"With the breakfast steak it will take about fifteen minutes, can you wait?"

"You're going to do it?"

"Of course. You're a free man, Audwin. You can have or do almost anything you want to. All we need to do is help you protect yourself for a short time."

"Last night I asked you what I must do to help you. Can you tell me now?"

"We have been investigating the two men you mentioned and two more."

"Penrod Griswold and Roderick Selig. Those are the other two. Ten years ago, I would have been on your list. The big five. The five who had fathers who went into the big war common workers, and came out with more than twenty million marks each. Almost ten million dollars."

When the food came, he looked at it, ate some, then stopped.

"I made them furious and they tried to hide me away from society for the rest of my life. They had guns and dogs and fences and all the money in the world to keep me drugged and locked up. It worked for ten years. Do you realize how long ten years is just sitting there and staring at a white wall?"

Kat watched him, but didn't speak.

"I'll tell you exactly how it feels sometime. Today I want to walk down the street. I want to buy something in a store. I want to whistle at a pretty girl, I want to go to a movie. Damn, how I've missed the movies."

"Was there some specific reason they shut you away in the sanitarium, Audwin?"

"Oh, yes. Yes indeed." He laughed for the first time that she had heard. He blinked back wetness and then rubbed his eyes. "Yes, they didn't like what I was doing with my own money."

"I don't understand, Audwin."

"I was giving it away. I gave away about thirty million

dollars before they realized it. My brother found out
first. Two of our smaller firms went into bankruptcy and
he didn't know why."

"What did you do with the money?"

"I gave it back to the Jews. First I used the record and
found as many of the survivors as I could. I gave each
survivor family two hundred thousand marks. No expla-
nation, no hint at why they were getting it. Most of them
were in America by that time. Then in six months I ran
out of names so I simply funded various Jewish benefit
groups, and Jewish charities in Poland and in Israel.
Then Berthold found out.

"By that time I had hidden the black box where they
would never be able to find it. It was my life insurance
policy. I told them that. They forgot it over the years, I'd
guess. They still don't know where the box is."

He pushed the breakfast away and she put it outside
the door. He motioned her to come back to the table.

"They stole the money. My father was one of them
who stole all that money from the Jews."

"The Jews in Warsaw?" she asked.

Audwin looked up and smiled. "Yes. You must know
a lot more about me and the big five than I had figured."

"We know a lot, but we can't prove much. We hope
that you might help us there."

He watched her critically. Her eyes were clear and
steady. At last he looked away. "I could, I could. I'll have
to think about that."

He sipped at a cup of coffee, filled his cup, and sipped
again. Audwin smiled as he looked up at Kat.

"You are a most patient woman, Kat. I like your
name."

"Thank you. What can you tell me about the Transportation Corps of the Nazi Army back in 1942?"

Audwin watched her a moment, then shook his head.
"Not yet. I want to walk the street, to go shopping, to
buy some clothes of my own and a good pair of shoes.

You don't know how long I've wanted a good pair of dress-up shoes."

Kat nodded. "Yes, I think I can arrange that. Two of us will go with you, to protect you. Do you remember Siegfried?"

"Oh, yes. He came to see me at the clinic now and then. A truly evil man."

"He will be looking for you, and I'd guess about a dozen more like Siegfried. We'll go to a small shopping center, would that be all right? It will be some distance from here."

By the time they walked out of the clinic, Roger was there with the keys to a car.

"Shopping time, Mr. Derrick. Right this way."

They went to a shopping area that had men's clothing stores, an ice cream parlor, and stores of a dozen kinds. They had a thousand marks with them and spent most of it. Audwin was so pleased he kissed Kat on the cheek on the drive back.

"The money?" he asked. "Don't worry about the money. When this is over I'll have half a billion marks to play with. I'll pay you back for whatever I spent today."

Roger drove the car to a new building, three miles from the company headquarters. It was for security reasons, she told Audwin.

"Siegfried knows about the other place. He could raid it at any time. You'll be safe here. We'll have four men here at all times. This might not last much longer."

It was an apartment house that Marshall owned. They had Audwin in the middle on the tenth and top floor. Kat had the apartment on one side and Roger, Hershel, and Duncan were in the one on the other side. All were stocked with dishes, food, blankets, TV sets, and radios.

Kat got Audwin settled in his apartment and asked him if there was anything he wanted.

He nodded. "You asked me about Warsaw. I should

tell you. Twice my brother and I got Dad drunk and asked him about Warsaw and how he made all his money. He told us in detail."

Kat nodded. "I'd like to hear. Would you mind if I record this?"

"Please do. I've been wanting to tell somebody for years. As you know it goes back to July of 1942."

⋆ TWENTY-FOUR ⋆

Grant Zedicher straightened his shoulders and quick-
ened his step as he marched through the street toward
the former women's clothing store that was now the
headquarters of his sector of the Nazi Transportation
Corps. He entered the building and looked up at the
huge Nazi flags and banners that covered half the walls
of the two-story-high room. A six-by-eight-foot picture
of Adolph Hitler hung directly in back of his desk, which
sat on a two-foot-high platform. The building had once
housed displays of dresses and other women's clothing.

Sergeant Fritz Hoffman stood near the desk and had
three men sitting calmly on chairs to the left. Yes, three
more. Good. He motioned to the sergeant who went to
the first man in line and spoke to him a moment.

By then, Captain Zedicher sat behind the desk, had
taken off his hat and put it nearby and laid his Luger
pistol on the desk near his right hand. The very presence
of the weapon tended to cow anyone who might become
unreasonable.

A man came in front of the desk and stood stiffly erect. Zedicher looked up and saw the anger and terror mixed on the man's face. He looked down at the form on his desk.

"Herr Sheperstein?"

"Yes. I'm here about a way to keep me and my family off the train."

Zedicher stared at the man. "Why do you think that is even possible? Who told you?"

"Several men. It is common knowledge among those who have some savings, some money. Is it true?"

Captain Zedicher frowned. "Do you think more than one man would know about it, if it were not true?"

Sheperstein shook his head. "No, sir. That's why I'm here. I'm not a rich man. I will give you every mark I have. Everything I own to keep off that train."

"How much do you have?"

"Just over twenty thousand marks. It is in gold coins and diamonds. Some very fine diamonds."

Zedicher waved his hand. "How many in your family?"

"Just myself, my wife, and two children."

"That's not enough money for a whole family. Do you know the risk I take doing this, saving your skins from the train? If the SS catches me I would be shot on the spot, sitting here at my desk." Zedicher watched the Jew. He had long ago come past the point where he considered the Jews as human beings. They were vermin who needed to be exterminated for the benefit of the greater Aryan race. They were cattle who had to be moved from one place to another in cattle cars when they were available or in boxcars. He looked at the man again and cleared his throat. "So, can you raise another ten thousand? If you can bring it all to me by this time tomorrow, your family will be safe and transported out of Poland to Switzerland. Do you understand?"

"Yes, yes. Tomorrow. I'll get the ten thousand somehow. Thank you. Thank you, Captain."

Zedicher waved him away and motioned for the next

man to come. They limited the numbers to three now. It was August and the clearing of the ghetto in Warsaw was tailing down. There had been more than two hundred thousand Polish Jews from Warsaw sent off on the trains so far. There would be another sixty to sixty-five thousand more sent, then the easy money program would be over.

Zedicher did not know where the trains went. He had heard something about the "final solution" to the Jewish problem. But he had never been there and seen it himself. He did his job. He filled the trains on command. That was the end of his responsibility.

That evening, he and others of the Transportation Corps had dinner together. This was unusual since only four of the eight men were officers. The four enlisted were vital in the machinery they had set up for this operation.

Zedicher checked his team. He had selected each man carefully three months ago before the deportations started. They had meshed like a well-oiled machine. There were Selig, Griswold, Streib, and Hoffen, all enlisted, and vital in the operation. Lieutenant Derrick was his second in command in the Transportation Corps and in their small escape route to Switzerland. Lieutenants Doerfler and Mandheim rounded out the eight men in the conspiracy.

Griswold brought in a black box and placed it in the center of the table that the meal had been served on. The box was nothing special-looking. It had been crafted of sheet steel, had double hinges on the lid, and was roughly one foot wide, two feet long, and eighteen inches high. Inside it had been lined with aluminum and brazed in place so it was watertight. The outside had been painted a dull black and it had handles on each end for carrying.

Lieutenant Derrick spoke first. It was in hushed tones in an especially secure building. The food was brought in on special orders. Derrick held up his hand for quiet.

"Gentlemen, we have reached a milestone. We have now converted our holdings into diamonds, and that in total, the estimated value of our gems is slightly more than forty million marks."

There was quiet cheering and grins all around the table. "Yes, that would be about five million marks for each of us, if the war were over tomorrow. But it won't be. There is a deadline we must be aware of, however. The last Jews will be on the train from here by the last day of August. By that time there will be only fifty thousand Jews left in the ghetto. At that time, our work here will be over, and we probably will be broken up as a unit, and men assigned to different corps or even sent to other special services."

"Can we speed up our operation?" Selig asked. "Take ten men a day through the system instead of three, and still only send three a month to Switzerland?"

They looked at Captain Zedicher. He nodded. "Good idea. We must build up our profits as quickly now as we can. We have only a month left. We must work faster. Spread more rumors about our 'service.' Let's have two guards in the headquarters building at all times. We know that some of the Jews still have handguns. We don't want any accidents."

Lieutenant Mandheim stood and the others listened. "This all brings up a serious situation we must resolve well before the end of the month. We haven't talked much about what we do with the diamonds, once our time here is finished. I'm open to ideas.

"As I fear, we will be broken up as a unit. I've seen it happen before. Half of one of my groups in France was shipped out to an infantry company. We must be ready with firm plans what we will do with the box now, and how we shall assemble after the war is over."

They all talked about it and at last Derrick took the floor.

"Gentlemen. My grandfather has a small farm north of Berlin about thirty miles. The ground will be there no matter what happens to Germany in this war. We will win, of course, but even if we don't, the land remains after all of the buildings and residents have been blasted into hell.

"My suggestion is that near the end of our tour here, two of us travel to Berlin on pass, take the box with us, and bury it in a known spot on the farm. It will remain there until after the war and we assemble to open it and distribute the fortune that will be inside."

Again the men all looked at Zedicher. He nodded. "Yes, it's a good plan. Something along the lines I was considering. This is better since one of our families owns the land. Instead of two going for the planting of our money crop, I suggest four of us go. That way we will have a better chance of one or two of the four who will be alive after the end of the war . . . win or lose. We must be realistic. I've been in combat and I know how easy it is to die in a war."

The men agreed and it was decided. There would be no written map showing the location. The exact spot would be memorized by each of the eight men in the group, and nothing written down, ever.

The next day Matthew Sheperstein talked with everyone left in the Warsaw ghetto who owed him money. He had not been pressing anyone. Most thought that once on that train it would be the end of their lives as they knew it. Most thought the trains would go to labor camps. Those who could not work would die. Most of those who could work would be poorly fed and worked to death. What good would money do them?

At last he told two of his oldest friends about his chance to get his family out of Poland, out of Germany to Switzerland. They gave him all the money and jewels they had. They knew they did not have enough to ransom their own families.

Sheperstein felt better than he had in months. Perhaps now he had a way out of this hellhole, away from the butchering Nazis. He told his wife and two daughters. There was a chance they could escape.

The next day he talked to the guard at the door and had a short visit with Captain Zedicher.

"I have the money, an extra fifteen thousand, five more than you asked for. It is in cash and jewelry."

Zedicher's frown softened a little. "Did you bring it with you?"

"Oh, no. I understood I would bring it the day you told us to come for the transport."

"Right, which is tomorrow."

"Isn't there a train due to go out tomorrow morning?"

"There is, but don't worry, you'll be safe enough. I'll bring you in here, send the train on its way, then you'll be safe inside a motorcar with shaded windows and on your way to Zurich, Switzerland."

"What time tomorrow?"

"Seven o'clock. The train will leave at ten. Bring no more than one small suitcase for each of you, the same as the others for the train. That way you won't stand out from the rest."

Sheperstein hurried home with a song in his heart. At long last they would be free. He could get back to his trade of watch making. Switzerland, yes, and then maybe get transport to England, perhaps America. He was so excited he couldn't talk.

The next morning the four Shepersteins went to the side door of the Transportation Corps headquarters. The same guard, Private Selig, was on duty. He told them he knew who they were. They were brought into the room. No one else but Captain Zedicher was there. He smiled, held out his hands, and Matthew Sheperstein gave him the small cloth bag with the gems in it and a thick wad of currency, all German marks.

The captain counted the bills, evaluated the diamonds, and nodded. "It isn't enough, but we'll let you go through. Just so no one knows how little you have contributed."

"No one else knows, Captain."

"Good. Now, I'll have to ask the four of you to stay outside, for a few minutes. Some important army officials are coming and I can't let you be seen in here. Stand in front."

Private Selig took them out and told them where to stand. They huddled against the front of the building. They could see the train waiting across the Umschlagplatz, the deportation point. Lines of Jews came from three directions and were loaded into the boxcars. The parents shielded their daughters from the scene so they would not ever have to remember seeing it.

A half hour later four armed men came down the street in front of the Transportation Corps office. They were pushing thirty men, women, and children in front of them, heading them for the train. On a signal from Selig, two of the men rushed over and prodded the Shepersteins, telling them to move in with the group.

"It's time, you'll have to move to the trains now. We have told you."

"No, we're supposed to stay in this area," Matthew said. "Captain Zedicher told us to stay here."

The two Nazi soldiers hesitated. A quick shake of the head from Selig told them the story, and they prodded the four Shepersteins, down toward the train.

"This is a mistake," Matthew Sheperstein called out. He motioned to one of the soldiers. "The captain said for us to stay there for a minute, then we have an interview with him. He wants to see us. You must take us back."

The soldier swung his rifle and hit Matthew on the shoulder.

"Shut up and do as you're told, or I'll shoot you down right here. You understand?"

Matthew nodded and caught his daughters' hands and hurried them along with the others. It was a short walk. Then they went up a short ramp leading to one of the boxcars on the railroad tracks.

"No, no, there's been a mistake," Matthew screamed. "Captain Zedicher himself said he wanted to see us in his office. We must go back there at once."

Several men and women behind him pushed ahead and he moved up the ramp toward the boxcar door.

"No, no, we're not supposed to be on the train," Matthew screamed.

Just after he said it, a soldier clubbed him on the side of the head from behind. His wife caught him and two others helped drag his limp body into the boxcar.

More and more people crowded into the car. A man helped Matthew Sheperstein lay down at one side, his head in his wife's lap. He came back to consciousness slowly. He blinked, looked at all of the people. The boxcar lurched as the train moved a foot, then stopped.

"No, no, it's a mistake," Matthew shouted. "We're not supposed to be here. It's a mistake."

A man knelt down beside them and put his hand over Matthew's mouth.

"Please, sir, don't make a scene. The Nazis will come in either shooting or clubbing with their rifles. I've seen them do both."

Matthew nodded. The man moved his hand.

"But we're not supposed to be here. I paid Captain Zedicher over thirty-five thousand marks to take us to Switzerland. We have to get off the train."

The man beside him took a long breath and shook his head.

"It's no mistake, my friend. No mistake. I have talked to three other families this morning. Each family gave money to Captain Zedicher, one over half a million marks. They were promised that they would be taken to Switzerland by car. All three of those families are on this train. He lied to you. Captain Zedicher lied to all of them. Only God knows how many he duped."

Matthew Sheperstein heard the man; he nodded a moment, then sat up. This time he didn't shout.

"It's a mistake," he said. "It's all a mistake. We paid thirty-five thousand marks to Captain Zedicher to be taken to Switzerland."

He waited a minute, then he said the same thing. His

wife caught him and rocked him back and forth. Matthew Sheperstein kept repeating the same three sentences word for word until he went hoarse and couldn't say a word sometime late that night as train fifty-seven rolled along across the Polish countryside toward Treblinka.

⋆ TWENTY-FIVE ⋆

On the top floor of the apartment house, Kat stared at Audwin Derrick as he continued telling her about the bribery, deceit, and lying to wring all the money the Nazis could from the Warsaw ghetto Jews.

"I can't imagine what it must have been like for those Jewish families," Kat said. "Things had been so bleak and hellish for so long, then the threat of the trains and a possible way out. Then the realization that they had been lied to and they were going on the trains anyway."

"The whole thing was so horrifying to me, once I learned the truth, that it took me a month to get over it. I was physically ill. For a week I thought I was going to die. The doctor couldn't find anything wrong with me. The family all knew that my father had been an army clerk in some army office in Berlin all during the war. He told everyone that his record there was open, he had nothing to hide.

"When I realized that he was lying, that he had been

one of the men who helped to slaughter six million Jews during the war, I nearly lost my mind.

"I had known about the box before. My brother said our father gave it to him to keep one day when he was an old man. The box contained some mementos from the war he told him. An old uniform, some brass, and I think an old pistol. The box was in one of our company safes for years. I thought nothing about it.

"After I knew about my father's part in the Warsaw shipments of Jews to Treblinka, I began to evaluate everything. One day I took out the box and looked inside it. There was an old uniform, that of a captain in the German Army, and the pistol and some brass and posters. There also was a single edged ledger, much used. In it one of the men had written down the exact names and dates and the amount of money paid by each of the Jews they had taken bribes from or stolen from.

"There it was in black and white by the hands of the men who had done the crime. Name after name after Jewish name and the money, some only a few hundred marks, one over four million. I took the book out of the box and kept it. Gradually I made my plans to try to locate heirs of the men who had paid bribes. I would repay them tenfold what they had lost."

"Could you find any of the heirs?" Kat asked.

"Only a few who had returned to Warsaw after the war. These must have been the few who actually were taken to Switzerland by our fathers back in 1942. I found about twenty, and I took money from the company by faking payments to our regular suppliers. It was all anonymous. I gave each family two hundred thousand marks each, about four million total."

"Your brother didn't know you did this?" Kat asked.

"No, or he would have stopped me. Then I began donating huge sums to Jewish charities and benefits in America and in Israel. By the time Berthold found out, I had given away more than thirty million marks."

"They stopped you?"

"Yes, Berthold knew first and he told the others. They wanted to kill me. He stopped them. I had taken the black box, put the ledger back inside, and hidden it. That turned out to be my life insurance. If they killed me, they never would find the box, and the evidence against them that could ruin their reputations and perhaps bring down their huge companies."

"Audwin, you said there were eight men in on the scheme in Warsaw. Now there seem to be only four huge corporations. Why?"

"After Warsaw, the men from Captain Zedicher's group were split up and sent to other transportation units around Germany. They lost track of each other, but each one knew about gathering at the Derrick farm north of Berlin right after the war was over.

"When Germany lost the war, the troops came home. They waited a month but only four of them came back. They learned later that the other four had been killed in the final battles of the war."

"So they dug up the box?" Kat asked.

"They did. It was exactly the way they had left it. Two of them still alive had been part of the group of four who buried it. Inside were the diamonds and precious stones. No bank notes, which were worthless after the war. They had planned well. Little by little they sold the diamonds. When they were through they had over forty million marks, enough to give each of the four survivors ten million marks free and clear.

"The men went their separate ways, but kept in touch, helped each other, manipulated bids, worked together on contracts and projects. They had families, all became remarkably rich, and all died without regret or remorse."

"So the second generation took over and kept building up the firms," Kat said.

"Yes, all went well until I discovered where the family's money really came from."

"What about your family?"

"I was a bachelor for years. I married late. We had no children. Then when they put me in the sanitarium, they told my wife that I had gone insane and she quietly divorced me and the company gave her a large settlement. She moved to Paris and became a painter."

"So, is that part of your life over?"

"Yes. There wasn't much love there in the first place, I know now. It seemed prudent to be married and have a family."

"What will you do?"

"First, I'll get the book for you. I would expect that you will make certain demands of my brother and the three others in the conspiracy.

"I will not be a hunted man for the rest of my life. I will make my peace with my brother, and take over half of the companies to run as I see fit."

Kat came alert when he mentioned the book. "You remember where you hid the box, and you'll take us there to help you recover it?"

"Oh, yes, I certainly will. I want to see the look on the faces of those four when I show them the book and you're there to tell them what they have to do to make up for the sins of our fathers."

"Is the box far away, Audwin?"

"No, not far. But we should go tomorrow. It's back in the home soil, in the old Derrick farm that's still in the family, about thirty miles north of Berlin." He smiled. "Oh, yes, it's going to be worth all ten years in that hellhole just to see Berthold's face when I show him the book and then give it to you."

Kat nodded, trying to think of all sides of the situation. "Audwin, would Zedicher and your brother guess where you had hidden the box? Would they guess that you put it back on the Derrick farm?"

"They might. These men are not stupid. That animal who works for them, Siegfried, is smart and a killer. I heard a lot about him since I've been in the sanitarium."

"Audwin, I need to talk to the others in my group."

He frowned. "You never told me who you people are. Why did you help me? What's this all about?"

She explained their group's purpose and how they began simply to find out why a young man was killed in Berlin when he began asking questions about his grandfather and how he bribed some Nazis in Warsaw to get to Switzerland.

"From there it just grew and grew and we had a full-scale investigation that kept reaching high into German industry."

"I've got some ideas how we can blackmail these guys to do some good things," Audwin said. "But first the proof, the black book in the black box."

"Will it take more than two hours to drive up there?" Kat asked.

"Not that long. Didn't I hear shooting last night? You people came with weapons?"

"We can take care of ourselves. We know Siegfried will have some of his soldiers with him. I better talk with my boss about this and get it set up."

Audwin turned on the TV set. "I'm not going anywhere. Not until tomorrow morning. I'm making plans what I'm going to demand from the big four. Are they going to be in for a surprise."

Kat went to her apartment next door and called the workroom downtown. Wade picked up the phone.

"Hey, Audwin is hot to get moving. He wants to go up to the Derrick farm north of Berlin tomorrow morning. He asked if we could go along while he digs up the box. He says it has all the proof in it we'll need to make the big four whine and run for cover."

"He asked us to go along?" Wade said.

"True. He's furious at his brother and the other three. Says he has a pile of demands for them or he'll reveal all that their fathers did to steal the money."

"Will Siegfried and his guns guess where it might be hidden? Will he be up there waiting for us?"

"A possibility. We better take the armored Mercedes.

"Shouldn't be a problem. Siegfried knows our address. My guess is that Siegfried is boiling and that he must think we have Audwin here. He could make a try getting him back tonight."

"You want all of us to come back to reinforce you?" Kat asked.

"No, two of you stay there. Send Roger and Duncan back here, now. If anything happens tonight, we'll be ready. You okay there?"

"Remarkably well. I've got it all down on tape, and Audwin is just mad as hell at his brother. It should work out fine. Oh, tomorrow morning. Can you pick us up here at seven? That would get us through traffic and out into the country early. The two armored cars, right?"

"Right. See you at seven in the morning with the rest of the crew."

Wade had sent the Export/Import workers home at noon. Now he and Ichi looked over the layout.

"How would you attack this place, Ichi?"

Ichi scowled. "I'm being inscrutable," he said. "For an all-out attack I'd break out the two four-foot windows on each side of the door and go through there. No way to stop an invasion there. Then I'd use flash-bang grenades, then go in with my manpower. I'd want at least four men, probably six to do the job. He's been in here before and knows there's more to it than this. So he'll have some kind of explosives to work on doors and back panels hoping to break through into the secret area."

"So we all use MP-5s and cut them down," Wade said. "We can have another cleanup from the CIA. I talked to them early on. They said they can keep us out of police hands one more time and move any bodies we don't want seen."

"Sounds right to me," Ichi said. "What time is the appointment for Siegfried to come calling?"

"Anytime after midnight."

Siegfried fooled Wade and the Specialists. He hit the

back door with dynamite a little after nine P.M., blew the
door off, and sent four men into the parking garage and
special weapons section. All weapons were locked up but
the invaders were halfway down the hall to the workroom area and the apartments before Wade heard the
alarm and hurried his men through the locked doors
from the front of the building into the Specialists' lair.

Wade and Roger flattened against the sides of the hall
and waited. One man dressed all in black poked his head
around the end of the hall from the garage area and
eased it back. The second time he poked his head out at
the same place, an MP-5 spat out a single round and a
gout of blood flew out the back of his head as the 9mm
round slammed through it.

All was quiet for a moment. Then in the half-light of
the hallway, Wade saw a grenade bounce down the floor
his way.

"Grenade," he shouted and he and Roger dove away
from the cross corridor to the long hall and waited.
Nothing happened. They edged back to look down the
hall from opposite sides and saw the bomb lying twenty
feet away.

Just then a single round from a rifle blasted into the
grenade, exploding it, sending showers of shrapnel blasting into every corner and crevice in the hallway and the
connecting area.

Wade ducked just in time, but felt a slicing streak of
fire along his shoulder. Two men ran up the hall toward
them.

"Cut down their legs," Wade said. He fired the MP-5
low and to his relief heard Roger's subgun chattering as
well. Four three-round bursts later, the two men screamed,
dropped to their knees, and crawled back the way they
had come.

When Wade heard the alarm that indicated the rear
door had blown, he sent Ichi and Duncan around the
block to the back door to determine how much damage.
The attack came so early that the Specialists hadn't

even put on their Motorola radios. They would be handy to have right now. Wade didn't know if his second team was at the rear of the plant. He couldn't be sure how many men had attacked them. They had three fewer now who could fight. If they came with six, they could still have three.

There was no way into the rest of the complex except down the hallway. A moment later, Wade heard the distinctive stutter of an Israeli Uzi submachine gun. Then there was a moment of silence. Quickly the stammering of the H & K MP-5 came in reply. Good, his boys were on duty.

"You hit by that grenade?" Wade asked.

"Just a scratch," Roger said. "We moving up?"

"Yeah, be ready with full auto assault fire if we need it. Ready?" Roger nodded. They stepped into the hall and ran forward. The corridor had never seemed this long before. After forty feet it branched two ways and they slid into the safety of the branches and looked ahead. To the left they could see from their second-floor level the company's eight vehicles, the ammo room, and the weapons room.

A man dressed all in black tried to take the stairs to the far side, but a single shot from an MP-5 brought him down. He screeched in pain and rolled down the steps dropping his weapon on the stairs.

"You've lost four men, Siegfried. Time to cut and run. I'll pull my men off the rear door. Take your wounded out that way and we'll call it a standoff."

A dozen rounds slammed past where Wade had edged up to the side of the balcony. The slugs cut into doors and walls of some of the apartments.

"Fuck you, Wade Thorne. Come and blow me out of here if you can. I've got grenades stuffed in two of your car's gasoline filler tubes. All set to blast off when I pull the string. This whole damn place will blow sky high and—"

A single shot sounded and the speaker stopped suddenly. There were four beats of silence.

"Okay, okay. Damn that hurts. Tell your gunmen to back off. We're coming out. Two wounded, three hunkered down. You can have the KIA. He's no damn good to me."

"Ichi, Duncan," Wade called from the second floor. "Give him some rope. Let him out the door. Watch the bastard."

All was silent then. Wade heard a groan. He looked over at Roger flat on his belly peering over the ledge at the ground floor.

"Two men with leg wounds heading for the back door," Roger whispered. Wade couldn't see them. "One more with his weapon slung, running for the door." Another pause. "Last joker turned and brought up his Uzi. Siegfried is charging for the back door."

Gunfire erupted again. The stutter of the Uzi, then the chatter from the MP-5.

The sounds died and it was deadly quiet below. Someone yelled in pain.

"Skipper, looks like Sieg and his guys are gone," Ichi called. "All clear below, clear out back."

Roger and Wade went down the steps cautiously. They saw a man lying near the back door, doubled over an Uzi. He didn't move. Quickly they cleared the rest of the building, then put up a temporary man-sized rear door.

Wade took out his cell phone and dialed the CIA number. Someone picked it up on the first ring.

"This is in the clear. I'm Wade Thorne, calling for J. August Marshall. We need a silent cleanup at the rear entrance to the Marshall Export/Import. You were here before. We have two problems."

The person on the wire wasn't sure what to say.

"Get the duty officer on the line quickly." A moment later Wade went over it again punching up the J. August Marshall connection. It was done.

Wade closed the cell phone and looked over the place.

"Ichi, check the vehicles. Be sure there are no grenades booby-trapping them. At least they didn't see our armored cars. They are in the other garage." Wade walked around. The damage could have been much worse.

"Roger, let's look at that scratch of yours."

Roger peeled out of his shirt. The jagged piece of shrapnel still stuck out of the wound. A bloody slice three inches long bled a stream of red life fluid. Wade grabbed a first aid kit from the closest vehicle and wrapped the wound tightly with a bandage. Then he assembled some material and went to work to bandage up the wound properly. A doctor would have to take out the iron and stitch it up. He hoped that the CIA doctor made house calls.

"Roger, you going to be ready to lock and load to-morrow morning?"

"Because of this little scratch? Did I tell you about the time I was in the SEALs and we were in Iran far behind the government troops when this band of about fifty . . ."

Duncan chuckled. "The last ten times you told us that yarn there were a hundred and fifty of the Arabs all with submachine guns."

Roger snorted. "Hell, I don't want to make it sound worse than it was. See these hundred and fifty Iranian crack troops had us pinned down in this dry wadi and they moved up behind an armored personnel carrier. I told our lieutenant that . . ."

Wade went to help get the door pasted back together. It was going to be a long night. The CIA had two bodies to take care of and the doctor might not be here at all. Then he had to be ready to go in the morning. He'd call Kat. At least they could postpone the trip up north a couple of hours.

★ TWENTY-SIX ★

The armored limos arrived at the rear door of the Specialists' headquarters in Berlin at six forty-five the next morning. Wade checked them over.

They were as ordered. They had steel protection around the engine and in all side panels. All the glass in the car was two-inch-thick bulletproof. The undersides of the rigs were steel-plated to protect against land mines. They were as close to a tank as you could drive on public streets. The most recent addition was the new tires that had such strong sidewalls that they could be shot full of holes and still stay operational.

He took a heavy load of guns and ammo. All six of them would be using the HP-5 submachine gun. They would have one sniper rifle, a Stoner SR-25. Wade loved this weapon. It was actually a U.S. Army M-16 modified to fire the 7.62mm NATO cartridge. It was designed for accuracy with a heavy but free-floating barrel, and a bipod attached to the front of the receiver to keep any strain off the barrel. His had a twenty-power scope and a twenty-round magazine. The weapon weighed ten and a half pounds unloaded.

He put in various other munitions: a dozen HE and

four WP 40mm grenade rounds, two tear gas grenades, two fragmentation grenades, a pair of shovels, and extra ammo for the four different kinds of pistols the Specialists carry.

Wade knew that the Zedicher army had automatic weapons. He wondered what else they had. He fully expected to find Siegfried and his men waiting for them at the Derrick farm. It was the most logical place for the box to be hidden. They probably had looked for it all night.

Siegfried would be boiling with rage. He had been beaten twice in the last two meetings. He would want to make certain he didn't lose this time, or his job with Zedicher would be history.

Wade made certain he had ten loaded magazines for each of the MP-5s and ten magazines for the sniper rifle. What else?

Roger came up and looked over the weapons.

"Looks like old times in the SEALs."

"But no boats or rebreathers," Wade said.

"How about a fifty for long range? We've got that fifty-caliber sniper rifle, my old buddy the McMillan M87R. Handy little tool."

"We don't want to shoot down any choppers."

"Hey, Siegfried may have hired one. They can afford anything."

Wade shrugged. "Bring along your fifty. It could be a help. Anything else we need?"

"That chopper would be handy, but we probably don't need it."

They picked up the rest of the crew, met Kat, Audwin, and Hershel, and headed north. Audwin directed. Kat translated. Hershel, their best wheelman, drove the lead car. Wade went with the first rig, with Roger, Uchi, and Duncan in the second.

It took a little over an hour to penetrate the countryside north of Berlin. Wade asked some questions early on. He found out that there were three entrances to the 240 acres of woods, streams, and farmland.

"He says the main gate would almost certainly be blocked if Siegfried gets there first," Kat translated. "He suggests we use the west gate. It's the least used one."

"No dirt roads," Wade said. "These rigs have a ground clearance of about three inches."

"He says it's a paved lane, no trouble for the low-slung car," Kat translated.

A few miles later Audwin talked to Kat again, who relayed his thoughts to Wade.

"Audwin says he isn't interested in killing anyone. There has been enough killing. He says our objective is a two-story red barn toward the north part of the ranch. There is a good road all the way to it."

"First we get inside," Wade said. "My guess is that Siegfried will have some company waiting for us at all three of the gates. That will be helpful since it cuts down his troops at any one place."

They rode in silence until Audwin told Hershel to take the next off ramp. He talked more and Kat turned to Wade.

"He says it's about five miles up this country road. Paved, so no problem. We'll go past on this far side of the estate, then curve around to the west gate. He hopes there will be nobody there."

Each of the Specialists had on a Motorola. Wade made a radio check and got back five responses.

"Ichi, we're looking for a two-story red barn. We'll be going into the estate at a side gate, maybe not so many visitors. Stay ready."

"Roger that."

"Remember, we're in sealed units. We can't shoot out of these rigs. We absorb what they offer and move on."

"How about just out of range of their long guns we stop and I unlimber the big fifty?" Roger asked. "I could take out any transport they have. That way they couldn't reinforce anywhere."

"Sounds reasonable. It all depends on the situation and the terrain."

Four of the men chimed in on the age-old military axiom and they laughed. But it was all too true.

"Ahead about a mile," Kat said, cutting into the laughter. "Audwin says it's on the left. A small house, a gatehouse, and a shed. No barn. Nowhere to hide a lot of power."

They watched as the house ahead on the single lane paved road came into focus. They couldn't see anyone around it. As they approached they could tell nothing blocked the driveway into the place. The house looked vacant.

"Car behind the house," Kat shrilled.

"Two cars behind the shed," Wade reported. "Once we get off the road here, gun it straight ahead down the blacktop, Hershel. We have to hope they don't have a leftover bazooka or an RPG."

They took the first rounds from an automatic rifle around the back of the house. The rounds chipped paint and nudged the two-inch glass and bounced off.

"Hit it," Wade yelled. The heavy car picked up speed slowly. Now it took rounds from the whole right side. Wade could hear the rounds hitting the tires, felt the air swoosh out, and the armored rig dropped two inches. The new tires weren't made for this extra weight. Maybe ten miles run flat.

"Razor strip just ahead," Kat bellowed. "It could shred all the tires."

Hershel jerked the wheel to the left and only the rear right tire went over the strip much like the ones police use to stop runaway cars. The dagger steel spikes pierced the right rear tire, letting the rest of the air gush out of it, but the big armored Mercedes rolled along.

Then they were a quarter of a mile away. An occasional round bounced off the big car.

"Stop it here," Roger said. "I'm ready with the fifty. Two rigs are starting to follow us."

The car stopped and Roger rolled out of the car, the big McMillan cradled in his arms. He had a five-round magazine loaded and locked. He rolled once, came up with the bipod legs spread, and five seconds later got off the first shot. He watched through the twenty-power scope as the round hit the sedan in the radiator and must have blown it away and continued on to mess up the straight six block. The car wavered, then jolted off the blacktop road into a field.

Roger had worked the bolt for a fresh .50-caliber armor-piercing round. He sighted in. The second car had stopped and two men ran over to the injured one. Sitting duck. Roger put his next round into the side of the engine and saw metal and glass fly as the engine gushed a huge cloud of steam. The third car moved quickly then and skidded behind the small house to deny Roger another target. He put one round through the back door of the house, then sprinted for the big Mercedes with a rear door open.

"Two down, boss. The third one hid behind the house. They'll go slow coming after us."

"But the word must be out. They will have radios to warn the others. How far to the red barn?"

"Two miles," Kat said after she asked Audwin.

"How far from the other gates is the barn?" Wade asked.

"Four miles to the main gate, six to the east gate," Kat said.

"Not far enough. They're moving this way right now. Find out if there's one road from the gates to the barn."

"Yes."

"Where does it join this road?"

"A mile from the barn."

"When we hit the junction, we'll split up. Roger, you copy?"

"Copy, Cap'n."

"Roger, your car will stay at the junction, or slightly this side of it wherever your tactical senses dictate. You're our roadblock. Use the fifty with them as far down the road as possible. A mile, a half mile. Put their vehicles out of business. Then maintain the roadblock if any of their troops come up the road."

"They'll split into groups and go around us," Roger said.

"Agreed. So as soon as you kill their vehicles, drive back to us at the barn and set up a perimeter defense."

"With three guys, Cap'n?"

"You'll have five or six, maybe seven if Audwin can shoot. Best bet we have right now. Depends how many men they have."

"Sounds familiar, Cap'n," Roger said.

"Here's the fork in the road. Set up that fifty. We'll see you three in the barn."

Audwin saw the red barn ahead and said something to Kat.

"He says pull around to the back. There's a wagon-sized door there."

"Ask him if the box is inside the barn," Wade said.

"He says it is, and not hard to find. Ten minutes at the most."

"Let's hope so and then we can button up and move out of here."

They all heard the rifle rounds hitting the armored car at about the same time.

"Then again, it might not be that simple," Hershel said. "I make it two rifles inside the barn."

"This rig is our best cover. See if you can drive it right inside the barn through that wagon door."

The rear door hung open. A pickup truck angled toward it but there was room enough for the Mercedes to brush the pickup aside and slide into the barn.

For a moment it went dark, then the interior lightened as their eyes got used to the lower light level. The two rifles fired from the left. Hershel and Wade slid out the right-hand doors with their MP-5s. Wade went to the front fender and peered around. Hershel looked past the rear

fender. Wade sent a dozen rounds toward some bales of
hay where he figured the riflemen were. There was no
response.

Kat wormed out of the front seat on the right side
with her MP-5. She moved up behind Hershel who
trailed six rounds just over the tops of the bales of hay
twenty feet away.

"What are they trying to do, get themselves killed?"
Kat asked.

"Not sure. There's a small door back there that's protected. They could slip out there and be away free."

"Maybe they did."

Both rifles lanced three rounds into the mix, three
slamming under the rear of the Mercedes and three
under the front. Wade had the heel of his boot almost
torn off by one round. He returned fire with a dozen
angry rounds.

"Give it up," Kat called in German. "You're surrounded. This is nothing worth dying for."

Six more rounds were shot into the air. Kat sniffed,
then again.

"Fire," she whispered to Hershel. "Get the car and
Audwin out of here." She saw Wade react to her talk and
knew that the mike picked up on his Motorola.

"Yes. I can hear the orders now. If they come to the
barn, that must mean the box is there so burn the place
down and we destroy the box."

"Grenades?" Kat asked.

"One each." Kat reached inside her shoulder bag and
took out an HE grenade and pulled the pin.

"Now," Wade said on the radio. They both threw the
deadly fragmentation grenades. Four point two seconds
later the fuses burned down and the grenades exploded
almost at the same time just beyond the bales of hay.

They heard shrapnel whining over the hay and into
the roof.

"I'll get it," Wade said and sprinted the twenty feet for

the baled hay. Kat was right behind him, her MP-5 up covering anyone she saw. Two of the bales had been knocked down. They found both men just in back, riddled with sharp, jagged chunks of steel. The fire they had set was six feet wide and growing. Wade made sure the men were dead, then looked at the fire.

"We better get that knocked down in another two minutes or the whole damned barn is one big bonfire." He charged ahead and rolled a stack of six bales of hay on top of the blaze in the loose straw. That put out half of the fire. Kat stomped out some of it and beat down more with a handy gunny sack.

Five minutes of stomping and flailing, the last of the flames were gone. All that was left were smoke ghosts heading for the roof and the swirl of blue-tinged air that eddied around the doorway.

The Motorolas came on.

"Sounds like you guys are having all the fun," Roger said. "The bad guys just showed over the first little rise. About a mile off. I'm lining up my first shot. Near as we can tell there are four vehicles. I don't know how many men that makes, but too damn many. Okay, I'm sighting in. Yes, no windage. First round." They heard the deep crack of the round in the chamber as the heavy chunk of armor-piercing bullet screamed out the long barrel toward its target, a vehicle a mile down the road.

"Shit, missed it to the right. Recalibrating, ready with another round, yes, looks better. No change in target location. And fire."

In the barn, Wade helped Audwin out of the armored car. Kat spoke softly.

"Now is the time to get the box." Wade looked around. There were stalls to the left where horses evidently were still kept. The hay would help feed them. On the other side several farm machines were parked in a row. Audwin went toward the horse stalls. There were no animals there now. He walked up to the feed box with a sloping wooden top. The box was four feet square and contained a mix of alfalfa and grains and probably some molasses, Wade figured.

Audwin pointed into the box.

"Got the sonofabitch," Roger shouted in the Motorola without realizing it. "Right in the kisser. Blew his damned engine to hell and gone. Now where is the next one?"

Kat looked puzzled. "You mean it's in the feed box?"

She had asked him in German. He shook his head and jumped into the feed bin digging out the mixture with a bucket and dumping it on the barn's dirt floor.

"The box must be under all the feed," Kat said. "We better all dig."

It took them three or four minutes to scoop the rest of the feed out of the big box, then Audwin pawed at the wooden floor. He found a loose board and pulled it out, then a half dozen more until they could see the dirt. He asked Kat for a shovel. They brought one from the armored Mercedes. He dug down a foot and hit something. He yelped.

"This is it," he said in German. Kat translated.

Wade stepped into the box and finished the digging. He pried the black painted box up on one end, then tugged it out of its long-time home. He lifted it out and Audwin took it and set it on the barn floor.

The Motorola spoke again. "Damn, the fuckers are splitting up. One going right, two to the left. I'll take the left ones. Just get a new sight, moving at an angle, so I lead the little bastard just like in Iran."

They heard the big gun fire and a shout of glee from Roger. "Two down. There are four, no five men walking, trying to get a ride in the next machine. That's my next target. They are still a mile and a half from the barn."

Audwin lifted the top of the box and showed them the contents. The old uniform with captain's bars, a Luger pistol, some German WWII medals, and a three-hole single-edged ledger. He opened it and pointed to the rows of neatly inscribed names, dates, and amount of marks tendered.

"The bastards," Kat said, fury pouring out of her. "Now I really believe they did it all."

"Move," Wade said. Kat carried the black book, Wade had the box, and they hurried back to the rolling fortress. They all rushed inside and Hershel started the engine.

"Damn, missed. Hey, guys, a big black Mercedes got past me on the right. He's swinging toward you. It's about half a mile off on some kind of dirt service road. No more targets. I lowered three of them, the men are over a mile away. I've counted fifteen. The black Mercedes moved faster than I thought it would. Sorry. Moving your direction."

"Any other way out of here?" Hershel asked Audwin. Kat took the answer and shook her head.

Hershel backed the heavy rig out and had just started to turn it around to head back down the road when a blur came at them out of the north. The heavy Mercedes from the enemy slammed into the armored car at thirty miles an hour. They didn't see it coming. The Mercedes was heavy enough without armor to jolt the front wheel off the axle, to smash in the left front fender grinding it against the armored steel around the engine, and to smash the radiator free of both sets of hoses.

None of the passengers in the armored car had on seat belts. Kat flew out of the front seat and flailed into Hershel who had a flash of a warning and held on to the steering wheel in a death grip with both hands. He absorbed Kat's force and kept her from being injured. Wade had just sat down in the driver's side seat and was slammed away from the door and dumped on the center of the seat and unharmed.

Neither car could move. They were nearly welded together.

Wade looked out the window. The far ones had been crazed with cracks but his side was unharmed. He realized they couldn't jump out of the car. The other car had let out its men before the crash and now they surrounded the armored rig.

Siegfried came near Wade's window. He held a strip of cloth a foot long. It was dripping wet.

"Gasoline," Wade said softly.

He saw Siegfried mouth the words "gas tank," then move to the rear of the car where the filler tube was. Once that burning gasoline hit the vapors in the big gas tank, the whole armored car would explode and become an instant funeral pyre for everyone inside.

✭ TWENTY-SEVEN ✭

ZEHDENICK, GERMANY

Kat saw the dripping cloth and recognized the words "gas tank" as well on the lips of the man she guessed must be Siegfried. She pushed down on the door handle gently, then rammed the heavy door open with her foot. The edge of the door hit Siegfried in the knee and side and drove him to the ground.

His men stood around without direction. Nobody told them to shoot into the car if a door opened. Kat pumped off four rounds from her automatic but didn't hit anyone and jerked the door closed and locked it.

Siegfried scrambled to his feet. He had lost the swatch of cloth he would have used in the car's fuel filler tube. His knee was shaky, he held his side as if he had a broken rib. With a savage intensity he looked around for the cloth, found it, and stood again.

Now he stared at the big car, snapping a cigar lighter. Each time a three-inch blue flame shot from the device.

"If he gets within a foot of the fuel cap, we all bust out of here shooting our subguns," Wade said. "He's moving, we better get ready."

"Doesn't a rig like this have a locking gas cap?" Kat asked. "I can't see it from here, but I'd bet a bucket of schnapps that it does."

"Hell, yes, it does," Wade barked. "The drivers asked me about putting more gas in when they arrived."

"Where's our SEAL?" Hershel asked on the Motorola.

"Roger, where the hell are you?" Wade asked his radio.

"We just came over the brow of the hill behind you. Small problem I see. We've got six guns here on line, ready to fire. Stay buttoned up."

Just as Roger said it, the people in the wounded armored car saw Siegfried walk to the front of the big Mercedes where the hood had popped open. He took his lighter and set on fire a towel that must have been gasoline-soaked. It flashed into fire and he threw it into the engine compartment.

"Could hit the fuel line and we'll be in trouble," Wade said.

The gunfire from outside came through then. Siegfried turned at the sound of the firing and caught a bullet in his left shoulder. He raced behind the welded-together vehicles.

Two of the opposing forces went down to bullets. A half dozen dropped their arms and held their hands high over their heads. Wade watched the smoke and fire from the engine. So far just the towel burning, he guessed.

The army came marching in. Roger held an MP-5 in one hand and the Stoner sniper rifle in the other and both blasted out instant death. Ichi had up his MP-5 in one hand and his .45 automatic in the other. Duncan steered the big car with one hand and fired out the window with the MP-5. It made a devastating noise to anyone not used to a war.

Siegfried ran a zigzag pattern to the front door of the barn and dove through. Four of his men ran for the barn. Two more went down with wounds and three surrendered.

Kat, Wade, and Hershel slid out of the wounded tank

and bent low behind it until Roger brought his army up to them. Wade ran around to the front of the Mercedes. The fire had burned out. The fuel line had not ruptured. The threat there was over.

Two shots came from the back of the barn but missed.

"What took you so long?" Wade barked at Roger.

"Well, there was this little German girl," Roger began. Then he grinned. "You got it?"

"Right," Kat said. "It's in the car with Audwin."

"We lost one of our vehicles," Wade said.

"Yeah, so, we gonna sit here and let them have tea and crumpets in there?" Roger asked.

"Let's put about a hundred rounds into the barn, then we'll get some voice going," Wade said.

The six Specialists found firing positions around the three vehicles and on a word from Wade began shooting. Wade dug into the backseat of the dead Mercedes and found the two tear gas grenades. He gave one to Roger and held one himself. He gave a cease-fire and nodded at Roger. They threw the two grenades. Roger's went in the small door in front. Wade's bounced off the windowsill and fell outside. The breeze blew toward the barn.

Two minutes later three Germans came rushing out the door rubbing their eyes. Then one more came out.

"At least six went in there," Wade said.

"Around each side," Roger said. Ichi and Wade went right, with Kat right behind them. Roger, Duncan, and Hershel charged around the other way.

Wade got in back of the barn in time to see two figures running into some trees fifty yards to the left and down a slight hill. One was tall with red hair. Siegfried.

"We have two runners, Ichi on me. The rest clean up the barn and safeguard that book. Let's go."

Ichi, the fastest runner in the Specialists, and Wade charged down the hill toward the fleeing pair. They kept twenty yards apart. Ichi surged ahead, then slowed for Wade. They came to the trees and expected a bush-whacking, but nothing materialized.

"Siegfried is still in a panic. He'll start thinking better quickly. We've got to watch out." They came to a small rise with the ground slanting up seventy-five yards ahead of them to the top of a ridge. Just as Ichi and Wade started up the hill, automatic weapons opened fire from above. The two dove for cover. Wade found a downed log he squirmed behind, and Ichi discovered the pleasures of foot-high boulders on an open slope. The firing lasted for twenty seconds, then stopped. Neither man was hit.

"Surprises," Ichi said. They ran up the hill spreading thirty yards apart to make it harder to ambush them the next time.

At the top of the slope they stopped. Ichi turned his head slowly, not breathing. He turned and pointed north, uphill. It was away from the barn and the other buildings they could see now behind and below them. It was the wildest part of the estate.

It was all uphill now. Ichi concentrated on the ground. At first the trail was easy to follow. Two city men floundering through the woods.

Ichi came to an open spot in the brush and woods and surged into it, then darted back behind a two-foot-thick tree. The shooter was too anxious and shot at the spot where Ichi had been. Ichi grinned. "Old Indian trick I learned," he said.

They went around the open spot working through trees until Ichi picked up the trail again. Almost at once there was a shot. Ichi grabbed his shoulder and dove behind a tree. Wade had his MP-5 on full auto and he sprayed the area ahead where the shot must have come from with eighteen rounds. He heard a scream, then a long sigh. He checked Ichi. The bullet had dug through his shoulder, probably bouncing off a bone.

Wade put a quick bandage on the wound to stop the bleeding. "You're out of it. Go back to the car for a real bandage and get that bleeding stopped. I can't do it here." Then Wade charged up the hill. He found the dead

German sagging behind a tree. He had two rounds in his forehead.

One on one.

Wade moved uphill more cautiously then. He could see the trail, bits and pieces of the woods' flooring of leaves and mulch disturbed. A small shrub or grass bent over from a footstep. He came to a section with car-sized boulders.

Wade stopped at the first one and listened. He could hear nothing moving ahead of him. He took a protected position behind the big rock and called.

"Siegfried, don't you like an even fight? Is that why you ran off like a whipped cur? Do you still like to kill women and little girls, Siegfried? Or is throwing young men off a cliff more to your taste?"

Wade listened closely, but nothing made any noise.

"I'm coming to get you, Siegfried. Just you and me now. Nobody to get in our way. No government to tell us what to do. No sense of outrage over a lost eye or a lost family. Just you and me."

A scream of rage from somewhere ahead. Siegfried had angled to the left. Higher in the rocks, Wade found the first traces of blood. Three drops on a flat rock. They splattered. Must have come from up high, a shoulder. Did he see Siegfried get hit? He couldn't remember.

Across the rock field, and higher yet, into timber again, sparser now, less underbrush. Pine trees of some kind. Why no shot from Siegfried? Had he lost his weapon? He had a pistol on his belt when he played with the gasoline-soaked rags. Surely he'd pick up an Uzi. Wade shook his head. He'd heard enough Uzis shooting at him today to last for a serious number of years.

Ahead he heard a cough. Siegfried? Maybe he was hurt more than it had seemed. Wade moved faster then, didn't move as well from cover to cover. He was mid-way between a substantial tree and a large rock when a weapon ahead stuttered three times. Something hard and hot hit Wade's left shoulder and powered him backward a step, then he lost his balance and he fell. He dropped the MP-5 and caught himself, rolled half over and stopped. In a heartbeat he leaped back to his feet, grabbed the submachine gun, and dove behind a tree.

Damn shoulder. It hurt like fire. He looked down and saw blood. He tried to hold out his arm to see the wound better where the round went through his shirt. Moving his arm created an open hearth of pain that boiled through his shoulder and into his brain. He gasped. He slung the MP-5 and pulled out the big handkerchief they all carried. They joked about them but they made excellent emergency bandages. Most of them had used them before. He wrapped it around his sleeve, under his arm, but there was no way to tie it. He remembered his grandmother putting a bandage on a finger. She wrapped it tightly, then had both ends and tied them together. He had one end and no way to tear it. After this both ends of his kerchief would be torn down four inches.

He kept the so-called bandage in place by holding his arm against his side, and moved ahead. He didn't know if the bleeding had stopped or not.

Fifteen minutes later he saw Siegfried entering some brush less than a hundred yards ahead. He carried an Uzi and he moved with some hesitancy. Wade didn't see a bandage.

Wade hurried again. He charged from cover to cover now, knowing he had to close the gap, get within good range for a shot. He'd take out Siegfried any way he could. Any unfair advantage would be gladly accepted. This was not an Olympic sporting event.

They came within range of each other suddenly. The terrain had grown increasingly rocky, now they were on an upslant that took some handwork to make it up some of the shale stretches.

Wade came into the last slant upward of fifty yards. It was shale and slab rock, hard enough to navigate without someone aiming an Uzi at you.

Wade saw Siegfried who had evidently been to the top and was starting down. Maybe there was a drop-off, something impassable. The Uzi barked. Wade dove for cover, missed it, and the round missed him. He took careful aim and sprayed three rounds at the big German. All missed.

Wade swung behind a ledge and waited. He checked his magazine. Good time to change. He felt in his pocket. Nothing. In the big pouch at the back of their action jackets he always carried three loaded magazines. Now there were none. He groaned. His quarry in sight and he was almost out of rounds. He took out the magazine in the MP-5 and hefted it. Three, maybe four rounds left and one in the chamber. He pushed the magazine back in place, shifted the lever to single shot, and waited.

Rocks rolled. They slanted well away from Wade. There wasn't enough really loose material to make a killer slide anyway. He took a look. Siegfried had moved down twenty feet to a depression where he had ninety percent cover. Not exactly pistol-shot range. He checked his pockets again. No extra mags for his .45 autoloader. At least he had the twelve-round magazine. He had fifteen shots left. He'd have to be careful. Siegfried might guess at his lack of firepower and charge. Might.

He waited fifteen minutes. Siegfried hadn't moved.

"It's over, Siegfried," Wade shouted. "Throw out your Uzi and your handgun and you live."

The Uzi came up and six rounds slanted off the rocks around where Wade's head had been.

"Come and get me, asshole."

"It's all over. We have the box and the book. We can put several people away for murder. The trolley ride is finished."

Three more rounds from the Uzi slapped rock near Wade.

He waited a half hour this time. "Getting thirsty up there, Siegfried? You come down and we'll give you all you can drink and eat. The war is over. The reign of King Zedicher is over, too. You're going down hard, but you'll be alive. How many men have you killed, Siegfried?"

There was no answer.

"Probably thirty, maybe thirty-five. You were good at it. Too damn good. Now, the game is over. The final hand is played out. You've lost again."

Siegfried charged. He evidently had left his hole and worked down the slope silently as Wade waited. Now he was ten feet away when he stormed over the shale and dove at Wade where he sat below his protective shelf of rock.

⋆ TWENTY-EIGHT ⋆

The first hint Wade had that he was in trouble came with a scream from Siegfried as he dove over the lip of the ledge and smashed into Wade. He had just put down the MP-5 and checked his watch.

Siegfried landed on Wade's side. Automatic survival instincts took over and Wade slashed at the form on top of him with the side of his hand, landing the blow on the side of Siegfried's neck. The big man grunted and wrapped his arms around Wade who struggled to bring up his .45 autoloader. He couldn't get it out of the holster.

Siegfried screamed again as Wade jolted his fist into the attacker's bleeding shoulder that rested inches from Wade's face. Siegfried's left arm relaxed a moment from the surge of pain and Wade exploded upward, getting his feet under him and throwing Siegfried off of him. Wade rolled and slid down the rock slab six feet.

Both men drew their pistols and covered the other.

"I've got a full magazine, Siegfried. Where do you want the first six?"

"I'll put two through your head so it won't matter where you try to aim," the former East German agent spat.

"It doesn't have to be this way, you can live, Siegfried.

Put down the weapon before you bleed to death from that shoulder."

"Bastard! Go ahead, shoot me, I won't go to prison. I'd die in a week there. Go ahead and shoot me." He pulled up his aim to Wade's head and his finger pulled on the trigger.

Wade waited as long as he dared. The man was going to shoot. He changed his aim from midbody to right shoulder and fired. The second before his round went off, he heard the startling click of the hammer of the other man's weapon hitting an empty chamber.

Wade's round slammed into Siegfried's right shoulder, staggering him backward.

"Empty," Wade said.

"You were supposed to kill me."

"Better luck next time." The two men stared at each other. "You're an easy man to hate, Siegfried."

"So go ahead. Now's your chance. You've got rounds."

Wade watched him. He didn't look so big, so terrible, so deadly now as Wade had thought about him being for years. Any of those early Cold War days he would have killed Siegfried without another thought. Now that he had him under his gun, it was different.

"Shoot, damnit," Siegfried bellowed.

"Considering it. You owe me big time. You owe Vivian and Chrissy. You owe the Silokowskis. You owe that CNN reporter you killed. Maybe we all should get a piece of you. Yeah, I like that. So move on down the slope. Oh, Siegfried. Be careful you don't slip and fall. I wouldn't want you to miss your trial or your hanging because you had stubbed your toe."

Siegfried glared at him and began working down the shale and sheet-rock slope. It was slow going. They made it to the tree line and Wade relaxed a little. He had taken the empty automatic from Siegfried but hadn't patted him down. That would be too dangerous right now.

They worked into the heavier tree growth. It seemed a long way back to the barn. Twice Wade caught himself getting light-headed. He was sure he hadn't lost that much blood. He carried his left hand inside the buttons on his shirt to take pressure off the shoulder.

Twice Siegfried stumbled, brayed in pain, and hit the ground. He had lost blood from wounds in both shoulders. Wade watched and waited. He didn't offer to help the big man get up. Wade stayed a safe six feet away, watching him. Was he getting ready to make a dramatic, desperate move or had he given up? Wade wasn't sure. It was hard to read Siegfried right now. Half of him was pain and hurt and anger at losing, but there still had to be the killer instinct that had made him such a dangerous international hit man.

They went through more trees, across the little meadow where Ichi had been bushwhacked, and faced a steep downhill slope when Siegfried stopped. Without warning he turned from six feet away and charged.

He covered the distance in less than two seconds and Wade looked up in surprise as the big man was three feet in front of him. He tried to lift his .45 auto but there wasn't time. He triggered a round that hit the dirt in back of Siegfried, then they were locked together with the larger man's arms wrapped around Wade and falling to the ground.

Wade lost the .45 in the fall and couldn't find it. His MP-5 over his shoulder fell away and all he had left was the five-inch blade in its sheath on his right hip. He surged upward and tipped over Siegfried. As they rolled, Wade pulled the knife free and waited for a chance to use it. He was still locked in the bear hug and they rolled again.

Wade hissed in pain as they both came down on his wounded shoulder. Then he got his hand free and pounded it four times into the bloody gunshot wound on Siegfried's shoulder. The German bellowed in pain and swore in three languages. He let go with the crushing hug and smashed his big fist into Wade's shot-up shoulder.

Waves of pain surged through him and he saw the daylight begin to fade, then he struggled to remain conscious and blew away the darkness and rolled again until he was on top of Siegfried. He spread his legs to maintain his position.

Before he could lift his hand with his knife, he saw Siegfried's arm flash up with a shiny four-inch blade in it. Wade slashed at the arm with his knife, felt the blade slice in through shirt and cut into flesh. Siegfried screamed and dropped the blade.

Wade brought his knife down and held it six inches over the other man's face. Siegfried's free hand darted up and caught Wade's wrist and began forcing it upward. Wade brought all of his strength and used his on top position to bear down. Slowly he reversed the direction of the blade and millimeter by millimeter he forced the double-sharpened point down toward Siegfried's throat. The big man's eye went wide as he saw where the blade was pointing. He bellowed in anger and made one last surge with his left hand to push away the knife. Then his hand buckled and Wade's knife slashed down.

Wade's wrist bounced off Siegfried's hand and jolted the blade sideways. Before Wade could stop it the blade made a slashing cut across Siegfried's one good eye. The German killer screeched in agony, and raw terror, then passed out.

Wade rolled off him, stared at the sliced open eye. He'd never seen such a terrible wound. The eye was ruined. Siegfried was blind. He tied the German's hands together in front of him with the last plastic riot cuff from his back pocket.

Immediate surgery might save the eye. Wade changed his mind at once. The blade had slashed deeply across the eye socket. It must have sliced more than halfway through Siegfried's eyeball. There was no chance his sight could be saved.

Wade used the Motorola. "I'm on the hill about five hundred yards above the barn, almost due north. I need some help. We have one man dead, and Siegfried badly wounded. He can walk. Two of you closest get up here and bring the big first aid kit."

Wade waited five minutes, then gently slapped Siegfried's face until he regained consciousness. Almost at once he screamed and passed out again. The third time Wade brought him to, he stayed awake.

"Kill me now, damn you, or give me your automatic so I can do the job. I'm blind now, I know it. I won't be blind and in prison, too. Shoot me, you bastard, Thorne. I'm glad I killed your wife and daughter. I enjoyed it, yeah I loved it. You hate me because I did that so kill me now before anyone else comes. Shoot me, you sonofabitch!"

Wade tried not to listen. He made a wad of cloth from a piece of his shirt and put it over the bullet wound in his shoulder. It stopped most of the bleeding. The light-headedness came back. He hadn't lost that much blood. From one little rifle bullet? He'd been cut up three times that much and hiked out of it. Damn, why was this different? He grinned. Yeah, that had been when he was twenty-two. He wasn't twenty-two anymore.

Duncan and Roger came puffing up. Twice they had called on the Motorola. Wade bellowed out a call for them to follow. They stared at Siegfried where he lay. They shook their heads and looked away. Duncan had the first aid kit. He put a compress over Siegfried's eye over his protest, and wrapped it fast with a bandage around his head. The shoulder wounds were easier to treat on both men.

It took them almost an hour to hike down the slope to the red barn. They had to lead Siegfried. The situation below had stabilized. Kat had taken the weapons from the prisoners and run them off to walk back to wherever they came from.

The black box and the black book and Audwin were safe. He had toured the old barn and now sat on the grass soaking up the surrounding country he hadn't seen for a decade.

"I'm moving back out here," he said. "This is where I want to be for the rest of my life."

"Might be hard to run Bavaria Limited from here," Wade said.

They all squeezed into the remaining armored car and headed for Berlin. They went out the side gate where they came in. No one was there.

BERLIN, GERMANY

Kat had used the cell phone, and by the time the car reached the home office's rear door, there were two police cars and the CIA's safe doctor waiting for them. They all knew each other. The doctor made a preliminary examination of Siegfried's eye and called an ambulance to take him to a hospital. Kat had given the police enough evidence and promised more evidence on Siegfried to tie him to the CNN reporter killing. The police arrested him and he landed in the prison ward of the hospital.

"He's lost the eye," the doctor said. "But we don't want him to get infection in there. It's so close to the brain that it could spread and we wouldn't be able to try him for murder and put him away for a hundred and fifty years of darkness."

Wade's shoulder wound was dressed and his arm put in a sling. It was only three in the afternoon.

"Good day's work," Wade told the crew. They all split for showers, clean clothes, and food.

Later that afternoon, they studied the record book. They found John Silokowski listed along with the 4.5 million marks. Each listing was followed by initials evidently of the man who had taken the bribe. In the Silokowski entry the initials were GZ.

"Nice way to put a noose around your neck," Kat said. "Keep detailed records of your crimes."

"Yeah, but what can we do with it?" Wade asked.

"We can't turn it over to a war crimes court. You can't prosecute a son for the crimes of his father. I'd bet that there isn't a single legal means we can use to get back at these people."

"We'll think of something," Kat said. "First we have to gather all of the evidence we have against Siegfried on the two killings we know about, George and the CNN guy. Let's get all we have down in black and white to turn over to the police. Roger, see if you can find that homeless man down in the jungle. He could be pivotal to the case. Then we'll need the names and addresses of everyone who saw Siegfried in that little village where George was killed."

Roger took a car and left.

One of the secretaries from the front office brought back the three morning newspapers. All had large front-page stories on G. B. Zedicher and the new foundation he had just created to help the homeless. He would build twelve area homeless shelters and job training centers around Berlin. The original outlay of cash was said to be over twenty million marks. The move was hailed by the Berlin mayor and the German Chancellor.

"What the hell is he up to?" Wade asked.

Before anyone could answer, someone turned up the sound on the TV set.

"A spokesman for Mr. Zedicher said this is just his way of giving back to the city that has been so good to him and his family. He said at one time he was homeless, after the war. He knows what it feels like. He wanted to do something beneficial to some of the unfortunates out there in the city.

"'I hope the homeless slums in our city will vanish quickly,'" Zedicher said. A spokesman said the first contracts have been signed and work starts tomorrow on the first Homeless and Job Training Center in the downtown area."

Wade walked to the TV set and back to his desk.

"Maybe we should give G.B. an update on the day's events. That might just make his day."

Kat made the call. She went through three different numbers and two secretaries. At last she found the right one.

"Yes, I'm calling for Siegfried. He's been hurt. Is Mr. Zedicher busy? Siegfried said to report directly to him. I think he'll take the call."

He did, a moment later a low man's voice came on.

"Yes, this is G. B. Zedicher. I understand something has happened to Siegfried?"

"Yes, Mr. Zedicher. He was shot in the shoulder and also lost the sight in his right eye. He's blind now."

"My God, how did it happen?"

"You know where and why, Mr. Zedicher. Oh, we still have Audwin Derrick. He's safe and untouchable. We have the black box and the book inside it. There is some damage to the Derrick home farm but not extensive. You're going down, Zedicher. We know you ordered George Silokowski killed and the CNN news reporter killed. You're going down."

Kat hung up the phone and almost purred. "Now that was fun," she said in German, then translated it. The Specialists all laughed.

Then they found more stories in the morning newspapers about Zedicher's bounty.

"He gave twenty thousand books to school libraries," Ichi said.

"He's been appointed to the board of directors of a big Berlin hospital after he donated six million marks for a new surgical wing," Hershel said.

"Whatever he's up to it's a masterfully choreographed campaign," Wade said.

Audwin was with them in the workroom. He had no idea what the good works meant. "He's working on something sneaky, low-handed, and mean," Audwin said. "Oh, my brother isn't going to be happy with me. Can I stay here with you people until this is all sorted out?"

"Of course you can," Kat said. "You might even be able to help us."

"Just remember, with G. B. Zedicher, anything is possible. Don't think that any kind of terrible thing is impossible for him to do."

Wade grinned. "Hey, people, how about this. He puts on a PR campaign, so can we. We promised CNN an exclusive on this. Let's give them a call. We can show them the black book and some of the list of those who gave bribes to Nazis in Warsaw in 1942. We won't say who the Nazis were then or who their heirs are today. But we'll ask the German public to come forward if they know anything about this forty-million-mark plunder by Nazis of the common Jewish residents of Warsaw."

Kat nodded. "I like it. I'll give them a call right now. Maybe we can make the eleven o'clock news."

They did. The story stirred up a controversy and it would be talked about for days. They didn't reveal any names of those who took the bribes, but hinted that they knew about some of them and what they were doing today.

The Specialists went to bed happy that evening, but their joy turned to bitter brew when they heard the morning telecasts.

"G. B. Zedicher, billionaire owner of Zedicher International Limited, was appointed by the Chancellor last night as the new Minister of Finance of the German Republic. He will serve as temporary minister until he is officially confirmed by the sitting legislature."

Wade threw his ballpoint pen at the wall. "So that's what it's all about. He'll be running one of the biggest budgets in the world. He must think there's room for a wholesale batch of bribes and ways to steal money from the government for himself.

"This would make him one of the most powerful men in all of Germany. Somehow we've got to figure out a way to stop him."

✳ TWENTY-NINE ✳

The Specialists stared at the TV screen as the announcer went on to list the qualifications that Zedicher had for the job. Somebody snapped it off.

"So how do we stop him from grabbing it all?" Duncan asked.

"We go talk to Siegfried," Kat said. "We get him to give up Zedicher. Yes, he killed those two people, or more, but he did it on the explicit and direct orders of G. B. Zedicher. We'll get him indicted for murder and that will get him unappointed in a rush. The only problem will be getting Siegfried to rat out his employer."

Kat and Wade spent all day in the hospital, but Siegfried was not in any condition to talk. His doctors had operated and removed the eye. He was recovering.

The third day they made it past the doctors and talked to Siegfried. He lay in his bed listening to a stereo, a better one than Wade had ever seen.

"What the hell do you two want?" he asked sharply.

"We want you to help save your country."

He laughed. "I'm not much of a patriot of United Germany."

"It's G.B. we want to talk to you about. Did you know about his politics?"

"The appointment. Yeah, I heard it came through."

"We can ruin him and his whole family and his business and put a rupture in the German economy that won't heal for twenty years. All we have to do is tell the whole story on CNN about the four Nazis who looted those Polish Jews."

Siegfried thought about it a minute. "He told me even if you found the book, you wouldn't have the guts to expose him. Too much money involved. He figures the big four control almost twenty-five percent of the business in Germany."

"Why should we care," Wade said. "This isn't our country."

"Why should I care, I'm blind and I'll never get out of prison."

"That's why. We might be able to work a deal with the prosecutors. We're turning in the evidence against you. We have some clout."

"House arrest out in the country somewhere. A real house, a garden, birds, all the music I can listen to, something like that?"

"Whatever we can bargain for. We want Zedicher."

He frowned past the bandages. "Want him for what?"

"He ordered you to take care of George Silokowski, and the CNN reporter. He's just as guilty of murder as you are. We want him for murder, not for the crimes of his father."

"Uh huh." Siegfried hit some buttons and changed the music from stern and martial to something soft and flowing.

"I tried to kill myself last night. Guard stopped me. Bastard. Now, you're starting to get me interested in living again. I can get Zedicher on two counts of murder. How about three?"

"Who?"

"The former Minister of Finance."

"The accident on Krueger was no accident," Kat said.

"Oh, yeah. That was a good one."

"Keep it to the two. With three we'd have trouble with the prosecutors."

"Deal," Siegfried said. "Let's do it today before I change my mind."

Kat left the room and called the German prosecutor's office. She at last found the pair assigned to the CNN reporter's murder. She talked to them for five minutes. They invited her to their office. She and Wade both went. They soon had the head prosecutor for all of Berlin.

He shouted and glared at Kat, who sat poised and confident. At last he threw down his clipboard and stomped out of the room. The man and woman prosecutors grinned and shook hands.

"We've got it. House arrest in the country. No restraints. He checks in with local police twice a day by phone. He will have a locator chip surgically implanted in his neck. We've got him."

The next day they called the police and told them the story. The police responded with two detectives, a video camera, and two tape recorders and operators. The taped interview with Siegfried in his room lasted for three hours. The prosecutors were there, too. Siegfried gave them chapter and verse on the two killings, and how he was specifically ordered to kill the men by G. B. Zedicher. Yes, he would swear to that in court.

Kat and Wade went back to the office with a bottle of champagne. Kat called CNN with the exclusive.

That afternoon on CNN the story broke about the testimony linking G. B. Zedicher to the two murders. The rest of the Berlin media had bulletins, broke into local and national programming with the news.

At five o'clock the Chancellor went on TV from his office and announced that he was withdrawing the name of G. B. Zedicher for the office of Minister of Finance.

An hour later, police arrested Zedicher in his office. He'd been too busy that afternoon to watch the news on TV.

That's when Kat popped the cork out of the champagne bottle and they all toasted the Specialists.

"One last task on this operation," Wade said. "We work out some arrangements with the big four industrialists to make some payback to the Jewish people. Let's get some ideas, then we'll call them all together for a little bit of old-fashioned negotiations."

The Specialists kicked around ideas all afternoon. They called in the two lawyers who were on retainer by J. August Marshall in Berlin to handle his affairs.

After a quick positioning of the lawyers they all got down to specifics that could be done under the law and still protect the huge corporations from going into bankruptcy and perhaps bringing down the German economy with them.

"There has to be some kind of a secret search done to find as many living relatives of these bribed victims as possible," Hershel said. "This must be done and monitored and certified by you gentlemen."

That idea was agreed to by all.

"Say they find a thousand different families who are direct descendants of those who got to Switzerland and those who didn't," one of the lawyers said. "What kind of compensation? How much should each family receive?"

They settled on a hundred thousand dollars equivalent in German marks or Euro currency, whichever was in use at that time.

"That's only a hundred million if they find a thousand, which they won't," Duncan said. "They can afford a lot more than that. That's just twenty-five million for each of the four firms."

From there the discussion turned into funding of Jewish synagogues in Poland. "I have no idea how many such religious groups there are in Poland," Wade said.

"That will be part of you gentlemen's job. If there are a thousand, five thousand, it will be your job to set up a formula for compensation." He paused. "I'd think another hundred million should be used here."

Audwin sat in on the talks and listened attentively. They had been speaking in both English and German with some translations both ways.

Audwin cleared his throat and they looked at him. "Yes, I agree. The first two plans are good. You realize the four industrial complexes you're talking about are worth more than fifty billion dollars each. This is like a beesting. I would suggest that you quadruple the payments. At least four hundred thousand dollars to each family heir, one family group per victim listed in the book.

"Again, at least four times as much money rebuilding, establishing, and funding Jewish temples and places of worship in Poland, especially in Warsaw. I don't know how many Jewish people have returned there, but there must be some by now. I'll shut up now and listen. I love all of this."

One of the lawyers looked up. "I assume that there must be total and forever security on the actual names of the corporations involved in these projects. No hint of a scandal must be visited on these four companies."

"Right," Wade said. "We had visions of a quarter of the economic strength of Germany going down the tubes."

The other lawyer chuckled. "They ripped off forty million dollars' worth of gold and diamonds. A lot of cash, but that's just a pimple on the behind of the Swiss bankers and the gold they took in from Jewish people who never lived to reclaim it. Some think that the total of that original Jewish gold plunder was well over three hundred billion dollars. Now that's a lot of money."

They kicked around the idea of reparations to the Jewish community and at last came down to Jewish charities and direct grants to Jewish organizations and welfare groups in Israel.

Audwin took the floor again. "I would hope that the cost to each of these four corporations would be in the neighborhood of a billion dollars each. That's enough to get their attention. I'm sure that you two gentlemen will do a good job in hiring people to make these searches to check out charities, etc. However I am offering my services as a third party in the legally constituted steering committee to see that these plans are carried out."

"But, Mr. Derrick. Won't you also be one of the subject firms? I mean you must own half of Bavaria Limited."

"I also gave away thirty million of my firm's money to Jewish charities ten years ago before my brother caught me."

Wade stood. "Yes, I agree with Mr. Derrick. He should be one of the three on this group. Now, is there anything else? I assume that you gentlemen will draw up the needed papers for this three-way control, and that you will be compensated for your services, not from the various funds, but by your regular employer. That will be true for any help needed in researching these heirs of the names in the book. We have copied the names and you will have them. The book itself will be kept by Mr. Marshall in the London offices. Is there anything else?"

The meeting broke up.

Audwin tried to phone his brother at the company, but he was out.

"He won't take my call," Audwin said. "Maybe tomorrow."

An hour after the meeting ended, J. August Marshall walked into the workroom. Only three of the Specialists were there. The others were found and assembled.

"Lady and gentlemen. Congratulations on your work. I heard the news about Mr. Zedicher. Couldn't have happened to a more fitting candidate. I trust in good German fashion he had a chain of command and of succession in his company. His oldest son, I would imagine, will quit his auto-racing career and return to the company.

"You must be Audwin Derrick. I've worked with your firm on several occasions. If you're having any trouble with your brother, I'll be glad to help you over this awkward part.

"Now, Audwin, you may listen, but your lips must be sealed about what you hear from now on."

"Yes, sir, Mr. Marshall. You can rely on me."

Marshall turned to his team. "Again congratulations on a difficult one. It was a long-range crime, but you put the pieces together nicely. I'll want to know the details about payback to the families and the Jewish community.

"Now, moving on. We have a problem. For the past six months the CIA and the NSC have known about a plot to steal from the United States two to eight functional nuclear weapons. We're not sure if these are to be conventional bombs, missile warheads, or field artillery warheads.

"This week an active attempt was made on one of our aircraft with a full load of nuclear bombs on a training flight. The attempt failed. There was no publicity.

"Now we know of at least two more tries at capturing nuclear weapons. This is just the start. The nation or combine of nations or perhaps some now unknown private consortium is trying again to capture a workable nuclear weapon.

"The President has asked for our help. We're not about to turn him down. Get things wrapped up here today. We'll fly back to London in the morning and then be heading for Washington, D.C., later in the day. This one has been marked urgent, with a critical time factor. So let's get cracking."

About the Author

Chet Cunningham, an army veteran of the Korean War, experienced combat firsthand as an 81-mm mortar gunner and squad leader. He has been a store clerk, farmworker, photographer, audiovisual writer, and newspaper reporter. A former freelance writer, he has published 283 books—mostly action, historical, and western novels. He was born in Nebraska, grew up in Oregon, worked in Michigan, went to college in New York City, and now lives with his wife in San Diego.

If you enjoyed *Plunder*, be sure to look
for the next in The Specialists series

BROKEN ARROW

coming soon from Bantam Books

Here's a sneak peak . . .

CHAPTER ONE
Lebanese Coast

Wade Thorne looked over the rail of the weather beaten freighter as it steamed southward at fourteen knots through the placid Mediterranean Sea. He couldn't see the lights of Lebanon to the east, but he knew they were there. Thorne leaned his 6-foot 2-inch and 195 pound frame against the rail. Squinting into the pale darkness, he soon saw a forty-foot fishing boat angling toward them, materializing out of the wispy fog, birthed by the uncertain moonlight.

Right on time. He liked that.

The ex-CIA agent checked his gear. He had only a backpack and two weapons slung over his shoulders. Beside him a woman stirred.

"Is that our pick up boat?" Kat Killinger asked. She was five feet nine, slender and dressed as the man was in black pants and shirt; blotches of dark cammo marred her beautiful face. She also had a black backpack but only one automatic weapon, an H & K M5 9mm submachine gun, slung over her shoulder. Her long dark hair had been braided, coiled, pinned and concealed under a black knit hat.

"Yes, this should be our friends," Wade said. The

fishing boat powered along thirty yards off the side of the freighter, three quick flashes of light stabbing toward the Specialists.

Wade sent two flashes back from a penlight, and both the figures at the rail relaxed a little.

"It could still be a trap," Kat said. "They would be delighted to grab a couple of US spies on their turf."

"That's why we lock and load," Wade said. He pivoted down the weapons one at a time, chambered a round, pushed on the safety and swung it back. Then he returned both weapons over his shoulders. He heard Kat do the same, and then they watched the boat come alongside.

"I was just getting used to this freighter's sickening diesel exhaust smell," Kat said. "What is this little boat going to smell like?"

"Fish," Wade said with a grin. "Live, dead, and rotting fish. Fish scales, fish guts, fish fillets, and lots of fish bait. Don't worry, we shouldn't be on board long."

They had a simple assignment. Wade reviewed mentally it as they waited for the boats to latch together. They had firm information that one of the terrorists involved in the Marine Headquarters bombing in Beirut in 1983 had surfaced in the southern Lebanese city of Sur, and was continuing to plan terrorist activities. Mr. Marshall had a contact in Sur who would meet the Specialists and direct them to the terrorist's house.

The name of the terrorist was The Hammer. Six different countries wanted him for murder, arson, and bombing. Mr. Marshall had instructed the Specialists to go in and bring in The Hammer for trial in England.

The fishing craft bumped against the side of the freighter and gunned its engine to match the speed of the larger ship. A crewman dropped down a line fastened to a cleat on the freighter. It was caught below and tied it to a fitting at the bow. The big ship continued its forward speed. Two heavy bumpers along the side of the fishing boat cushioned the steel against steel contact. A crewman dropped a rope ladder from the freighter and it was at once secured to the rail of the forty-footer below.

"Let's choggie out of here," Wade said. The two moved to the freighter's rail where the rope ladder had been tied off. Wade went down first. The ropes swayed and slammed against the side of the freighter with the movement of the big ship. It reminded him of the times he had gone down a rope net from a fifty-foot training tower. He hit the bottom of the ladder, stepped onto the fishing boat rail and jumped to the sloping deck, skidding a moment on a fish fillet carcass. He swung his MP-5 up, clicked off the safety, and covered the three men who stood on the other side of the boat.

Wade snapped off two phrases in Arabic.

The correct answers came back at once in the same tongue. Wade gave the rope ladder two jerks and Kat crawled over the rail and down the rope ladder as if she did this sort of exercise every day. Twice the rope and her body swung away from the big ship and then slammed back into the side of the freighter. She remembered to let go of the rope at the instant of contact, then grabbed it again quickly. She soon was stepping over the rail and onto the fishing boat.

One of the three Lebanese held his hat over his chest and nodded. Wade could smell the results of the day's work of catching, cleaning and icing down the fish. The Lebanese man's face showed plainly in the weak lights on the craft and Wade could see that the wind and water reflected sun had turned his skin into the shade of old leather. He figured the fisherman was about forty. The man had small brown eyes peering from under heavy brows and with a bushy, black moustache.

"Welcome. We are on time, no?" the captain asked in English.

"You are on time. Good. How long to the dock?" Wade asked.

"My English is good, yes? We are about an hour to the dock or another place if you want."

"We need a safe landing, where no one will see us," Kat said.

The captain turned to her, his eyes flashing. "Oh, a woman. A most brave and courageous woman. I congratulate you. In my country women are not as . . . as free, can't dress . . ." He stopped. "Now, we must leave."

One of the men untied the line from the fishing boat's bow and threw off the rope ladder. At once the big ship surged away from the smaller one. The second man had moved to the cabin and the fishing boat turned and slanted toward the east at full cruising speed. Wade watched the glowing green phosphorescence of the wake. By the action of the water he figured they were making about ten knots. Good.

The captain with the windburned face and probing eyes rubbed one hand through his thick, dark hair. "We wish you well. We come to same place at dusk for three days. Yes?"

"Yes," Wade said. "Half the pay when we land, the other half when we get back to the freighter."

"Yes, yes. We can do it. We fish only a little. My family thanks you. We wish to help."

"You have children?" Kat asked.

"The captain beamed. "Oh, yes, six. Three of each. All so bright and happy. It takes much money these days just to feed so many."

Kat took a pair of small but powerful binoculars from her pack and watched to the east. They sat on a hold cover and Kat kept telling herself to forget the smell of fish. It was everywhere. So far she had beaten down two surges of bile. She would not throw up. She would not. It was enough she would smell like fish for a week.

A half-hour later, they saw the coastline.

The town where they would land was Sur, the ancient Phoenician port of Tyre, that was a bustling trade center as early as 3,000 B.C. Wade wondered if there would be anything left from those early days nearly 5,000 years ago? Some stone wharves? A stone dock?

"More lights than I expected," Kat said. "This is not a huge town."

Wade motioned for the captain to come over.

"How big is the town of Sur?"

"About fifty thousand. Many fishing boats."

"Can we get in without being seen?"

The Lebanese frowned, preened his moustache and then rubbed his face with his right hand. "We go to a small wharf away from big docks, no?"

"Yes," Kat said.

The captain looked up quickly, then smiled. "I am not used to . . ." He stopped. "I have a friend repairs boats. He has dock away from big ships. We go there in dark. No one see. Yes. It is good."

As the boat approached the harbor, the two Specialists went into the cabin so they wouldn't be seen. Both sat on the floor and put on their G-16's, their improved short distance person-to-person radios. The belt unit was the size of a beeper, and had wires that went under the wearer's clothing to the back of the neck where a wire disappeared into the ear with a small earpiece. Another wire wrapped around the neck with a throat mike. The throat mike was not as sensitive as a lip mike, but much easier to wear and not as prone to being knocked off. They checked the radios by tapping the mikes, then left them on and waited. Wade could see lights now and the sides of tall ships beside them as they worked into the port. He knelt and looked out the forward window.

Dozens of ships of all sizes seemed jammed into the port. Then a waterway opened to the left and they veered that direction away from the rest of the ships. Ahead he saw only blackness.

Three or four minutes later Wade felt the ship nudge against a dock and come to a stop. The Captain stepped into the wheelhouse and smiled in the soft light.

"We are here. The dock is empty. Go in safety."

Wade handed him an envelope with highly prized US bank notes and repeated the instructions.

"Here at dusk. The next three days."

"As you say, so it shall be," the captain said.

They crept out of the wheelhouse to the deck and then to the rail. The fishing boat was tied to a stone wharf. Wade saw that this dock was moss covered and did seem to be 5,000 years old. Kat looked over the rail and scanned the narrow dock that fronted an equally narrow street. A hill climbed into the darkness just off the road.

She quartered off the area and checked each grid. After two minutes she lowered her binoculars and nodded.

"Nobody out there unless they are top-notch professionals," she said.

"Let's go," Wade said and they stepped over the rail onto the ancient stones and hurried toward the road.

Both moved quickly along the street that wound around a small hill, then slanted down into a half-commercial, half-residential section. They saw only three streetlights ahead over several blocks. The buildings were a wild mixture of modern concrete block structures beside stone and mortar houses and buildings that looked a thousand years old. The street here was dirt with no sidewalks. Wade could see no telephone poles or light poles. Only an occasional building had any lights on inside.

Both of them had memorized the maps and instructions. But looking at a map and seeing the real town was a lot different. The town of Sur was larger than they expected. A quarter of a mile down the road they found a landmark in their instructions. There were almost no street signs. They found a three-story building made of stone with a sign on top.

Most of the town here was still dark with a streetlight only every four blocks or so. It was a little after 1 a.m.

A pair of headlights illuminated the street ahead of them and they darted into the doorway of a building and let the rig roll past. It was a police van with two men in it.

They turned down the street by the tall building. The map said to go two hundred yards until they came to a large rock house with a dry fountain in front of it. The man they were to meet lived three houses farther on from the big rock house and on the same side of the street. A numbered address would have been a lot simpler.

They worked ahead slowly until they found the large rock house with the dry fountain. It was across the street from them. They had seen only three men on the street. There were almost no cars or vehicles. Pausing, they looked at the target house. It seemed quiet. No lights. The place was small, maybe four rooms, Wade figured. Built of stone on the outside, probably brick or stone walls inside. There were two windows on the front and the side that they could see.

This was the home of their contact who would lead them to the terrorist. They watched the place for five minutes, saw no activity. No one went up or down the street. They heard one vehicle far off.

They both walked across the dirt street and up to the house, then turned in sharply and hurried to the back door they had been told to use. Kat tried the door. It was unlocked. She looked at Wade, then she jerked open the door and rushed inside with Wade right behind her. There was no sign of anyone inside. Moving silently, they cleared the first room, a kitchen, and then into the rest of the house.

Quickly they cleared two more rooms, and found no one there. Wade wondered where their contact was. They opened the door into the front room.

"Blood," she whispered. "Lots of blood." They used their penlights and moved into the front room. The small lights revealed a nightmare of blood: splatters and drops, stains across a wall, smears along the floor. On the dining room table they found what was left of their man. The fingers on his right hand had been cut off. His left arm amputated. A bloody axe on the floor beside it. A hundred slices and cuts criss-crossed his body. His throat had been slashed, and his eyes gouged out.

Kat picked up the mutilated arm and put it on the

table, shining her flash on the wrist. The numbers 1289 had been tatooed into the flesh.

"Our contact," Wade said.

A moment later, windows in the room exploded in a shower of glass as bullets jolted through them. Wade and Kat dropped to the floor out of range of the killing slugs. Before they could react, they heard rounds hitting the wooden front door. Then more bullets slammed through the broken windows and dug small grooves in the stone and plastered inside walls.

Someone kicked in the front door and a deadly spray of hot lead spewed from an automatic weapon ripping into the table.

Kat had her MP-5 up and fired a six-round burst into the spot a foot above the muzzle flashes of the weapon at the door. They heard a grunt, then a scream. Kat and Wade crawled to the front wall to be out of the line of fire. So far no one had pushed a weapon through the broken windows.

At once more rounds poured through the door and front windows. Kat moved to the corner out of the danger zone.

She tapped her throat mike twice for the "OK here" signal. She heard two taps in response then a whisper in her earpiece.

"Flash-bang, on three." There was a pause. Then her radio spoke again. "One, two, three."

Kat closed her eyes and put her face to the wall, then held her hands over her ears. The non-lethal weapon bounced once outside the front door, then went off with a series of six skull splitting explosive sounds that drilled through the brain and rendered anyone nearby deaf for two to three minutes. They were followed by six intensely brilliant strobes of light that penetrated eyelids and blinded the terrorists around the front of the house.

Kat "saw" the strobes of light through her hands and felt the thundering pulsations of sound. Wade charged out the front door as soon as the last strobe died and gunned down two men he found writhing on the ground. Another man rushed toward the front of the house and Wade sent a six round burst after him.

Two weapons at the rear of the house continued to fire. Wade stepped back into the front room, then slid toward the door into the middle room, crawling through to the kitchen where he could see out the back door. One muzzle flash appeared twenty yards away in the back yard near a trash pile. He sent a dozen 9mm rounds at the area and saw the weapon lift up and the man fire off three rounds in a death spasm before he fell.

Wade listened to the silence, and heard a man running down the street.

He went back to the second room where Kat was looking through the contents of the room that hadn't been trashed.

"Should be an address or a hint where the terr lives around here somewhere," Kat said.

Wade used his pencil flash and joined in the search.

"If this guy was any kind of a professional, he wouldn't have written the address down," Wade said. "Which makes it all that much harder for us." They continued to look for any clue for five minutes but couldn't stay much longer. Either the police or terrorist reinforcements would be there soon. Then Kat had an idea.

She went back to the body and looked at the man's face. It was unmarked. She used both hands and pried his teeth apart. But there was nothing inside his mouth. He would have screamed a lot while they tortured him.

They looked in the last room, sparsely furnished with a table set up with a pallet and oils, an unfinished picture on an easel.

Wade looked at it. Then he grinned. "Look at that. Our contact was an artist. Perhaps this picture tells us something. See the large tower with a light on top? And the four houses in that shaft of sunlight? That has to be where the terr lives. Let's go find that tower."

They went out the back door and in the distance they

could hear the wail of sirens. Wade replaced his MP-5 magazine with a full one from his backpack. His second weapon, a Colt Commando carbine, the army's M-4A1, was tied over his back with a rubber cord. Kat, too, put in a new magazine and they looked at the wet painting.

"That tower must be a landmark of some kind," Kat said. "I hope the light stays on all night."

They looked around just outside the house.

"We need a small hill so we can see more of the town," Wade said.

"Maybe from the street?"

They walked to the street and began to look around when suddenly bullets began screaming over their heads and beside them as an automatic weapon across the street opened up on them from the killing range of less than thirty yards.